what
strange
creatures

what
strange
creatures

emily
arsenault

WILLIAM MORROW
An Imprint of HarperCollinsPublishers

WHAT STRANGE CREATURES. Copyright © 2014 by Emily Arsenault. All rights reserved. Printed in the United States of America. No part of this book may be used or reproduced in any manner whatsoever without written permission except in the case of brief quotations embodied in critical articles and reviews. For information address HarperCollins Publishers, 195 Broadway, New York, NY 10007.

HarperCollins books may be purchased for educational, business, or sales promotional use. For information please e-mail the Special Markets Department at SPsales@harpercollins.com.

FIRST EDITION

Designed by Diahann Sturge

Library of Congress Cataloging-in-Publication Data has been applied for.

ISBN 978-0-06-228323-8

14 15 16 17 18   OV/RRD   10 9 8 7 6 5 4 3 2 1

What strange creatures brothers are!
—Jane Austen, *Mansfield Park*

To Dan and Luke

Tuesday, October 22

W hat are you supposed to do on the second night your brother is in jail on a murder charge?

Should you watch *The Colbert Report*? Should you clean the black crud from behind your kitchen faucet? Should you make yourself a smoothie with protein powder?

I did all of these things, trying to forget the prosecutor's words: *Her body was found in a wooded area, about ten yards from the side of Highway 114. According to autopsy reports, she died of strangulation and also had a deep wound in her upper left thigh, consistent with assault using a screwdriver or scissors.*

But what was I *supposed* to do? Was I supposed to settle into the situation and practice saying things like, "Jeff? You didn't hear? He's in the clink. Homicide." Or in reminiscent fashion, with a long, throaty cough and the resigned wave of a cigarette: "Back when Jeff was still on the outside . . ."

Probably I wouldn't need to practice. Probably one grows used to saying these things, as the first nights turn into first weeks, then months and years. I'm a Battle, after all. And Battles get used to all sorts of shitty things—like noisy mufflers and bad lighting and generic plastic wrap that sticks to nothing but itself and your angry, frustrated fingers.

Police investigators obtained a search warrant for Mr. Battle's apartment and vehicle. In the trunk of the vehicle, in the spare-tire compartment, they found a screwdriver with blood on it.

Finally I settled on the dog bowls and cat dishes. Yes—that was what needed to be done next. They all had a fine layer of Iams crust on them, from days of hasty feedings—bribing the poor dears with wet food as I dashed home briefly between trips to Jeff's place, the prison, my job, the courthouse. Now I collected the dogs' metal bowls and the cats' delicate ceramic dishes, dumped them in a plastic tub in the sink with some Palmolive, and ran the water till it was scalding. I winced as I plunged my hands into the soapy water.

Police also found that Mr. Battle's trunk had been saturated with vinegar and an ammonia-based cleaning liquid.

Tears sprang to my eyes.

My brain struggled to find words to drown out the prosecutor's and came up with this:

And, daughter, don't be at all afraid, for it is a singular and a special gift that God has given you—a well of tears which man shall never take from you.

I recited the original words softly to myself:

"And, dowtyr, drede the nowt, for it is a synguler and a specyal gyft that God hath govyn the, a welle of teerys the whech schal nevyr man take fro the."

I'd memorized this sentence at a different time in my life, when feeling smart had been a misguided priority. It was comforting now—not for its content so much as the sound of the Middle English. I'd always liked its long-ago, faraway feel in my mouth.

After the dishes were done, I opened my dryer and folded a single towel and a single pair of underwear—gray boyshorts with slutty black lace unraveling at the backside. Had I been married when I bought these? I couldn't remember. The rest of the laundry could sit in the dryer for another day, but these I'd need now, as I'd noticed my underwear drawer empty this morning.

I carried them to my room and collapsed on my bed, where I used my cat Geraldine as a pillow. As I began to repeat those words under my breath, she slipped away politely, hopped off the bed, and retired behind the dust ruffle. Geraldine is not interested in being a therapist—she's always made that very clear.

Besides, she was right. This was no time for comfort. I needed to do something. Something for Jeff. But what could I do at this hour?

The black lace of the boyshorts—still in my hand—gave me an idea. There *was* something I could try. Something a little bit shadier than my usual comfort zone of indifferent to mildly degenerate. I used the underwear to wipe away a tear and snuffled back the rest that wanted to follow it.

Yes. I would try it.

I was willing to try almost anything for my brother.

Wednesday, October 2

Three Weeks Earlier

I can just *feel* myself becoming Margery Kempe—slowly and organically, as I creep toward middle age. I'm steadily getting crazier, more self-righteous, more contradictory to myself, more prone to deranged weeping fits. And maybe about to enter a celibate stage of life, but that's a separate matter.

I've not heard this ever proposed before: that the longer one works on a doctoral thesis, the more one begins to resemble one's subject. Maybe it happens only in the humanities. Because how much can one start to resemble a slime mold or the Tokyo stock exchange? I'll leave that question for the biologists and the economists.

In case you don't know, Margery Kempe was a middle-class Englishwoman who was born in 1373. She wrote what is thought to be the first autobiography ever written in English. Or rather she had it written. Unable to read and write herself, she hired scribes to take down her life story for her. She had fourteen children (though they don't factor much in her book), then convinced her husband that Jesus had told her she shouldn't have sex anymore and should spend some time traveling. She often wore white clothing to show her virtue—as per the instructions of God—even though it was highly unconventional for a married woman to do so.

The Book of Margery Kempe is her account of her visions and prophecies, her relationships with her supporters and detractors, her daily life in the town of King's Lynn, and her harrowing pilgrimages—to the Holy Land and elsewhere. She spent a great deal of time crying and wailing and carrying on about the sweet, sweet music Jesus made in her head, generally annoying her neighbors and fellow pilgrims and often pissing off church authorities. Still, she managed to avoid execution for heresy and lived to see old age and have her story documented. She was absolutely an eccentric and almost certainly a nut job.

You would think after seven-plus years of on-and-off trying to finish this infernal thesis, I'd get sick of explaining to people who she was. I don't. While I'm tired of my situation, I rarely get tired of her. When I started, my life was very different. I was younger and thinner, a full-time grad student, and engaged to a lawyer. I found Marge quirky and amusing. When I took a job editing Whitlock's Candles' catalogs and mailers—after my funding ran out and I stopped teaching undergrads—I thought it would be for a year or two while I finished writing the dissertation. My husband, Brendan, generously paid my grad-school fees as two years turned into three. Then I paid my own way after Brendan was gone.

Gradually my writing sessions produced fewer and fewer words as I sipped more and more Malbec in front of the computer, listening to Jeff Buckley sing "Hallelujah" on repeat. One marriage, one divorce, three boyfriends, and a bunch of other shit later, it's just Marge and me.

I felt my inner Marge creeping up on me on Wednesday while I was standing by the eggs in Stop & Shop, trying to decide if the ones fortified with omega-3 were worth the extra fifty cents. I had noticed also that the omega-3 ones did not say "cage-free," and I was wondering if this meant I'd always have to choose between my own neurological health and chicken happiness. And then I started to think more deeply about my word choice: "always." No, I wouldn't *always* have to choose, because I'd be dead before always came around.

And then this Adele song came on over the supermarket loudspeakers. You know the one—that super-popular one where Adele belts out *yoooouuuu* like gangbusters? I don't know what it's about, because whenever I hear it, I'm simply too overwhelmed with my own vague yearning to listen to the lyrics. I've always been a sucker for a good pop song—ever since I was eleven years old, when Casey Kasem's countdown would regularly reduce me to a puddle of inexplicable longing.

I started to wonder, right there by the eggs, if this would ever change. If I heard the Bangles' "Eternal Flame" on my deathbed in my old age, for example, would I still feel that same wistfulness? Would it give me comfort or fill me with despair?

I started to whimper at the very question and had to put down the omega-3 eggs. I began to cover my eyes, but a voice behind me said, "Excuse me?"

It was a young woman with a very full cart, baby in car seat affixed to the top. The baby was tiny and pink, with a hand-knit blue hat and the most delicate of closed eyelids. And his mother needed to get at the eggs. I muttered "Sorry" and stepped away. Sobered, as usual, by seeing women younger than me with children, I wandered across the aisle to the frozen entrées and selected a Lean Cuisine spinach and mushroom pizza for my dinner. Still, I found myself narrating my own actions in my head, calling myself "this creature" as Margery did.

This creature then decided to treat herself to some frozen yogurt. And then she felt better. By then Adele had stopped singing and this creature had come back to herself.

Mind you, Margery Kempe referred to herself this way presumably to remind herself and her reader, constantly, that she was a creation of God. I, on the other hand, do it only occasionally, and only because I am turning into a freak.

I was eating the last of the frozen pizza when my brother knocked on my front door that evening. I was glad to have gobbled up most of it before he arrived, because I didn't much feel like sharing. The crusts and the limp pizza box were in the trash before he'd made it into the kitchen.

"Hey," Jeff said.

"Hi there. What brings you here?" I asked.

"Bad time? Working hard on Marge tonight?"

"No. Hardly."

It wasn't that I wasn't happy to see him. It was only that it had been a few weeks since he'd waltzed in aimlessly like this—like he used to. His relationship with his new girlfriend seemed to be growing more time-intensive.

Boober came into the kitchen, yapping and dancing toward my brother with desperate excitement. Jeff bent down and tried to scratch behind his ears as he rolled onto the floor and nipped at the air.

"*You're* happy to see me, aren't you, Boob?" he said, then stood and opened my refrigerator. "Got any doggie bags?" he asked.

Jeff knows I go out often with my friends Megan and Tish. Chinese with Megan on Sundays. Mexican with Tish on Thursdays when she can get a babysitter or when it's her ex's turn to take the kid.

"Yeah. A chimichanga."

"You saving it for something?"

"No. The guacamole's turned a little brown. Not sure I want it anymore."

I don't at all resent my brother always eating my restaurant leftovers. In fact, I save them for him to be sure he doesn't starve. What bothers me is that he puts me through this charade of asking if I want them. I'm not creative enough to keep coming up with these bullshit reasons for why I'm not going to eat them.

Jeff took the foil dish out of the refrigerator and pulled off its circular cardboard top. "I didn't think you were into fried food like this."

"It was a low moment," I explained. "I got some . . . uh, thesis news this week."

Jeff glanced from the chimichanga to me, uncertain if he should dig in or politely wait for my news.

I handed him a fork. "They've given me a deadline—of sorts. They were hinting about it last spring. But it's finally happened.

"Eat," I said, and he did. He looked ravenous.

"The new department chair has decided to lay down the law

with me," I said, watching Jeff gobble the side of refried beans. "She called me in. Me and the other hanger-on. His name's Buck, and he's been working on a dissertation on *Robinson Crusoe* for like twelve years."

"You've mentioned him before."

"Yeah, well. The new department chair is making us each present pages and do a talk for our committees at the end of this semester. 'Wherein you will show significant progress,' she said."

"She said 'wherein' to your face?"

"Yeah. Can you believe that?"

Jeff shook his head. "I don't know how you can stand these people, frankly."

"Clemson told me he tried to fight for more time for me, that it wasn't fair to set an arbitrary deadline. '"Significant" is rather a subjective term,' he kept saying. But it didn't work. I feel bad that he felt the need to even try. At his age dear old Clemson shouldn't be wasting any breath on me."

"Is it gonna be doable?" Jeff asked. "The end of this semester?"

"I think it's going to have to be. I don't want to talk about it, really."

I closed my eyes for a moment, weary of the topic already. When I opened them, I watched Jeff use his fork to shave the brown off the guacamole. Then he slathered it onto his chimichanga half.

"Did I tell you I'm thinking of becoming a hoarder?" he asked.

"Really? Well, I'm thinking of signing all of my e-mails 'Namaste,' so I guess we're even."

"Except that I'm serious."

"Oh," I said, getting up for a glass of water. "Okay, then why don't you flesh this out for me a little more?"

"I think I'd do well to develop a deeper emotional relationship with material objects. Seems like there'd be some consistency there, at least." He took a big bite of chimichanga. "And I could do to be a little thriftier."

I shrugged. Thriftier than eating someone else's leftovers? "Maybe. Thrift *is* important. But the people on that hoarding show . . . What's it called?"

"I think it's just *Hoarders*."

"Okay. They don't seem happy. I've only seen a couple of episodes, but—"

"Well, that's the thing. That show. If it doesn't work out, you or I can call them. Then I'll get a free housecleaning and free counseling."

Jeff was struggling to cut through the rubbery old chimichanga with his fork. I got up again to get him a knife.

"Do you want therapy? Why don't you skip the hoarding and just get therapy, then?"

"I'd need a bigger motivator than I have now. If I were sleeping on pizza boxes and Chinese-food cartons, I might be motivated to take counseling seriously."

I sat back down, sighing heavily. "I'm not sure I'm the one you want to be talking to about motivation."

Jeff stopped eating for a moment. He regarded me with his big brown eyes. It was then I noticed that his face looked even thinner than usual. Perhaps, I thought, I should buy Chinese food every day and deposit it directly in the fridge so there would always be "leftovers" for him to eat.

He finished his food without replying. We don't say things like

"You can do it" to each other. That's not how our family operates.

"How's Kim?" I asked.

His new girlfriend was a pretty, bright-seeming waitress in her mid-twenties, whom he'd met in a night class I'd encouraged him to take. This Kim seemed oddly taken with my brother. ("Despite lack of gainful employment," my mother had squawked over the phone recently, marveling.) Things had moved fast. They were practically living at each other's place these days, from what I could gather.

Jeff wiped his lips with his fingertips. "Good," he said. "In fact, I was going to bring her up. She . . . uh, wants to take you out for dinner."

"Me?"

"Yeah. Uh." He picked up a hardware-store mailer from the kitchen table and ripped a square out of it. "Don't yell at me when I explain."

"Uh-oh."

"Are you free tomorrow night?"

"Why don't you explain first?" I said.

"She's going away this weekend." He began to fold the paper. "She has to go see her sister in New Jersey. And she was looking for a place to board Wayne."

Wayne was Kim's dog. I'd not met him, but Jeff had spoken of him with great admiration.

"Wayne is the puggle, correct?" A beagle-pug mix. I had no idea what their temperaments were like, since I didn't keep up with those trendy dog breeds.

"Yep," Jeff said. "I'd step up, but Mike wants me to help with a job up in the Berkshires. I'll be there with him one, maybe two nights. Kim's roommate refuses to deal with Wayne. I mentioned you might be willing to help her out. I was going to ask you a few days ago, but I forgot. Somehow I gave Kim the impression I'd *already* asked you and it was a done deal."

"You want me to board a puggle?"

He looked sheepish. "Can you?"

I wasn't exactly jazzed about it, but if it helped Jeff hold on to something that made him happy, I wasn't about to say no.

"I'm not sure Boober will like it, but it could be an interesting experiment. I've kind of wondered how he'd do with another dog."

"Yeah? You know, there's free steak at Wiley's in it for you."

"I can't let Kim do that." I don't let anyone more than a couple of years younger than me treat me to food or drinks. It makes me feel pitied and spinsterish.

"Yes you can. She gets a good discount."

Wiley's was the overpriced steak house and wine bar where Kim worked. It definitely wasn't a townie establishment. According to Jeff, she brought home amazing tips.

I shrugged. "I'll let her give me a discount, how about that? Either way, I think I can manage a puggle for a weekend."

Jeff looked up from his folding. "Thank you."

"Not a problem."

"So . . . you're thinking of getting another dog sometime, then?"

"If I'm going to be consistent, I'd need to have another breakup first."

He handed me the folded piece of catalog, which he'd fashioned into a little Scottie dog. Origami is one of his many talents.

"Lovely," I said, balancing it delicately on my sugar bowl. "Thank you."

"But you think that's what you'd do next? A dog instead of a cat?"

"I'm being real careful about who I date next, so I'm thinking there won't be another animal."

"Because another dog would probably be best, don't you think? To even it out a little?"

"What are you trying to say? Are you concerned about me becoming a crazy cat lady?"

"Sometimes," Jeff admitted. "But this is great, Theresa. About Wayne, I mean. I want to return the favor, too. Somehow."

"You'll take care of Boober and the cats the next time I go away, hey?"

"When'll that be?"

"I don't know. Maybe if I ever finish with Marge, I'll take a victory trip."

Jeff was quiet—perhaps thinking that neither of those things would ever happen.

"Hey, Theresa," he said after a moment.

I had a feeling I knew what was coming next. "Yeah?"

"I've been thinking I should eat more scones."

"Oh, yeah? Well, I'm thinking I might start singing softly to myself in the grocery store."

Jeff thought about this for a moment. "I've been considering giving myself a compliment whenever I hear a telephone ring."

"I've been thinking I should blog about how I'm not eating bacon this year."

He sucked in his bottom lip and didn't look at me. "I'm thinking of committing a random act of kindness. Either that or a senseless act of beauty."

I was too tired to go on.

"You win," I said.

He always wins anyway.

No, I am not a crazy cat lady. Nor do I intend to be one in the future, I reassured myself as I walked Boober that evening.

One dog and three cats might seem like a lot of animals for a single woman. But I had none when I was married because Brendan was allergic. So when we divorced, I treated myself to Sylvestress, my black-and-white Ragdoll cat.

I'd just moved into my little ranch house in the cheapest part of town—behind the municipal golf course. I got the house for a very good price, due to all the bad press the neighborhood was receiving at the time. A toddler had been injured by a stray golf ball. I made a big down payment from the sale of the comparatively luxurious house Brendan and I had occupied together. Between my job at Whitlock's Candles and the savings from the old house, the mortgage is manageable. And it's worth all the hassles of having my own place, partly because I can have as many animals as I want.

After Sylvestress I've added a new animal with each breakup since, significant or otherwise. I realize that this might seem like pathological behavior, but as I told Jeff, I plan to take any future relationships very seriously from here on out. Maybe no more men—and therefore no more pets—till I'm done with Marge. Maybe.

After Brendan there was Leonard from the biology department. Such smoking-hot good looks on that guy. It was nice while it lasted. He and I both started using Facebook a couple of months into the relationship, his old high-school girlfriend appeared, as smoking hot as he was if not more, and that was the end of that. A few weeks later, I went to the pound and adopted Rolf, my stately orange tabby.

Next was Ernie: skinny, sexy Roman-nosed Ernie with the generously paying IT job. He was a couple of years younger than me, but it didn't seem to make much difference at first. He moved in after six months. And it was a little paradise with Ernie for the first couple months of cohabitation. We went out to dinner a lot. When we didn't, I made rich, buttery suppers like scampi and chicken Kiev and lit candles and popped open bottle after bottle of Malbec.

But that was all before the pinball machines.

When the thrill of cohabiting wore off, Ernie bought a pin-ball machine and moved it into my basement: a machine from the eighties called Pin-Bot that we played every so often when we were bored. I didn't think much of it at first. Jeff sometimes came over and played it with us.

But a month later Ernie came home late with a friend of his, driving a rented U-Haul van. In it was another eighties-era machine, this one themed Elvira and the Party Monsters. They parked that thing right in the living room and proceeded to play it for a couple of hours, barely acknowledging my presence. Now, before you call me a shrew for letting this bother me, I suggest you go to an arcade and watch a couple of men playing pinball for an hour or so. If you're sensitive to these things, all that grinding and gyrating against the machine will make you wonder after a while.

Anyway, once his buddy left, Ernie told me that this was a

temporary move, that he was planning on selling Pin-Bot and relocating Elvira into its space in the basement.

But I had a feeling this might be a passive-aggressive assertion of his bachelorhood. Then he started spending late nights at this sports bar downtown that supposedly had some stellar, famous machine he couldn't afford.

When the third pinball machine showed up in my kitchen one Saturday—a monstrous yellow-and-black machine decorated like a taxicab, with a big light-up TAXI sign at the top and Mikhail Gorbachev as one of the characters—I decided we needed to have a frank discussion.

He was playing the machine while I was trying to talk to him, so it went something like this:

> Me: *I have a feeling you're trying to tell me something by moving this machine in here.*
> Pinball machine: *Yo! Taxi! Bing! Bing! Bing!*
> Ernie: *Don't be so sensitive. It's just a hobby.*
> Pinball machine: *HEY, COMRADE TAXI! YOU GIVE TO ME RIDE!*
> Me: *I mean, you know how much I like to cook, and this is sort of in the way. Seems a little inconsiderate, and I'm wondering if. . .*
> Ernie (jostling the machine, banging the flippers): *Damn it!*
> Pinball machine (in a Dracula voice): *Look out!*
> Ernie: *What did you say?*

When Ernie and his machines moved out, I got my wire-haired dachshund, Boober. I named him after Martin Buber, one of my favorite theologians from my English-and-religion dual-major undergrad days. I changed the spelling because I thought using the real one might be a little sacrilegious. And now whenever I date a new guy, I make sure to ask, "Do you now or have you ever owned a pinball machine?"

Last was Scott, a slightly older gentleman with dapper gray sideburns and a goofy smile and a savant-like knowledge of wild mushrooms and presidential politics. The week he seduced me with a fricassee made of handpicked chanterelles, however, my friend Tish spotted him in a deadbeat-dads poster at the post office. The following Saturday I went to the pound and adopted my sweet gray shorthair, Geraldine. She spends most of her time sleeping under my bed or gazing out my bedroom window at the golf course, but I find her curled by my side in the wee hours a couple of times a week.

So animals are my one indulgence. That and a weekly bottle of wine, which these days I tend to hide from Jeff when he comes over. Not because it embarrasses me but because he'd probably drink most of it.

Here's the story with my brother: He's one year older than me, and he's supposed to be some kind of genius. A standardized test he took when he was seven told my mother so. I've been hearing it ever since. And while Jeff has many enviable qualities—creativity, origami skill, loyalty, and super-fast metabolism—I've never bought that he's a genius. Maybe that's what drove me to become the nerd of the family—to bring home straight A's and get into the famous Thompson University, which we were always being told was off-limits to working-class townies like us. Maybe that's even what drove me to stay there long past the undergrad years, to decide I needed a Ph.D.: to let everyone know that I was, in the end, the smart one. But the why of entering a humanities Ph.D. program usually involves some sort of deep-seated but ultimately boring intellectual inferiority complex, so I won't go into it. I no longer feel I need a Ph.D., but Marge and I do need closure, I think.

How Jeff ended up a school-bus driver is an equally long story. But he didn't finish college, and he likes kids. That's the short version. And he actually liked his job. A little more than a year ago, however, he kicked an eighth-grader off his bus for making fun of an overweight girl. Made the kid walk all the way home—across town. The boy's parents—a lawyer and a law professor at Thompson—complained, saying Jeff had lost control of his temper, grabbed their son, and physically thrown the boy off the bus. All the other kids denied the parents' version of the story, but Jeff was eventually let go for "endangering" a student. The incident got some local press, and he had a lot of support—letters to the editor in his favor, a summer job offer from the owner of a local ice-cream-truck outlet—but was quickly forgotten. For a long time, he was at my house almost nightly, scrounging for food and drinking my wine.

When he met Kim a few months ago, he stopped coming around so much. I was happy for him. And I didn't need so much company after all. I had a dissertation to worry about, and my time was running out.

Thursday, October 3

We all went to Wiley's together in Jeff's black Buick—one of the few reliable things in his life. Supposedly the car was some kind of collector's model, and he took better care of it than he did of himself.

While Jeff drove, Kim brushed her hair and asked me about Whitlock's Candles.

"I *love* their candles," she told me. "Especially the ones that smell like laundry and air and stuff."

"The Fresh line?" We didn't have a scent that smelled like *air* per se. "Like Late-Summer Rain and Morning Linen?"

"Yeah. I think so."

"I named Late-Summer Rain."

I didn't say anything about Morning Linen. I'd argued that linen doesn't always smell good in the morning but had lost to the fragrance team, who'd been proud of the name.

"*Really?* Oh my God, that's cool. What a great job."

I couldn't tell if Kim's admiration was real. She didn't stop brushing her hair as she spoke. It was a rich brown-black, with scarlet highlights that were surely artificial. They suited her well, though, and matched her lipstick color. The light freckles dusted across her cheekbones gave her an impish quality that men surely found irresistible. One thing I liked about her was that her makeup wasn't always perfect. Each time I saw her—and I'd seen her only a handful of times, admittedly—something always seemed hastily applied. There would be a blip in her lipstick or maybe a patch of foundation below the ear not fully blended in. Today one eye's mascara was thicker than the other. Kind of a *Clockwork Orange* effect.

"How'd you get such an awesome job?" Kim asked.

"I don't know if it's awesome. But yeah, I'm lucky to have it. My friend Tish . . . her dad owns the company. He started it when we were kids. Richard Whitlock."

"Oh. Really? I thought Whitlock's Candles had been around, like, a hundred years or something."

"They want you to think that. It's all in the marketing. 'Whitlock's' sounds so Colonial, doesn't it? But Richard started the company in the eighties. It had about a hundred stores by the late nineties. Didn't you know Richard is Jeff's landlord, too?"

"You didn't tell me that, babe." Kim shoved her hairbrush into her purse.

"Whitlock's got a lot of real-estate investments around town."

I saw Jeff frown in the rearview mirror. He was watching me swallow a gag at the "babe."

"Theresa's being modest," Jeff said. "She always mentions that she knew Mr. Whitlock growing up. But he wouldn't ever have hired her if she weren't a really good writer."

I rolled my eyes. "I used to help Tish with her homework.

She couldn't diagram sentences, and neither could he. In his eyes it made me some kind of a genius."

"Old impressions die hard, I guess." Kim glanced out the window. "You didn't know it then, but it got you a job. That works."

"Yes," I said, trying to follow her gaze. We were stopped at a light. She was looking upward, at the top of a telephone pole or the clear sky behind it. "It does work. That's true."

Kim turned back to me. "What does that mean, by the way? Diagram a sentence?"

Jeff wouldn't let me answer. "It's something from the deep past," he said, "that you don't really need to know about. Like bloodletting. Like a card catalog."

"Somewhere in between those two," I said. "Right."

"You guys are cute," said Kim, and then she looked out the window again. She said it like she felt sorry for us.

We hung out at the bar while we waited for our table. Just as Kim and I were settling onto our barstools, Jeff spotted someone he knew and floated off with his oatmeal stout.

"Do you know Nathan?" asked Kim, indicating the dark-haired bartender working in front of the elegantly backlit wall of fancy booze bottles. "Have I ever mentioned him to you before?"

"No," I said.

"I think you'd like him."

I gazed at the Asian-character tattoo on the back of Nathan's neck. "Really? What makes you say that?"

"Well, it's not any one thing. But I think you'd like his attitude. He's laid back. And he's, like, sort of a radical."

As Nathan turned to give someone a beer, I noticed his sharp profile. He had a nice strong nose, which I liked. I didn't care much for the five-o'clock shadow. It was well manicured—a deliberate shadow, to be sure. But facial hair generally makes me nervous.

"And he loves animals, like you," Kim said, leaving the "radical" part unexplained.

"Oh, really?"

"And he's into, like, spiritual stuff. I bet he'd really be interested in that nun lady you're doing your thesis on."

Marge was no nun, but I didn't feel like getting into it with Kim. I didn't want to sound like a know-it-all. I'd probably already come across braggy about the candles.

"Maybe I ought to try to fix you guys up."

I sipped my wine and didn't reply. I wasn't sure if she was serious.

"I would've asked *him* to take Wayne this weekend. But he's got this snake, and that makes me nervous."

"Oh? A snake?" *Polite smile, Theresa. Remember that Jeff really digs her.*

"Yeah. He's got a really old greyhound, a couple of canaries, and a ball python. His dog is bigger, but I'd worry the snake would get out of his cage and think Wayne was food."

"A python? Huh."

"Yeah. It's pretty cool. It's all white and yellow, kind of pretty in a way. Jeff and I went over to his place a few weeks ago. He took it out of its cage and showed it to us. He really snuggles with that thing. Loves it as much as his other pets."

I took a longer drink from my wineglass. I wondered how I could seem that eccentric to Kim—that a dude with a python felt like a good match. Maybe it was all the flannel I'd been wearing lately.

"You don't need to fix us up, Kim."

She frowned. "No?"

"Deadly reptiles. That's a deal breaker for me."

Kim let out a big, fake-sounding laugh. Then she said nothing—just sipped from her cocktail straw.

"What's so funny?" I asked.

"I'm surprised to hear you say the term 'deal breaker,' I guess."

"Oh."

"I've got a couple, too. I understand."

She put her hand on my arm. I think my face tightened slightly, because she pulled it away quickly.

"For example?" I said, trying to recover by expressing a bit of interest.

Kim pawed around in her plaid leather handbag for a moment and came up with a cell phone. "For example, being an asshole," she said, tapping at the phone but trying to look casual about it.

These young folks irritate me, always looking at their phones. It annoys me in a fist-shaking, "get off my lawn" kind of way.

"Isn't that a deal breaker for everyone?" I asked.

"Not in my experience."

"And it's not something you know going in," I said. "Like someone owning a python, for example. The python's there from the beginning, if you choose to deal with it. An asshole, if he has any intelligence at all, hides it at the start. Then slowly reveals himself. After you move in, say."

Kim slid the phone onto her lap and covered it with her palm. I wondered if this was the new phone etiquette, like covering your mouth when you cough. "Some assholes. There are assholes of every kind out there, Theresa."

I forced a smile. Funny how this young thing was trying to school me about assholes.

"But the kind you're talking about . . . was that what Brendan was?"

I took a breath, surprised to hear my ex-husband's name come out of this young thing's mouth. She and Jeff had clearly discussed him, and Kim was trying for an intimacy I wasn't interested in having with one of Jeff's girlfriends. Not at this stage anyway. Women always seemed attracted to Jeff's very gentle heart for a few short months—before they liked to break it. If Kim stuck with Jeff a couple of years, boosted his confidence, encouraged him to get a job worthy of his talents, made him healthy breakfasts, and fattened him up a bit, then maybe. But not until then. And I wasn't interested in pretending in the meantime.

"No," I said. "He wasn't an asshole. It was a complicated situation."

Kim's gaze eased down to her Cosmopolitan glass for a moment. "Okay," she said, then took a sip.

We both watched Nathan move behind the bar. He was handling a bottle of Grey Goose in a ridiculously sexy fashion, sliding his left hand up the length of it as he tipped it and poured with his right.

"You know what I like about your brother, Theresa?" Kim asked.

"No," I said, then realized it sounded colder than I intended. "What?"

"I mean, aside from the fact that the first time we went out, he made a rose for me from the cocktail napkin."

I smiled. Jeff's full of million-dollar book ideas. Most recently he'd talked about a series of gluten-free mysteries. Before that was *How to Win Chicks with Origami*.

"The thing is . . . he's as good as he seems."

"Good?" I said.

"As kind as he seems. No more, no less. I realized while you were talking about the type that slowly reveals himself. That's not Jeff at all. He's as good as he seems." Kim hesitated and twiddled her cocktail straw. "Isn't he?"

I couldn't tell if she was trying to kiss up by talking up my brother—or really asking for my assurance that she was with a good guy. Naïve either way.

"In my experience," I answered.

Friday, October 4

When Jeff called to tell me he was on his way with Wayne, I put Boober in my bedroom and let out the two outdoor cats. A few minutes later, I watched as Jeff let Wayne out of the backseat of his car. Wayne was velvety brown and even fatter than I expected, but there was an unexpected lightness to his movement as he pranced up the driveway. His tongue hung out casually to one side, and he glanced amiably at my brother a few times as they walked.

Jeff took a little detour into the side yard to pick up a golf ball and stuff it into his jacket pocket. He used to be more consistent about collecting the stray balls and taking them to the pro shop for some extra cash. Lately he'd been remiss. There weren't too many piled up, though, since it was the end of the season.

"Hi, guys," I said as they entered the kitchen. I stooped down. "Are you Wayne?"

The puggle looked at Jeff.

"He really liked the drive," Jeff said. "He likes the car."

Wayne tilted his head, listening to Jeff.

"Didn't you?" Jeff deposited a brown bag on the kitchen counter. "Here's his food. It's a special formula for fatties. He's got a thyroid problem."

Wayne blinked, repositioned his paws, and cocked his head even farther to the side.

"I'll be right back. I've got his little bed in the car, too."

Wayne lowered his head to his paws and glanced from me to Jeff's retreating figure and back to me again, his forehead wrinkling, his bitty black eyebrows worrying up and down.

While Jeff went back out to the car, I knelt next to Wayne and held my hand out so he could sniff it. Then I patted him on his soft head.

"You don't seem like a Wayne," I said.

Wayne made a deep groaning noise and lifted his head again.

"Or maybe you do," I said. "I didn't mean to be presumptuous. I don't really know you yet."

Jeff returned with a plaid, fleece-lined dog bed—a very expensive-looking item that made me feel like a second-rate pet owner.

"I'd stay to help him settle in," Jeff said, "but Kim and I are both sort of in a rush."

"Get out of here, then," I said. "We'll be fine."

He did as instructed—even quicker than I expected. He was out of my driveway in about thirty seconds. Jeff rarely moves so fast, so I wondered what made my brother so eager to escape.

"Won't we?" I said to Wayne.

Wayne lifted his head, sniffed the air, and resignedly closed his eyes.

Monday, October 7

It was a sultry night in June when Margery Kempe told her husband she'd rather watch his beheading than sleep with him anymore. She told him so in response to a hypothetical question he asked her while they walked home from a trip together. (If a man came with a sword and was going to lop off my head unless I made love to you like I used to, would you let him do it, or would you sleep with me?) When John Kempe heard his wife's honest response, he declared: "*Ye arn no good wyfe.*"

In my final year with Brendan, those words echoed in my head quite often. That was the point when I ceased to find that passage amusing. I'd returned to this conversation between Marge and John many times over the years, trying to decide what I thought of it.

And I was reading it yet again while I waited for Jeff or Kim to come pick up Wayne.

Despite John's chagrin, it was on that very same trip that Marge finally convinced him to allow her to be celibate— after a few years of haggling. They sat under a cross and made a deal. She'd pay off some of his debts (she was from a wealthier family than he was) and agree to eat with him on Friday nights (which she'd recently stopped doing, as one of her many displays of faith), and he'd quit trying to get her into the sack. It was a pretty good deal for the times. That is, for a woman with fourteen children who was ready for some spiritual Me Time.

I looked at the clock. It was getting late, and still no word from Jeff.

My time with Wayne had gone more smoothly than I anticipated. I had Boober and Wayne take turns in the guest bedroom, making sure to give the sequestered dog plenty of attention.

I tried Jeff's number. No answer. I didn't know Kim's.

It was awfully quiet in my bedroom, so I went to check on Wayne. When I opened the door, I found him wrestling something with his paws. Seeing me, he stopped and cocked his head.

"What've you got there, boy?" I said.

It was an old leather journal of mine, in which I'd never written a word—a gift from Brendan years ago. I wasn't sure where Wayne could've found it.

The journal was made of a beautiful wine-colored leather. ("It's cruelty-free leather," Brendan had told me when I opened it. I still don't know what that means.) It had a lovely oak tree carved into the front, and the description inside said it was a "Tree of Life."

I've never been a journal type, but maybe I hadn't ever told Brendan so. Or he simply hadn't believed me. Interesting things tend not to happen to me, and I don't know how much eloquence I'd be able to get out of bad haircuts and candle-catalog layouts.

"Let me see that, Wayne."

When I yanked at the corner of the journal, Wayne growled.

"Don't growl at me, hon," I said sharply.

He dropped the journal and tilted his head at me.

"That's right," I whispered, scooping up the journal. "Cute becomes you more."

Wayne had chewed through the elegant branches of the tree. And the top right-hand corner of the cover was gone—he'd probably ingested it.

"That wasn't very nice," I said to Wayne, who sighed and plunked his body sideways on the carpet. "But I guess I was never going to write in it."

Wayne's pink belly rose and fell softly against the floor.

"But what if I'd written about all of my most personal experiences in here, Wayne? My deepest wishes?"

Wayne's little black eyebrows gave an obligatory twitch. Then he closed his eyes. I tossed the journal onto the pile of books on the bed—thrillers and romances and scholarly tomes about medieval women.

"I guess you're right about that. There's no sense in your feeling bad about it, because I *didn't*."

I sat on the floor and gently thumped his chest with my palm.

"Do dogs ever ask what if, Wayne?"

Wayne didn't open his eyes.

"I suppose I should ask Boober, too. But you'd be surprised. Contrary to his name, he's not a very deep thinker, I'm afraid."

Wayne sighed again.

"You know, if I told Kim about this, she'd probably want to buy me another steak. But I'm not going to. Because I don't really care about that thing. It just seemed expensive. That was the only reason I never threw it out."

Wayne was dozing now.

"You know, you're right. I should be working on Marge. You're right."

I stayed on the floor, patting Wayne's chest until the room grew cold and I grew hungry. The phone didn't ring, and Kim and Jeff never arrived.

Wednesday, October 9

Jeff sounded tired when he finally answered his phone late Wednesday afternoon.

"Oh, hey," he said. "I've been meaning to call you."

"Yeah? I've been trying you all day." I picked up a measuring cup and started watering the herb pots on my kitchen windowsill. "When are you and Kim gonna pick up this puggle? You can tell Kim he's awful sweet, but a neighbor called yesterday about how much he barks while I'm at work."

"Well. I can come get him right now if you want. But I don't know where Kim is."

I picked up a dead basil plant and tossed it into the trash, plastic pot and all. "What do you mean, you don't know where she is?"

"She's not back yet. She said she'd be back Monday and would call if it was gonna be longer."

"She didn't call?" I peered into the garbage and felt guilty for not recycling the pot.

Wayne wandered into the kitchen, his nails gently clicking *tsk-tsk-tsk* on the linoleum. He stopped in the middle of the room and stared at me.

"No. And I can't call her. Because she forgot her phone."

"How do you know that?" I reached into the trash and pulled the pot up, slipped the desiccated dirt and basil out, and rinsed it.

"She called me on Friday from a pay phone at a rest stop," Jeff explained. "Asking if she'd left her phone in my car. I checked. And she had."

"So you have her phone?"

"Yeah. It was shoved down into the passenger seat."

"Could you call her sister's?" I asked. "That's where she was going, right?"

"I don't have her sister's contact information. I've tried to figure it out. I know one of her sisters is named Brenda. So I was poking around online looking for a Brenda Graber, from New Jersey. But I don't know if her sister's married."

"I can't remember. . . . Are you on Facebook?"

"Kind of," Jeff admitted. "I only go on every couple of months and randomly thumb up shit to make people feel good about themselves. Like, people from high school who I remember having self-esteem problems."

"Is Kim on Facebook? That's why I'm asking. Because you could look through her friend list for her sister."

"I did that already. I couldn't find a Brenda."

"Huh," I said. "Well, since you have her phone, why don't you look for Brenda's number?"

"You're right. I guess I could do that."

It seemed odd to me that Jeff hadn't thought of this already. This is the thing about that genius IQ score, see?

"Didn't Kim have to be back for work?" I asked.

"I thought so. By the end of the week at least. I didn't know her exact schedule. I resisted calling for a couple of days, because I didn't want to give them a bad impression. But I broke down and called this afternoon. They haven't heard from her either. She was supposed to come in last night."

I gazed down at Wayne. He had lowered his head to his paws and was working his little eyebrows up and down. He looked as skeptical as I felt. There was something Jeff wasn't telling me, I was pretty sure.

"Do you want to come over?" I asked.

Jeff hesitated. "What, to pick up Wayne?"

"No."

I looked in the fridge. No doggie bags since Jeff had eaten the last one. I hadn't been very social lately since I was trying to commit to Marge. "Just to come over."

"I don't know, Theresa."

"I was thinking of getting some pizza and some beer tonight," I said quickly.

"Huh?"

"I'm having a taste for both."

"Well . . . if you want company."

"Yeah," I said miserably, hating myself a little for baiting my brother with beer. "Yeah, I do."

After we hung up, I ordered a medium pizza and went out for some Newcastle ale.

Rolf watched Jeff and me from the top of the refrigerator while we helped ourselves to pizza slices.

"I found Brenda's number," Jeff said. "Left a message. But

I found something else on Kim's phone. Something kind of weird. Pictures."

"Uh-oh," I whispered. "Are they pornographic?"

He snorted. "I wouldn't show them to you if they were."

He pushed a maroon cell phone across the table at me. I gobbled half a pizza slice before picking it up. On the tiny screen was a photo of a man and a woman on a street corner, eating hot dogs. Both were wearing suits. The man was gray-haired, a good decade older than the woman.

I pressed the side arrows to look through the next few pictures. They focused in on the man—some blurry, some clear. His mouth open. His mouth closed. Sinking his teeth into the hot dog. Dabbing his mouth with a napkin. Turning, presumably to the woman, and laughing. He was about sixty years old, on the stocky side, with deep-set eyes and almost no lips.

"Is this someone you know?"

"You don't recognize him?"

"Should I?"

"It's Donald Wallace."

I tapped my head with my fingertips. "Oh. Did he teach math at the high school?"

"Jesus, Theresa. *No.* Donald Wallace is running for Senate. In the special election next month. To replace Henry Rowan. Do you really have your head that far up Marge's ass? Did you even know that Rowan *died*?"

"Well, yeah. I did know *that.* So Donald Wallace . . . Is he the . . . Republican candidate?"

"Democrat. Good guess, though. The fact that you didn't know doesn't bode well for him. It's not looking that great."

"Do you care?"

"Of course I care. They need every single Democratic vote to pass the employment bill. They were counting on Rowan's, and now it looks like a Republican has a chance at that seat."

"And Kim cared, too? That's why she was up there in Boston taking pictures of the guy eating a hot dog? Are you *sure* this is him?"

"Pretty sure. Keep looking."

I hit the arrow some more. Same guy sipping a coffee. Then a whole bunch of shots of him using his palm to arrange a piece of his gray hair across his forehead. All of the photos were taken outdoors, from a far distance. He was never looking at the camera.

"This doesn't really do anything for me."

"It's him. Trust me. I know his face. He's on *Maddow* all the time."

Since losing his job, Jeff had become a cable-news junkie.

"So what's this guy's story?" I asked.

"He's the state attorney general right now," Jeff said. "He was local for a while. By local, I mean he was a prosecutor for our county ten or so years ago. Pelsworth County before that. Before he started moving up the ranks. People around here like him. But I think statewide they're having trouble getting Democrats excited about him."

"Well, apparently Kim was excited about him."

I slid the phone back to Jeff.

"Kim didn't care about politics," Jeff said, picking up the phone.

"Um . . . are you *sure*? Looks to me like she was sort of a groupie."

"Like she was stalking him, you mean?"

I contemplated my pizza slice. "I didn't say that."

"She never said anything while you guys were watching all your cable news together?"

"She almost never watched it with me. She really didn't seem to care."

"Huh."

"Okay. So that's the first thing I found on the phone. But I found something else."

"Ooh, what now? Joe Biden sipping a Slurpee?"

Jeff ignored me. "Text messages. I don't know the number. But look at them."

I did. One had come in on the day after Kim had left, at around 10:00 A.M. It said, I WAITED FOR AN HOUR YESTERDAY. WHERE WERE YOU? Another had come in about two hours later, saying, THAT VIDEO I SENT YOU. THAT'S JUST BETWEEN US. An hour after that: SO I'M JUST A FUCKING JOKE TO YOU? And a few minutes later, simply: FUCK YOU, KIM.

"That's . . . interesting. Did you try to call that number and see who it is?"

"Yeah. I got a mailbox-full message. But after seeing that, I couldn't resist. I looked at her last few calls. The couple of days before she left. I didn't recognize any of the numbers. None of them was labeled as people she knew. I called one of them right before I came over here. I got the voice-mail box of some reporter at the *Chronicle*."

"Did she know anyone at the *Chronicle*, that you know of?"

"No. The other numbers . . . I'm going to try them tomorrow, during business hours. Maybe even ask some of these people how they knew Kim, what she was up to right before she left. Would that be too . . . desperate?"

"I don't think so." I hesitated. "Do you think she thought someone in the news business would be interested in her hot-dog pictures?"

Jeff took a long and solemn swallow of beer. "I care about her. Actually."

The words took my breath away for a moment. We don't normally say this stuff outright in our family. Except occasionally about a deceased pet perhaps.

"I . . . know that."

"Then don't talk like that. Like she's stupid."

"I'm sorry. I don't think she's stupid. You come here with photos of a local politician chomping on a wiener and I might, you know, get a little punchy."

Jeff went to the refrigerator to get himself a third beer.

"Another for you?" he asked.

I shook my head. I used to match him. These days each drink of his diminished my thirst a bit.

Jeff closed the fridge but lingered there for a moment, still holding the handle. "All this makes me think of something odd she said the night before she left. I mean, I didn't think it was odd until now. But she asked me if there would ever be a circumstance in which I'd be willing to be paid for my silence."

"What?"

"That's what I said. I told her it was too general a question. Silence about what? It would all come down to that."

"And she said?"

Jeff came back to the table. "She told me I was asking too many questions. She said, 'That's the point of asking a hypothetical question. That you don't have to get too specific.' And I said that 'hypothetical' didn't mean nonspecific, and she got mad at me for implying that she was dumb, and then the conversation was over."

Jeff opened his beer, staring at Rolf on top of the fridge. "How does he get up there?"

"Rolf? Sometimes he jumps up onto the stove first. Sometimes he jumps directly from the floor. To show off."

"From the floor all the way up there? No way. He'd have to *fly*. And you can't fly, can you, Rolf?"

Rolf blinked modestly, then began to lick his outstretched leg.

"He's very athletic," I noted.

"There's no way he can jump that high."

"He does. I've seen it."

"Maybe you just dreamed it. I think you did."

I didn't reply. I was worried about Kim, and what it meant that she hadn't returned, called, or texted my brother. Maybe it had been too good to be true, this cute, easygoing-if-a-little-affected young lady who'd come into my brother's life and brightened things up where I'd no longer had the energy to do so. I felt as if Jeff and I had both been duped somehow. I was, after all, the one left holding the puggle.

What did we really know about this Kim? Jeff had met her in the Art of the Memoir night class I'd encouraged him to take last semester, because he was always saying he wanted to write a book of all his school-bus and ice-cream-truck stories. It was a very popular night class at the university that drew in students and dabblers of every age. Now I felt partly responsible for Jeff's meeting Kim—who was maybe turning out to be another heartbreaker.

"You told me a couple of months ago that you dream more about your animals now than about anyone else," Jeff continued.

What was wrong with Jeff and me, that nothing was ever quite finished for us and nothing ever quite worked out? Sometimes, when my father would scratch off a losing lottery ticket or arrive at the movie theater after all the seats had sold out, he would say cheerfully, "Oh, well. We're Battles. We're used to disappointment." Or worse: "We're Battles. What chance did we have?" Maybe we'd both taken these pronouncements more seriously than my father had intended. Maybe we somehow invited failure, on some deep and instinctual level.

"Do you think you dreamed it? Rolf jumping up there from the floor?" Jeff wanted to know.

"Probably," I said.

Thursday, October 10

At the office I spent the better part of the afternoon on a jade green Outdoor-category candle:

> *Dayspring Grass*
> *The smell of a freshly cut lawn breezing*
> *through your bedroom window after a long,*
> *lazy summer sleep.*

At the last minute, I changed "lazy" to "dreamy." Middle-aged women might not like the implication that they are lazy just because once in a while they get a decent night's sleep—just because once in a blue moon their husbands might drag themselves out of bed before them and mow the goddamned lawn.

Jeff's car was in my driveway when I arrived home. He'd let himself in, and Geraldine was curled up at his side as he sat in the darkening living room.

"How sweet," I said. "She likes you better than me. Where's Wayne?"

"Sleeping on your bed. I gave both dogs a walk."

"At the same time? How'd that go?"

Jeff shrugged and petted Geraldine. "Fine. Wayne couldn't care less about Boober. More of a priority for him was smelling that rotting stump in front of that red house down the street. I also took out your trash, by the way. Because it smelled like old Fancy Feast."

"Thanks," I said, looking through my mail and hoping he'd skip the crazy-cat-lady comments.

"Listen," he said. "I'm sorry you have to deal with Wayne."

"Don't be silly. I'm liking it so far. For the most part."

Jeff nodded. "So I called those numbers on Kim's phone."

"And?"

"And I found a few strange things. First of all, I got hold of the woman whose voice mail answered last night. From the *Chronicle*. Her name's Janice Obermeier. She didn't know Kim personally, but she said Kim had contacted her a couple of times in the past few weeks."

Boober pranced into the room, sniffed around Jeff's ankles, and gave a couple of commanding barks. Geraldine promptly got up from the couch and dashed down the hall.

"Contacted her about what?" I asked.

"Well, Kim told her she had some 'special information' about Donald Wallace."

"What information?" Boober barked again. I threw him a pull toy, and he began wrestling with it on the carpet.

"That's not clear. But apparently Janice Obermeier didn't feel that Kim was a serious source. So she didn't pursue it."

"But how would Kim . . . ?"

"I have no idea. But she said she had some video she thought was gonna go viral. The Obermeier lady thought it sounded odd, too. She seemed concerned when I said Kim was missing.

She said she'd wondered if Kim was . . . 'one hundred percent well' was the way she put it. She told Kim she'd give it some thought, but she didn't call her back. I got the feeling that's what she does when crazies call her looking for publicity. And then the next time Kim called, she left a message saying she had some *new* video footage she thought she'd be interested in. Some special footage she'd uncovered or something."

"You didn't know anything about this? Her calling the newspaper?"

"No. But the whole viral-video thing actually does sound like Kim. She has a kind of obsession with viral videos. Except she was usually interested in animal videos."

"Like the dog riding the skateboard?"

"Exactly like that. She was constantly filming Wayne, hoping he'd do something really charming she could put up on You-Tube and get a million hits."

I scoffed. "Like eating a two-hundred-dollar handbag? Something like that?"

Jeff shrugged. "He actually does cute stuff now and then."

"Even if it worked . . . to what end?"

"I don't know, Theresa. I never *asked* her. I thought it was kind of sweet."

"But she never mentioned Donald Wallace?"

"Never."

"And never Janice Obermeier."

"Nope."

"Did you look for any video on her phone?"

"Yeah. There wasn't any. But I wasn't surprised, since she has a handheld video camera she usually uses for her Wayne footage."

"Oh," I said, rising to find a snack in the kitchen.

Jeff followed me. "There's one other weird part of all of this that I thought would interest you," he said. "One of the other numbers . . . it was Zach Wagner."

Zach Wagner was a young instructor in the English department—my department—at the university. He taught the memoir class where Jeff met Kim. He occasionally wrote pieces for the *Chronicle* and the prestigious national magazine *Waltham's Review*.

"That's actually not that weird. He writes for the *Chronicle*, too. Did you talk to him?"

"No. I got his voice mail."

I fished in the cabinet for a box of Triscuits and watched Jeff open my fridge. He took out the leftover beer from the previous night.

"I was hoping you could do something for me," he said, rummaging in my utensil drawer until he found a bottle opener.

"What's that?" I asked, even though I already knew the answer. I'd been hoping he wouldn't ask.

"Talk to Zach Wagner. Ask him if he knows why Kim was calling him."

"Oh. Uh . . ." I would certainly feel like a creeper doing that. And Zach was pretty cute, which would make it doubly painful. "I guess maybe I could do that. But you could, too, you know."

"But he'd probably take you more seriously. You're, like, his colleague. You're on his level."

I suppressed a snort, lest Jeff think I was being snide again. "Not ex*act*ly . . ."

"Well, more than him and *me*, right?"

Negligible, I thought. "We don't need to quantify it. I'll think about it, okay?"

"Just offhand the next time you're on campus."

"I'm not on campus much these days. Not to mention how I'd manage to bring Kim up without admitting we were snooping on her phone—and what exactly do you think he's gonna be able to tell you?"

Jeff held his beer bottle with both hands and bowed closer to it as if confiding in it. "I care about Kim, and she's gone. Any clue would help."

I stared at the beer in his long, bony hands. For the first time in a while, I wished I had another to offer him.

"I'll consider it," I said. "In the meantime I think you ought to get a hold of her family. Don't you?"

"Yeah. I guess I should. I only met them once, and I don't think they like me. Once they heard I was looking for a job, it was over."

I expected Jeff to continue, but he was silent.

Boober skittered in. This time when Jeff tried to play with him, he nipped him on the hand.

"Boober!" I said, scooping him up, and taking his ear gently in my mouth.

"What the hell are you doing?"

"I bite him on the ear," I said. "It kind of brings him back to himself."

Jeff shook his head. "Did you hear what you just said?"

"Yeah. It's like a Zen thing for him. Look how calm and present he looks now."

"*Jesus*, Theresa."

"What?"

"I'm not going to say anything."

And he didn't. But he finished his beer before he left.

Saturday, October 12

Not just her family," my mother insisted over the phone. "The police. Your brother always takes everything personally. Well, what if it's *not* personal? What if something happened to her? What then? See, he needs to call the police, just in case. Do you want me to call him and tell him to do it?"

"No," I answered.

"If he doesn't do it, maybe you should."

"Probably."

"And if you don't, maybe *I* should. God, I wish he still drove a school bus."

I was surprised to hear my mother say this. She used to go around saying to people, *I've got two kids. One drives a bus and the other's a Ph.D. candidate.* As if the juxtaposition were hilarious. As if transporting children safely to school were comically unimportant in comparison to working a dead-end job by day and lurching anemically around a university library at night.

She stopped saying that a couple of years ago, presumably because her friends noticed that the word "candidate" was still included in the statement long after it should have fallen away.

"What does driving a school bus have to do with this, Mom?"

"Then he'd just be brokenhearted. Not brokenhearted *and* unemployed."

"He's still working under the table for Mike's cabinetry business."

As I said this, Wayne hopped onto the couch, over my lap, and up to the windowsill, snuffling anxiously.

"That's not a real job, Theresa. That doesn't even pay his rent."

Wayne growled. I wondered if he could hear my mother's voice and thought it was some sort of game bird.

"Well, I know. . . ." I sighed.

"I know you know."

I never used to call my mother before she moved to Florida with her fiancé last year. But these days it felt necessary. I halve my worry over Jeff by splitting it with her. And since he never calls her at all, questions about him usually occupy the space of the conversation that used to be about me and my romantic life.

My father calls only about once a month. Technically he still lives in Thompsonville, but most of the time these days he was off on a cruise ship. A couple of years after he retired from his job driving the P&H Oil truck, he got a job as "gentleman host" on a cruise ship. They pay older men to dance with the widowed ladies who go on the cruises. All those years my mother had dragged him to ballroom-dance lessons in their "let's try to save this marriage" stage had ended up giving him a pretty sweet deal for his retired bachelorhood. It was quite a good gig for a guy who'd spent most of his prior years griping about what shitty luck he had.

"I wouldn't say he's brokenhearted," I reassured my mother. "Maybe perplexed."

"Perplexed. Wonderful. Either way Jeff needs this drama like he needs a hole in the head."

"Like a hole in the head" is my mother's favorite all-occasion phrase about Jeff. *Jeff needs a history degree like a hole in the head. Jeff needs another drink like a hole in the head. Jeff needs a yoga retreat like . . .* You get the idea.

Wayne barked once sharply.

"Is that the puggle?" my mother demanded.

"Yeah."

"Tell him to shut his kibble hole."

Wayne took a deep breath and let out a full sentence of barks.

"He doesn't usually do this. I don't know what's up."

My mother worried for a bit more over Jeff's weight, Jeff's viability as a family man, Jeff's heating bill. By the time she got around to asking me if I was dating anyone, Wayne was barking too loudly for us to continue the conversation.

After I hung up, I saw my mailman come into the yard. At that point the barking reached a dramatic crescendo: a long, continuous ROWROWROWROW interrupted only when Wayne took an occasional gasping breath.

I decided to go out and greet the poor mailman—and apologize to him. I slipped out quickly and shut the door behind me, because Wayne was still going apeshit in the living room.

"Sorry about that," I said to the mailman as he handed me my *Bon Appétit* and an electric bill.

"You have a new dog?" he asked.

I'd never spoken to this mailman or seen him up close. He had a Tom Selleck mustache and jumpy little eyes.

"Um. I'm dog-sitting for someone."

"He's done that every day this week."

"Oh. Really?"

"Yeah. A couple of your neighbors have asked me about it."

"That's weird," I said. "Because he's relatively quiet when I'm home."

"Okay," the mailman said uncertainly. I tried to determine his age. Probably mid-thirties, like me. It was an odd feeling to realize this. Usually I think of mailmen as being much older than me. Mr. McFeelys and so on.

"I'm hoping he'll be back with his owner in the next couple of days," I said. "I'm sorry."

"Okay," the mailman said, then continued on his way.

It was true. I was hoping Wayne would soon return to his rightful owner. But I had a feeling that wasn't likely to happen. In fact, I somehow *knew* it wouldn't.

What sort of punk was Kim, lying to my brother like that and leaving her fat, special-needs dog with a near stranger? I liked Wayne okay, but I didn't want to do Kim any favors. I wanted to know where the hell she went and who exactly she thought she was. The longer she stayed away, the more she pissed me off. It was time to go looking for her.

Monday, October 14

Kim's apartment was in Barton Village, which was populated mostly by university grad students. I'd heard it was clean but had thin walls and dicey plumbing. I found Apartment B8, where Jeff had told me Kim lived with her roommate, Brittany—a grad student in sociology.

A young woman answered—overweight, but in a pink-cheeked, healthy-looking way.

"Hi there," I said. "I'm looking for Kim."

"She's not here. I don't know where she is."

"Are you her roommate? Are you Brittany?"

The young woman shifted slightly and stuck out her lower lip. Her lipstick was a candy red that looked similar to Kim's shade—only more skillfully applied. Her hair was pulled into a high, slick ponytail that dipped up cheerfully at the top and flipped at the end. It was the sort of ponytail I'd wasted many hours in high school trying to achieve, usually without success.

"Yeah," she said.

Of course someone named Brittany would get that ponytail exactly right.

"Have you heard from her recently?" I asked.

Brittany sucked in her lower lip again. I wondered how she managed to do it without messing up the lipstick. "Are you a friend of hers?" she asked.

"Sort of." I tried to sound casual. "A friend of a friend. She left her dog with me. And now I'm wondering where she is and when she's going to pick him up."

Brittany's eyebrows did a little jump. "She left Wayne with you?"

"Yeah."

"Oh. Are you Missy, then?"

"No," I said. "My name's Theresa."

"I assumed she'd left the dog with that boyfriend of hers. Or with Missy."

"No . . . uh . . . I've got Wayne."

"Oh, poor you," said Brittany, cocking her head. I wasn't sure if this was imitative of Wayne or simply her natural mannerism. "Wayne can be challenging."

"So Kim didn't say when she'd be back?"

"She said she'd be back Monday. I haven't heard from her."

"Are you worried about her? 'Cuz I'm starting to worry."

Brittany looked at her feet for a moment, then opened the door a bit wider. "Do you . . . uh, want to come in for a second?"

"Sure. Thanks."

I stepped into the living room, which resembled an IKEA showroom—all aqua and white furniture and carpet with brittle black end tables. Throwing off the freshness of the room was a ketchup-colored beanbag chair covered in dog hair.

"How's it going with old Wayne, then?" Brittany asked.

She perched on the very edge of the sofa and motioned for me to do the same.

"He's okay. He barks a lot when I'm not there, I'm told."

I sniffed at the air of the apartment. It smelled like Whitlock's Lemon Curd candle. Lemon Curd was another one of those candles I was responsible for naming. I'd convinced the fragrance team to change it from Lemon Zest, which I felt was too pedestrian. Curd was more British, and the older ladies love that.

"Yup. That sounds like Wayne. That's why I never let Kim leave him with me. One time, and never again."

"What happened?"

"He ate my favorite jacket."

"Leather?"

"No. Leather I could understand. Black denim. From J.Crew. What kind of dog eats denim?"

"Maybe there's something missing in his diet," I suggested.

Brittany scoffed. "That dog's not missing anything in the food department. What he needs is an obedience class. I've been telling Kim that for a *long* time now."

"So you and Kim are friends? Not just roommates."

Brittany rolled her shoulders, looking thoughtful. "Not really," she admitted. "I've told her that as someone who has to live with Wayne. Not so much as a friend. I don't mean I have anything against her. We're just not friends."

Brittany got up and walked over to the coat closet beside the door to the apartment.

"So if she was in some kind of trouble, she wouldn't call you about it?" I asked.

"No." Brittany pulled a black jacket out of the closet and carried it back to the sofa. "Not unless there was no one else for her to call, maybe. The thing is, I'm not so surprised she's saddled you with Wayne and then flaked out. She does stuff like that sometimes. I'm sure she'll turn up."

"What do you think happened?"

"If I had to guess, I'd say she reconnected with her old boyfriend."

Brittany thrust the jacket into my hands so I could see the jagged, stringy fabric where a cuff had once been.

"Wow," I said, holding it in my lap for a moment, hoping to appear sympathetic. "So her boyfriend. You mean Jeff?"

"Jeff? No. Is he the alcoholic? No. Her *old* boyfriend's named Kyle. All of Kim's drama always boils down to Kyle. That's my theory anyway."

"Right . . ." I gave my best knowing nod, trying to ignore the leaden feeling in my chest. I avoided the impulse to point out to Brittany the difference between alcohol*ism* and alcohol *abuse*.

"If she'd only cut it off with him, she'd probably be a lot happier. Sometimes you *can't* be friends."

"I know, I know," I said. Was the second "I know" too much, I wondered. Too fake?

"I think Jeff's onto the whole thing. I heard Kim talking on the phone with him once, and she's all like 'We just had to talk about one thing. We have a mutual friend, and she's having a problem.' Or some bullshit like that. 'I can't go into it, I can't go into it,' she kept saying. By the time she got off the phone, she was crying. I think that Jeff was really laying into her. Can't say I blame him, I guess. I *know* she still saw Kyle, still talked to him. And more than once."

"Why didn't she just end it?" I asked.

"Well . . ." Brittany cocked her head at me again. Maybe that was one too many questions. Maybe it sounded terribly naïve. Maybe anyone who knew Kim at all should have the answer.

"I actually don't know. She said he'd drunk-dial her sometimes, but what I don't get is why she would answer."

Brittany shrugged and folded her arms.

"So maybe if I could track down Kyle, I could track down Kim?" I asked her.

"I'd think," Brittany said, then clucked her tongue. "You ever met Kyle?"

"No." I folded Brittany's jacket and placed it between us on the couch. "You?"

"Nope."

"Now, what was his last name?"

"Mmm . . . Spicer? Yeah. I remember thinking it reminded me of cinnamon."

"And you think she's with him?"

Brittany shrugged again.

"Where does Kyle live?" I asked.

"I'm not sure, but he lives close. Maybe Ricksville. I know he works at Carpet World in Ricksville."

I nodded. I wasn't sure what I was going to do with this information.

"Did Kim happen to mention someone sending her nasty texts?" I asked.

"Texts?" Brittany shook her head. "No. I don't think so."

"What about Donald Wallace? Did she ever mention that name to you?"

Brittany looked at me like I was a lunatic. "Donald Wallace?" she repeated. "You mean the Senate candidate?"

"That's the one." I tried to sound casual.

"Uh . . . *no.*" Brittany twisted her lip to show how weird she thought I was for asking.

"So, then . . . this friend of hers . . . Missy? Do you think she'd know where Kim is?"

Brittany shrugged. "I'm not sure. I know Kim would walk Wayne with her sometimes. I never met her. Kim mentioned she was an old friend she'd recently gotten in touch with again."

"Do you know Missy's last name? Where she lives?"

"No. I just know that they'd walk Wayne in Higgins Park in Folston. She mentioned it to me as a nice place to jog, 'cuz I'm always looking for a place to jog besides the campus. I hate jogging on campus. But anyway, Missy's got a baby. They'd walk with the stroller and Wayne. Personally, I wouldn't want that slobbery thing near my baby. But whatever."

"Uh-huh," I said uncertainly.

Brittany hesitated, then gave me a sympathetic pout. "You know, I'm sure Kim will turn up. She'll show up all apologetic, all wanting big, sloppy Wayne kisses."

"Let's hope so."

"I'll tell her you were looking for her. If I hear from her."

"Thanks," I said.

Driving home, I considered the concept of enabler. It was something I'd been thinking about a lot lately. I never meant to be one, you see. I've noticed that there's little sympathy out there for enablers. Not that there should be a great deal, but this is something I wish people understood: It's a role that sneaks up on you.

A few years ago, I seriously thought that it was Jeff enabling *me.* I was the one going through a divorce, after all. Jeff would visit me with a six-pack and a carton of cashew chicken. Or I'd invite him over for spaghetti Bolognese—the recipe takes a dash of wine, and then we'd finish the bottle while we ate. And maybe another if I had one on hand. I really *liked* drinking then—more than I ever had before. It was the first time in my life when I felt as if I *needed* a bit of numbing each night.

After each of my subsequent breakups, Jeff was always there with at least a six-pack, and more often the makings of a Manhattan or an Old-Fashioned or whatever "vintage" cocktail (his phrase) he'd been meaning to try. I was usually too self-involved at the time to ask myself if he was drinking as much by himself—or with his friends—when I was between breakups.

But after he lost the school-bus job, the alcohol he'd bring to my place got cheaper and cheaper. Popov vodka and orange juice. Screw-top wine, then boxed. Sometimes I'd wonder where he got the money even for that. The word "vintage" was no longer used. When I'd stop by on a Saturday or after work, I'd often find him halfway through a bottle of something or dozing heavily on his couch.

If we were from a family that talked directly about feelings or worries or troubling behaviors or anything at all, really, this would perhaps have been when we would have talked about it. But we don't, so we didn't.

That's how it sneaks up on you, see?

And then you find yourself standing in a Lemon Curd–smelling living room with a girl with Twizzler lips saying your brother's a drunk. And it stabs you right in the stomach, because you knew a long time ago that this was coming but were selfishly afraid to think it. To think it for real—that is, in a way that required something of you.

As I pulled in to my neighborhood, I started to plan my evening: sad Lean Cuisine chicken, salad, maybe some frozen yogurt if it wasn't too freezer-burned. And Marge: work on the section about Marge's time in Jerusalem. A little wine. Then watch some DVRed *Mad Men* if I earned it with sufficient Marge work. Fall asleep with Sylvestress.

But when I reached my driveway, I couldn't bring myself to turn off my car. I let the engine idle for a moment. It wasn't, I decided, the monotony of my plans that made me reluctant. Lately, after the last couple of breakups, I enjoyed the monotony.

It was Jeff. Jeff in pain again. Me carrying on with Marge as usual and pretending all was fine in Jeff Land. I was used to it. But I didn't ever like it.

I set my GPS for Carpet World in Ricksville. It was only twenty minutes away.

The moment I stepped into Carpet World, I felt a little sorry for Kyle Spicer. I couldn't imagine coming, day in and day out, to this place of chemical stink. At least where I worked, you had a different cloying smell every day.

I approached the eager-looking young woman at the front desk and asked for Kyle. She pointed me toward a corner of the store where two men stood with a pregnant woman as she looked through a giant book of carpet samples.

"Which one is he?" I asked the woman at the desk.

"Tall one," she answered.

I watched Kyle talk to his customers. He had a big, perfect

toothpaste-commercial smile. I couldn't determine the color of his eyes—only that they were dark and oddly shiny, intensified by long eyelashes.

"Well, seeing as how this little girl's gonna be here sooner rather than later," he was saying, "I can set the order up right now. I'll put a hot rush on it, and I'll bet we can get it to you by Wednesday."

Kyle was handsome despite an unusually round face and a bad haircut. It was cut too close to his head, making it stand military-stiff at the top. Something in his hair—either natural sheen or some kind of product—made it look wet. He most definitely had the style of a salesman. I wondered exactly what a "hot rush" was.

He led his two customers to the front counter. While the guy of the couple bent over his wallet, shuffling credit cards, I thought I saw Kyle wink at the pregnant wife. She looked as taken aback as I was, so I probably wasn't imagining it. But then as he rang them up, it did appear that his right lid was a little twitchy. Maybe the carpet chemicals affected his eyes.

"Can I help you with something?" Kyle asked me as the couple made their way out the door.

"I'm actually here to talk to you about Kim Graber. I'm sorry to bother you at work, but I didn't know how else to contact you."

"About Kim?" Kyle's bright eyes widened into a stare. "What about Kim?"

"Well, she's a friend of a friend. I'm looking for her, and I was told you might—"

"I'm sorry," Kyle interrupted me. "I didn't catch your name."

"Margery." I swallowed. I didn't want him to associate me with Jeff, whose last name he very likely knew. "Lipinski."

The name had simply fallen out of my mouth. It was obvious where I got the Margery, but where did the Lipinski come from? Probably from Tara Lipinski. Figure skaters' names are often at the tip of my tongue. I've always kind of wanted to be one.

"Well, Margery," Kyle said crisply, "you're a friend of a friend. . . . Who told you to come see me, then? Which friend?"

"Her roommate, actually. Brittany? So I'm wondering if you've heard from Kim in the last few days?" I tried to sound casual, friendly. But Kyle looked unconvinced.

"The last few *days*?" he repeated. "No. I don't know what Brittany told you. I've never even met Brittany. But Kim and I aren't in regular contact anymore."

"So you don't know where Kim is?" I said.

Kyle squinted at me. Or his eyelid was twitching again. Hard to say which.

"Why would *I* know where she is? She has a boyfriend, you know."

There was something snottily adolescent in his tone that unnerved me. I didn't know how to reply.

"Maybe you should ask *him*," Kyle added.

"I've . . . uh . . . already asked."

"How about her family?"

"She's apparently not with them."

I was beginning to regret that I'd walked in here without much of a plan. Kyle stared at me. He may have been the first person I'd ever encountered whose eyes I'd actually describe as "piercing." I breathed carefully and shifted my gaze to the nearest wall, which displayed a rug with a red CLEARANCE tag. The rug was an ugly pink-brown. Like a raw hot dog.

"Do you know what her deal is with Donald Wallace?" I asked.

Kyle squinted again. In that moment I could've sworn his eyes actually sparkled. "Jesus," he said. "Why would you bring that up?"

"I don't know. I saw her pictures, and I was . . . concerned."

Kyle scoffed, then bit his thumbnail. "I told her it was a dumb idea," he said. His gaze began to dart around—from my face to my car parked right outside the storefront and back to me.

"What do you know about Donald Wallace?" He lowered his voice so I had to step closer. "Did she show you her stupid video, too? I mean, what she had done so far?"

"She was going to . . . but she didn't."

Kyle's face relaxed into a dull stare. "Why didn't she?"

"Because we didn't have a chance to arrange it."

"To arrange it?" Kyle folded his arms. I got the impression he was no longer having a conversation with me—just watching me.

"Yeah. We didn't have a chance."

Kyle drew a long breath into his nostrils. "Who the hell are you?"

"I'm Margery"—I involuntarily lowered my voice to a whisper—"Lipinski."

"Uh-huh. I got that."

Kyle raised both eyebrows, waiting for more. But I had nothing.

"Are you working for Donald Wallace or something?" he asked.

"What?"

"I really don't appreciate you coming here. I have a real job here. I know you all were harassing Kim, and maybe she deserved it for being a pain in the ass. But I don't have anything to do with their little project. I wouldn't dream of messing with Donald Wallace. The less I have to think about him, the better. I'm not even *voting* in this damn election. Have you been stalking Missy, too?"

"I'm not working for Donald Wallace," I managed to say.

"Whatever you're doing, you're not being honest with me. And I'd like you to leave."

I'd like you to leave. I'd never heard these words before. They froze me. They seemed words for a different sort of woman from myself. A raving maniac of a woman, perhaps. What would Marge do?

Another customer walked in—a bone-thin man in a loose necktie, gray dress pants sagging off his nonexistent behind, and thick, round glasses. He gazed around the store with buggy little neck movements, then stared at Kyle expectantly.

"With you in a moment, Mr. Bowles," Kyle said to him.

"I'm taking care of her dog, you see?" I said softly, feebly. I realized then that I should've *started* with Wayne. "I've got Wayne at my house, and I'm just wondering when she's going to pick him up."

Kyle wasn't listening. It was too late. I'd already botched this in a big way.

"If you're not here about a carpet, ma'am, I think you need to leave."

"Okay," I mumbled, feeling strangely shamed—perhaps due to the presence of a genuine carpet consumer.

Turning toward the door, I felt all their eyes on me: Kyle's, the desk girl's, Mr. Bowles's. I wasn't exactly sure what had just happened, but I didn't know how else to deal with the situation except to end it.

I pushed through the glass doors and hit the UNLOCK button on my car keys. After I'd put on my seat belt and started the car, I stole a glance into the store. Even through the glare of the glass, I could still see Kyle's little death-ray eyes shooting hostility at me.

I wasn't sure what to make of Kyle Spicer. He'd seemed a relatively reasonable guy—if a bit greasy—until I'd mentioned Donald Wallace. When he started to doubt I was telling the truth, his face had changed. In the moment I'd interpreted it as anger. Now that I thought about it, though, it seemed like it could have been fear.

Wednesday, October 16

Most of Thompson University's young academic stars made me want to puke, but Zach Wagner, admittedly, did not. The extent of his success was potentially sickening, but he was so friendly and down to earth that directing snide jealousy at him would just feel gratuitous.

Before he started teaching at Thompson, he'd won a few journalism awards. More recently—about two years ago— he published a well-received book. It was nonfiction, partly about his own brief experience in a juvenile-detention center as a teenager, partly about the juvenile-justice system in general. It was nominated for the National Book Award and even inched onto the *New York Times* bestseller list for a few weeks. Rumor had it he'd gotten a pretty big advance on his next book, but I was pretty far down the department food chain, so I wasn't ever sure of the accuracy of information once it reached me.

I'd heard parts of Zach's first book before it was even published—a few years ago, at a small department reading. The part he read—basically the story of how he got into the system in the first place—was pretty amazing. His mother's house was about to be foreclosed upon. As a fifteen-year-old, Zach had gotten the brilliant idea that if he staged an "accidental" fire, his mother could collect the insurance money. My favorite passage described the night he got the idea. He and his mother were watching the news—watching the Branch Davidian compound in Waco burn down while she polished her bowling ball and he ate pineapple chunks out of a can. Something clicked in his head when his mother said, "I'll bet they'll never really know what happened in that place." A week later he came home from school and found his old cat dead on the kitchen floor—probably of heart failure. Knowing a tiny bit about how insurance worked, and knowing that a dead cat in the rubble would make a fire seem a lot more believable—and probably grief-stricken over his childhood pet—he decided it was now or never, found some matches, lit a couple, tossed them on his upstairs bed, and then went outside to watch the house burn down. A neighbor called the fire department when she smelled the smoke. Two upstairs rooms were badly damaged, but the fire never reached the kitchen or the dead cat.

As odd as it might sound, he had the whole room laughing at this passage. The book was funny and humble and humbling and sad. Zach spent six months in juvenile detention and the next couple of years afterward mending his relationship with his mother.

I was still married when his book came out, so I didn't really notice then that Zach was attractive. But he is. Not *hot*, mind you. Cute. Softer than what I normally go for, but definitely appealing. He has pink cheeks, fine sandy hair slightly overgrown, and sandy eyebrows to match. And I appreciate his gently framed glasses in the grad-school sea of de rigueur hipper-than-thou horn-rims. Usually he wears these chunky, cozy sweaters that make you want to double-palm a chai and tell him all of your most sensitive secrets.

Zach's relative lack of academic trimmings made him more appealing to me as my dissertation dragged. But he caught my eye roughly around the same time he was nominated for the National Book Award. Of course I was too intimidated to talk to him after that.

Besides, it was also around that time that a stylish brunette started showing up for him at the end of his office hours. She resembled Kate Middleton. I promptly stopped eyeing him, as I certainly can't compete with a Kate Middleton.

Now I tried to puff myself up with fake confidence as I opened the heavy door of Phillips Hall. Zach was nice. At least I'd heard he was nice. Jeff had liked him a lot. Surely, then, he'd want to help—even if he was the pride of the English department and I was its shame.

As I entered the building, I could hear the Cloud-Nines practicing their signature tune on the first floor. I quickened my pace, hurrying for the stairs. Collegiate a cappella makes my brain cells ache.

I headed up to the English department's office on the second floor. The Phillips Hall smell entered my nose, filling me with a familiar dread. The building always smelled smoky-sweet—as if someone were burning a bouquet of lilies. I never could figure out where the scent came from. No one else ever seemed to notice it. Maybe it was the smell of my own incompetence.

I'd looked up Zach's current office hours online so I'd be sure to catch him. When I opened the door to the department lounge, he was standing there in front of the mailboxes. I watched him flip through a stack of papers, sigh, then look through them again. Today's sweater was navy blue with a chartreuse Charlie Brown zigzag across the front.

The floorboard under me creaked as I shifted my weight.

"Theresa," Zach said, looking up and pointing at me with uncertain recognition.

"Yeah," I said, surprised. "Yes. Hi."

"Are you looking for Dr. Clemson? Because he's not—"

"No. Uh. Not today. I came to talk to you, actually."

"Me?"

"Yes. About a friend. Kim Graber."

Zach pressed his glasses into the bridge of his nose. "Oh. Kim. Really?"

"She's kind of left me in an awkward situation. She seems to have disappeared, and—"

"Disappeared?" Zach looked startled.

Why didn't you start with the puggle? I berated myself.

"Well, see, she left me with her—"

"Listen. Why don't you come in?" Zach interrupted me and opened the door to his office—one of four choicest offices right off the lounge. Then he offered me a chair. "Do you want a glass of water or anything?"

"I'm okay."

"How about a cookie?" Zach extended a paper plate to me, piled with flat, crispy-looking cookies. "I forgot the baking soda, apparently, but they still taste pretty good."

I wouldn't have been tempted to take one, but since he mentioned he'd made them, I felt obliged. Zach lifted a wide-mouthed metal water bottle off his desk and unscrewed the top. When he gulped from it, water splashed out the sides and down the front of his sweater.

"Shit," he said. "I can't get used to these things. I switched from plastic because of BPA."

I tried to look sympathetic, since I couldn't think of a good response. I don't worry about BPA and such. I'm in my mid-thirties, so I figure I'm already doomed, as far as those things go.

"How do you know Kim?" Zach asked me. "You say she's *missing*? Have the police been notified? Is this serious?"

"Well . . . I'm not sure yet. But she's a friend of a friend. And she left her dog with me when she went away. This may sound like a small thing, but I'd like to be relieved of dog-sitting duty."

"Huh. That's *not* a small thing, actually. And I wouldn't have guessed she'd have a dog."

"Why's that?"

"I don't know. A dog requires a certain amount of . . . what's the word I'm looking for? Oh, I don't know. Maybe she seems more like a cat person. Maybe that's all." Zach's face began to redden over his fleshy white cheeks—endearingly, like a Campbell's-soup kid. "A friend of a friend, you said?"

"The friend was my brother, actually." Zach's bashfulness made me want to be sincere. "Her boyfriend."

"Jeff is your brother?"

"Jeff Battle," I said.

"I know. I just . . . never knew *your* last name. Everyone around here just calls you . . ." Zach hesitated. "Theresa."

He'd nearly said *St. Theresa*, the poor fool. I'd of course heard it before. Nicknaming was a gentle form of disowning in the department. The other dissertation lifer—the *Robinson Crusoe* guy—they called Gilligan.

"Yeah, my last name's Battle. And Jeff's my brother."

"Jeff was in my night class last year."

"I know. I encouraged him to take it."

"I liked Jeff a lot. His pieces for my class were very entertaining."

"His pieces?"

"His responses to my prompts."

"Oh." I shrugged. "My brother never lets me read anything he writes."

"Does he write much? Now that the class is over?"

"I don't know. He usually has a few creative projects going at once. I'm never clear what they are at any one time."

I wasn't sure how true this was anymore. But I wished it still was.

"Well. It wasn't till Kim came to me a few weeks ago that I realized she was dating Jeff. Not that it was any of my business. But she mentioned she'd met her boyfriend in my class. I think that may be a first for me. First match made in my class."

"You never know."

"You never do." Zach pressed the bridge of his glasses again.

I thought I saw him looking at the cookie in my hand, so I took a bite.

"Don't finish it if you don't like it. I made them for one of my classes. I usually do something like this when I've given them a lot of work. So they won't hate me. This week I gave them three nights to read *Sister Carrie*. Did you ever do stuff like that when you were teaching?"

Was he kidding? My students were lucky if I remembered their names and brushed my teeth.

"No," I answered.

"Good for you. It's probably unprofessional. Bringing food into the classroom. You know, I had a professor when I was an undergrad. A real dick. He rarely gave anything but C-pluses and made people cry during their presentations, and everyone hated him. But at the end of the semester, you know what he did?"

"What?"

"He had us all to his *house* on the last day of class. For a *pizza party*. I mean, we all had to go because he was a stickler about attendance. We all had to go to his creepy house and have beer and pizza with his creepy wife because he had decided he wanted to see what it felt like to be one of those 'likable' teachers. I would've had way more respect for him if he'd simply embraced being the dick that he was. Sometimes I think I need to remember that."

"Cookies with no baking soda are a good compromise," I offered. "Between embracing your dickishness and being a pizza-party professor."

Zach frowned at the paper plate. "Nobody ate them."

"So, uh . . ." I looked at the cookie in my hands, then took another bite. "Kim came to you. . . ."

"Yes. For help on a personal project. Did she tell you about it?"

I paused to finish chomping on the cookie. "Sort of."

Zach scratched his head. "Okay. What did she tell you?"

I knew I needed to do this delicately. I didn't want Zach suddenly blowing a gasket, like Kyle.

"That it had something to do with the election," I said. "I mean, something to do with Donald Wallace."

"Yes. She was putting together a video about some of his

cases. Cases he prosecuted in which she thought there might've been wrongful convictions. Some kind of YouTube thing—like a homemade campaign ad."

REALLY, now, I thought. That wasn't what I was anticipating at all. That sounded rather ambitious and academic for Kim. I'd expected something more in the category of catching Wallace at a strip club.

"Are there really so many wrongful convictions?" I asked, doing my best to hide my surprise. "On Wallace's record?"

"I don't think so. But *she* thought so. She had this idea in her head that there were."

"And this idea came from where, exactly?"

Zach took another drink from his BPA-free water bottle, this time very carefully. A tiny, deliberate sip.

"Did she tell you anything about the Jenny Spicer case?" he asked.

Spicer. Kyle Spicer.

"No." I tried to look casual. Oh, *God*. Maybe Zach could see the scene at Carpet World being replayed in the black of my dilating pupils. "But that sounds familiar, though. Jenny Spicer . . ."

"It was a pretty notorious case. Donald Wallace prosecuted it in the early nineties. A young girl was murdered. But the guy they convicted—they released him later. Like ten or so years later, I think. DNA evidence didn't match him. Kim probably talked to your brother about it at least."

"Um . . . I don't know if she did or not. All I know is that she . . . uh, mentioned to Jeff that she had talked to *you* about her Donald Wallace thing."

"What did she say about that?" Zach asked.

I thought about this for a moment. I'd already adjusted the truth just a bit—to avoid discussing the whole business with Kim's phone.

"Nothing. She just mentioned that she called you," I said.

"Yup." Zach sighed and swiveled his chair gently. "She did. A few times, actually. I agreed to meet with her about it a few weeks back. But when I heard the details, I was reluctant to get involved. Clearly she's passionate, but . . . but it's an odd situation."

Zach screwed his bottle closed and plunked it on his desk. I waited for him to elaborate, watching the bottle form a wet ring on the student paper beneath it.

"It's sad to me, frankly," Zach continued. "Obviously Kim has a serious issue with Wallace's ethics. And good for her, calling that into question, if that's what she really believes. But this idea she had for how to go about getting attention for the issue? Making a video? It struck me as wrongheaded."

Wrongheaded. That word never sits well with me. It always makes me think of *The Legend of Sleepy Hollow.* Zach seemed to notice my face twitch when he said it.

"I mean, it felt like a wasted effort. How about writing a letter to the editor and leaving it at that?"

"Did you suggest that to Kim?"

"Yes. Of course. She said she'd do that once she had the video online."

"And she thought this video of hers was simply gonna take off? And stall Wallace's progress in the election?"

Zach shrugged and put his palms out. "That was the general idea."

"And how were you supposed to help?"

"She wanted me to give it some press in the *Chronicle*—and in *Waltham's*, even. Once she had it loaded up. That was part of it. The other part was . . . well, in my book, one of the kids I'd featured had a brush with Donald Wallace. She was sort of caught up on that, too. The kid's story interested her. This kid named Dustin. Plus she thought that connection would raise *my* interest in her project, I guess."

"Kim read your book?" I was impressed to hear this. She hadn't struck me as much of a reader.

"Well. Part of it. My sense was that someone had shown that one section to her because of the vague connection to Wallace. But that may have been what brought her to my class originally. Reading part of the book."

"Do you think there's any chance this could've worked? Her project, I mean? With your help?"

"I doubt it. Surely Wallace could've countered with something from the other guy's past. He's not exactly an angel either." Zach hesitated. "Now, I don't know what your politics are. . . ."

"I don't really have politics," I admitted.

"Okay. Well. I recognize that Wallace is a career politician. With all career politicians, you're gonna find some shady shit if you dig a little. It's a cliché to say it, but I imagine that's true of both candidates. I'd just as soon have Wallace win. We need that employment bill to pass."

I was quiet. I didn't know much about the employment bill. I wonder sometimes how these people can keep up with current affairs *and* their academics. Smart people exhaust me.

"Is that a terrible thing to say?"

"No, no," I said, hoping he wouldn't ask me to elaborate.

"I mean, the Jenny Spicer case is troubling, I understand . . .

but I don't think that's entirely Wallace's fault, by any means. And damn it, a Republican in that seat . . . oy."

Zach rubbed the side of his face, then mushed his palm over his mouth and down his clean-shaven chin. "You should stop me. I'm digging myself into a hole. Ethics are ethics, and I should care. I *do* care. But I'm trying to explain why I didn't want to get involved."

"Do you think, for Kim, it was about the . . . uh . . . employment bill? About wanting a different outcome than you do? Wanting a Republican in that seat?"

Zach sighed and shook his head. He grabbed his water again, unscrewed the top, then screwed it closed without drinking. The metal made a soft *eek-eek-eek* sound.

"No. She mentioned to me that she usually votes Democrat, when she votes. Which I had a feeling was not all that often. She didn't even seem to know what the employment bill was. But she was angry, regardless, that no one was giving the Spicer business much press in the election. For her it was very much about Wallace, and it was personal. She knew that little girl Jenny Spicer growing up. That was what it was about."

"Oh. Jesus."

Eek-eek.

"Didn't I say that earlier?"

"No. . . . How terrible for her."

"Oh. Yeah. She was a childhood friend of Jenny's. When she was killed. I think Kim was a year or two older than Jenny."

"You'd think she'd have appreciated Donald Wallace at the time."

Zach shrugged. "At the time, maybe. I don't know how much a kid could appreciate or understand the legal process under those circumstances. But in any case she has obvious reason *not* to admire him anymore. She may see his overzealous prosecution of . . . now, what was his name? The kid they convicted? Andrew something. She may see that as the reason they never got the *real* guy, see? I mean, if she's going to be fair, she needs to blame the police, too. *All* of the adults in that neighborhood who wanted to pin it on some creepy teenager and be done with it. Not only Wallace."

"Uh-huh," I said.

Eek. Eek. Eek.

"Look up Jenny Spicer. You'll get a good sense of it."

"Okay."

Zach tipped his head back and drank, spilling water down his Charlie Brown zigzag. "Shit," he muttered. "Hey. You know what else you might want to look at? Did your brother tell you about my class blog?"

"I think so. You had all the students post some of their assignments or something?"

"Yes. They all posted their responses to the memoir prompts on a class blog. I posted a few of my own, too."

"Huh," I said. My students never got anything like *this* from me either.

"I used to have them read one another's pieces and comment on them. But I shut that part down after a while. It got nasty a few times. Those undergrads can be pretty ruthless."

As Zach was saying this, my phone began to vibrate in my bag. I wrestled it out from under a Marge notebook tangled in a set of earbuds. Jeff's cell number was on the screen.

"I'd better get this," I said, jumping up and stepping into the English lounge.

"Hey there," my brother said when I answered.

"How're you doing?"

"Uhh . . . not great. I'm thinking of walking home."

"Walking home from where, Jeff?"

"I don't feel that great."

"From where, Jeff? Should I come get you?"

"I've been talking to the police."

"Is that where you are? The police department?"

"No. I'm in the bathroom."

"The bathroom where?"

"Stewie's."

I put a finger up to indicate to Zach that I'd be right back. Then I hurried out to the hall.

"Stewie's the bar?" I asked.

"We don't *know* a Stewie, do we? Hey . . . that rhymed."

"What happened at the police department?"

"They brought me in to answer a few questions. Something's happened to Kim."

"What? What's happened?"

"They're not sure, I guess. But her car's been at this hotel for a few days, and they can't find her."

"Hotel where, Jeff?"

My question was interrupted by a groaning sound on Jeff's end.

"I'm coming for you now!" I shouted into the phone.

I hung up and ran back to Zach's office. As I grabbed my jacket, Zach pulled a Post-it off his desk and scribbled a Web address on it.

"Here's where my memoir-class blog is up," he said. "I've got it categorized by semester, since I keep it up for students to look at for inspiration. Your brother and Kim were last spring, I think. Right?"

"Yeah," I said, taking the note from his fingers. "I'm sorry. I have to go. Thanks for chatting with me, though."

"I thought maybe it would be interesting for you—to read what Kim wrote about Jenny Spicer. While you're at it, you should read some of your brother's stuff. It's pretty good. . . . Hey, are you all right?" Zach asked.

"Yeah," I said. "But I've *really* got to go."

Once I'd cleared the English lounge, I ran out of Phillips Hall.

When I arrived at Stewie's, Jeff was nowhere to be found. Thankfully, a guy I knew from high school was there, and he agreed to check out the men's room for me. Jeff came out looking sickly but relatively steady.

"Hey, Theresa," he said when he saw me. "Did I tell you I'm thinking of cutting the crew necks off all my T-shirts?"

I decided it best to drive him home, and he didn't protest. On our way to his neighborhood, he told me more about his police visit.

"So you never called the police yourself. They came to you?" I asked.

"Right," he said. "I mean, I did call her family. And they didn't seem all that concerned. If they had been, I might've done things differently."

I turned onto Amber Street, where Jeff lives in one of four apartment houses that the Whitlocks owned in town. They usually rented the apartments to older undergrads at the university. Likely Jeff was behind on his rent, but the Whitlocks probably were glad to have him around to keep his eye on things. He mowed the lawns for them and reported to them if any tenants were doing anything unsavory. At least they probably *assumed* that he did.

"So they told you she checked in to a hotel *where*?"

"In Rowington."

Rowington was all the way on the eastern side of the state.

"What was she doing there?"

"I don't know. They thought *I* might know. But she never checked out. She left all her stuff. Her clothes and everything. And they found her car a block or two down the road at a Denny's."

"Oh my God."

I glanced over at Jeff, who closed his eyes.

"Is that where her sister lives?" I asked, unnerved by his quiet. "Rowington?"

"No. New Jersey, remember? They grew up in Fairchester. But her sister lives in New Jersey now."

"Where's Fairchester?"

"East. But not as east as Rowington. About an hour from here."

I parked the car. "So she'd definitely lied to you about where she was going."

Jeff stared at the front porch of the house. "I guess so."

"So she left her *car* . . ."

"Her car and almost everything, she left. Her makeup case open on the bathroom counter at the hotel."

"What about her purse and stuff?"

Jeff shook his head. "Well, I've got her phone. But it looks like she had her purse with her, wherever she went. I think she'd probably have had her laptop with her, too. 'Cuz she was always watching viral videos. That wasn't in her room either. There wasn't any sign of violence, though, they said. But it doesn't make a lot of sense to skip out on your hotel bill and then leave your car. That's not cost-effective. And the issue isn't the bill. If it was only about the bill, the management just would've charged her credit card. When they found her room like that and no one came back, they were concerned that there might be some trouble. And then, when the police came, they made the connection with the abandoned car. The police down here are also investigating, since Kim's from here. They talked to her roommate this morning, and she gave them my name."

I wondered if Brittany used the word "alcoholic" when she spoke to the police.

"You're quiet," Jeff said.

"Let's talk about it more upstairs," I replied.

Jeff collapsed into a kitchen chair while I rummaged in his fridge for the makings of a halfway decent meal. To my surprise I found two packages of those nifty little crescent rolls that come in a can—a childhood favorite of Jeff's. Plus there was some cheese and a few apples. I decided to make tea and lay all this stuff out on a plate for picking.

"I'm sorry," I said, pulling the seal on the crescents and popping them open. "I'm sorry this is happening. I don't know what else to say. Kim's a sweet girl. And I hope she's okay."

Jeff and I were silent for a minute or two. I turned on his oven, found a cookie sheet, and started laying out the crescents.

"Remember . . .," I began, thinking about how Jeff had loved these canned Pillsbury products when we were kids. He especially loved the yeasty way they smelled raw, right out of the can. One time he stole a raw biscuit and kept it in a Sucrets box so he could sniff at it as he went to sleep. When our mother found the rotting contents of the box under his pillow, she came pretty well unglued.

"Remember what?" Jeff asked, his voice so weary it came out more a sigh than a question.

"Nothing," I said.

We didn't speak as the rolls baked. When the timer went off, Jeff stood up and took them out of the oven.

"Eat in the living room?" he asked as I sliced the last of his cheddar cheese.

I shrugged yes and followed him in with the food.

Jeff clicked on *The Rachel Maddow Show.*

"I've got a crush on her," Jeff told me, turning up the TV as he nibbled an apple slice.

"Isn't she a lesbian?" I asked.

Jeff put his apple slice on a napkin and set it on the arm of his couch. "It's not that kind of crush."

"Oh," I said. I decided I didn't need clarification. Maybe he was still a little drunker than I'd originally assessed. I gobbled a roll and tried to follow the pundits' discussion about the budget crisis.

When the show was over, Jeff clicked off the TV before the first commercial came on. Without the blare of cable news, the silence in the room felt sudden and oppressive.

"When are you gonna move somewhere you can get a pet?" I asked Jeff.

"You know, Theresa, I've admired how you've been able to

embrace pet ownership after poor Jedi. But I still don't think I'm ready."

Jedi was our childhood dog—a Lab mix my mother got us as a divorce-consolation aid when I was ten. Jedi struggled with a mysterious skin condition that affected his hindquarters, which were often shaved or scratched raw or both, depending on the severity of his rash and the amount of spare cash my mother happened to have on hand for vet bills. He wore a dirty, dented Cone of Shame for at least a quarter of his life. When I was about fourteen or fifteen, I was too ashamed of his appearance to walk him around the block. I'd sneak him behind our toolshed when my mom thought I was walking him, giving him a stick to chew on and whispering, "Sorry, Jedi. Sorry."

"Well. Jedi had a good life. Most of it anyway."

Jeff frowned. He doesn't like to talk about Jedi much.

"And it's been, what, fifteen years since he died?" I said.

"Maybe I'll be getting a ferret soon."

"A ferret?"

"Yeah." Jeff sighed. "I think maybe I'm a ferret guy waiting to happen."

"People with ferrets are . . ."

"Creepy. I know. That's what I'm saying. Plus, ferrets require a lot of attention. I'm already unemployed. Maybe I should go for it."

"A ferret is not the answer," I said.

"After a ferret then maybe I'll start playing World of Warcraft."

"Don't talk like that."

"Well. It's a little difficult to stay positive right now."

"I understand."

"Theresa . . ."

"Yeah?"

"The police were asking me all sorts of questions."

"Yeah. I can imagine."

Jeff picked up a roll. "Questions I wasn't expecting."

"Like?"

"Like where I was all weekend."

"Why wouldn't you expect that?"

"It wasn't the question itself." He peeled a layer of flaky pastry, then put it back down on the plate uneaten. "It was how they asked it."

"And how was that?"

"Like they wanted something from me they weren't getting. Like I should know what happened. They even asked me that. 'What do *you* think happened to her?'"

The emphasis on "you" jangled my nerves.

"And what did you say?" I asked softly.

"The only thing I could." Jeff shrugged. "That I don't know. But I've been going over it all day. What the possible answers could be to that question."

"And what have you come up with?"

"Um . . . she ran off with another man. A man with a much nicer car than hers."

"Wouldn't she have brought her makeup?" I asked.

"Theresa, be kind."

"I'm not being unkind. She *did* leave her makeup, did she not?"

"And her clothes. Her suitcase."

I decided not to try to come up with some Pollyanna explanation for this. Jeff was right. It didn't look good.

"Or she went out to get a quick bite at Denny's and some psycho snatched her."

I nodded. This seemed more plausible than her running off with another man and not bringing any spare clothes. More plausible, but a whole lot darker.

"You said they didn't find any wallet or purse in her room?"

"Right."

"So it looks like she went out for something, intending to come back soon."

"Right," Jeff repeated, more quietly now.

"Did Kim take walks much? Or jogs for exercise?"

"Jogs? No. She belongs to the gym on Cedar Street. Walks sometimes."

"Did you tell the police that?"

"They didn't ask that. If she walks. They wanted to know about the last time I had contact with her."

"And that was the Friday she left, right?"

"Yeah. When she called to ask if she'd left her phone."

"You told them that?"

"Yeah."

"And what'd they say?"

Jeff let his gaze catch mine, but just for a moment. "They asked me to give them her phone."

"And did you?"

"Of course."

"Did you show them those weird pictures?"

"No. But I assume they'll see them."

I began to wonder who else the police would be questioning. I wanted to ask Jeff what he knew about Kyle, but I couldn't figure out how. It was probably best for him not to know about Carpet World for the time being.

"So now you don't have those numbers you were so curious about?" I asked.

"Well, they're in my phone now. Since I called them all. And I know who they all are. Except the one who sent her those texts."

Jeff put his palms to his forehead and leaned his head back, closing his eyes. "I take it you haven't gotten around to talking to Zach Wagner yet?"

"Actually, I have," I said, and told him about it.

When I was finished, I asked Jeff if Kim had ever told him about Jenny Spicer.

He shook his head. "I knew she had a friend who was murdered when she was a kid. She wrote about it once for Wagner's class. She said they never figured out who did it. It sounded pretty horrific, and I never asked her about it. She didn't mention that it was a famous case. She didn't ever mention Donald Wallace."

"Where's your laptop?" I said.

"I don't feel like looking that up right now," Jeff mumbled. "Do you understand?"

"Oh. Of course." I stared at the limp leftover crescent rolls, feeling terribly insensitive. Naturally, at this moment, Jeff wouldn't want to read about a young girl's murder.

"And this video project she was doing? She didn't mention it at *all*?"

"No. Never a word. She had her video camera all the time, but like I said—she mostly just took footage of Wayne. Although . . . you know, she *did* go over to Nathan's a few times recently."

"Nathan the bartender?" I asked.

"Yeah. The guy she works with. The guy with the snake, you know? He's also a videographer. Does weddings and stuff, and films some local bands, too, I guess. And, like, VHS-DVD conversion for people's old wedding videos. She went over there a couple of times because he has some fancy video-editing software. She told me she was doing a voice-over. Some video she was really proud of. Of Wayne eating a taco."

Jeff wrapped his apple slice in his napkin and said, "Jesus."

"What?"

"It sounds so stupid, now that I say it. Of course she was lying to me."

"Do you think that she . . . ?"

"I don't want to talk about this anymore tonight. I think I need to go to bed."

April 25, 1993
The Daily Leader
Abbott Found Guilty of Spicer Murder

FAIRCHESTER, MASS.—After four hours of deliberation at the Pelsworth County Courthouse yesterday, the jury in the Andrew Abbott murder trial handed down a guilty verdict.

Abbott, 18, will likely face life in prison without parole after being convicted of strangling nine-year-old Jenny Spicer of Fairchester last fall. Sentencing will take place on

May 9, when Abbott is expected to receive a sentence of at least fifty years.

The verdict brings to a close a two-week trial of a case that has shocked the community in Fairchester and surrounding towns. A large crowd outside the courthouse watched as Abbott was led out in handcuffs and leg shackles and loaded into a police car on its way to the county jail.

"Andrew Abbott had a highly inappropriate relationship with a little girl half his age," said Assistant Prosecutor Natalie Trevor during a press conference after the trial.

"When he became convinced that she was going to tell her parents, he killed her and tried to make it look like a random act of violence. This young man is a highly disturbed individual, who considers himself a Satanist. Now, whatever else that means, it meant for him that he could use an innocent young girl for his own sick purposes and then dispose of her. There is no morality, no remorse in a belief system like Andrew Abbott's," she said.

Trevor prosecuted the case alongside Donald Wallace, the Pelsworth County district attorney.

Members of Spicer's family, who attended each day of the trial, were visibly pleased and relieved when the verdict was announced but declined to comment for this article.

Spicer disappeared on October 17, 1992, while walking home from a friend's house. Her body was found near the Davis Reservoir the following week. An autopsy concluded that she had been strangled.

Abbott confessed to the killing when investigators questioned him on October 26, then later recanted. During the trial Abbott's attorneys argued that the confession was made under duress, but they failed to convince the jury.

One young witness testified to seeing Abbott with the victim in the hours before her disappearance. Others described an inappropriate relationship that had been developing between Abbott and Spicer. Prosecutors also presented evidence that Abbott had molested Spicer, and several witnesses testified that Abbott was engaged in occult practices.

Two classmates of Abbott's from Fairchester High School testified that he admitted to killing the girl and described her final moments.

February 26, 2006
The Daily Leader
DA Drops Charges—No New Trial for Abbott

FAIRCHESTER, MASS.—County prosecutors will not pursue a new trial for Andrew Abbott for the 1992 murder of nine-year-old Jenny Spicer, Pelsworth County District Attorney Joshua Broderick announced yesterday.

During a 1993 trial, Abbott was convicted of strangling the young girl, but he was released from his fifty-year sentence in December when new DNA evidence suggested that he was not the killer. A judge then ordered a new trial for Abbott. With the district attorney declining to retry the case, the charges are dropped and Abbott is exonerated of the murder.

"Nearly fourteen years have passed since Jenny Spicer's

tragic death. Witnesses' memories have faded, the original lab technician who examined the hair evidence has since died, and it would be very painful for the Spicer family to have to go through all this again," Broderick said in a statement released yesterday.

Part of Abbott's conviction rested on two hairs found clutched in Spicer's hand. Initial analysis in 1992 found the hairs to be "consistent" with Abbott's hair—a determination made through a microscopic hair-comparison process, which was standard before DNA testing.

In late May, DNA tests performed on two hairs showed they did not match Abbott's hair. His lawyers worked for two years to get the DNA testing. Appeals Judge Catherine Beckwith granted the request after Abbott's lawyers pointed out that two unsolved murders and one unsolved disappearance of young girls in the Pelsworth-Wellport area between 1995 and 2001 had similar circumstances to the Spicer case and suggested she had fallen victim to a serial murderer.

Meanwhile, two young witnesses recanted some of their testimony from the original trial, claiming now to be unsure of their statements that they saw Spicer with Abbott on the afternoon of her disappearance. Abbott's family has long maintained that his confession was the result of fatigue and police intimidation after a six-hour-long interrogation. The New England Project for Justice has been providing representation for Abbott since 2002.

"If they really thought Andrew Abbott was guilty of Jenny Spicer's murder, there is no way in hell they'd be letting this go," said Abbott's attorney, Harriet Chambers.

"We're just happy it's over," said Abbott's sister, Stepha-
nie Reece. "We were thrilled when the conviction was overturned last year. Ever since then we've had this hanging
over our heads—the chance they'd try to bring it to trial
again. Now we know he's home for good."

Andrew Abbott himself was not available for comment,
nor was anyone from the Spicer family.

It was still early when I got home, so I went online and read all
about Jenny Spicer, Andrew Abbott, and Donald Wallace.

Reading these articles, I felt I did have a vague memory of
the case around when I was a teenager. Most of the articles
about Andrew Abbott and Jenny Spicer were from 1992 and
between 2004 and 2006. Abbott's conviction was overturned
in late 2005. It seemed he was freed more quietly than he was
convicted. While the DNA evidence was apparently pretty
damning to the case against him, remaining questions about
the appropriateness of his friendship with Jenny kept him from
being celebrated as an innocent man finally set free.

Still, in 2006 there were a couple of relatively high-profile
articles about Andrew Abbott—including a feature in a national newsmagazine. The article depicted Abbott as a loner
kid of ambiguous sexuality who was immediately suspected
by his neighbors and the local police department "because he
was different." Naturally, he wore a lot of dark clothing and listened to Iron Maiden. He'd had to repeat a grade in elementary
school due to "academic setbacks and social difficulties," so he
was still in high school at the time of Jenny's death even though
he was eighteen. It had come out during the trial that he'd had
therapy at age thirteen for depression and inhalant abuse.

The feature contained a picture of him at the time of the trial. He had stringy brown hair that reached his shoulders and a long, narrow face with pockmarked cheekbones and an unusually large beak of a nose. His mouth was slack and open, his eyes dull and empty.

In a picture from 2006, Andrew Abbott appeared much more alive. He had a fresh haircut, and looked more muscular, better fed, and better dressed in a forest green polo shirt. He wasn't exactly smiling for the camera, but he was regarding it with a calm and serious expression.

The article ended with a quote from Andrew Abbott:

> "It's not about blame. I don't think any one person is to blame. It was a perfect storm, sadly. I don't have time to figure out who deserves the most blame. I've wasted too much time already to bother with that."

A couple of years later, his lawyers reached a settlement with the state for $150,000 in compensation for his imprisonment, although the state "denied liability," whatever that meant.

The mention of the young neighborhood witnesses gave me a creeping suspicion about Kim. I did a Google search for "Kim Graber" and "Andrew Abbott." Nothing useful came up. After I adjusted it to "Kimberly Graber" and "Andrew Abbott," an article from 2005 came up. I searched the page for Kim's name and found this:

> At the hearing, two of the young witnesses from Abbott's original trial—Kimberly Graber and Melissa Bailey, now in their early twenties—stated that they were no longer confi-

dent of their prior claims that Abbott had preyed on Jenny. Bailey, who testified in 1992 that she had seen Abbott and Spicer together in Abbott's backyard on the afternoon of her disappearance, now said that she had fabricated the encounter but that her parents' and investigators' attention encouraged her to embellish and repeat the story. Graber's statement was more ambiguous, saying that she was no longer sure of the statements she made in the days and weeks following Jenny's disappearance and death. She had originally told police that Jenny Spicer had told her that Abbott had molested her. "I was little and I was confused," Graber said. She went on to say that Abbott had befriended all three of the girls that summer and sometimes "sat with us at Jenny's picnic table and helped us draw pictures of horses and unicorns." But that was the only detail about the relationship she could remember with any degree of confidence.

Pretty intense. And now I was pretty sure who this Missy was whom both Brittany and Kyle had mentioned. Missy as in the nickname for Melissa, most likely.

If Jeff had known about any of this, he had done a pretty good job of keeping it to himself. More likely Kim hadn't told him. That was one humdinger of a skeleton to have in the closet, after all—to have been involved in one of those old Satanic Panic cases. Painful childhood stories are one thing—but you start talking about Satan and all bets are probably off.

I remembered watching Geraldo Rivera's Satan special with Jeff when we were kids. My parents must've been distracted by their divorce at that time—otherwise I'd like to think they wouldn't have let us watch it. I couldn't recall exactly how old we were, but I do remember Jeff and me eating little packaged chocolate puddings while we watched it by ourselves. I probably would've been scared if Jeff hadn't kept making fun of all the mullets. It had been a deliciously depraved evening, like few others in our childhood. And yet no one I knew—not even my old friend Tish, who was often self-righteously gullible when we were kids—*really* seemed afraid of Satan worshippers.

But Kim had been younger. Very young. And a girl her age had been murdered.

Then I looked up "Kyle Spicer." I couldn't find anything that connected him directly to the case, but one article mentioned that Jenny had two older brothers. That sounded about right. Kyle had looked to be older than Kim but younger than me. I began to feel like a heel for bothering him at the carpet store. I would think that if you'd had something so horrific happen to someone in your family, you might have a hair-trigger response to strangers and weird intrusions.

Next up was Donald Wallace. A basic search made it clear he was a pretty famous guy in our state. If I weren't oblivious of politics, I probably would've known his name by now.

He'd been considered a shoo-in for Massachusetts' U.S. Senate seat for some time now. Now that Henry Rowan had died, there'd be a special election. Wallace had been attorney general of the state for six years. Before that he was the D.A. in two different counties—in nearby Pelsworth County for seven years and then a county closer to Boston for another eight. In both places he'd tried a number of well-known cases, several even more notorious than the Jenny Spicer case. There was an abusive-nanny trial and a triple murder, among others.

In any case it seemed to me Kim was right that the media wasn't talking about Andrew Abbott much now—during the special election. His name showed up in a few right-wing blogs as ammunition against Wallace, but no one seemed to focus much on him. Maybe it was because Wallace had washed his hands of the case when he'd switched counties. He was no longer serving the Fairchester area once Abbott's new lawyers had started trying to appeal. Or maybe it was because of the doubts people continued to have about Andrew Abbott's character. He wasn't exactly a poster boy for the miscarriage of justice. Or maybe it was a bit of media bias. Whatever the case, Kim clearly had an agenda to bring Jenny Spicer and Andrew Abbott into the current political conversation.

Was Kim—a waitress without much more than a tragic past and a penchant for YouTube—the right person to make this happen? She apparently thought so.

I wasn't sure I understood her motivation, but I admired her confidence.

Thursday, October 17

I spent most of my afternoon reading through the final copy for our Limited Edition Christmas Cookie Candles, which were set to hit the shelves in just a few weeks. Mr. Whitlock wanted them released at Christmas only every few years, so people might someday clamor for them the way they did for the McRib. This year's cookie scents were Chocolate Crinkle, Gingersnap Spice, Cranberry-Almond Biscotti, and Peppermint Macaroon. I prayed that my work on these descriptions was sufficient. Truth be told, I hate all candles that smell like baked goods. I would never say so at work, but I simply don't understand them. Who wants their house to smell like a torturous batch of cookies that is never going to come out of the oven? That no one ever gets to eat?

I spent my final half hour at the office gazing out my cubicle window at the Whitlock's corporate parking lot. Beyond that, above the trees, I could see the tip of the wick of the giant red replica Whitlock's candle against the gray afternoon sky. It marks the Whitlock's flagship superstore. As per an agreement with the town of Thompsonville, it is lit only during the holiday season, in the evenings. So I never see it lit while I work.

As I write at my desk during the day sometimes, I imagine it lighting spontaneously, filling the Thompsonville sky with a blinding but nourishing glow. And I picture myself weeping and wailing at the sight of it. It's not a *wish* I have per se. It's just a scene that plays out in my head when my mind begins to numb from candle copy.

I don't believe in miracles, but boredom tends to fuel my imagination for them. When I was in church as a kid, I used to stare at the crucifix and silently ask God to confirm his existence by shooting lasers out of Jesus's eyes. He never obliged, and I was always oddly surprised that he didn't. What everyone else in the church would make of it if it happened was not something I usually concerned myself with.

When I got home, Jeff was there fixing the crank on my kitchen window. I'd asked him to do it a couple of months ago, then forgotten about it.

"Sorry about yesterday," he said.

"Sorry for what?"

He rolled his eyes. "Come on, now. How was work?"

"Fragrant," I said. "Any news about Kim?"

"No."

"I looked up the Jenny Spicer trial last night."

"I figured you might. I did this morning."

"So that explains her interest in Donald Wallace. I think she may have had a reason for lying to you. She probably felt ashamed. You saw she testified as a kid, didn't you?"

Jeff nodded and stepped over to the kitchen table without looking at me. "Since we were talking about Zach Wagner, I meant to show you this."

He picked up a few papers from the kitchen table. He'd also brought a copy of Zach's book. I recognized the black-and-white cover with its silver medallion. It was a very restrained book jacket—with a simple picture of a bed and a narrow window on the front, and no author photo on the back. *Juvie* was scrawled across the front in all lowercase letters.

"I brought these. Kim left all this on my desk."

"When?"

"I don't know. She doesn't have a printer, so she always prints stuff at my house."

I took the printouts from him. Sylvestress came in and twined around my ankles as I looked over the stuff.

Most of the printouts were articles about the shooting death of a man named Todd Halliday. His wife claimed he was killed by intruders in their home, but she was convicted of the murder in 2006.

"I'd seen that stuff on my desk a couple of weeks ago but didn't ask about it," Jeff said. "Kim's always printing out a ton of stuff. Girl doesn't know how to bookmark. She's not very high-tech. Anyway, it looks like she was really interested in that one case. Where the mom shot the dad. I found Zach's book under all this stuff. She'd marked a bunch of pages in the section about Dustin Halliday. Even highlighted some stuff."

"Dustin Halliday?"

"One of Susan and Todd Halliday's two kids. He was in juvenile detention a few years after his father was killed, and he was one of the kids Zach put in his book. In the book the kid keeps saying the prosecution got it wrong—that his mother wasn't guilty."

"Zach did mention that she was interested in him." I flipped through the papers again. "Donald Wallace prosecuted that case."

"She never even *mentioned* Wallace to me," Jeff murmured, picking up Sylvestress. "Not when I was watching all my news shows. Not ever."

Sylvie pawed at Jeff's chest and leaped out of his arms.

"Sylvestress hates drunks," Jeff told me.

"Oh, I wouldn't say that," I protested weakly.

"I would," Jeff said.

I couldn't decide if he was joking, so I didn't reply.

"Are you hungry?" I asked.

"No," he answered. "I didn't come here for food. Just to show you this stuff—and to apologize."

"No need to," I said, feeling awkward—like I didn't know him all of a sudden. Like he was a stumbling waiter to whom I needed to be overly polite and reassuring.

I knew how to deal with the Jeff of Our Many Mutual Disappointments. But Jeff with a potential tragedy in his life—the tragedy that Kim seemed to be turning into—that person I wasn't sure how to speak to.

"I think I'm gonna go home now," he said. "Watch some news."

I started to say, *You don't have to*, but stopped myself. He knew he didn't have to.

Boober watched him pensively from the living-room window as he got into his car. Unable to pretend I was motivated enough to work on Marge, I read through the printouts about the Halliday murder.

It felt, at first glance, more straightforward than the Andrew Abbott case. At least Satan wasn't involved. Susan Halliday was convicted of killing her husband with his own gun. Sadly, her two boys—twelve and fourteen then—were at home at the time of the shooting. Dustin—the younger of the two sons—woke up when the gun went off, but his older brother, Trenton, slept through it and awoke right before the police arrived. Susan Halliday claimed that two intruders had come into the house, her husband had confronted them with his handgun, there was a struggle, and he was shot in the neck.

It obviously wasn't a very believable story. There were no fingerprints on the gun, but Trenton Halliday claimed that he saw his mother wiping down the gun as the family waited for an ambulance to arrive. Additionally, for almost a year Susan Halliday had been sleeping with a coworker of hers at the Department of Motor Vehicles. Donald Wallace and his team made a great deal out of that. Several character witnesses spoke of what a devoted mother Susan was, but no one could deny that the Hallidays' marriage had been strained for several years.

Dustin claimed to have run into the living room in time to have seen the intruders—a black man and a long-haired white man—leaving the house. But his testimony apparently wasn't credible. He was confused on the stand and contradicted himself several times. Once he testified that the white intruder looked straight at him and said, "Close your eyes, kid." When a young female prosecutor on Wallace's team questioned him, he claimed not to have seen either of the intruders' faces. He was also unclear as to whether the intruders had dropped the gun (and his mother had picked it up) or taken it with them when they ran.

A local editorial criticized both the prosecution and the defense teams for putting the brothers on the stand, calling it "grotesque" child abuse to set them against each other at such a young age. The writer seemed particularly concerned about Dustin. Though he didn't come right out and say that Dustin was emotionally unequipped to give accurate testimony, he implied it.

One of the articles showed a picture of Susan coming out of the courthouse. She had a round face with loose-looking skin that had perhaps been tanned too long and too often, a large pointy nose, and a disproportionately cute pixie haircut. Maybe that part was special for the trial. She looked more scared than diabolical to me. But I don't have a great aptitude for reading faces, so it was hard to say.

I picked up Zach's book. Kim had bookmarked the section about Dustin and marked off a few different parts of it with a squiggly line of blue ballpoint pen. The first passage she'd marked was this one:

> "We were mostly a regular family. My mother used to watch Lifetime all damn day. Next thing I know, I'm living in one of their movies."
>
> This is how Dustin Halliday describes the way his life changed when he was twelve.
>
> "When I look at how kids have their same old lives still, like the kind of life I had, I think it's funny what they don't know. They don't know that a couple of guys

can randomly decide to walk into your house and your life and shoot everything to hell. Change everything."

Dustin's insular suburban life ended on the night in 2005 when his father, Todd Halliday, was shot in the family home. Within forty-eight hours, Dustin's mother, Susan Halliday, was arrested for murder. The case was notorious in the state. Local news stations had extensive coverage of the trial, which was also featured on the television newsmagazine *Headline*.

"Sometimes I think I should sell my story," says Dustin. "But usually I think that not enough people care enough to buy it. People cared about the murder and the trial. But not so much about my brother and me after the trial was over. Maybe if we were younger and cuter."

Days after Susan Halliday was arrested, Dustin and his older brother, Trenton, were placed within the care of a family well known to Trenton. Michelle and Tom Barbieri, the parents of Trenton's closest school friend, offered to take them in.

During the trial, however, the boys fought a great deal, and Dustin developed significant behavior problems at school and at home.

The Barbieri family did not feel they could keep both brothers. Trenton was thriving at the local high school, while Dustin was failing most of his classes. Social services made the decision to separate the brothers and try Dustin in a new home. Dustin ran away from two homes before he was placed in a group home.

After that the two brothers took very different

paths. While Trenton focused on school and became closer to his foster family, Dustin began to rebel—he started smoking pot, then taking Ecstasy. Soon he was selling both to other kids.

Zach had spent a great deal of time in each section profiling not just the kids he featured and their daily lives in detention but their families and backgrounds. In the section about Dustin, he'd given a few pages to his brother, Trenton. Kim had marked most of it:

Dustin's brother, Trenton, visits him every couple of weeks. On this particular Saturday, he's telling Dustin about his telemarketing job.

"You have to decide if your approach is going to be aggressive or pathetic," says Trenton, now nineteen years old. He attends the Salinsburg branch of the state college and works as a telemarketer on the evenings when he doesn't have classes.

"That's how you make it in that job. You grow a thick skin, first of all. Because every ten calls or so, you're going to get people telling you you're the scum of the earth. But beyond that, if you want to make any sales, you learn that you have to talk over people like an asshole or talk soft and sad so people feel sorry for you. Some people go with one or the other, always. But I do it call by call. From the moment I hear their voice. There's something instinctual about it. When I hear the hello, I make a decision. Aggressive or pathetic. It keeps it interesting."

Telemarketing was Trenton's first job when he was

seventeen. He was good at it, so he kept at it. Now he works that job in addition to one as a customer service representative at Medialink Cable Company—similar work, he says, though better-paying and less stressful.

"Anything but food service," he explains to me. "Anything."

Most of his earnings go toward his tuition at college, where he is now a junior, majoring in marketing. He shares a two-bedroom apartment with three other students, which keeps his rent low. The Barbieris occasionally help him out when he runs into financial difficulty.

He says he wished his brother were as lucky as he has been. He hopes he can help Dustin when he gets out of detention—after he himself graduates and gets a full-time job and a place of his own.

"Dustin—he had it tougher because this all happened when he was younger. But he's old enough now to face reality. I wish I could help him with that. But I've figured out that that's something no one can really help you do. You need to be ready to realize you've been bullshitting yourself."

Admittedly, I'd only skimmed most of the parts of Zach's book that weren't about Zach himself. I didn't remember these brothers very well.

And the last portion Kim had marked was this:

Dustin maintains his mother's innocence all these years later—a position to which he attributes some of his difficulties with the Barbieris.

"They didn't want me to ever talk about it. Or at least they didn't want me to talk about it except in the way they wanted."

By "they" he means "the social workers—and the families, at least some of the time. It's frustrating to have to live with someone who doesn't want you to ever say what's on your mind."

He says he finds that more people here in juvie are willing to listen to his thoughts about the murder than people on the outside are.

For one, there is Sharon Silverstein, who teaches English and history in the detention center's high-school classes. She has encouraged Dustin to write about his parents. Usually he's done so in the form of songs. He isn't willing to share any of his songs.

"They're shitty," he says. "I need to hone my craft a little more. Maybe I can buy a guitar when I get out. My parents promised me one, back in the day. But obviously that didn't work out."

Another good listener is his classmate Anthony.

Dustin and Anthony are both sixteen. Though they don't seem to acknowledge it, they are perhaps drawn to each other because they are two of the few inmates in this facility from a white suburban background.

"Anthony's the only one I've told everything about what happened with my parents," Dustin says.

Anthony and Dustin sit together in the dining hall at lunchtime.

"There were a lot of things the police didn't want to

pay attention to," says Dustin. "They weren't listening to what I was really saying. I was a confused kid. It's their job as the adults to read between the lines and make sense of the story, not try to confuse me more and catch me in a lie. I'd just watched my father die. Then you're gonna treat me like that?

"And there was other shit the police never followed up on. There was a holdup at a convenience store a few blocks away two nights before my dad was shot. A black guy and a white guy. Very unusual for our town, that kind of thing. Just like what happened at our house was very unusual. But that was real and ours wasn't somehow. How does that make sense?"

Dustin pauses to shovel grayish peas into his mouth.

Anthony looks bored. He has clearly heard this speech before.

"You ought to take all this stuff about what your parents did and what you did," he says to Dustin, "and when you get out of here, you write it down and you put it in some object. Put it in an old mug you used to drink out of. Or tie it to an old lamp that you used to have in your room. And you put it in your head that that story is that thing. And you throw that thing in a river, or bury it, or just toss it in the garbage somewhere if you don't want to get all ceremonial about it. So then whenever you want to think of that story, you think of it like the mug or the lamp or whatever. It's just a thing you used to have in your life. But that you don't have anymore. You can remember it. But it's not significant. It's not a part of you. It's not you."

"It is me," Dustin insists. "Maybe less when I get out than before. But it's still me."

Kim had underlined and scribbled exclamation points next to the lines that said:

"There were a lot of things the police didn't want to pay attention to," says Dustin. "They weren't listening to what I was really saying. I was a confused kid. It's their job as the adults to read between the lines and make sense of the story."

I thought that was interesting, given Kim's history and given that both she and Dustin had likely been dealing with the same adult during the height of their difficult young lives: Donald Wallace.

Friday, October 18

I was trying my damnedest to concentrate on Marge, reviewing a chapter that has always intrigued me. In several spots in the book, Marge tells little stories that, in her view, prove she has an occasional gift for prophecy. In this particular chapter, the priest-scribe who took down her story becomes a character in her narrative.

Apparently he was often testing Marge's supposed gifts to make sure he wasn't wasting his time documenting her life. On this occasion he was taken with a young man who had a sad story. He came from far away and had no money or friends. He couldn't go home because he'd accidentally killed (or gravely injured, he wasn't sure which) a man in self-defense. While the priest felt sorry for this well-spoken and good-looking young man, and felt he deserved his assistance, Marge predicted he was bad news: "For many speak and seem very fair outwardly to people's sight—God knows what they are in their souls!"

The young man ended up borrowing money from the priest and taking off, never to be seen again.

It was one of many I-told-you-so's in Marge's book. What

interested me most about it, though, was the glimpse it gave of Marge's scribe. There seemed to be humility in his inclusion of that story. Still, many Marge enthusiasts wondered, as I did, how much of himself—or his opinion of her—ended up in the book without Marge's knowing. Did she ever have anyone read back to her what he'd written? Did she have a sense of how nuts she sometimes sounded?

As I worked, I sipped on Malbec and played Jeff Buckley's "Hallelujah" from my iTunes. An hour into it, I heard a light knock on my door. Jeff didn't wait for me to yell for him to come in, and I put down my glass when I saw his face. There was suffering in his expression. His eyes were red, his face slightly blue. I wondered if he'd given himself another nasty hangover.

"Hey," I said. "I've got a nice chicken with garlic sauce for you in the fridge."

He stared at me. There was something unrecognizable in his gaze. This was no hangover.

"Kim's dead," he said.

He collapsed on the carpet next to Wayne.

"What? Jeff—"

He took Wayne's ear in his hand and stroked it. "Her body. They found it near Rowington."

He pulled Wayne's paws into his lap. His shoulders shuddered, and then he began to cry.

The few available details were grim.

Kim's body was found near Highway 114, which was a rural highway about thirty miles from the hotel where she'd been staying. There were obvious signs of strangulation, according to the police statement. They wouldn't say, though, if there had been a sexual assault. In fact, they didn't say much of anything else. There would be an autopsy in a few days.

Jeff had found out about her death from another waitress at Kim's job. Kim's family had let them know down at Wiley's, and a waitress friend of hers had come by to see how Jeff was holding up. She found Jeff at his apartment, watching MSNBC, oblivious. No one had contacted him.

As Jeff explained all of this, Wayne got up and wandered off. I wondered if he sensed the nature of our conversation.

"This whole time I was just waiting for her to come back." Jeff drew circles in the carpet with his finger. "And cursing her. Saying terrible things about her in my head. Because she had lied to me."

"You couldn't have known," I kept saying.

After I'd said it about three times, Jeff finally looked at me.

"You don't know the half of it," he said. "You don't know even a tiny fraction of it. Of how much I was starting to resent her."

I didn't know what to do with this. I knew more than he realized, since I'd talked to Brittany.

"Do you want to explain what you mean?" I asked.

"No. Not right now." Jeff stared at the carpet. "Maybe I could take Wayne home with me tonight."

"What about the no-pets rule?"

"It's for one night. They'll never know about just one night."

"He might bark." What a dumb thing to say. *Just let him take the damn dog, Theresa.*

"He probably will. But it's just for one night."

I didn't say anything more. I fetched Wayne's leash and his special-formula dog food. Then I found Wayne himself nestled on my bath mat, gnawing on a DVD case: the first season of *Homeland.*

I sat on the mat with him and stroked his soft head. He growled at the threat against his new plastic possession. I removed my hand and talked to him gently for a few minutes—about his mistress, about grief, about being good and quiet and gentle with my brother tonight. Then I was silent. After a couple more minutes, he dropped the DVD case and twitched his eyebrows at me.

"Ready?" I whispered. "Good puggle."

I brushed my teeth, then found Sylvestress and deposited her on the bed next to me. I didn't want to sleep alone, and watching her clean herself always cheered me up. She performed sweeping, dramatic licks to each long lock of her luxuriant fluff. It was more elegant and more entertaining than the quick, businesslike manner of my shorthair cats.

Once Sylvestress closed her eyes, I slid my laptop onto my lap and noodled around online for a while. When I felt ready, I typed in the address for Zach's class blog. First I glanced at the syllabus: Nabokov, Annie Dillard, Maya Angelou, Tobias Wolff, Mary Karr. Fun stuff. It was the sort of class I'd never gotten to teach, as I'd always toiled away in Composition 101. But then I'd never published a book or won any awards.

There were seven written assignments for the semester. Each time one was due, students got to pick between two prompts Zach had written. The prompts were sometimes clever, sometimes cheesy, sometimes academic:

Recount one story shared orally that has come to act as central "myth" for your family.

Write about a "first" that was significant to you in some way—e.g., first job, first kiss, first day of school.

Write a conversation between your present-day self and a younger version of yourself.

There was something for everyone—from the jaded junior English major to the senior citizen auditing night classes. I admired Zach for the effort he'd put into the course. I'd had trouble when I was assigned the more diverse night classes. My assignments were always too easy or too hard, and someone was always either rolling their eyes or having a panic attack.

I randomly clicked on a midsemester assignment.

How did you mark time as a child? Illustrate how you marked the passing of time through one specific memory from your childhood.

OR

Describe a transitional moment in your childhood or adolescence.

The student responses were alphabetized by last name. I didn't feel quite ready for Kim's yet. So I clicked Jeff's first and found this:

When I was five and my sister was four, our father worked long hours and our mother worked two jobs.

Our babysitter, Mrs. Vernick, would always watch *The Young and the Restless* right before she'd walk me to the corner for the afternoon kindergarten bus.

I was young and restless myself, always fidgeting on the couch and trying to think of ways to engage Mrs. Vernick, to pull her gaze away from the television. I'd start knock-knock jokes or try to touch my nose with my tongue or pull my turtleneck over my face, but no dice: Vernick had seen it all before. One time I looked down at my feet and noticed that my white socks were quite visible below my red corduroy cuffs.

"Hey, Mrs. Vernick," I said. "Look! My pants are getting short. It must mean I'm growing."

Mrs. Vernick barely glanced up from the couple smooching on the TV and replied, "Your pants aren't getting short. They're the same size they always were."

"But I'm growing," I repeated.

"Yeah, you're getting taller. Sure."

I beamed at this surprisingly positive reply. And as I stepped onto the school bus that day, I pointed to my ankles and announced to the driver, "Look at how short my pants are! I'm really growing."

I don't remember the driver's exact response, but I recall that it was enthusiastic.

Of course, I'd been told up till then that I was growing. Kids grow. Everyone knew that. A little tiny bit every day, so you didn't usually notice it while it was happening to you. But this was the first real, tangible dramatic evidence I'd seen of it. The pants came halfway up to my calves, practically! It was like magic, it was so true.

I pointed it out to my teacher and all my friends: "I'm growing!"

The statement became more and more exuberant as the day went on.

I'm growing. Growing! GROWING!

When my mother got home after supper that evening, she announced she needed a Diet Coke.

"Can I get it for you?" I asked excitedly, feeling very grown up indeed.

"Sure." My mother shrugged.

I hopped up and got her a glass and poured her soda from the ever-present two-liter bottle in the fridge. I handed her the red plastic cup and watched her sip tiredly, put down her cup, and wipe her mouth, then her eyes. I thought of telling her, as I'd told everyone else that day, that I was growing. But she seemed the one person I didn't need to tell. She was my mother, after all. Of course she already knew it.

My mother took another sip and studied me. For a gleeful second, I thought she was going to observe, too, without my having to prompt her, that I was growing. Growing. GROWING!

"Why are you wearing your sister's pants?" she asked.

I looked down at the pants. They were red, just like a pair of mine. But I noticed now that the button and fly were a little different than I'd remembered them.

I'd spent the whole day wearing my little sister's corduroys.

"Oh," I said.

By the time I'd finished reading it, Rolf had positioned himself on my chest, purring like a Harley. I let him stay. Jeff's piece saddened me even more deeply than I'd already been this evening. Typical Jeff—hopes dashed by little realities. What scared me now was that this thing with Kim was no *little* reality he was dealing with. And, more so, that this time there was going to be no laughing his way through it.

I clicked on Kim's response for the same assignment.

Fourteen.

When I was a kid, it was all about fourteen.

When I was seven, I couldn't wait to be fourteen. Mostly I just liked the number. It had an appealing evenness to it: twice my age. And someone had told me that was the age you could become a cheerleader, so I was sold on it.

I remember asking my mother often, "When I'm fourteen, can we go visit Grandma?"

My grandma lived five miles away from us. My mother misunderstood the question. She'd get all teary-eyed and say, "Of course, honey. If we can."

What I meant was that I wanted to make sure I'd have the opportunity to show off my fourteenness. And who better to show it off to than my grandmother—my favorite person in the world. I was aware that people's grandparents sometimes died, but at the time I didn't think that sort of thing could touch me.

For several years I was counting down to fourteen. Seven years to go. Six years to go. Five.

When I was ten, I wanted it desperately. It was going

to be so awesome, so teenagery, so sophisticated. Surely I'd date boys and kiss them. I'd wear cool jewelry and cut-off jean shorts with red tights, and matching lipstick, and black boots.

I believe I forgot about fourteen sometime around the age of twelve.

When I got there, I didn't really bask in it. I got a few zits. I got an F in geometry and an A in music. I went to homecoming with a sophomore who had beautiful eyes and a bad haircut. I visited Grandma often enough, but I don't remember her being particularly impressed.

This response surprised me. It was short, yes, but I liked it. It had a jadedness to it that resembled Jeff's, actually—and that I hadn't seen in Kim in person. Suddenly her chemistry with my brother made more sense to me. Suddenly—but too late.

I didn't feel up to reading Kim's piece about Jenny Spicer. Too many depressing stories running into one another. I'd read it tomorrow, maybe. Instead I peeked at Zach Wagner's sample response for the same week. He'd responded to the transitional-moment prompt:

To me, "Money for Nothing" will always taste like a mouthful of smoldering ash.

It was playing in my father's truck when I had my first cigarette. We were stalled by the roadside after a fishing trip. I was nine years old, and it must've been boredom that motivated him to offer me a puff.

By that time my parents had been divorced for a few years and I saw him only about twice a year when he came out from California. I had few opportunities to show him how tough I was, and earlier that morning I'd failed to do so: I'd refused to cut my own hook out of a live fish. So this I had to do, no matter what.

I put that cigarette to my mouth and inhaled. It burned so badly that my mind went blank for a moment. I'd swallowed a mouthful of hell. My throat was on fire. My father watched me as I coughed and sputtered. He didn't smile or frown—just turned up the radio and waited for my next move. Dire Straits was singing about money for nothing, about chicks for free. I held on to that cigarette, though. I squeezed back a couple tears of pain. I put that thing back up to my lips again. If I could swallow lima beans for my mother, I could do this for him. I took another puff.

My father smiled. "Great song, huh?"

There was more, but I stopped reading. Deeper and deeper depression. I'd clicked on Zach's piece to cheer myself up, but unlike the personal parts of his book, it felt more sad than funny. Even though he'd invited me to read the blog generally, reading this piece felt like an intrusion.

I looked at all the other students' responses to the time prompt—even flipped over to the responses of students from other semesters. I really liked the question, and it was comforting to read of others' quirky childhood perspectives. There were a fair number that talked about time being experienced as a "countdown"—days till Christmas, days till summer, days till a father returned home from serving abroad. One kid wrote of his certainty that all dogs died exactly at age twelve and his grim countdown as his family's bulldog mix inched toward the inevitable. There were an almost equal number of essays about "marking time" with something besides a calendar or a clock—hair growth, report cards, a father's Friday lottery tickets, a yearly box of crayons worn to nubs. My favorite was one that explained how the writer thought as a preschooler that daylight was generated by collective sleep—and each night he felt compelled to force his eyes closed and do his part.

In that spirit I shut my laptop and did my best.

I was in my kitchen buttering my toast when I saw a woman in white moving across the lawn, holding a basket. Despite her Coke-bottle glasses and zip-front velour robe, I knew it was Marge. She was collecting golf balls. My first impulse was to duck and hide. What if she saw me? What would I say? And what if she told me I was going to purgatory? Or even hell? She liked to tell people where they were going in the afterlife, and she was pretty certain of herself when she did.

Before I could move, she turned and looked at me.

"Hello?" I whispered, heart pounding. She said something back, but I couldn't hear it at first. I opened the window.

"I wore a hair shirt for a while," Margery was saying, "but he told me to stop wearing it."

"Who?" I asked.

"Jesus," she answered. "Remember? He said, 'I shall give you a hair shirt in your heart, which shall please me much more than all the hair shirts in the world.'"

I recognized this as a direct translation of a line from *The Book of Margery Kempe*.

"I've always had trouble believing he said that to you, Marge."

Ding-dong.

Just as I was saying this to her, I heard a doorbell ring. But I didn't have a doorbell.

Marge seemed to sense my confusion. She put down her basket and pointed toward my front door.

Ding-dong.

"Answer it," Marge said.

I went to my door, but no one was there. I checked to see if there was a new doorbell installed but found nothing new.

Ding-dong.

My eyes flew open. It was my new ringtone. I'd chosen it a few days ago, to replace the barking-dog one I'd had before that. When Jeff had made me feel like a freak for biting Boober's ear, I'd decided to ease off the pet trappings a bit.

I grabbed my phone off my nightstand. Jeff was calling. It was 2:00 A.M. I'd slept for about an hour.

"Hey," I said.

"Were you sleeping?" Jeff wanted to know.

"Um . . . I'm gonna have to go with yes."

"I think I ought to tell you sooner rather than later," he said. "I lied to the police."

It was like this, Jeff explained. Kim had one of *those* relationships with her ex-boyfriend: one of those relationships that never truly ends. You could tell by the way she talked about him, for one. She'd known him since she was a kid. They'd broken up just two years ago. But he was the whole reason she'd even been here in Thompsonville. She'd moved to this part of the state with him when he'd gotten the managerial job in Ricksville. He was a serious part of her life and her history.

And she made no secret of the fact that he called every so often, to "check in."

None of this bothered Jeff—until recently. A few weeks back, she said she was going to visit her sister in New Jersey. A couple of days later, when she got home, she showed Jeff a picture on her phone—of Wayne nosing a jar around her kitchen, trying to lick the last bit of peanut butter out of it. When Jeff closed the picture window, he saw a text from Kyle.

The text said something like, IT WAS NICE SEEING YOU THIS WEEKEND. I MISS YOU.

Nothing terribly romantic or racy. But definitely suspect.

"Wouldn't that make you wonder?" Jeff asked.

"Sure. Of course," I admitted. It seemed to me Jeff was a little more adept with his girlfriend's phone than he needed to be, but I decided not to point that out, under the circumstances.

"So the next time she said she was going to see her sister, of course I was skeptical."

"Okay."

"*And* she wanted me to take care of Wayne. I wondered, am I the big stooge here? Believing her *and* taking care of her dog while she goes off and cozies up with some other guy?"

Cozy up. Nice euphemism, I thought. I was pretty sure I'd used the phrase on more than a few candle descriptions.

"So I told her I was busy. It was a lie at first, but then that job with Mike came up."

"Okay. So you were gone all weekend anyhow. No big deal."

"I was gone, yeah. But I wasn't at that job the whole time."

"Where were you?"

Jeff said nothing.

"Are you still there?" I asked.

"Yeah," he answered.

"Where *were* you?"

More silence. He was scaring me.

"Just spit it out," I said. "Jesus, Jeff. Is this how you acted with the police?"

"I followed her."

"Jeff!"

"Yup, yup, yup," he sputtered, "I know."

"You don't drive fast enough for that."

Jeff's style of driving is a bit geriatric—from his days driving the kids to school.

"It was tough. I had to speed a little. Out of my comfort zone. But I kept up with her. All the way to Rowington. Once I saw we were going that far north, I should've turned around and gone home. 'Cuz then I at least knew she wasn't going to Kyle's. But we weren't going to New Jersey, obviously. So I was still curious."

"Just curious?"

"Okay. I was angry she lied to me. I still wondered if this trip had something to do with Kyle."

I switched on my bedside lamp, thinking I might have an easier time processing this information with a bit of light.

"You followed her all the way to that hotel?" I asked.

"Yeah. And I spent the night in the parking lot."

"Do you think she met Kyle there?"

"I didn't see him there. Her door was to the outside. So I saw her go in when she checked in. No one came to her door after that. Not that night anyway."

I rubbed my eyes and got out of bed. "What if she saw your car?"

"I don't think she did. I parked pretty strategically. I did doze off at around five in the morning, for like an hour. But I doubt anyone came in or out at that hour."

"Okay, so . . . why do you think she was there? Did you see anything that would help you answer that?"

"No. Not at all. But around seven I left. I had to get back on the highway to meet Mike in time for the job. What I did do, though, was call Carpet World after nine. To see if Kyle was there. He wasn't, but the girl who answered the phone said he'd be in by eleven. By then I was too busy on the job to check and see if he really was."

"So you're going to go tell the police all this, I take it?" I was pacing my bedroom floor by now.

"I guess. But I'm not sure how. Should I wait and see if they come and ask me about it again?"

Something about this question made me a little queasy. "I don't think that's a good idea, Jeff."

"But if I just show up and tell them I lied to them, that looks pretty bad."

"Looks worse if they figure it out themselves."

He paused for a moment. "But maybe they won't."

"Maybe," I said. "This isn't good, Jeff."

"No shit, sis."

Usually it made me giggly to hear Jeff use curse words. They generally came out of his mouth all wrong—like a kid pronouncing a foreign word in a language class. This time, however, he sounded expert.

"I'm glad you told me." I wasn't entirely sure of this, but it felt like the right and sisterly thing to say.

And then I told him to try to get some sleep—knowing, of course, that neither of us would.

Monday, October 21

On my desk the next morning was my next assignment: Travel Candles. They were small candles in cute tins, with just a couple of hours of burn time. *"Available only in our most classic scents,"* said the memo from the marketing director.

With this sort of thing, I always started with the same question: *Who buys this shit?*

The head of marketing had told me that they were popular for weddings—as favors or in "care packages" or gift bags that couples put in the hotel rooms of out-of-town guests. This intense bridal consumerism was so far from my world that I had no idea how to get on its level. Who else, I wondered, might be convinced they needed a travel candle? I checked the price. They were very cheap compared with our other candles.

Hmm. Something about small indulgences going a long way?

The second thing I usually do, if I'm having difficulty relating to the product, is purge myself of any annoyance I might have toward its potential consumer. Just a line or two, scribbled out on a scrap of paper before I got to work on my computer:

It's kind of like an Olive Garden for your nose. Wherever you go, you never have to smell anything new. You can have Pumpkin Spice and Holiday Cheer running hard through your limbic system, always.

I ripped the paper to bits, threw it into my wastebasket, and got to work.

A little indulgence goes a long way, I typed.

Sure, "goes a long way" was a cliché. But since this was a travel candle, it could work. And your typical Whitlock's Candles fiend probably didn't mind a little bit of cliché. In fact, she probably found it comforting. Yes. Comforting. That was what this was really about:

A little bit of comfort that can go a long way. Toss one or two of these in your travel bag and enjoy our classic scents on the go.

"On the go" was all wrong, of course. We didn't want to be sued for injuries if some bonehead decided to burn our candles on his morning commute. You really do need to think of these things in my line of work.

My desk phone rang. It was a call from outside the building.

When I picked up, I was surprised to hear my friend Tish's voice.

"Theresa. Has Jeff called you today?" She sounded frantic.

"No. Why?"

"I think he's in some kind of trouble. My brother was there a little while ago, replacing the dishwasher on the first floor. Four police officers are there. They're searching Jeff's apartment, his car."

I took a deep breath and tried to keep my voice steady. "Are they still there?"

"I don't know. Hughie had to go to work after that. He called me from his cell. He called me 'cuz he thought you'd want to know. After this I'm calling my dad and telling him you'll need some time. So you don't need to ask. You can just leave if you need to."

"Oh. Uh, thank you, Tish. But do you think I should go over there if Jeff hasn't asked me to?"

There was a long pause on Tish's end. "Uh, Theresa?"

"Yes?"

"Whatever you decide to do right now, it sounds like you might need to get Jeff a lawyer. You know that, right?"

"Yeah. Right."

"Do you know who you would call? If you needed to?"

"No. Maybe I'll call my divorce lawyer and ask her for a recommendation. Would that be a good way to do it?"

"I don't know. Probably. Yeah, start with that. And keep your cell phone on, will you? I'll call and check in."

After I hung up, I grabbed my keys and jacket. As I stood up, I stared out the window at the wick of the giant fake Whitlock's candle. For two seconds I willed it to burn for me. It didn't. I pushed in my chair and crept wordlessly out of the office.

While I was parking next to Jeff's place, one of the stoner undergrads from the second-floor apartment came out to greet me.

"Your brother saw you drive in." He flipped his slick black bangs out of his eyes. "He's up in my apartment watching TV. You can come up if you want."

The kid seemed rather blasé about the fact that Jeff's apartment and car were being searched by a bunch of police officers. I tried to convince myself that maybe he knew better than I did. Maybe it was no big deal to have four uniformed law officers rummaging through your shit. Maybe this sort of thing happened to stoners all the time.

Jeff was wearing the same sweater he'd had on yesterday—the thin gray one with the holes at the elbows—and watching CNN. A dusty blonde with smart glasses was grilling a chinless congressman. Wayne was curled up next to Jeff, dozing.

"Jeff?" I said, waiting for him to look at me.

"Why aren't you at work?" he asked, staring at the television.

"I'm gonna . . . uh, leave you guys so you can talk," the stoner piped up. "I've got a paper to finish this afternoon."

"Good luck with it," I said, hoping that would encourage him to leave the room.

"I'll be out of here as soon as they're finished," Jeff told him.

"Take your time, man. This really sucks."

"I heard you might need some help," I said, sitting on the edge of the couch as the kid slipped down the hall.

"I appreciate that, Theresa. I really do. But this is happening. I don't think there's much you can do." Jeff paused and turned up the television. "Actually, why don't you take my phone?"

"Why?"

"Just take it. I think they're looking for any excuse to arrest me."

"Why would they do that? They don't have any . . ."

Jeff finally met my gaze. I'd never seen him look so awful. His eyes were so red and puffy they looked sore, and he had some sort of white ointment or toothpaste mushed into the stubble on his chin.

"*Take* it. And keep calling the first number I've been calling. That's the person who sent Kim the weird text that day. I've been thinking if I can figure out who that was, I could figure out what she was—"

I heard a door slam outside. Jeff started at the sound of it.

"Do you think they're gonna want your phone?"

"Eventually, maybe. Yeah. But for now just take it and get that number out of it."

"He's upstairs, in the second apartment!" I heard someone shout outside. I slipped the phone into my purse.

"What're you watching?" I tried to sound casual.

"The news, Theresa," Jeff mumbled.

"What's the news?"

"Do you really want to know? You who haven't voted since 2004?"

"That election was very scarring for me," I answered. "All that time I spent watching debates, hearings on Iraq—wasted. If I don't get involved like that again, I won't be disappointed so badly again."

Jeff rolled his eyes.

"It happens to be true," I said. "I can't handle it."

He smiled weakly. We both knew we were only half in this conversation, killing time till the cops were done. And it had been foolish of me, in this moment, to remind my brother how little I can handle.

"That's never stopped you with relationships," he said anyway. "Why, then, do you let it stop you when it comes to responsible citizenship?"

"That's not fair," I said. "Because—"

Heavy footsteps in the stairwell interrupted my answer.

"Because?" Jeff asked me, his eyes wide and frantic.

I'd forgotten what I was going to say. "Because . . . attention to relationships is, like . . . uh, responsible participation in your own life?"

There was a sharp knock on the door. They didn't wait for an answer. Stoner emerged from his bedroom as the first policeman entered the apartment.

"Hello, Officer," said the stoner, in that slow, faux-polite way stoners have.

The first officer had a giant paunch, the second had the beefiest upper body I'd ever seen.

"Where's Jeff?" asked Officer Pec. His chest seemed to bulge at the pronunciation of my brother's name.

Then he caught sight of my brother, who had just stood up.

"Jeff Battle," said Officer Paunch. "You are under arrest. For the murder of Kimberly Graber."

Officer Pec grabbed Jeff's wrists. Jeff didn't resist. But he said, "Why? Why now? What makes you think—"

"You have the right to remain silent. . . ."

I picked up one of the remotes on the couch and hit the power button. It didn't do anything. It must have been an old remote, or had old batteries, or else it was the DVD remote. The officer finished reading Jeff his rights. A commercial came on. A red cartoon bear was struggling to wipe his behind. A red mama bear was offering him a superior toilet paper. I grabbed another remote, hit the power button over and over again, then hurled the remote at the television.

"Ma'am?" one of the officers said. "I'm going to have to ask you not to—"

"I'm just trying to get the TV off!" My heart was racing, and

I was struggling not to scream the words. Wayne began to howl.

I slipped past the police officer and hit the power button on the actual television.

"It's okay, Theresa," Jeff was saying. They were leading him to the stairs.

"I'm getting you a lawyer," I said to him. Meanwhile the stoner stood there gaping at me. "Remember you don't have to talk to them till after you speak to your lawyer."

The smaller officer held Jeff's thin wrists against the back of his sweater.

"Where are you taking him?" I asked Officer Paunch, who was bending down to grip Wayne by the collar.

"The station, ma'am," he replied.

"Here in town?"

"Yes, ma'am."

"I'll follow you there," I called down to Jeff. He and the other officers were already almost all the way at the base of the stairs. I don't know if he heard me.

"Do you mind if I come back for the dog in a little while?" I asked stoner dude.

He shrugged. "No problem."

We both stared out the window, watching the officers guide Jeff into a cruiser.

"Man, this really sucks for you guys," the kid said.

"But we're used to disappointment," I mumbled.

"What?"

"Nothing," I said, then tore down the stairs to my car.

I didn't realize that my heading to the station after Jeff would do him no good. They wouldn't let me see him. His arraignment would probably be the following day, I was told, and I could see him after that. He had been arrested on account of some "evidence of his involvement." I sat at the police station for three hours, but they didn't tell me anything more. Once I'd finally given up for the day, I circled back to the stoner's place for Wayne.

Soon after I arrived home, Tish showed up with her three-year-old daughter, Penelope.

"I came to see if you were okay," Tish said, handing me a greasy bag from our Mexican place. "And I thought you might not want to cook."

"I'm not okay," I admitted, putting the bag directly into the fridge.

"Did they appoint Jeff an attorney for the arraignment?" she asked.

"Yeah. I'll be looking for a different one in the meantime. My divorce lawyer gave me some good tips. There's this guy Gregson who I think would be good."

"I'm hungry, Mama," said Penelope.

"You just had a snack, honey."

"I don't think it was enough." Penelope put her finger to her lips in a gesture of thoughtfulness. "I think I'm still a little hungry."

Tish and I both gazed at Penelope for a moment. I think she could sense that we were both too tired to negotiate with her. Penelope picks up on a lot of things. Penelope, truth be told, sort of wigs me out. I've never mentioned it to Tish and never would, but her oval face and her haircut remind me of the *Shining* twins.

"I think you had enough, hon," Tish told Penelope. "And you can let Mama talk to Theresa for a few minutes."

"Can I watch TV?"

Tish turned to me. "Do you mind?"

"No," I said. I turned on the TV and flipped around the channels till I found a cartoon.

Penelope put out her hand—for the remote, I think. I pretended not to notice.

"Have you called your mom?" Tish asked. "Does she know Jeff was arrested?"

"I haven't called her yet."

"Theresa, you need to," she said gently.

I couldn't help but wonder if Tish was here for me or for Jeff. She'd always had a weird little crush on him—ever since we were kids. It was only after her divorce that she'd become more obvious about it. A murder charge might finally make short work of that, though.

"I know, I know," I said. "I just need to take an Advil first, or something. I think I'm getting a migraine. Hearing my mother screaming won't help that."

"And I'd imagine your parents could help pay for the lawyer. Now, regarding work—I've told my dad not to expect you for the next couple of days at least. So you can tend to this."

"Thanks," I said.

I studied Tish's face. Her black hair was stylishly cut, as always, but she looked almost haggard these days. It seemed she got thinner and thinner since she'd become a mother. Penelope hadn't let her sleep through the night till she was two. And even after that there always seemed to be some worry about Penelope that kept Tish in stress mode: Penelope biting, Penelope telling other kids her dad was a priest, Penelope putting valuable objects in the toilet. I knew it was small of me, but sometimes I missed the plumper, more carefree Tish.

"*Who* was arrested?" Penelope asked.

"Mama and Theresa are talking," Tish said. "It's a private conversation. Now, have you called your dad?"

"I'm not sure how to get a hold of him. His boat is in Sardinia right now, I think. Or somewhere around there. I never pay attention to his itineraries anymore. All I remember was him saying Sardinia. I'll have to call the cruise line and figure out how to get in touch with him."

"Did he rob a bank?" Penelope demanded. "Are the police gonna shoot him?"

"Nobody robbed a bank, Penelope." Tish turned to me again. "Do you want me to help with that?"

"Or did he set somebody on fire?" Penelope grinned at her mother. "Were they screaming?"

Tish shook her head and rolled her eyes toward the ceiling for a moment.

"I'm not going to acknowledge that, I don't think," she whispered to me.

"Tough call," I whispered back, shrugging. "No. No, you don't need to stay."

My mother repeated, *What are you talking about?* for about ten minutes.

Then she went ballistic and put her fiancé, Ned, on the phone so I could explain everything again to him. Then they had to hang up so she could freak out all over again.

Ten minutes later she called back for the details.

"Where's your father?" my mother demanded when I was finished.

"He's in Sardinia."

"Naturally. Sardinia. Where is that?"

"It's in the Mediterranean."

"Oh my God. Poor Jeff. We've gotta get him out of there. Have they set a bail?"

"They do that at the arraignment," I said for the third time. "Tomorrow."

"I'm flying up."

"You won't make it in time for the arraignment."

"So what? I'm flying up as soon as I can. I knew this Kim was going to be trouble. I knew it was going to end in heartbreak."

This declaration shouldn't have annoyed me, but it did. "Mom, she *died*."

"Yes, I understand that, Theresa. It's still heartbreak, isn't it?"

"I'm pretty tired," I said. "Let's talk first thing tomorrow."

"I might be on my way by then. Ned is looking for flights now."

"Even better," I said.

"This mailbox is full and cannot accept any messages at this time. Good-bye."

Before bed I tried the number on Jeff's phone, as he'd asked me to do. Still a full, unidentified mailbox. And I hated that bitchy way she said *"Good-bye."* With that crisp tone, she may as well have said, *"Your brother's in jail and all you're doing is calling this dead-end number? You're worthless. Good-bye!"*

I was too depressed to brush my teeth or put on pajamas. I crawled into my bed in my work clothes and tried to put myself to sleep thinking of my hypothetical kid.

He's exactly Penelope's age.

Because as it happens, Tish and I got pregnant around the same time—back when I was married. When I went in for my first appointment at nine weeks, there was already an audible heartbeat. I remember feeling close to this little being right away—and terribly excited that it wouldn't be only Brendan and me anymore. I also remember that when I found out was right around when Michael Jackson died. It seemed weird to me that my child would grow up in a Michael Jackson–less universe. How would I ever explain Michael Jackson to him? How could you explain him to anyone who had not experienced him historically? Maybe I thought about such things to block out more consequential parenting anxieties. In any case I lay awake at night going over my long-winded explanation in my head: *He was very talented from a young age. He was very famous. Probably more famous than anyone should be, before they're old enough to decide for themselves if they want it. . . .*

Only Brendan and Tish knew. When I went back to the doctor at fourteen weeks—right before I was about to tell everyone else—the heartbeat was gone. They estimated it had stopped at around twelve weeks. I remember thinking that that clever little soul must've read my thoughts and decided that breaking the monotony of my marriage wasn't a job he was up for—or the life he was looking for. And frankly, I came to respect that. Eventually.

At the time I was disappointed, but I didn't cry. It was all too abstract, still, at fourteen weeks, for me to cry. I could tell that Brendan was relieved. And I couldn't forgive him for it. Not that I tried. I didn't want to. I was too lazy. That was when I knew it was over.

Whenever I see Penelope, though, I think about this kid. Less intensely than I used to, but still consistently. I always think of him as a boy. He's a quiet kid with a pointy chin, horsey teeth, and a fruit-punch mustache. He likes to build elaborate towers with his blocks, and Penelope comes over and knocks them down and describes the broken bodies beneath the rubble. My boy doesn't seem to mind. He's chill. He's all in his head. He barely hears what she's saying. When she gets really graphic, he tries to divert her attention by talking about Dora the Explorer.

I've never named the kid, because that would be creepy.

Creepier even than Penelope.

Usually I try my best *not* to think of him at night. Anything but him.

But on this night he was a more comfortable thought than Jeff in jail.

I picture the kid kneeling in one of my kitchen chairs. I'm feeding him a fried-egg sandwich like the kind my father used to make for Jeff and me. When I'm not looking, the kid slips out the egg and feeds it to Boober. I pretend not to notice. I sip a cup of coffee while he eats his ketchup and bread.

As my brain succumbs to exhaustion, cartoon mama bears and baby bears begin to dance clumsily around us, twirling strong and reliable toilet paper. We try to ignore the bears—Boober, the boy, and me—but they are brighter and more real than we are, somehow. We don't want to fade in their presence, but the more we try, the more we do. I let go of my coffee cup, I let go of everything, and we're gone.

Tuesday, October 22

A uniformed officer brought Jeff into the court-room, holding him gently by the arm. Even though Jeff was wearing a blue jumpsuit, I felt comforted for a moment by the officer's white hair. He reminded me a little of Rusty the bailiff on the old *People's Court*.

When I allowed my gaze to fix on Jeff, though, a wave of reality swept over me: He was in shackles. This was not the damned *People's Court*, and I needed to stop looking for little reassurances everywhere.

As I tried to refocus my attention, everyone began to stand. I stood with them. The female judge entering the room looked to be about my mother's age—with more sensible hair than my mother, however, and natural, un-plucked eyebrows.

"Thank you," she said. "Please be seated."

At that point the clerk read a string of numbers. All I could understand was the phrase "murder in the first degree," which he said twice.

"Good morning, Your Honor." A woman in a perfectly

tailored gray suit stood up. "Jessica Dorrin for the Common-wealth."

A portly bald man at the table in front of us stood up and turned to the judge. The thick, layered flesh at the back of his neck reminded me of a shar-pei. "Good morning, Your Honor. Patrick Marsh on behalf of Mr. Battle."

I've always wanted a shar-pei, but I'd probably never be able to afford one.

"Mr. Battle, how do you plead to this indictment?"

Patrick Marsh nodded to Jeff.

"Not guilty," Jeff said.

"Your Honor," said the woman prosecutor, stretching her arms out wide and tapping her fingertips on the edge of the table.

As she turned to the judge, I could see she was about my age. Her layered brown hair framed her face quite symmetrically, as if it had been cut that very morning.

"We are prepared today to outline for you the seriousness of the crime as we address the question of bail."

This woman sure had her shit together. *She* could have a shar-pei if she wanted one. But I'd bet she'd rarely be home to pet it.

"Proceed," said the judge.

"Kim Graber—Mr. Battle's girlfriend—was first suspected missing on October ninth, when personnel at the Best Western in Rowington reported her belongings abandoned in one of their rooms, which coincided with a report of her vehicle abandoned at a Denny's restaurant on the same road—Fillmore Street in Rowington. When Mr. Battle was questioned as to her possible whereabouts, he informed police she had told him she had gone to see her sister in New Jersey and he had not seen her since October fourth. On October eighteenth Kim Graber's body was found in a wooded area, about ten yards from the side of Highway 114. According to autopsy reports, she died of strangulation and also had a deep wound in her upper left thigh, consistent with assault using a screwdriver or scissors. Investigators Neely and Clement ascertained through E-ZPass records that Mr. Battle had in fact driven to Rowington on the very day Ms. Graber had. Additionally, Mr. Battle had given police a false alibi—Michael Lansing, who employs Mr. Battle occasionally at Lansing Cabinetry. According the Mr. Lansing, Mr. Battle was late for his job on Saturday, October fifth, and he could not vouch for Mr. Battle earlier in the weekend. Upon learning this, police investigators obtained a search warrant for Mr. Battle's apartment and vehicle. In the trunk of the vehicle, in the spare-tire compartment, they found a screwdriver with blood on it, which late this morning tested as the same type as Ms. Graber's—A-negative. Additional DNA tests are being performed."

I began to feel dizzy—and then I felt Tish squeezing my arm—more out of shock than a desire to comfort, it seemed, but it brought me back to full consciousness. *Between this news and Tish's fingernails, this creature thought she might cry out.*

"Police also found that Mr. Battle's trunk had been saturated with vinegar and an ammonia-based cleaning liquid. We believe that Mr. Battle was angry at Ms. Graber for a recent romantic encounter with her ex-boyfriend, Kyle Spicer."

As she continued, I heard a light weeping coming from the seats on the other side of the courtroom. A middle-aged lady was hunched over her giant brown leather purse, tearing at a tissue. A young woman with Kim's dark eyes and hair was sitting next to her, touching her lightly on the shoulder, staring at the judge. I felt dizzy again. Despite the quiet of this room, the prosecutor's words were difficult for me to hear—as if being spoken underwater, or into a glass jug.

"According to some of her friends, this had been a source of tension between herself and Mr. Battle in recent weeks. The evidence here suggests very strongly that Mr. Battle followed Ms. Graber to her Rowington hotel and killed her in cold blood.

"Your Honor, we also believe that given the nature of the charges, and given that Mr. Battle has willfully undermined the police investigation into Ms. Graber's death, it's appropriate to ask that he be held without bail. Additionally, we think Mr. Battle is a flight risk. His father works overseas and has contacts in several different countries. He is currently in Sardinia."

I took a deep breath. I was pretty sure I was losing my mind. Kim's eyes. Sardinia. *The People's Court.* Shar-peis. No bail. Could they *do* that?

I didn't hear the prosecutor's next few words, but I heard her say the words "bail hearing."

"Counsel for Mr. Battle?" the judge said.

Mr. Marsh stood up. "I'd ask that Mr. Battle be held without prejudice until we can have a bail hearing."

"All right," said the judge. "Let's set the bail hearing for October twenty-fourth."

"What just happened?" I asked as the grandfatherly officer led Jeff out of the room.

"I think they're deciding bail on Thursday," Tish said.

"But I thought they were supposed to do it *now*," I whimpered.

"I thought so, too. But I'm not sure how it works. I think you ought to let me ask my dad's lawyer to help."

I got up and shuffled from the courtroom. Tish followed me down the hall and out to the front steps of the courthouse.

"That's nice of you, Tish."

An elderly man walked by us, reading the front page of a folded newspaper as he walked. He smelled yeasty and sour. I stared after him.

"Should I?"

A young woman in shiny black boots walked by next, texting and sighing. Then an older lady with a stroller, pushing a toddler of ambiguous gender. The child was blond and smiling and shaking a plastic container of goldfish crackers. A couple of goldfish crackers flew in our direction.

"Theresa?"

For a moment I wished to be any one of these people passing by. Anyone but myself. "I don't know. All I know is I want to talk to my brother."

I stooped and picked up one of the goldfish.

"Maybe this is good luck," I said.

"I've had those pelted at me for a few years now," Tish said. "I can assure you it's not."

There were several security hoops to jump through at the county detention center, but once I got to the visiting area, it wasn't what I expected. There was no security glass separating Jeff and me, and we didn't have to talk on the phone.

There was a row of booths—blue plastic seats attached to the floor and a square white table. We sat facing each other, like we were eating a really awkward meal together at McDonald's—with an armed guard.

"I'm separate from the convicted prisoners," Jeff assured me. "They keep the people awaiting trial separate."

"Still, I bet you've met some interesting people," I whispered.

"Yeah, just like summer camp," he said, fingering the top button on his jumpsuit. "Friends to last a lifetime."

I decided not to point out that neither of us had ever been to summer camp.

"Can I bring you anything?" I asked Jeff. "I mean, next time?"

"Like what? Magazines and crosswords, you mean?"

"I don't know. Like anything you want. Can you watch MSNBC in here?"

"Uh . . . yeah. There's a room where we can watch TV. So far I haven't piped up to ask them to switch it to *Rachel Maddow.*"

"Can I bring you doggie bags or something?"

"No." Jeff looked exasperated by the question. "You can't bring food."

"How's the food here?"

He flashed me a big, fake smile. "It's *free.*"

"What did you have for dinner last night?"

He pressed his palms into his eyes and rubbed them slowly. "Jesus, Theresa. Do you really want to know?"

"Jeff. You need to talk to me."

"Fine. American chop suey."

"No, I mean about . . ." I took a deep breath. "Well, for one thing, what's with the screwdriver?"

Jeff leaned back in his seat and closed his eyes. "I don't know," he said.

"What do you mean you don't know? How did it get there?"

"I think the police must've planted it." His voice was on the verge of breaking. "I can't think of any other way."

"The police?" I said. I had the vague sensation of my neurons misfiring. I rarely disbelieved anything Jeff said. But my brain wasn't quite letting in this process as it was supposed to.

"Um . . . so they figured out that you followed her."

"Yeah. From my E-ZPass. Like they said. I guess you were right about them figuring it out."

The way my brother said it—and the way the guard looked at us as he spoke—made me squirm. So I decided to change the subject to something that had been bothering me.

"You didn't notice that Kim was acting weird lately? She must've disappeared a few times in order to take those pictures, call that reporter, and whatever else she was doing."

"I did notice. That was why I thought she was fooling around with Kyle again."

I chose not to ask about the "again" part of this. "And that's why you followed her to Rowington."

"And that's why I followed her to Rowington," Jeff repeated quietly.

"I think this obsession she had about Donald Wallace *was* connected to Kyle, actually," I said. "It sounds to me like they had a messy relationship."

Jeff shrugged. "Good for them. Kim liked messy. Messy excited her."

His words stunned me for a moment. Jeff never spoke that way. At least not to me.

"You're pretty certain she was cheating on you with him?" I asked him.

"Certain? No. I'm not certain of anything right now, Theresa. Except that I'm fucked."

"No you're not. They'll figure out who really did it."

"Not if they've already decided it was me."

"I don't know if that's accurate yet."

"Look at me, Theresa." Jeff flapped the arm of his blue jumpsuit. "*Look* at me. You think I'm being punked here?"

"I'm sorry. You're right. Maybe some of them have decided. But we need to help them realize they've gotten it wrong."

Help them realize. How psychobabble-sunny I sounded. I wouldn't be surprised if Jeff wanted to slug me. I rather wanted to slug myself.

"How do you propose we do that?" he demanded. "Has it crossed your mind that some of them might not even care about getting it right?"

"It's not like you have enemies in the Thompsonville police department. Why wouldn't they want to get—"

I didn't finish my sentence. I thought of Donald Wallace—a man so powerful and ambitious that he might as well be from a foreign land, if not made of an entirely different substance from Jeff and me. What if our scrappy little Kim had been more of a threat to him than we realized?

We're Battles. What chance did we have?

"Is there any way you can think of that could help us find out more about Kim's project?" I asked. "About her relationship to Donald Wallace?"

"I don't think there was a 'relationship.' Do you know something I don't?"

"I didn't mean it like that."

Jeff put his head down in his hands, clawing at his hair for a moment. The corrections officer turned and stared at him.

"Jeff!" I snarled, and he stopped, setting his hands on the table again. "Why do you think Kim didn't tell you about *any* of this?"

"I don't know, Theresa. I've been asking myself that. I mean, I'm unemployed, for God's sake. I could've helped. It would've made my day to have something to do, and she probably knew it. I could've helped her with the—" He stopped.

"What?" I said.

"You could ask Nathan, maybe. He might know more than I do. Probably does."

"Nathan the bartender? Nathan the python guy?"

"Yeah."

"Was Kim paying him to help her or something? Or were they such good friends he was willing to help her for free?"

"I don't know. The time he helped her with the Wayne footage, I know she bought him a six-pack in exchange. So they weren't close enough that she didn't feel she owed him *something*."

"Kim mentioned that all three of you hung out once. Does that mean you were sort of his friend, too?"

"No. It was kind of weird, actually. I mean, his snake was there and everything."

"Okay, but aside from that. Was he . . . reasonable? If I went into the restaurant and asked him about it, do you think he'd be forthcoming?"

"I don't *know*. It depends on whether he thinks I did something to Kim. If he knows who you are, he might not want to help you."

"But maybe if he has any material or contacts, he could be convinced to give it to the . . ."

I almost said police. But that led me to wonder how they'd respond to an avenue of investigation that involved the state attorney general. Reading those articles about what had happened to Andrew Abbott didn't give me a great deal of faith in the system my brother had just entered.

"You need to tell your lawyer everything," I said.

"I have. There's not a lot to tell."

"Is there anything else you wanted to tell *me*?"

Jeff laid his hands flat on the table before us and pressed his fingers outward, as if carefully folding an imaginary piece of origami paper.

"I wanted to tell you to please not let Mom lose her mind over this."

"I can't promise that. You know that."

"Then I wanted to tell you to try to make sure Dad doesn't come blasting in here asking me questions about the showers."

I couldn't promise this any more than I could the one about our mother, but the words startled me nearly speechless. I imagined my father here at this very table, saying to Jeff, *Well, we're Battles. . . .*

Fucking hell.

"I'll see what I can do," I whispered.

My mother didn't need a ride from the airport. She'd arranged her own rental car and driven it straight to the detention facility. Then, after she got to see Jeff, she carted herself over to my place. I put on a strong pot of coffee when I saw her car, then watched her march up my driveway.

She gripped a white pastry bag and pulled her purple fleece tight around her chest. As she walked closer, I could see she had on a thin pineapple-printed dress and pantyhose. You'd think she had never lived in New England. Her hair was in her usual full-bodied bob, however—sprayed into an immovable brown helmet. I wondered if she'd even once rested her head on the flight.

I greeted her at the door and gave her a hug.

"Hey, honey." She steered me inside. "When'd it get so damn cold around here?"

"A couple of days ago, the weather kind of turned," I told her.

"I called Springer, Norris, and Rice before my flight." My mother handed me the white bag as we entered my kitchen. "Set up an appointment for Jeff with Gary Norris. He'll be visiting Jeff this evening. He thinks Jeff has a good chance at bail. He said it might be high, but that the D.A. is being ridiculous thinking she's going to have him held."

I peered into the wax bag. Glazed doughnuts from Donut Dip, my mother's favorite townie establishment. Thompson grad students went there only ironically. The jelly doughnut is the most ironic of all doughnuts.

"They wouldn't let me bring those in to Jeff," she explained.

I nodded and poured us each a mug of coffee. "Is he good, this Norris?"

"One of the best defense attorneys in the state, my research tells me."

"Expensive?" I said.

"Ned's helping," my mother answered. "He's got a lot of money squirreled away."

I'd always figured as much, not that it was any of my business. But I'd been to their house in Key West once and knew that my mother couldn't have paid a fraction of the mortgage on her school-secretary pension.

"I can help," I told her.

"That's sweet of you. But I think your father and I can spare it more than you, don't you agree?"

I wasn't so sure that was true. If I had kids, it would be different.

"I don't have a lot of extra expenses," I reminded her.

My mother ignored me, biting into one of Jeff's doughnuts. "When the hell is your father getting home?"

"I just got a hold of him early this morning. He's going to get off the ship when they stop in Sicily, but it might take him a couple of days to arrange the flights home."

"Sicily," my mother muttered, then snorted her disdain.

Boober came sniffing into the kitchen.

"There's my little granddog," she said, leaning over to pet Boober. "Did you miss me, honey?"

Boober gobbled down the doughnut chunk she offered him.

"You know your brother loves your critters as much as you do." I could hear that my mother's voice was almost breaking.

"I know," I said. "With the possible exception of Sylvestress."

"We both know your brother wouldn't hurt a fly." Her lip trembled for a moment, but then she steadied it, took a breath, and licked a bit of frosting off her doughnut. "But I've never thought he's had instincts about dangerous people, dangerous situations. He'll trust anyone. I think he didn't realize what kind of people Kim was involved with."

I wasn't sure where my mother was going with this.

"What kind of people do you think Kim was involved with, Mom?"

"Theresa . . . the sort that would do something like this. To her and to Jeff."

I didn't meet my mother's gaze. Had Jeff suggested the same thing to her, about the police possibly planting evidence? It seemed not. But it sounded like she'd already begun to form her own equally implausible explanation in her head.

"Do you think Kim did some drugs?" she asked me.

"Some drugs? Like what kind of drugs, Mom?"

She shrugged and flicked doughnut glaze out of her pinkie fingertip. "Well, I don't know. Does it matter?"

"No, Mom. Jeff wouldn't go out with someone into serious drugs."

"That's what I'm saying, hon. He wouldn't *knowingly*."

"Usually you can tell when someone's into something serious."

"But your brother—"

"Jeff would be able to tell. And if, for the sake of argument, he couldn't . . . *I* would."

"How many times did you meet her?"

"About . . . four, I think."

My mother shook her head, closing her eyes for a moment. "He didn't want to talk much when I went to see him this morning."

"Can you blame him?" I said before realizing how nasty it sounded.

"He doesn't know anyone in there, doesn't get to see anyone much all day, and then someone comes to visit him and he doesn't want to talk? If I were in there, I'd sure as hell want to be able to *talk*."

I managed not to say, *I know you would*.

"It may be difficult for him to talk about what's happening."

"Well, of course I know that. I mean, I know that rationally. But I would feel better if he'd say more."

"He had American chop suey yesterday," I offered.

"Well, isn't that a fucking relief," my mother snapped.

She stood up and stared out the window. After a moment I heard her begin to sniffle. Surely she would start to cry at any moment if I didn't do something to stop it.

I quietly lit a Morning Glory votive on my kitchen table, then said, "You know, there was this brief period in Marge's life— twelve days—when she was plagued by visions of penises."

"Penises?" My mother turned around to frown at me. "Theresa, why do you tell me these things?"

"Men of all kinds—laymen and priests, whatever—coming straight at her from all directions, showing her their privates."

"Uh-huh?" My mother picked up her coffee and rolled her eyes.

"And she prayed to God and asked him to make it stop. But he made her endure it for twelve days. An angel came to her and explained that the visions were a result of her doubt. She had doubted that God had really spoken to her in the past. She had wondered if it was actually the devil. And now God was going to make her suffer through this so she would appreciate, when it was over, her usual beautiful messages from him."

"Uh-huh," my mother repeated. "And this relates to your brother how?"

I took a long sip of coffee, racking my brain for an answer. "These past few days I haven't felt as if this was really happening. I feel like it's fate deceiving us all somehow."

"Fate? Or God, Theresa?" My mother returned to the table, eyeing me warily.

One of her worst fears for me is that I'll take this Marge stuff too seriously and become a holy roller someday. Mom's never been much for religion. When Jeff and I were growing up, my father would pack us into the cab of his Ford pickup every Sunday for Mass at St. Margaret's. Whenever we asked why my mother didn't join us, we were told that there wasn't room in the truck. Several times Jeff and I volunteered to ride in the back to accommodate her. In fact, that was a particular childhood dream of mine for a while—arriving at Mass in the back of that truck, hair flapping in the wind, waving to a jealous Tish as she got out of her parents' station wagon.

My father would take Jeff and me to Cumberland Farms after church—assuming that our behavior was good, which it usually was—to pick out a bag of candy or chips.

How nice, my mother would remark when we arrived home. *Cheetos for Christ.*

"I said fate," I insisted now. "I didn't say God."

"I've probably asked this before, honey, but don't you ever think that Margery woman was a lesbian?"

"No, she was just . . . medieval."

"A lot of nuns are lesbians, you know. Did you know that?"

"She wasn't a nun. I've told you that about a hundred times."

"Who gives a shit, Theresa? The more you tell me about her, the more I wish someone *did* burn her at the stake. There. I've finally said it."

My mother actually said it every couple of months.

"I mean, if you're so interested in eccentric middle-aged women, why don't you call *me* more often? How about that?"

"You're not really that eccentric."

"I hope you're not getting woo-woo on us. I really hope not."

"Why do you hope that, Mom? Woo-woo people are *happy*. And what's wrong with that?"

"They only *think* they're happy."

"If you think you're happy, you *are* happy."

"Theresa, I'm going to stop you right there."

"Yeah?"

"I'd appreciate if I didn't have to hear about your friend Margery. Not today. Not tomorrow. Not till after your brother's gotten out on bail, and probably not after that either."

I'd actually brought up Marge on purpose, because it was less painful to see my mother angry than to see her cry.

"I'll try," I said, and reached for a doughnut.

After we had Chinese takeout, my mother left in the early evening. She was going to try to sleep, she said, because she hadn't slept since I'd called her with the news of Jeff's arrest.

We'd run out of things to say, so I was eager for her to leave. Once she was gone, though, I desperately wanted her to come back. Still, I resisted calling her. If she really thought she could sleep, I didn't want to get in her way.

I turned on the television and looked for the most mindless show possible. I settled on a cooking reality show, but I couldn't absorb it. Then I tried cleaning and laundry and harassing my pets.

Two days till Jeff's bail hearing. And after that—what next?

I choked down half a smoothie, washed the cat and dog dishes, and folded a pair of underwear. After all that I found myself on my bed, crying and reciting some words from Margery Kempe and wondering desperately what I could do for Jeff at this hour.

The idea came to me suddenly. I'd go find Nathan the bartender and see what I could get out of him. It was after ten, but he was probably still on duty.

Nathan was serving a group of boisterous undergrads when I arrived at Wiley's.

Watching him from my barstool, I realized something about him that I hadn't fully registered the time I was with Kim. With his tight jeans, silly earring, and five-o'clock shadow, he resembled the late-eighties George Michael. Back then, when I was in elementary school, he was one of my earliest, most primitive experiences of sexiness. I'd found him mostly irresistible but slightly, inexplicably gross. Did I have the same notion of sexy all these years later? I wasn't sure. I never thought I'd have an opportunity to test it.

While I waited for Nathan's attention, I took out my phone and tried the mystery number from Jeff's phone again.

"This mailbox is full and cannot accept any messages at this time. Good-bye."

"Whore," I muttered as I closed the phone. I put my head in my hands and rubbed my temples.

"Tough day?" someone asked. I looked up. It was Nathan.

"Sort of," I admitted.

Damn. This wasn't how I'd intended to start with him—by looking depressed. Men don't generally dig that.

"Yeah?" Nathan said.

He's into, like, spiritual stuff, I remembered Kim saying. *I bet he'd really be interested in that nun lady you're doing your thesis on.*

"Yeah. I . . . um, met with my dissertation adviser."

"Dissertation? You're a Ph.D. student?"

"Yup."

"What's it on, can I ask? Your dissertation?"

"It's on a medieval text. By a woman named Margery Kempe. Heard of her?"

Nathan shook his head. "I feel like I've maybe heard that name before, but I can't say I know anything about her. Was she a mystic?"

I was surprised by the question. "Um . . . kind of. But you might be thinking of Julian of Norwich. Sometimes people associate the two. She and Margery Kempe actually met once."

"I've never heard of Julian of Norwich."

"Oh. Well, she was an English mystic who lived at the same time as Margery Kempe. She was an anchoress—she lived in seclusion. But Marge—Margery Kempe, she was a married woman. More of an eccentric holy woman than a mystic."

I was trying not to sound like a smarty-pants. Surely Nathan got tired of smarty-pantses around here. I knew the feeling.

"Huh. An eccentric holy woman. That sounds cool. But listen—what can I get you?"

"Do you have Blue Moon?"

"Absolutely," Nathan said, and then dashed off to get it.

"But did she have, like, mystical visions?" he asked as he plunked down my beer.

"Well . . . yes . . . sort of. She was very controversial in her day. Some people thought she was a heretic. Her main expression of her relationship with God was through screaming and crying all the time. Some modern scholars think there was probably some sort of mental illness involved."

"What do you think?"

I smiled—enigmatically, I hoped. Probably I ended up looking reptilian, but I figured that might help me in this particular case. "I'm still working that out. But I do think, crazy or not, she pulled off something very rare for her time—committing herself to a religious vocation as a married laywoman."

Nathan nodded and then moved toward the back of the bar to wipe a counter.

"So it must be a sad time around here," I said. "I heard about the girl who worked here."

Nathan continued to clean. "Yeah. It's been a shock."

"Did you know her very well?"

He shrugged. "She was a nice girl. It's a tragedy."

"So you were friends?"

He tossed his rag into a bin under the counter. "Kind of, yeah. I'd rather not talk about it, though."

I nodded. An older couple approached. The man busting out of an argyle sweater vest, the woman with lots of sparkles on her ears and wrists that nonetheless did nothing to improve her scowl. Undergrad parents, I guessed. Probably better tippers than I was. Maybe better conversationalists, too. Nathan went to them, and I wondered if I'd lost him.

Ten minutes later—after I'd finished my beer—he returned.

"Are you a div student?" he asked.

"English literature."

I wasn't sure, but it seemed as if he was a tiny bit disappointed.

"But I'm very spiritual," I added.

Nathan hesitated. "Why are you smiling?"

"I don't know," I said. "Am I smiling?"

"No. Not now, I guess. Anything else for you? Another Blue Moon?"

"Um . . . I was thinking maybe a cocktail." I looked on the specials board. "Pomegranate mojito? Is that something you recommend?"

He lowered his voice. "Not really."

"What *do* you recommend?"

God, this was so embarrassing. I wondered if I seemed as desperate as I was. First Margery Kempe, then cocktail recommendations. It had been a few months since I'd flirted with anyone, so I wasn't sure if this was a step in the right direction.

"Ever had a Jasmine?" Nathan asked.

"Yes," I said. Jeff had been on a Jasmine kick a few months before he was fired—back when he could afford to try fancy cocktail recipes. "Actually, that sounds pretty good right now."

"All right, then. Any particular kind of gin?"

"No," I said, since I wasn't exactly up on my gins.

"So what *kind* of visions did she have?" Nathan asked as he mixed my drink.

If the way to this guy's heart was—miracle of miracles—with Marge stories, I had this one in the bag. I started with Marge's first vision. Right after the difficult birth of her first child, she went slightly insane—saw demons breathing fire and felt them clawing at her. She tore at her own skin and cursed everyone around her and wanted to kill herself. It may have been a very severe postpartum depression, perhaps postpartum dementia. She had to be tied to her bed for months. But in the middle of this, Jesus came to her in a purple silk robe, sat by her bed, and told her he had not forsaken her. This calmed her, and she made a sudden and miraculous recovery.

Nathan pressed his sexy George Michael butt against the back of the bar and listened carefully. I sipped my Jasmine as I spoke. It was so strong that I was light-headed by the time I got to the part about the purple robe. When I was done with that Marge story, Nathan asked for another.

I happily told him about the time, years later, when Marge was on her pilgrimage to Jerusalem. Along the way all her fellow pilgrims got so annoyed with her weeping and self-righteous lectures that they abandoned her. But she forgot all these troubles—at least temporarily—once she arrived in Jerusalem on a donkey. When she caught sight of her destination, she thanked God for granting her desire to see the city and asked that he also one day grant her desire to see heaven. He promised her fulfillment of that wish as well. So happy was she with this exchange that she nearly fell off her ass.

"That's practically a direct translation of the original Middle English," I added when Nathan looked skeptical.

Soon after that, I told him, as Margery looked upon the Mount of Calvary, she had such powerful visions of Christ's suffering that she fell to the ground and rolled around and flung her arms about and gave out loud, shrill cries. These cries were different from the weeping she'd been prone to already in her life. This was the first time she experienced a great wailing scream that she could not control—and that would be her trademark for many years to come. It was a turning point for Marge. After that, Marge was no longer simply annoying to the people around her. She was insufferable.

By the time I was finished with my Jasmine, I had Nathan's number. And we had a date for the following night.

Wednesday, October 23

I managed to doze for a couple of hours, but I woke up around 4:00 A.M. and couldn't go back to sleep. Once a little daylight started to glow around the edges of my blinds, I knew it was hopeless. My eyes stung with exhaustion as I made a pot of coffee.

The half-and-half was slightly curdled, but I fished out the biggest chunks with my spoon and drank the coffee anyway. I wondered if coffee was served in jail. Then I wondered about breakfast in jail generally. Did they serve eggs and meat? Or more of a Continental spread?

My stomach was starting to develop a sour feeling. I buttered a piece of toast, took a single bite, then pushed it aside. I couldn't do this for a whole day more—sit around wondering. I needed to get out and talk to people about Kim. Who else would know about her project? There was Nathan. I was working on him, of course. And there were those guys Dustin and Trenton Halliday. But closer to Kim's history was Missy.

According to Kim's roommate, Melissa Bailey probably lived in Folston—if Bailey was still her last name, which it probably wasn't. I popped onto Facebook for the first time in months. I found Kim's account quickly through Jeff's list of friends, then looked at her list. There was a Melissa Bailey Corbett, married to a Tanner Corbett. A quick search online confirmed that Tanner Corbett lived in Folston, on West Street.

I got up from the kitchen table and found Wayne sleeping in his L.L.Bean bed. Next to him sat my Tupperware butter dish, mangled with bite marks on one corner. I thought I'd put the butter back in the fridge after I made my toast, but it appeared I had not.

"Get the hell up, Wayne," I said. "We're going to see a friend of yours."

When I started the car, Wayne was sitting in the backseat, tongue reservedly hanging one-quarter out. He sighed when I put on my Brandi Carlile CD, then set his paws up on the door's armrest and snuffled at the window.

"Good boy, Wayne," I said. "You like the car?"

"Uff-uff-uff," he said, noncommittally.

By the time I was on the highway, I could no longer see him in the rearview mirror and assumed he'd fallen asleep. Just as I was getting off on Missy's exit, though, Wayne came bounding over the front seat console, slapping me with his heavy tail.

"I really don't appreciate that, Wayne!" I yelled, pushing his behind into the passenger seat as the GPS ordered me to get into the left lane. I steadied the wheel as I approached the light at the end of the ramp.

Wayne put his front paws on my leg, puffed up his chest, and glanced around the intersection—as if he'd just caught sight or scent of a squirrel. I pushed him away again and took a left. Wayne kept trying to get onto my lap and look out the driver's-side window, scratching up my corduroy skirt with his long black nails. I'd thought Missy would be more likely to talk to me if I looked nice. But it would backfire if I had ripped tights and bloody knees.

I managed to push Wayne away until we reached the Corbetts' address. The house was an old tan saltbox with a spooky black metal eagle hanging over the door. Folston was known for these sorts of homes—small Colonial houses near the charming downtown full of yarn shops and bakeries. Brendan had once suggested we look at houses here, but I could never figure out what people did in Folston, aside from knitting, eating muffins, and going to its famed annual Shakespeare in the Park.

"Don't blow this for me, Wayne," I said, gripping his leash as I locked my car door.

Before Wayne and I reached the steps, a tiny redhead came to the door with a baby in her arms. The woman was thin-limbed and freckly, with little color behind the freckles. I couldn't see the baby's face—only swirls of soft red hair around the back of its perfectly round head.

"I'm sorry to bother you," I said, before the young woman said anything. "I'm a friend of Kim Graber's. I was hoping you'd be willing to talk with me. I wasn't sure how to get your number. . . ."

"You've got Wayne, I see. I saw you from the window." The woman bounced the baby gently. Her expression remained neutral.

"Yeah. Kim actually left him with me the weekend she . . . disappeared. I've had him since. You've met Wayne before?"

"Yeah. We all took a couple of walks together once. Me and Zoe and Wayne and Kim. Now, what's your name?"

"Theresa," I said. "And are you Missy?"

"Yes," Missy said. The baby turned and stared at me. She had a thinnish face for a baby and blue eyes like her mother's. Everything was like her mother's, in fact. I tried to guess her age—probably about six months.

"I'm sorry, too," Missy said. "I don't know what she told you. But she and I weren't really close. I mean, I'm still in shock about what happened. I assume you were close friends, since you've got Wayne here."

I glanced down at Wayne, who was pulling out all the stops: tilting his head, arranging his eyebrows in a contemplative expression. Missy cracked a hint of a smile.

"I was wondering," I said slowly, "if you would be willing to talk to me about this Donald Wallace thing she had going on."

Missy didn't take her eyes off Wayne.

"Would Wayne like to take a walk now?" she asked. "I could put Zoe here in her stroller."

I was surprised how game she was. "It's not too cold?" I asked.

"Zoe and I walk every day," she said. "Unless it's raining hard or something. She might be getting tired soon, but we can try."

Missy disappeared into the house for a couple of minutes. When she came out, she had on a stylish black double-breasted coat. Clutching the now-bundled baby in one arm, she dragged an enormous stroller down the steps with the other.

"Can I help you?" I said, as the carriage landed on the sidewalk with a plastic crunch.

"I'm fine," Missy said, buckling Zoe into the stroller. "I assume you know how Kim and I knew each other?"

"I know that you were friends when you were kids." I took a breath. "I know about Jenny."

"Yeah." Missy pointed in the direction she wanted to go. "Well, we grew apart after Jenny Spicer died. Like in high school. Kim was sort of a drama queen. I was more a nerd. I kind of hid from any kind of attention. Especially attention that came from the Jenny thing. Now, you know about Kyle, right?"

"Yes," I said. "But how long were he and Kim together?"

"Like forever. Like since Kim was old enough to say she was 'going out' with someone. When she was around twelve. I guess he'd have been around fourteen. They were together from then until just a couple of years ago. The only reason I know this is because Kim and I were back in touch just recently. Facebook, you know? And then her Donald Wallace project."

Wayne stopped to sniff a garbage can at the end of a driveway. We both watched him for a few moments before I spoke again.

"So she was doing interviews with people who were involved with Jenny's case. I know that much."

"Yeah." Missy frowned. "She was, like, *so* sure some newspaper reporter was going to be all over it and give her all this publicity. I had my doubts, but I did agree to be interviewed. I didn't really want to, but . . . I felt bad for her."

"Why?" I asked.

Missy paused to adjust Zoe's knit hat, pulling it to cover an exposed ear. Zoe smiled at her mother's touch. "Because it seemed like she thought this would make her feel better about everything that had happened with Andrew Abbott. Like this would somehow redeem her. Like if she somehow helped defeat the guy who prosecuted him, that would absolve her a little bit. It was kind of twisted, but . . ."

Wayne stopped again, this time to sniff a dark spot on the sidewalk. We all stopped with him.

Missy sighed. "It's a pretty hard thing to have in your history, that you helped put a poor kid in jail for twelve years because he was on the weird side. Now, I tried to be as honest as possible at the hearing in 2006. I did the best I could with that. I tell myself I was a kid in 1992, but I was basically an adult in 2006. I did the right thing when I was old enough to know better. Kim—I don't think she felt that way. Because when you look at what she said at that hearing, it was like she didn't want to completely stop believing what she'd said as a kid. Or to *start* believing she could've been lying as a kid. Or she wasn't sure how to testify in a way that didn't upset Kyle. So for her that hearing wasn't maybe as cathartic as it was for me."

Missy stopped walking for a moment. "I love that house. Isn't it pretty?"

She was pointing at a small yellow house with an especially pointy roof and spindly blue trim curling along the sides.

"Yeah," I said, though it made me think of the witch's house in "Hansel and Gretel."

"You should see it in January, with all the icicles hanging off it."

"Cool." I shuddered.

Missy started pushing the stroller again. "Now, what I was starting to say about having something like that in your history. If there's one other person in the universe who knows what it's like to have the same nasty skeleton as you . . . it can be kind of hard to decide how you feel about that person. You never want to see them or think about them again, on one hand. But on the other, they're all you'll ever have if you want someone who can relate."

"And this is how you felt about Kim?"

Missy nodded. "And presumably how she felt about me. Now, this is going to sound weird. But I'll try to explain. A year ago or so, I saw that my husband had done a couple of Google searches on our computer. 'Star athlete injury.' 'High-school sports injury changed my life.' Because the thing about my husband is that he was going to be a big college football star, supposedly. Scouts from different universities came to check him out playing, whatever. But then he got this awful knee injury and it was over. Real sad *Friday Night Lights* kind of stuff, he says. He jokes about it now. But when I saw those searches, I thought, he's looking for people who had the same sort of thing happen. How funny. Those people actually exist for him. I mean, if he wants to find them. He can find a kind of tribe, if he wants. But I'll never have a tribe for what happened when I was a kid. Now, me, I could do a hundred Google searches and all I'd ever come up with is Kim."

I'd never considered finding "my people" online, so I didn't know how to reply. Maybe it was a generational thing. What would I type in anyway? "Wasted-youth medieval mystic"? "Divorced cat lady no Ph.D."?

I peered in at Zoe, since she'd been so quiet. Her eyelids were drooping. I thought of remarking on her cuteness, but Missy began to speak again.

"It's like she and I were the only two kids trapped in the same creepy attic. You don't want to think about the attic at all. But when you do, you're kind of glad someone else was there."

It was rather an unsettling metaphor. I had to look away from Zoe's urchin face for a moment.

"Where does Kyle fit into all this, though?" I asked. "What about him? Wasn't he there, too?"

"Kyle didn't ever testify. Kyle didn't ever say incriminating things about Andrew Abbott. Kyle has suffered a lot. But that's because he lost his sister. It's different for him."

Wayne groaned in surprise, then nearly yanked my arm out of its socket trying to dash into the yard in front of us. I looked up to see the rear end of a gray cat slip under a hedge.

"Can I ask you a question?" I said to Missy when Wayne quit barking.

"Yeah?"

"Who do you think first gave you the idea that it was Andrew Abbott? Where did that come from? Was it how the adults talked about him? Or the first police officer who questioned you about Jenny?"

"I feel bad saying this now. But I remember pretty clearly. It actually came from Kim. Kim started talking about Andrew kissing Jenny and all that. I kind of followed along, I think. Kim was always more sure of herself . . . talking to adults, telling them what she thought they wanted to hear. Making things sound good to them."

"Where do you think *Kim* got the idea?"

We hit a corner. Missy made a sharp turn with the stroller, and I followed her. I was curious if we were making our way to the park, but I didn't want her to skip this question.

"I have no idea. But Kim was kind of . . . fast, you know? You talk about kids picking up adult things. . . . She would've been one to pick up on it if the grown-ups were creeped out by Andrew. Me, I was kind of clueless. I never, ever would've thought anything was wrong with him showing us how to draw horses. You . . . uh . . . know about that part, right?"

Wayne sighed and glanced up at me, as if to say, *Do we need to talk about this?*

"Yes. Well, basically. So . . . when she wanted to interview you for her video, what kind of stuff did she want you to say?"

"Oh, just talk about Andrew Abbott, and how he was wrongfully convicted, and how I wish more people were talking about that in the media, with Wallace running."

"Wouldn't Andrew Abbott or his family or friends be better people to interview?"

"Of course. But I don't think Kim could ever get them to sit for her stupid video."

"Did she ask?"

"You know, she never said. I assume not. I assume she'd have told me. I think she was maybe too afraid to ask. Too ashamed of herself. I hate to say that now, but it's how I felt about it." Missy sighed. "I mean, ultimately I just wanted to say to her, 'You want to feel better about what happened to Andrew Abbott, go to him directly and fucking apologize, for Christ's sake.' Excuse my language."

"Did you ever do that yourself?" I hesitated. "Apologize to Andrew?"

"I did after the hearing. In 2006. Or—I tried."

"What did he say?"

"He said that he didn't blame me, so I shouldn't apologize. That for him it was all about the adults who had done this to him. But at least he was willing to talk to me." Missy shrugged.

"So it might not have been very satisfying for her. But at least then she could've said she tried. That's the thing about Kim. It was maybe more about drama than principle. I think she thought that this was gonna be Wallace's 'forty-seven percent' video or something. And she'd, like, have all the glory of being the one to take him down."

"Do you think she had any footage on her video that would be even remotely damaging to him?"

Missy stopped walking for a moment, thinking about my question. Zoe gave a little cry of protest, and then Missy began to move again. She stared down at the baby. I wasn't sure if she was trying to will Zoe to stop fussing or just avoiding my gaze.

"It was hard to take Kim seriously sometimes," she said. "So I'm not sure how to answer that question. But I think, in the end, she stumbled into something that might've been difficult for Donald Wallace after all."

"And what was that? Do you want to say?"

She walked in silence for a moment, then asked, "Did Kim mention Colleen Shipley to you?"

"No."

"Colleen Shipley was Donald Wallace's assistant, back when he tried Jenny's case."

"Okay."

"And Colleen Shipley, I was surprised to hear, was willing to talk to Kim. But not on camera."

Missy pushed the stroller over a deep crack in the sidewalk. Zoe began to fuss again. Missy produced a purple pacifier from a plastic bag in her pocket and popped it into Zoe's mouth.

"This is where it gets messy. Colleen Shipley gave Kim a few old VHS tapes. Of her and Wallace talking to me and Kim when we were kids."

"Colleen *had* that?"

Missy shrugged. "I'm just telling you what Kim told me. I had my issues with Kim, but I don't think she'd have made that up. And she offered to let me watch them. I said no thanks. I just don't want to watch that shit at this stage of my life, you know?"

"I can understand that," I said. "But . . . what happened to the videos themselves? Did Kim show them to anyone else?"

"I don't know," Missy said. "I know that she'd put what she found—or some of it—on DVD, because that's what she offered me—DVDs. Probably she saved it on her computer or somewhere, too, since she'd somehow transferred it to digital format. Or gotten someone to do it for her."

Nathan the bartender came to mind—Nathan and his wedding-video services. Putting that aside for a moment, I asked, "Do you remember talking to this Colleen lady, back when you were a kid? Talking to Donald Wallace?"

"Only vaguely. I felt, back then, like I had to say the same thing so many times. I didn't know when I was talking to important people and when I wasn't. But . . . Kim kept asking me if she could put some clips of the old tapes in her video."

I thought of the journalist that Kim had apparently contacted—Janice something—who'd thought she was a little crazy for calling her claiming to have "special footage."

"What clips?" I asked. "Something specific?"

"I don't know. She said in general they made Wallace look like an asshole."

"But was there something illegal that he did?"

"I don't know. I think Kim hoped so. But I don't think she was sure. She wasn't exactly a legal expert."

"Was it legal for Colleen Shipley even to *have* the tapes?"

"I don't know. I didn't ask Kim that. I wasn't really so focused on that. More on what Kim was gonna do with them now that she had them."

"So did you say yes? To letting her put clips with you in them on her video?"

Missy shrugged. "Not exactly. I mostly avoided the question. At first I tried to convince myself that her interest in the whole thing might burn out before the election was even over. In the last week or two before she died, I started to realize that might not happen. Although it seemed as if her interest was shifting."

"Shifting?"

"The last time I saw her, she was talking more about those guys Dustin and Trenton. The Halliday boys."

I didn't expect to hear those names out of Missy's mouth. "She told you about them?"

"A little bit. Do you know much about their case?"

"I've read all the articles I could find."

"Yeah. So did Kim. Her idea was that Donald Wallace got their mother convicted wrongfully, too. It seemed like a long shot to me. What happened to Andrew was a total travesty, I know. But I don't think Wallace's career was *full* of convictions like that. I'll bet most prosecutors have put one or two innocent people in jail. As I was saying, Kim maybe wanted to find more people like herself. I think she was attracted by the idea that Dustin was like her—that he was somehow another victim of Donald Wallace's ambition."

"She considered herself the victim in all this?"

"Oh, I don't know if that's accurate. It was more like . . . she needed Donald Wallace to be the villain. She needed a boogeyman. Andrew Abbott wasn't it anymore. So Donald Wallace was his replacement."

We were headed back toward Missy's house now.

"You don't need a boogeyman?" I asked.

"You know, that's an interesting question. I stopped needing one when I had Zoe. Because now I've got about a thousand little boogeymen. And none of them is Donald Wallace. Let me just put it that way."

A thousand little boogeymen. As we took our final steps to Missy's house, I chose not to ask Missy what some of those were. I knew what she meant.

As soon as I got out of Missy's neighborhood, I pulled in to a Wendy's. At the drive-through I ordered a double cheeseburger and a couple of waters, plus an extra paper cup. In the parking lot, I fed Wayne one of the meat patties while I ate the remainder of the sandwich.

"This is called emotional eating," I explained to Wayne. "At least for me. For you it's a reward for being a detective dog. That Missy probably would've slammed the door in my face if it weren't for you. But she saw you and she spilled. So thank you."

Wayne swallowed the last of his meat patty and yawned. I poured half a bottle of water into the paper cup and held it out for him while he slurped.

When he was finished, I put the cup in my cup holder and started the car.

"I'm feeling lucky, Wayne," I said once we got on the road.

Using my Bluetooth, I tried Jeff's mystery number again as I drove.

I so thoroughly expected that hag to pick up and tell me the mailbox was full that I nearly hung up before I gave her a chance. This time, though, she said, *"You have reached the voice mail of . . ."* Then there was a pause, and I was so startled I nearly lost my grip on the steering wheel.

"Dustin Halliday," said a male voice.

I hung up quickly.

"Did you hear that?" I said to Wayne, who was *uff-uff-uffing* in the backseat again. Talking to Wayne helped me keep calm.

I steadied my hands on the wheel.

"I suppose I could've left a message," I said. "But I'd better come up with a plan first. Right?"

In the rearview mirror, I could see Wayne licking an old hoisin-sauce stain on the backseat.

"But by now he's probably wondering who the stranger is who's been calling and hanging up. I wonder if he's ever going to pick up?"

I pulled in to my driveway and let Wayne out of the car, holding his leash. He led me around the yard, snuffling through the brown leaves that I would need to rake soon. Usually Jeff helped me with that.

A cold gust blew through the yard. Wayne raised his head and sniffed at it. The leaves—the few that weren't mushed into the lawn—rattled softly. The brisk air seemed to clear my head of some of the sticky lethargy brought on by the fast food.

Of course I should pursue Dustin Halliday—but carefully.

And of course I should talk to Zach Wagner a little bit more about Dustin before I planned my approach. My brother was an accused murderer. Zach's success and my failure were irrelevant now. I didn't care what Zach—or the English department—thought anymore. I cared about Jeff.

I tugged at Wayne's leash, and he obliged. Inside, before I had my coat off, I opened my laptop, went to the English department's Web site, and found Zach's e-mail address.

The Spellman Hall student lounge was crawling with undergrads. Maybe it was the weather—suddenly colder than the relatively mild autumn we'd had up till now—compelling them inside for the lukewarm flavored coffees on offer at the student café. Back when I was working on my master's, I went in for the Pumpkin Spice. These days it felt to me like drinking a Whitlock's candle.

Zach had agreed to meet me after his late-afternoon class, but I was early. I settled into one of the cube-shaped coral chairs and passed the time going through my coat pockets. I'd taken this coat out from storage just a couple of days before. It still had year-old cat hair on it and year-old tissues in the pockets. Plus a cough drop that likely predated my divorce. The last thing I found was a glove—half hidden in the torn lining of the coat. It was a knitted hippie glove, chunky with white and purple yarn from Pakistan, and it was turned inside out, its innards curling out like a tangled old telephone cord.

I'm a bit of a compulsive picker. Not like scab picking or nose picking, thankfully. Knitted things, mostly. Anything with little knots or ties—I have to untie them. Particularly when I've got some stress going on. And those chunky hippie gloves—they're full of tight little knots on the inside. Brendan had given me the pair at our first Christmas. I'd lost the right one years ago but kept the left around for picking. The thumb and palm were full of holes that I'd untied and retied last winter.

So now I set to work picking at the middle finger—a couple of tight knots right at the tip. I listened to two undergrad girls chatting two seats away. Both of them were pretty in a button-nose sort of way. Both of them had their hair done up in beautifully messy ponytail buns of the sort I've never been able to pull off without looking like Bertha Rochester.

"I LOVE pizza. I mean, REAL pizza," the smaller of the two girls was saying. "But I can't eat that dining hall stuff. Not AGAIN. And I'm SO sick of SALAD bar. I'm NOT doing it tonight. Not TONIGHT. I can't WAIT to go down to Annie's and get a bagel with TONS of cuuuh-REAM cheese."

"Oh, choke on it," I muttered, then bit at the stubborn middle-finger knot.

I heard a chuckle behind me. I turned and saw Zach Wagner. At least I remembered to remove the glove from my mouth before greeting him.

"Hi," he said. "How are you holding up?"

"With respect to what?" I asked. I wondered how much he knew.

"With respect to what's been happening." Sinking into the chair across from mine, he lowered his voice. "I heard about them putting off setting your brother's bail."

So he knew everything. Of course. He read the newspapers.

"I'm surprised you showed up, then." I tried not to mumble the words.

"What makes you say that?"

All I could do was shake my head.

Zach leaned forward, clutching his hands together and still

speaking softly. "I haven't made a judgment on your brother—I hope you know that. I'm just surprised you still care about Kim's project . . . under the circumstances?"

"I don't think the circumstances and Kim's project are unconnected."

Zach touched one of his bushy eyebrows, looking embarrassed for me. "How's that?" he asked.

"I think Kim walked into something more dangerous than she realized, and it maybe got her killed."

Zach nodded slowly, letting this sink in as he leaned back in his chair.

"I have to be honest with you, Theresa. I'll help you in any way I can, but I don't want to get your hopes up. I don't think anyone cared much about Kim's project. Besides Kim."

"Would you be surprised to hear, then, that Dustin Halliday was sending her threatening texts the day she disappeared?" I asked.

Zach's expression changed from pitying to surprised. "Are you serious?"

"Yes."

"Like, 'I'm gonna kill you' kinds of threats? Or more in the manner of 'Girl, I'm gonna unfollow you on Twitter'? What are we talking about here?"

"He was definitely angry at her about something. Swearing. He seemed . . . insulted. Maybe she'd asked him something that offended him. Or that made him feel threatened. And there was a reference to some kind of footage."

"How do you know this?" Zach asked.

I explained about Kim's phone.

"Does she have e-mail on her phone? Was he e-mailing her, too?"

"It's not a smartphone, so I don't know."

Zach frowned. "I hadn't realized she'd tracked him down. I knew she wanted to, but I thought she'd have trouble."

"Because?"

"Well, when I was interviewing him for the book . . . he didn't seem stable to me. I'd felt pretty strongly he might have some trouble adjusting once he got out. He didn't seem like someone who'd get a nine-to-five and a listed home phone number."

"Unstable? How unstable? Like . . . violent? Remind me why he was in juvenile detention?"

"Drug distribution. Habitual. I think it was, like, his fifth offense. Violent? Not in my brief encounter with him. Troubled for sure. But that doesn't necessarily mean he'd be violent."

"Uh-huh," I said. I was vaguely disappointed by this answer. "Now, why was Kim so interested in Dustin? Just because he'd been involved in a Donald Wallace case, too?"

"And because he thought his mother was unjustly convicted." Zach shrugged. "That was my impression."

"It seems like he talked about that when you interviewed him for the book. His belief that his mother was innocent."

Zach nodded. "A little. I tried to put in enough about that to show the source of some of Dustin's emotional difficulties, without letting the murder case overshadow that whole chapter. When Dustin would talk about it, he was very convincing. But then when I followed up on a couple of things—like this idea that there were a black guy and a white guy partnered up and going on a crime spree in his neighborhood, robbing a convenience store that week or whatever . . . it's not true. Yes, there was a holdup in town that week, but it was committed by a white kid acting alone, strung out on drugs."

"Did you mention this to Kim?"

"Yeah, we talked about it. She said she wanted to talk to Dustin herself." Zach pulled an opened bag of peanut M&M's out of his coat pocket. "Have you let the police know? About Dustin harassing Kim?"

"No, not yet," I said. "Did she mention to you some 'special footage' she had?"

"*Special* footage?" Zach repeated.

"She mentioned to some other journalist that she had special footage. Did she mention that to you?"

Zach reached two fingers into the M&M's bag and drew out one orange candy. He bit off half of the M&M, leaving the bottom half—with peanut attached—still sitting delicately between his fingers, like a tiny hatched egg. He stared at it for a moment, then ate it.

"Actually . . . *yes*. By then I was trying to distance myself from the project, but yes. She was going on about some old VHS tapes she got or something. It sounded a little wacky. I have to admit I . . . told her I had a meeting to get to, the last time we spoke."

Zach offered me the bag of candy. I shook my head.

"I kicked her out of my office," he continued. "Pulled the snooty-professor card, I'm sorry to say. I've got a lot on my plate right now, with my book's deadline approaching. And I was just tired of her coming to me with this weird shit. Is the other journalist you're talking about Janice Obermeier?"

"Yeah," I said.

"Because I gave her Janice's name and number. It was a sort of passing of the buck, to be honest. I wasn't really sure Janice would be interested, but she *does* do more political stuff than me. *And* more sensationalistic material sometimes."

"Did Kim tell you anything about these old tapes?"

"Something about when she was a kid. Footage of herself as a kid, I think? It didn't sound like anything important." Zach began to probe his M&M's bag again—maybe looking for a particular color.

I took a breath. "What if she had footage of herself and one other underage witness being questioned by Donald Wallace and his assistant in 1992?"

Zach's hand froze in his M&M's bag. "What're you saying?"

"What if Donald Wallace's assistant had this footage in her private possession and gave it to Kim recently?"

"Really?" To my satisfaction, Zach looked genuinely intrigued.

"Yes. You would consider *that* important, right?"

Zach returned a brown M&M to the bag and looked thoughtful.

"Don't worry about getting my hopes up," I added. "Just say what you think."

Zach leaned back in his chair and took a deep breath. "Well, it would depend on a couple of things."

"Like what?"

"Like if this footage was used in Andrew Abbott's trial, for one."

"I don't know that yet."

"And if there's anything in it that would make Donald Wallace look bad."

"I don't know that either. I don't have the footage. I only know that Kim had it."

"Now, *that's* interesting. How do you know this? Did Jeff tell you this?"

"No," I said. "Someone else did."

"Maybe you ought to tell Jeff's lawyer. Does Jeff *have* a lawyer yet?"

"Yeah. So now, when you say you don't think anyone cared about what Kim was doing . . ."

"Yeah. You got me. I didn't realize she had anything like *that*."

"Right. So with that in mind . . ."

"I'm not gonna suddenly say someone cared, Theresa. I'm not gonna say it was tied to her death. But it makes it a hell of a lot more complicated, for sure. I wonder how far Kim went with this. If she got Donald Wallace's assistant to take her seriously, then she got further than I thought."

"I think Donald Wallace may have known about her," I offered. "Or at least some of Donald Wallace's people did."

Zach looked puzzled. "What makes you think so?"

I was too embarrassed to mention my conversation with Kyle at Carpet World. "Just conjecture," I murmured. "Listen, I wanted to ask you a couple more things about contacting Dustin."

Zach twisted his M&M's bag closed. "Do you think he's somehow connected to this business with the assistant?"

"Oh. Well, no. I hadn't thought of that. Whatever else was happening, it looks like Dustin was angry with Kim. Everything else aside, it seems worthwhile to get to the bottom of that. How do you think Kim tracked her down?"

Zach shrugged. "She came to me for contact information, but I didn't have it. The best I could do was give her some fairly recent information about the brother. Trenton Halliday."

"How recent?"

"Well, I had a bit of contact with him when the book came out. He wrote me to thank me for portraying his brother in a fair way. It surprised him, I guess. Anyhow, we ended up having a couple of beers. But that was a few years ago now. I told her I thought he still worked at the same cable company, and I guess she found him through that. But it turned out to be a dead end, she said—that Trenton hadn't seen his brother in more than a year. So I have to assume she found Dustin some other way."

"Wasn't there also a teacher that Dustin was close to?"

"Sharon Silverstein?" Zach nodded. "You could try her, too, yes. I think I might still have her e-mail address. So I could send that to you. Doesn't seem likely, though, that he'd keep in touch with an old teacher but not his brother."

"Well, you never know. Maybe there's bad blood between the brothers. And how about Dustin's little friend?"

"His little friend?" Zach raised an eyebrow.

"I forget his name. I'm grabbing at straws here anyway, but he had this friend in juvenile detention that was mentioned in your book."

"Oh. Right. Anthony. You know, often those relationships don't last after the kids get out. That was my experience anyway. I didn't stay friends with any of the kids I met when I was . . ." Zach trailed off and shrugged.

I decided not to make him finish his sentence, since it was clearly an awkward subject. "Anthony wasn't his real name, was it?"

"No. Only two kids used their real names. Dustin and one other kid."

"Why didn't you simply change all their names?"

"I left it up to them. Dustin was a special situation, because his mother's case was so well known anyway. The details would've been recognizable to a lot of readers."

"And therefore he didn't want his name changed?"

"He was an odd one. He said he'd *only* participate if I used his real name. Isn't that weird?"

"I guess."

Zach opened his bag of candy again. "Dustin had an interesting spirit. He was articulate, in his own frenetic way."

He pulled out a brown M&M and followed the same procedure as before—carefully bit off the top half of the chocolate, leaving a peanut with a cap, examining it, eating it. Was he inspecting each peanut for quality? It was cute, in a woodland-creature sort of way.

"I got some flak for putting a kid with such a sensationalistic story in the book," Zach added with a shrug, "because it supposedly detracted from the main issue. But it made for good variety in the book. You don't want everyone's story to sound the same."

"No," I said. "No, I suppose you don't."

I wondered how *my* stories would sound, were I a student in Zach's class. Would they sound exactly like my brother's? A dozen variations on, *We're Battles. What chance did we have?*

"Anyway, did you tell Jeff's lawyer yet? What you've been up to? What you've found so far?"

"I have yet to determine if he'll think this line of inquiry will be useful."

"I see," Zach said. "Well, I'm sure he'll find it interesting.

Particularly the stuff you're telling me about the assistant and the footage. You really ought to tell him that."

I nodded. We were both quiet for a moment.

"Listen, can I buy you a coffee or something?" Zach offered.

"No thanks. I'm fine. Too upset for caffeine, actually."

"Now, can I ask . . . how's your brother holding up?"

"Hard to say," I answered. I didn't feel like talking much about Jeff. Even if Zach had spent a little time in a correctional facility himself. "He's kind of quiet when I visit him."

Zach was distracted by my hands. "What're you knitting?" he wanted to know.

I shoved the glove between my thigh and the chair.

"I'm not," I said. "I'm not knitting."

His eyebrows crinkled inward as he nudged at the bridge of his glasses. Probably it was difficult to make appropriate small talk with the sister of an accused murderer.

"Um. Do you still have Kim's dog? Does her family know you have him?"

Well played, I thought. Relevant but not too painful.

"Maybe. I saw them at the arraignment. What, was I going to go up to them in the courtroom and be like, 'Listen, folks—I know this is kinda weird, but can you come pick up the dog?'"

"Right."

I hesitated. "I had a couple more questions for you about Kim's project, actually."

"Sure. Don't know how much I can answer, though."

"Okay. Well, did Kim ever mention Kyle to you? Kyle Spicer?"

"Kyle Spicer? No. A relation to Jenny, I assume?"

"I assume, too. But he was Kim's boyfriend for a long time apparently."

Zach grimaced. "That's kind of icky. I had no idea."

"Never mentioned him?"

He shook his head. "No."

"How about a Melissa Bailey? Missy Bailey?"

"No. Wait. You know, I think there *was* a Missy in her piece about Jenny Spicer. If memory serves. Did you read that yet?"

"Not yet," I said. "Did you know that Kim was involved in the original investigation? The trial?"

Zach shrugged. "I got the sense that might be the case. But I never asked her outright. It didn't seem appropriate. And she didn't ever come out and supply that information."

I looked at my hands. My thumb and forefinger were raw from so much picking.

"What *are* you doing?" he asked.

"I just like to untie the little knots."

"So it's the opposite of knitting."

"I guess."

"You're an unraveler."

I thought about this. It sounded better than "a picker." It was bullshit, of course. But it was elegant bullshit.

"Yes."

"I suppose the world needs unravelers as much as knitters."

I smiled. Only an academic would say such a thing. "I don't think so, Zach."

"Well, it needs a few, probably."

"In case there are ever too many sweaters? Too many home-made hats?"

"I meant unraveling more generally."

"Of course," I said. "A general unraveler. And while we're making these sorts of observations, I like how you eat your candy."

"I've always done it this way." He seemed surprised that I had noticed. "Since I was a kid. My parents always used to buy me a package on Saturdays, when they'd do their boring errands, like the drugstore and the dry cleaners. I'd try to make them last the whole trip."

"I always eat the red ones and the blue ones first," I admitted. "Because then what's left are the colors they had when I was little."

"That's funny," Zach said. "I like blue the best. They feel the freshest. Space-age, even. Like an astronaut power pellet."

"Chocolate is for comfort," I said. "Not for efficacy."

"You've obviously never watched a Snickers commercial."

I glanced at the clock. As much as I would have liked to lose myself in this repartee, I had Jeff to think of.

"I should go now. There's only an hour left that I can see my brother."

"I won't keep you, then." Zach paused. "He's lucky to have you."

"Can you send me that teacher's e-mail address?"

"Sure thing. And let me know if you get a hold of Dustin, will you? I'd feel better if you didn't try to confront him on your own."

"I thought you said he didn't seem violent."

"He didn't. But when I sent Kim to Trenton, I didn't have any idea Dustin would end up harassing her. It would just make me feel better if you were cautious."

"I'll see if I can even find him. Then I'll worry about that."

I put on my coat to signal that I was ready to end the conversation.

Zach stood up with me. "Good luck, Theresa. I'll be thinking of you."

As I walked away, I wondered about that statement: *I'll be thinking of you*. I often said it to people myself—when they had sick family members or when they lost their jobs. I now wondered what good all this thinking ever did anyone. Under these desperate circumstances, I might have preferred a prayer over a thought. But I wasn't in a position to be picky.

My father was already visiting with Jeff when I arrived at the prison.

"I wasn't sure what time you were getting in," I said, hugging him.

"Decided to come here first thing."

His glasses—the ones he'd gotten right before he left on his latest cruise—startled me. Our father had recently discovered John Lennon glasses, and neither Jeff nor I had had the heart to tell him they weren't flattering. We'd figured that one of the bolder cruise biddies might break it to him.

Dad's hair seemed whiter than the last time I'd seen him. In the last couple of years, it had eased from gray to white. One of his ears was sunburned and peeling. He'd either fallen asleep in a half-shaded spot or put sunblock on one and then forgotten the other.

"You're okay?" Dad asked.

"Kind of," I said.

"Your brother's got some good news. Isn't that right, Jeff?"

He said it as if Jeff had come home with a Pinewood Derby trophy.

I turned to Jeff. "What's this?"

"Oh, I was just telling Dad—"

"They've found some skin under the girl's fingernails," Dad interrupted. "They're sending it to a lab for some DNA testing."

"How long does that take?" I asked.

"Gary Norris thinks it'll be a couple of weeks."

"When the results come back, they'll know it's not you." Dad rubbed his kneecaps with anticipation.

Jeff scratched at the stubble on his chin. Did they provide razors in prisons? I wondered. Shampoo? A toiletry kit?

"Let's maybe talk about something else for now," Jeff said. "How was Sardinia?"

"Oh." Dad looked surprised but game. "Beautiful. Of course."

"One of your top five?"

"I don't know. It would be if I were a beach man. But I'm more of a forest man."

"Then you've taken the wrong job, I think."

"They don't pay you to dance in the forest."

"Maybe someone would. Maybe you ought to look for a job like that."

"Maybe I ought to."

"Another million-dollar business idea."

I watched as my father and brother had this exchange, their lips barely moving, their eyes never actually focusing on each other. They'd started speaking to each other this way when Jeff was a teenager. I wondered why my mother and I couldn't make bizarre, meaningless small talk like this. My mother had to end every conversation wishing either that Marge had been burned or that I'd stayed married.

"Dad," Jeff said gently, "I need to talk to Theresa about something. But I'll see you tomorrow, okay?"

"I wonder how soon after the hearing we can post the bail?" Dad said.

"Mom and Theresa have got that worked out, I think." Jeff turned to me. "Right?"

"Yeah, we've been working through it. Depending on how high it is, we can possibly get Jeff out a few hours after they set the amount. Gary Norris is anticipating it won't be prohibitively high."

Gary Norris. This name would be an important part of our family discussions for a good while now, I supposed.

"I'll call your mother," Dad said with a nod. He seemed reluctant to get up. But he did, slowly. He squeezed Jeff's arm. "Tomorrow," he said.

On his way out of the visiting area, Dad paused at the snack vending machine by the door. He gazed at it for a moment, then pointed at it and gave Jeff a questioning look. *Do you want anything?* Jeff shook his head. My father raised his hand good-bye and disappeared.

The words "Cheetos for Christ" crossed my mind, making me both hungry and despairingly sad.

"What's going on? Something?" I whispered. "Or did you just want to get rid of him?"

"The DNA test, Theresa."

"What about it?"

Jeff gnawed on a hangnail before answering me. "I wasn't able to talk to him about it like I meant to."

"What do you mean?"

"I was trying to prepare him for the possibility . . ." Jeff shook his head.

"The possibility that it's gonna be your DNA?"

"Well, I don't know how it works. But the morning before she left . . . well, you know."

"She . . . uh . . . scratched your back?"

"Um . . . something like that?" Jeff stared at the smudged tabletop between us. "Our relationship was . . . like that."

"Would it need to be something more violent?" I said, avoiding his eyes. "For there to be enough skin?"

"I'm not sure."

"Did you ask Gary? Um . . . Gary Norris?"

"Yeah. He wasn't sure either. He's looking into it. He said probably not. And especially if she'd showered in between, and all that stuff."

"I see."

"Maybe you ought to try to be with him. When the news comes in. Or tell him what I just told you."

I couldn't quite imagine how such a conversation with Pops would go down.

"I'll try," I said anyway. "Was there anything else you wanted to talk about?"

Jeff finally met my gaze. "I've got an adjustment to one of my million-dollar ideas."

"What's that?"

"*How to Win Chicks with Origami*. Let's change it to *How to Survive Prison with Origami*."

I tried to smile. "Limited market, I'd think."

"In any case, I made a friend by folding him an elephant."

"I would be careful with that. Do you think someone might take it as a sort of courtship?"

"I'm not folding any birds or flowers. And you're overthinking it right now. It's just a little county facility, with people awaiting trial separate from the convicts. I won't need to worry about the Bubbas till after the trial, when they throw me in maximum security."

"That's not gonna happen."

Jeff didn't reply.

"We're going to deal with this, Jeff. You're just the guy they stuck it on."

He squinted at me. "Who's 'they'?"

"Whoever wanted to shut Kim up."

He gave me a weak smile. "You think that's what this is? Big, bad politicos pinning their shit on the unemployed loser?"

I was beginning to feel unequipped for this discussion. "Well, what do *you* think it is?"

Jeff shook his head and said nothing. After a moment he wiped his eye with his index finger, rubbing away a tear.

"This isn't going to sound rational," he said. "But I don't know what it is. All I can think is that it's my shitty destiny finally catching up with me. It doesn't need to make sense. This is just where I was always going to end up, somehow."

This was a very Jeff response. I could've accepted it if he were behind a bowling alley's shoe-rental counter or cleaning birdcages at Pet City. Not sitting in the county detention center. Even *my* defeatism has its limits.

"We're going to figure this out. *I'm* going to figure this out."

"Who's going to believe you?"

"Zach Wagner is helping me."

"Really?" Jeff looked surprised.

"Yes." It was kind of an exaggeration, but it made my efforts sound rather expert. I needed Jeff to take me seriously, for both our sakes.

"I like Zach," Jeff admitted.

Good. "Me, too."

Jeff had truly seemed to perk up at the mention of Zach. So I decided not to mention Nathan.

I had plans for Nathan. But after our conversation about

Kim's giving him a "back scratch," we'd probably both had enough inappropriate sharing for one afternoon.

"Hey, Jeff," I whispered.

"What?"

"I'm thinking I might start putting rainbow sprinkles on all my food."

Jeff sighed deeply and rubbed his left eye so hard I could see its red insides.

"Go ahead, then," he said.

I had about an hour before my date with Nathan at Stewie's, and I spent it in front of my computer, Googling.

Zach was right. Dustin Halliday probably wasn't an easy man to find. My searches turned up nothing useful. There was a dentist in California by the name of Dustin Halliday, but that obviously wasn't the same guy. My Dustin didn't appear to be on social media, and I couldn't find any sites that mentioned him in a particular school or job.

Dustin's brother at least had a defunct-looking Facebook account and appeared to be working at Medialink Cable Company, as Zach had mentioned. There was a company e-mail address listed for him.

I kept my e-mail to him simple—saying that I was trying to get in touch with his brother and would appreciate contact information. I supplied my cell number and told him to call anytime. Before I sent the message, I changed the setting on the account so my name wouldn't show up in his e-mail box. I was using my old Yahoo! account with the address Marge410, so I signed it Margery Lipinski. There was a slim chance, after all, that Trenton would know something about my brother's arrest.

It turned out that the e-mail address of Sharon Silverstein—Dustin's old teacher in juvenile detention—was also readily available through a GED program where she worked, so I hadn't needed to beg Zach for it—although he had sent it to me, as promised. With her I was a little more forthcoming, vaguely referencing my contact with Zach but not explaining the motivation behind my interest in Dustin. I signed my own name.

When those notes were sent, I hit REFRESH a few times, hoping for a quick reply. Nothing.

There was also Colleen Shipley to think of—Donald Wallace's old assistant. She was potentially one of the more promising sources of information, so I needed to plan the approach carefully. Assuming there weren't many Colleen Shipleys in this general part of Massachusetts, I found that she now worked in real estate. I located her e-mail address but wasn't sure if I should contact her that way. It seemed a very sensitive thing—her giving Kim old footage that probably shouldn't ever have been in her possession. I wasn't sure if I believed that it had happened. But if it had, an e-mail from a random stranger might spook her or put her on the defensive. I'd have to give some thought to my approach.

I refreshed again. It had been ten minutes and still no replies.

It didn't feel like I was doing nearly enough, what with Jeff in a prison cell fashioning toilet-paper farm animals to ward off fellow inmates.

I found Zach's book and flipped through the Dustin section again. His father's murder and his mother's trial were discussed in relatively general terms—many of the articles Kim had found were more detailed. Zach's book mostly discussed Dustin's crimes—drug possession and distribution—and his life at the detention center. The parts Kim had marked—about his brother, his teacher, and about his relationship with his friend Anthony—were the exception. I wondered if she'd focused on parts that would actually help her *find* Dustin. As Zach had mentioned, it was a long shot—but that probably wouldn't have kept Kim from trying, if she didn't have many other leads.

Then I looked up the section about Anthony—Dustin's friend. While most of the other kids came from situations of poverty and often neglect or abuse, Anthony had every advantage growing up. His parents were clearly quite educated and seemed to be much better off financially than most of the families of the other kids profiled.

When Anthony was sixteen, he'd been involved in the beating death of a gay classmate.

In Zach's interviews with Anthony's mom, she talked a great deal about "the teenage brain": how it was not fully formed and how teenagers often had issues with impulsivity. I wondered if she had seen the same *Frontline* on the subject that I had. It was probably a comfort to her—having scientific assurance that her son was possibly not a violent psycho in the long-term sense.

The story of Anthony's crime was disturbing nonetheless. Supposedly his victim—whom Zach had renamed "Liam" in the book—had hit on Anthony at a party, and three of Anthony's friends encouraged him to lure the boy out to his car for a "drive." They drove to an empty parking lot behind an office complex and beat him until he was unconscious. Autopsies revealed that a particularly bad blow to the back of the head—likely sustained when one of the other boys slammed his head against the pavement—had probably killed him. Although Anthony had driven the car, he was not thought to be the main perpetrator of the beating. Anthony and two of his friends got lesser sentences, all claiming that their one friend "Patrick" had been the main aggressor—while they'd only intended "to scare Liam a little bit."

Anthony was sentenced to two years in juvenile detention, to be released at age eighteen.

Kim had actually marked one part of Anthony's section—again with her wavy blue squiggles—in which he'd tried to explain his thinking the night of the beating.

> "I think that a big part of it was that Liam picked me out to harass. If he'd been harassing someone else, I think I could've been cooler about it, you know? If it happened to someone else, I'd have told that person, 'Hey, just tell him you're not interested. Or tell him to go to hell, if you want. And then walk away.'
>
> "But since it was me, I somehow wasn't able to do that. In the moment it felt very personal. Like, I was so sick of that shit. Just because you're a little quieter, a little smarter, a little nicer, people think you're gay."

"So your friends wondered about your sexuality?" I try to clarify. "And you went along with them to put a stop to that?"

"I don't know what other people wonder," Anthony replies, a hint of impatience in his voice. "I just know I was angry. Not only at Liam. At the boxes people wanted to put me in. That night I didn't want to be a nice guy. I wanted to tear the fuck out of that box, in a big way."

"Do you wish now that you had told the guys no when they challenged you to trick Liam?" I ask.

"Well, yes. Of course."

"Would you say you're afraid of gays? Or they make you angry?"

"Neither. I'm not like that at all."

"But do you think there was real anger in what you did? Anger at people different from you? Or was it just about the moment, about the other guys?"

"There was anger, yes. But it wasn't at people different from me. It came from somewhere deep inside me, I think, and had nothing to do with Liam. I feel like I came to my senses, though, when I saw Patrick whaling away at Liam. Like, what have we done? How did I get here? But by then it was too late."

"Do you think you are in control of your anger now?"

Anthony sighs before answering. "I hope so."

Kim's squiggly line ended there. In the margin she'd written *"April 12."*

I didn't know the significance of the date. Maybe she'd figured out the date of Anthony's incident?

This part of the book differed from the rest, as it was perhaps where Zach had asked the most direct questions. More often he quietly let the kids speak for themselves. Here it felt as if Zach were trying to get more remorse out of the kid than was going to emerge organically. If I were Kim, I'd hesitate to track such a person down. But then Kim didn't strike me as a big hesitator.

I couldn't remember news of a hate crime like this in Massachusetts recently. But the book had come out two years earlier, and Zach had probably done his research a year or two before that. And Jeff was right—I had my head in the sand when it came to current events. I was perhaps even worse back when I was married—back when I was working harder on Marge.

Without the real names of the victim or any of the kids involved, I couldn't look up the incident.

I opened up a new e-mail to Zach.

"Hi, Zach," I typed. Then I realized how obnoxious I felt asking him for another favor. Instead I decided to put it in the form of a question. *"Thanks for the Sharon Silverstein contact. Just wondering—did Kim ever ask you for the real name of the kid 'Anthony' from your book?"*

Polite sign-off, then more tapping the tabletop as I waited for my answers. I distracted myself from the dead silence by going onto Zach's class blog. Scanning through a couple of Kim's pieces, I found one with the name "Jenny."

"Dreams" by the Cranberries

Whenever I hear it—and I really try not to, but the most painful songs have a way of snaking into your car and your consciousness, into the background of every other bar scene of every other movie you've ever watched—I think of my old friend Jenny.

The three of us would dance to the Cranberries—Jenny, Missy, and me.

We got "Dreams" from Missy's older sister. Missy's older sister was cooler than mine, although I was cooler than Missy. Figure that one out.

I would lip-sync, and Jenny and Missy would do backup and dance. I was ten, and they were eight and nine. So I was in charge, always.

Jenny would do an exaggerated swirling sort of dance with a sly smile—what Missy's sister called "an interpretive dance." We didn't know what that meant, except that it was funny. While Jenny would interpret, Missy would just hop up and down, pumping her skinny little arms. We would do this for hours in Missy's garage after school that fall.

Jenny was pretty.

Probably if she'd lived to the double digits, she'd have been beautiful.

But when you're nine, pretty is all there is. Pretty is where it's at. And Jenny was there. Blond hair to her butt. Bright blue-green eyes. Light skin, but with a healthy pink glow across the cheeks. She always wore a shiny pink-and-silver jacket to match. Remembering her now, it feels like she was doomed from the start. Girls like that get snatched up, don't they?

Maybe you don't believe that. But it's what happened to Jenny. She disappeared one Wednesday, and they found her body on the following Sunday. The details aren't important. We all know what happens to girls like that when girls like that are snatched up.

Where would she have gone from there anyway? Such girlish perfection?

Jenny was so pretty and Missy so small and so innocent. Jenny didn't know what a pimple was, and she never would. Missy didn't know what a French kiss was. I have to believe now she does. Can't be sure. A year or so after Jenny, we stopped being friends.

Oh, Missy and Jenny with their "-y" names, so delicately feminine. Next to those lullaby names, "Kim" felt like the crank of a wrench or the sound of a broken metal appliance being thrown off the back of a pickup truck.

Sometimes Jenny and Missy didn't feel real to me—even back then. Sometimes I was afraid of them knowing me. Me: a whole year older than Jenny. Two years older than Missy. A lifetime. I wasn't shocked by parents fighting or dogs humping couch cushions or older boys who threatened to kick each other in the nuts.

When Jenny died, I felt it was meant for me. I realize, of course, how self-centered that was, but I was ten, so I try to give myself a pass.

I was the one things happened to. I was the oldest. I was the one who told them things. Now Jenny knew more than any of us ever should. "Any" in the universal sense.

I guess this is more about three girls than about a song. More about one girl than a song.

When I hear "Dreams" now, I don't hear the words. I don't hear its upbeatness or its optimism. I don't really even hear the woman singing it. The song dissolves into a memory of three girls—and then, ultimately, of one girl.

There is, in the end, only Jenny. Pretty like a girl on TV. Pretty like a girl who won't last. Old as I was at ten, how is it I didn't know that? How is it that of all the things I told her, I couldn't tell her this? How is it that I didn't open that door?

There is only Jenny dancing.

Interpretive dancing.

I can't interpret her dance. All these years later, I still don't know if I want to.

For several minutes I stared at the line *"When Jenny died, I felt it was meant for me."* It gave me a chill.

Still no answers to my e-mails. I glanced at Jeff's piece for that same week's assignment. The prompt was about a childhood or an adolescent memory associated with a song.

"Stranger on the Shore"

Occasionally, when I was in high school, he'd let me drive before I had a license—to the grocery store for his cigarettes and honey cough drops. And then, later, I'd take him out for lunch once a week. And occasionally I'd let him drive. Well into his eighties, he still drove. Technically. It was a swervy, slow-motion, white-knuckle kind of experience, but I owed it to him.

My grandfather always played gentle instrumentals in his car. There was a particular clarinet song that came tootling over his speakers every so often and turned my insides into vanilla pudding. I'd stare out the window and think about sharing an umbrella with my future wife, flying kites with my future kids, drinking beer at bonfires with my retirement buddies. I missed them like they'd already happened.

I didn't know till after my grandfather died what the song was. He left me his black Buick Regal Grand National with all his cassette tapes still in it. I listened to them all, and it was the one marked "Acker Bilk."

I was strangely relieved to hear it once I found it. Without lyrics to quote, how would I ever have found the song online? By Googling "clarinet song that sounds like a long-remembered Hawaiian honeymoon"? The song might have been lost to me forever.

But now I had it whenever I wanted, should I ever want it: "Stranger on the Shore," by Acker Bilk.

For a time I listened to cheer myself up whenever I was down—about a lost job or a lost girlfriend or wasted opportunities—to remind me of my grandfather, who lived through the Depression and the war and never seemed depressed about anything much.

It didn't work. It only reminds me that I am not him. That I wasn't smart enough to ask the secret to being him while he was still here. That there is no secret anyway. That his way of being had begun to fade before I was even born.

Now I reserve the song for whenever some famous old dude dies. Some famous old dude I thought would always be there. Johnny Carson. Andy Rooney.

I got an ulcer when Dick Clark died, because I knew I'd be lost on every New Year's from then on.

I might get another when Jim Lehrer dies. Or Bill Cosby. Or Jimmy Carter. Or Paul Simon. God help me then. Because I'm not sure how many more times I can listen to "Stranger on the Shore."

This sounded to me like Jeff talking after about three drinks. It needed some editing. I looked up Acker Bilk on YouTube and began listening to "Stranger on the Shore." Thirty seconds was about all I could take. It made me think of our grandfather at my wedding, struggling to eat a slice of fancy cake with a shaky hand. Worse was the reminder that my brother's and my hearts seemed to break in all the same odd places.

I refreshed my e-mail. Nothing.

There wasn't much time left till I had to meet Nathan at Stewie's, and I still had to decide what to wear. My fanciest date clothes were all mashed into a pile at the dark end of my accordion closet. I sorted through them until I found my translucent black V-neck top with the shiny gray lining. Front and center it looked rather conservative, but when you moved, the trashy underlayer whispered sexual possibility. It was brilliant fourth- or fifth-date attire.

This was only a first date, of course, but these were desperate times and I wanted to get into Nathan's place as quickly as I could. I slipped it on with my jeans and glanced in the mirror. Apparently Geraldine had also recognized the beauty of the blouse, as it was hairy across the left shoulder and boob. I took a sticky roller to it, put on some lipstick, and headed out.

I tried to keep the Marge talk to a casual minimum, but Nathan kept asking questions. I'd meant to tell only a light story or two, about a few of Marge's many adventures in Venice and Rome, on her way home from the Holy Land: The hunchbacked Irish beggar who escorted her from Venice to Rome and put up with all her crazy shit until she decided to show her devotion to God by giving away all her money, including some she'd borrowed from him. ("Yes, she borrowed from a beggar," I said when Nathan gave me a funny look.) The woman who had a Jesus doll that she'd let other women dress up and kiss—appropriately nutty company for Marge. And the German priest who understood her English and whose German she understood in turn, not because they knew each other's languages but miraculously, through the power of prayer.

The conversation grew long when I mentioned that it was at this point in her journey home—in Rome—that Marge had her vision of her marriage to Christ. Nathan had a fair number of questions about that.

"So it was, like, a divine union, then? Her nirvana in a way?"

"I wouldn't say that, no," I replied. "It wasn't like Marge's self dissolved into the divine. It was a wedding fantasy, with Jesus as her groom. And there's no feeling that the post-wedding Marge is any more enlightened or less egocentric than she was before."

I described how she envisioned a wedding attended by all sorts of saints and angels. And after the wedding Marge began to smell sweet smells in her nostrils, hear sweet songs in her ears, see delicate white flecks dance in front of her eyes, and feel a burning warmth in her chest. These she considered "tokens" of God's love. And in a very suggestive passage, she explains that God tells her:

> *You may boldly, when you are in bed, take me to*
> *you as your wedded husband . . . and boldly take me*
> *in the arms of your soul and kiss my mouth, my head,*
> *my feet as sweetly as you want.*

"This is where Marge starts to make people feel a little uncomfortable," I said. "Talking about Jesus like that."

"Does she make *you* uncomfortable?" Nathan wanted to know.

"No," I said. "I think maybe Marge misunderstood some aspects of the mystical experience. I mean, not that I'm a good one to dictate the terms. But that's partly what makes her interesting. How many of us have a perfect understanding of what it means to be a person of great faith?"

"But it sounds like what annoyed people is how overconfident she was about it," Nathan pointed out. "*She* would never admit to misunderstanding."

"She was quite self-righteous, yes," I said. "But she had a fair amount of self-doubt, too. That's why she was often traveling around and speaking to various priests and anchorites about her experience—to reassure herself of its validity. Anyway, give me bumbling Marge over a real saint any day. Saints are perfection, and it can be difficult to learn anything from perfection. Marge is real. She can at least show us some of our spiritual folly."

"Okay, I get that." Nathan finished his beer. "What has Margery taught you, then?"

I thought about the question for a moment. The more I thought about it, the more it felt like a kick in the stomach. Seven years later, maybe she hadn't really taught me anything.

Thankfully, Nathan didn't wait for an answer. Instead he beckoned our waitress so we could order second drinks. After that I segued from Marge's wedding into questions about his wedding videography. And after thirds he asked me to his place. I tried to be coy about agreeing, and he gave me his address. We drove in our separate cars.

I couldn't see the color of Nathan's house in the dark. But the property looked pretty well kept. Leaves raked. Light glowing on the front porch. Neither of these things necessarily disqualified him from being a sociopath, but they were comforting nonetheless.

Not that there had been signs that he *was* a sociopath. But I didn't usually move quite this fast, and it was fear of sociopaths, more than morality or reserve, that kept me from it.

I met Nathan on his porch.

"Before you come in," he said, "I think there's something you should know."

I had to bite my lip to keep in a nervous giggle.

"Why are you smiling?" he asked.

"I'm not smiling."

Nathan stroked his George Michael shadow. "Well, you should know that I have a snake."

"A snake?"

"Yeah. I realize that can be a problem for some people."

"I can imagine."

Nathan bit his lip. "Is it for you?"

"Well . . ." I was still feeling my last drink, I was pretty sure. "How big is the snake?"

"Almost five feet. Which is on the long side for a ball python."

"Oh? Bonus."

He stared at the key in his hand. "Do you still want to come in?" Bashfully sly or slyly bashful. Either way I found it attractive.

"Hmm. Does this snake have a cage?"

"Of course. It's very secure."

I hesitated. "Maybe I ought to go in and have a look."

"Good for you." Nathan grinned and unlocked the front door. He led me through a decent-size kitchen. Clean, I noted, but not compulsively so. Country-cottage cabinets painted a cheerful yellow. His style or a previous owner's? An old girlfriend's?

"Here she is," Nathan said when we arrived in the living room.

The glass cage took up nearly all of one side of the living room wall. It had reddish wood chips on its bottom and large rocks in the corners. In the middle were plants that resembled bonsai trees. I couldn't see the snake at all.

"Big cage," I said. "Lucky snake."

"I wouldn't agree to have her unless she had a nice big enclosure."

"Uh-huh," I murmured. I wasn't sure if this was standard python-owner braggadocio or what. I stepped closer to the cage. Curled up under one of the plants was a tight spiral of white reptilian skin with soft yellow-orange blotches—wrapped in a disk about the diameter of a teakettle. Her head wasn't visible.

"What's her name?" I asked.

"Peaches and Cream."

"Oh, my." I sighed.

"She's an albino. I didn't name her. She's a secondhand snake."

"You couldn't rename her?"

"I didn't feel right about it. She had that name for seven years before I got her."

"How long do these things live?" I asked.

"Twenty to thirty years."

"Wow."

I stared at the snake. She looked very clean. I wondered if pythons required baths of some kind. I stopped just short of picturing Nathan showering with Peaches and Cream. Such an image might very well set me to weeping—Marge style.

"Did you . . . um, always want to be a snake owner?" I asked.

Nathan glanced at Peaches and Cream and then back at me. Then he let out a long, wheezy smoker's laugh that so startled me that I began to laugh, too.

"No. She's . . ." he began, then dissolved in laughter again. He sat down on the couch, wiping a tear from his eye.

"What's so funny?"

"Just the question. The way you asked it. You're trying so hard to be nice about it."

"Not *so* hard. I don't *hate* snakes. At least not like some people do."

"Truth be told, Theresa, she's a stray. That's all. Think of it that way. She was abandoned, and no one else would take her."

"Abandoned?" I said.

"A buddy of mine took her in when his friend—the original owner—went to Iraq. When the friend got back, he had a lot of problems. To make a long story short, he couldn't take the snake back. My friend kept him as long as he could, but then his girlfriend got pregnant and they wanted to move in together. She didn't want a snake in the house with a baby."

"Makes sense," I said.

"Yeah. It does. Anyway. No one else was volunteering. So I did. Peaches is mild-mannered. It's some work, but it's not *that* big a deal." Nathan brushed my arm with his hand. "You have pets?"

"Yeah," I said. "Does she eat live mice?"

"Frozen and thawed. Not all pythons will. But she's fine with it."

I opened my mouth to ask for the details but decided that

wasn't a conversational direction I wished to pursue. I made a mental note to refuse anything that came out of Nathan's microwave, whatever else happened this evening.

"Do you mind if I use your bathroom?" I asked.

"Sure," he said. "Second door on the left. Just to let you know, though—that's where I keep my two canaries. It's a big bathroom, and the light in there is really nice early in the day."

One of the two yellow canaries *chip-chip-chipped* at me while I brushed my fingers through my hair. The other hopped around in the cage but said nothing. On my way back to the living room, I peeked into the two rooms along the hall. One was a bedroom, the other an office with two computers, a DVD player, and a bunch of other electrical equipment I couldn't identify. There was a video camera on the office swivel chair and stacks of DVDs popping up randomly around the carpet like mushrooms.

"You did something with your hair," Nathan said as I returned.

"Just combed it."

Nathan brushed the hair from the side of my face. "It looks good."

I leaned close to him. "Thanks."

He kissed me. Strong, determined, but soft on the finish. A pinot noir of a kiss. And his shadow beard didn't bother me as much as I thought it might.

I nudged him onto the sofa, and we kissed again. I felt giddy until I looked up at the glass cage and saw that Peaches and Cream had lifted her head and begun to unfurl herself. Her eyes were bloodred. I nearly screamed, but then I turned back to Nathan, reminding myself—*albino*. She's an albino. Of course her eyes are red. She can't help it.

"Can I ask you a question?" I touched his silly earring.

"Sure, beautiful."

I felt my buzz fade a bit. Flattery makes a tiny part of my brain disconnect. For me it's like hearing nails on a chalkboard. And who calls a woman "beautiful" like that these days? What did he think this was? An episode of *CHiPs*?

"Do you remember the George Michael album *Faith*? The video where he's dancing by the jukebox?"

"Nope."

"Oh, come on. His most famous album."

Nathan shrugged. "I don't know it."

"Are you kidding? 'Cuz I was going to say you have the same style as him. I mean, your hair's not frosted, but the facial hair and the jeans and the earring . . ."

"I have to admit that I have some pretty big holes in my . . . uh . . pop-culture knowledge."

"I'll say. How old are you?"

"Thirty-four."

"Oh. Same as me." I was a year older, but close enough. "How could you not know who . . . ?"

"I grew up in a Hare Krishna commune. We didn't leave till I was ten. When did this George Michael thing come out?"

"Hare Krishna? Like the orange robes at the airport?"

"Like that. But I didn't spend any time at any airports. We grew up on a farm."

"Wow." I considered this while he raked his fingers into my hair. "Were you bald? With one of those little ponytails?"

"Listen. I probably shouldn't have said anything. But I find it easier sometimes." His hand got tangled in my hair, slid down my neck, and came to rest on my back. "You wouldn't believe how many conversations you get lost in. When you didn't have TV or Santa Claus or the mall. It's easier to just explain than to try to fake it."

"You could've said you didn't have MTV."

"I could've. Since that's true." Nathan's hand drifted up and down my back. "But the truth is even easier. In a way."

"Are you a Hare Krishna now?"

"A Hare Krishna who works as a bartender? No, Theresa."

"I guess that was a stupid question. Why did you leave the commune?"

"It was complicated. My parents didn't agree with some of the choices the people in charge were making."

"Are your parents still Hare Krishnas?"

"No," Nathan whispered, then kissed my neck.

"Did you go to regular school, growing up?"

"No. Well, not till junior high."

He kissed me on the mouth again—stronger this time.

"Wasn't that hard to—"

"Do you really want to talk about this right now?"

"Kinda," I admitted.

"Kinda? Oh, right. You study religious freaks."

"No I don't. I only study one freak."

"I see," Nathan said. He let his hand fall from my back. As he moved, I could smell him—a combination of wine, patchouli deodorant, and something unidentifiable that made me think of gray wolves.

"How about we discuss it later?" he asked, gazing at me with his sharp brown eyes.

They weren't a dark brown. They were almost yellow around the edges of his irises. Why did I think I knew what wolves smelled like anyway? I'd watched a lot of wildlife documentaries, and I was rather fond of the gray wolf. But still—that didn't quite explain it.

"Promise," I whispered, leaning into him and taking a deep breath. There it was again.

Nathan pulled me close. I allowed my gaze to meet his. The yellow in his eyes felt warmer, somehow, than anything I'd seen or felt in days. Weeks, even. Jeff, my parents, Peaches, and Zach all drained gently out of my head. I thought about Marge for a moment—about how there was a time in her life when Marge would weep whenever she saw a handsome man, because it would make her think of Jesus. I thought I might weep now, but it had nothing to do with Jesus. *This creature started to hear Jeff Buckley's "Hallelujah" pipe up somewhere in the back of her brain, drowning out everything else.*

"Promise," Nathan echoed.

He said it flatly, parroting so immediately that he almost certainly didn't know what he was saying. But the look in his eyes was so hungry that I didn't care.

When Nathan was asleep, I slipped out of bed and got half dressed. Wearing just jeans and a cami, I tiptoed into Nathan's office and sat in front of the computers, taking care so his office chair wouldn't squeak. Once I was closer, I saw that it was actually only one computer—a Mac laptop—and two large additional screens. When I opened the laptop, the screen was already open to CNN online—a story about government surveillance.

I clicked on the Finder and typed in *"Kim."*

There was a folder on the desktop titled "Kim's stuff."

Too easy, I thought. I glanced around me, heart pounding, half expecting Peaches and Cream to pop out from behind the screen or under the lampshade, jaw unhinged. But all was still and silent.

Opening the folder, I found two files. They were titled "Wayne" and "Wallace." I clicked "Wallace."

In that folder there were a few videos. The first was called "Wallace draft." Everything after that was labeled "Wallace stuff 1," "Wallace stuff 2," and so on. As the video began, I tapped the volume down low so it wouldn't be audible in Nathan's bedroom. Pictures of Donald Wallace flashed on the screen. Some of them were identical to the ones on her phone—him eating a hot dog, an ice cream. Others were less grainy—him at a hearing of some kind, him behind a podium with his fingers clawed in a dramatic gesture. In most of them, his mouth was open. All of them were unflattering.

Then a fortyish woman appeared on the screen, the back of a restaurant booth framing her head. She had a wrinkled little mouth and wore glasses with oversize frames. At the bottom of the screen, it said, *Pamela Bolduc, Andrew Abbott's cousin.*

"It was like Kafka," she said. I could hear the sound of forks on plates and restaurant chatter in the background as she spoke. Her picture dissolved, and these words appeared, white against a black screen: *Donald Wallace's Most Famous Conviction.*

The picture lingered on these words for about seven seconds too long, and then the woman appeared again, saying:

"My cousin spent twelve years in jail. The DNA from the scene shows that he probably wasn't even there. It was someone else. But did they say, 'We made a mistake'? Did they say, 'We're sorry'? No. It disturbs me that we have a system that doesn't have to do that. That has no room for self-reflection or remorse.

"I hold the Fairchester police department and Donald Wallace responsible for what happened. They decided who'd murdered Jenny Spicer before they'd fully investigated all the possibilities. They pursued my cousin because he was different."

The black screen came on again, with the white block words: *"An innocent young man was jailed for more than a decade."*

Then Pamela Bolduc continued, "I am a registered Democrat, but I will not be voting for Donald Wallace in this election. I will never vote for Donald Wallace. Because I believe there is a difference between commitment to justice and commitment to one's own ambition. Donald Wallace has the latter, and my cousin was the collateral damage."

Then Donald Wallace appeared—this time in actual footage rather than still pictures. He was outdoors, on a city street.

"What are you talking about?" he said.

His low voice went nasal at "talking." His thick brown-gray hair flopped out of place as he dashed away from the camera's view. It was jumpy footage, probably taken from a phone.

Then a young man appeared, standing against a brick wall outdoors. His boyish brown bangs flew sideways in the wind.

"Everyone who was involved in the prosecution of Andrew Abbott should be ashamed of themselves. And yes, that includes Donald Wallace," he said.

"Ryan Janik, New England Project for Justice," read the label below his head shot.

Ryan Janik dissolved, and new white letters appeared: *"Another troubling conviction"*

Next was an elderly-looking man in a wing chair. He was

quite wrinkled, but his hair was shiny and dark and sculpted. He reminded me of a rubber Ronald Reagan mask.

"I still believe that something went wrong in the Susan Halliday case. Justice was not served," he said.

"Frank Boynton, Esq., Public defender (retired)" was his label.

The jumpy footage of Donald Wallace appeared again.

"No. *No.* I don't have a comment," he said. Then his tall, black-suited frame disappeared behind a revolving glass door.

The white letters appeared after that, this time saying:

"A mother of two imprisoned. A family torn apart."

"My mother probably won't ever get out of prison. For a crime she didn't commit," said the next guy who appeared onscreen.

"Dustin Halliday, Susan's son," read his subtitle.

I leaned in close to the screen, examining the young man's features as he spoke. His eyes were a deep-set, transparent blue. His small nose and white coloring against chapped red lips made his face seem delicate. There was a skater-dude quality to his hair—though if such a thing as a skater dude even exists anymore, I don't know. In any case he looked like a creepy old mannequin wearing entirely the wrong wig.

"There *was* an intruder in our house that night. I know. I was *there*," he was saying. "And there was evidence of it, that the prosecutors chose to keep to themselves."

The video ended abruptly there. It actually seemed like a decent start. A little hokey, but that was the nature of campaign ads. The beginning of Kim's wasn't much better or worse than any real ones I'd seen.

She had sort of danced around the edge of the topic of Andrew Abbott—hadn't talked to anyone really close to Andrew himself. A cousin? Was that as close as she could get?

I wondered if Kim had even told this cousin who she was. And that Ryan Janik character looked young enough to have been a toddler when the case was tried. Still, the draft was provocative enough to make a potential viewer want to look up the Abbott case himself. And I was interested to see that Kim had apparently approached Donald Wallace in the flesh.

The stuff about Susan Halliday was a little clunkier. Kim had convinced people closer to the case to talk to her, but a son and the lawyer of the convicted woman saying "she didn't do it" wasn't exactly compelling evidence of her innocence. It was a stretch to call it a "troubling conviction." Perhaps Kim had had more planned.

I breathed carefully, straining to hear any movement in the hall. Then I clicked on the next video, labeled "Wallace stuff 1."

The wrinkled lawyer who'd spoken in the second-to-last clip appeared again, in the wing chair as before.

"Look at the two brothers," he was saying. "The younger one—he was the one who was awake when it happened. He's never wavered on his story. He's always maintained he saw two intruders. It's the older one who turned against his mother. Wallace and his team worked on him for long enough. But that one never woke up, never left his bedroom."

"A lot of people think Dustin was coached by his mother," Kim said.

"If you were in that courtroom and heard both those kids testify, you'd know which one was coached. The older one. Whasisname?"

"Trenton?"

"Yes. Trenton."

"Hold on a second," Kim said. She appeared to be zooming out on Boynton. From the wider view, his shirt was visible: blue plaid and rumpled, with the sleeves rolled up tight at the elbows. He looked surprisingly buff for a guy so wrinkled.

"So you're saying the prosecution team coached Trenton."

"Can't prove it. I'm just saying it seemed like it."

"Do you think Trenton was hiding something?"

"I wouldn't go that far. He was only a kid. I simply didn't feel the version he was saying was real. It felt canned somehow. And I still believe that something went wrong in the Susan Halliday case. Justice was not served. That's the bottom line for me."

"Was there evidence that there was an intruder in the Halliday house the night of Todd Halliday's death?" Kim asked.

"Evidence? Hell yes. Their living room was all ripped up, and their bedroom."

"Why would intruders go in while the whole family was here?"

Go Kim, I thought. Kim was surprisingly direct with her questions. What was a little old law degree and a lifetime of lawyering to be intimidated about?

"The Halliday family hadn't been in the home for a while. They'd been staying with family for a couple of months because of the repairs after that house fire they had. Likely the two intruders thought no one was home. That's why Todd died, you see. Because he surprised them."

"And they shot him with a gun purchased by Mr. Halliday one year earlier."

"You've read the court transcript. You read what happened. There were two of them and only one of him. They put their gun to his head and told him to hand his over. He tried to turn it on them, but there was a struggle and he got shot in the neck.

Now, didn't you say you wanted to focus on the kids in the case? Justin and Dustin?"

"Trenton and Dustin. Yes."

Frank Boynton looked at his watch. "And you had this theory that Donald Wallace was like some kind of Svengali with the kiddies."

"Well, I didn't say that. But I think some of his methods in preparing his younger witnesses for trial were unethical."

"You know what I think? I think it's unethical to bring kids into the trial process, period. Unless it's last-ditch, absolutely necessary. Granted, Wallace made his name prosecuting crimes against kids, so it's hard to get around it there. But in this case I don't know if it was really necessary."

"You were the one who put Dustin on the stand, correct?"

"Yup. Like I said. Necessary. He was the only real witness besides his mother," Kim said.

"Have you kept in touch with any of the family?" Kim sounded hopeful. "Like Dustin?"

"Kept in touch? No, dear." The old lawyer harrumphed.

"How do you feel about Donald Wallace running for Senate now?"

"How do I feel about it?" Boynton shrugged and stuck out his lower lip. "I dunno. Doesn't surprise me. He's an ambitious guy."

"Are you going to vote for him, can I ask?"

"Sure. Better than the alternative, put it that way."

"Hold on a sec," Kim said, and the picture jiggled.

"Surely," Boynton said.

The video ended there.

When I clicked on "Wallace stuff 2," Missy Bailey appeared, laughing.

"God!" she said. "You want me to say all that again? This is torture, you know."

"Just the part about how they talked to us for like five hours," Kim said.

"Well, more like two or three in my case," Missy said. "But they were more interested in you than me."

I thought I heard the groan of a shifting box spring. I hit PAUSE and listened. When I heard it again, I closed the file and tiptoed back to the bedroom. Nathan was awake in the bed—still lying down, still shirtless, but staring at his phone.

"Oh, hey." He yawned and reached for a glass of water next to his bed. "What're you up to?"

"You fell asleep," I said. "I just went to look at Peaches and Cream some more. And check my texts."

"I can take her out of the cage if you want to get a better look."

Nathan's gaze was fixed on the floor as he said this.

I looked down to where he was looking. Both of our sweaters—his stylishly grungy brown pullover and my nubbly cream hoodie—were piled there where we left them, arms tangled. My phone was half visible on top, falling sideways out of the sweater's front pouch pocket.

"Oh. No, thanks."

Nathan saw me looking in that direction.

"It buzzed while you were gone," he said. "I think you got a text message or something."

"Okay," I said, sitting on the bed, holding my breath.

Nathan tossed his own phone on his bedside table, next to an Eckhart Tolle book with a shiny orange cover.

"Who texts you at this hour?" he asked.

"Nobody, usually," I said. "It's probably one of those payment reminders or something."

"Looks like you started to get dressed. Do you want to leave?"

I hesitated. "Do you want me to leave?"

"No. But it doesn't need to be awkward if you want to leave."

"I don't," I said.

But when I moved closer to him, he felt clammy to me. I wondered if I felt the same to him. It was as if he'd jinxed us by using the word "awkward."

"Tell me about the farm," I said softly.

"The farm?"

"The farm you grew up on."

And he did. He told me about a couple of cows—Lalita and Rukmini. They were beautiful brown cows, and he learned how to massage their udders and milk them. He liked Lalita so much that sometimes he'd visit her even when it wasn't chore time—in the kids' brief free time—after classes but before the evening meal.

It didn't sound quite real, but I didn't care.

"It sounds beautiful," I whispered.

"Some of it was," he murmured, without opening his eyes.

"What wasn't?"

"I don't want to say right now. It'll wake me up, talking like that. And then I won't be able to get sleepy again. Tell me another story about that Margery lady instead."

Thursday, October 24

Since Nathan was almost asleep already, I told him a quickie—about the time there was a great fire in Marge's town of King's Lynn. The townspeople, normally exasperated with Marge, begged her to wail and weep to her heart's content, on the off chance that God was in fact listening. She advised a priest to walk toward the fire holding Communion wafers, then followed him to the door of the church. When she saw the flames, she cried out for God to help. She went into the church, still weeping and begging. Soon three men also came into the church—all with snowflakes on their cloaks. A snowstorm had begun, and it would put out the fire. God had answered her prayers. At least that was how Marge saw it.

When I finished, I couldn't tell if Nathan was asleep. I closed my eyes for a few minutes and tried to listen carefully for his breath. I must've dozed off with him, because when I opened my eyes, there was early daylight seeping through his bedroom blinds, a smell of coffee in the air. I inhaled it indulgently as I sat up and stretched. For a brief and groggy moment, I fancied my life a Folgers commercial.

Snake dude was not a bad lay, I could hear the Folgers guy singing. *And she's got her brother's bail hearing later today. . . . The best part of waking up . . .*

"Oh, shit!" I began fumbling for my cell phone.

"What is it?" Nathan popped in, shirtless and holding a mug. At his feet was a very old-looking greyhound, whom I hadn't seen the night before. "This is Jasper, by the way. He was sleeping in the basement last night. He's pretty much deaf, but he's a sweetheart."

"What time is it?" I asked.

"A little after nine."

"Oh, God."

"I would've woken you up, but you said you had a couple of days off or something, right?"

"Oh. Yeah. But I have to be somewhere else. I didn't think I'd sleep this late. Usually I wake up at six forty-five. Internal clock."

"Maybe something in my house reset your clock," Nathan said, scratch-pinched his chest hair, then sipped his coffee.

This struck me as a creepy thing to say. Something—like what? Snake charm? Sexual energy? A carbon monoxide leak?

"Can I pour you a cup of coffee?" he asked. "I have a travel mug you could take."

I threw on my sweater, then my coat. I gathered my shoulder bag and phone. "No thanks. I don't have time."

"I'll call you later?" Nathan said.

All at once I felt suffocated by the sweaty smell of Nathan's sheets and itchy at the sight of his ample chest hair. Marge's hair shirts came to mind. I wasn't sure I wanted him to call me later. But then I still had a few more of Kim's files to look at.

"Oh. Sure. Yeah."

I didn't mean to sound so casual. But there was Jeff's hearing to worry about. I could still possibly make it.

"Talk to you later!" I called as I headed out of the house.

"Okay!" Nathan called after me.

I only had a moment to assess whether this was mockery or exaggerated enthusiasm. Probably not. The Hare Krishnas were likely not a sarcastic people. I was admittedly pretty ignorant on the subject, but it seemed a fair guess.

Once I hopped onto the highway, it was only three exits to the courthouse. I revved the engine to seventy-five after I got onto the highway ramp. Ten seconds later I had to slow it down to a stop. There was a backup of cars, and I couldn't see what was happening. Even if this cleared up soon, I was going to miss the first few minutes of the hearing.

"Damn it," I muttered. While I waited, I checked my phone.

I'd forgotten about the text message that had come in in the wee hours. I'd expected spam and didn't recognize the number. But it said, SORRY, I DON'T KNOW WHERE MY BROTHER IS. HOW DO U KNOW HIM? TRENT H.

The traffic began to crawl a bit. I tossed the phone onto the passenger seat, then fought and swore through the traffic knot. When I got to downtown a half hour later, I had trouble finding a parking space and didn't bother to feed the meter.

As I raced up the courthouse steps, I heard someone shout my name.

It was my mother—headed toward me, the heels of her pumps clicking on the concrete.

"I stayed here to meet you. Ned and your father were eager

to work out some of the details. But I knew you were on your way." She shivered and rubbed her upper arms. "Where have you been?"

"I got stuck in traffic. There was an accident, and they had only one lane open."

"Jeff got bail, but it's high." She did a little hop to warm herself.

"How high?"

"Two hundred thousand. We have to come up with twenty thousand of that. Gary Norris has already put your father in touch with a bondsman. I think we can have him out tomorrow. Maybe the next day. It depends on how fast we can all get the money organized."

"How're we going to come up with that?"

"Ned's helping me. And your father is putting up five thou he says he can take out of his retirement, but it takes twenty-four hours to process the withdrawal. If you can throw in a couple thousand, it'd help. Then we'll work out the details later. We'll get most of it back. Except for the fee."

"Whatever it takes," I said. "I have about twice that in the bank at the moment."

My mother nodded stiffly, distracted. She hadn't really heard what I'd said. Part of her mind would probably be held captive as long as her son was.

"Whatever it takes," I repeated.

This time I said it for myself. Saying it made me feel better about last night. I couldn't give my brother as much money as my parents could. But I had other resources—other plans.

My mother reached out and grabbed me by the arm, clutching at my elbow till it hurt.

"Is Jeff happy that he was granted bail?" I asked.

"Happy? No, Theresa."

"I mean, did he seem relieved to you?"

"I didn't get to talk to him yet today. There was just the hearing, and then they took him back in. It was short. Gary did a good job."

"Two hundred thousand? That's a good job?"

"There's only so much he can control, under the circumstances."

My mother's grasp moved up my arm. "You're skinny these days," she said.

"Thank you," I replied.

"It wasn't a compliment."

She finally removed her hand. I wanted, then, to apologize to her for mentioning Marge's penis visions the other day. But she'd asked that I not mention Marge at all. I decided the best way to apologize, for now, was to respect that.

I dropped my mother at her hotel, then went home to check on the animals.

Boober greeted me at the door, yipping wildly. Just as I stepped inside, he peed on the floor.

"That's the right idea, sweetie," I said. "Hold it till I get home."

I found his and Wayne's leashes and brought both dogs outside.

Boober ran circles around my legs while I checked e-mail on my phone. Zach had written back early in the morning:

Hi, Theresa, Yeah, Kim did ask about Anthony. I'd like to talk to you about that. I didn't give her his name because of confidentiality issues. Also, I found something Kim wrote for the class that might interest you. Do you think you'd have time for a coffee sometime in the next few days?

I answered, asking him to suggest a time. Aside from taking a couple thousand bucks out of the bank for bail, my day was wide open.

The teacher Sharon Silverstein had written back as well, saying she had a free period in which she could call me if I wanted. I untangled Boober from around my ankles and typed back that I'd be waiting for her call.

After that I switched to texting and wrote back to Trenton Halliday, DUSTIN IS A FRIEND OF A FRIEND. I HAVE HIS PHONE NUMBER, BUT HE'S NOT ANSWERING MY CALLS. I typed in the number I had for Dustin and asked Trenton to confirm it.

"We're going to see about this Dustin Halliday," I said to the dogs.

Wayne snuffled his approval, then barked at a leaf skittering across my driveway.

I lost a few hours doing laundry, filling dog bowls, eating pickles out of a jar in the fridge. When Sharon Silverstein called, I found myself ironing a pillowcase.

As I began to ask her about Dustin, I turned off the iron and wandered into the living room.

"No, I haven't kept in touch with Dustin since he finished his time," Sharon told me. "Zach's right that he confided in me a lot. But once he got out, that was it. The kids don't tend to want to drop in at the detention center to reminisce."

"Right," I said, feeling stupid. Of course they didn't.

"Oddly enough, though, I've heard through a different kid that Dustin's been living in downtown Marist Park with one of his old buddies from detention. Troy Richardson. I ran into Troy at Shaw's supermarket a couple of months ago. He was working there."

"Troy Richardson." I circled the living room, dusting the tabletops with my pillowcase. "A friend of Dustin's?"

"Yeah. They seemed pretty close."

"Was he one of the kids Zach Wagner profiled in the book? The one he named 'Anthony'?"

As I asked these questions, I watched Geraldine march into the middle of the living-room carpet. She does this for only one reason.

"Troy? No. Troy wasn't in the book, I don't think. I didn't know all the kids in the book."

"Oh. Okay. So this is a different friend? Not the Anthony kid?"

Glurp. Glurp. GLURP. Geraldine's stomach heaved up and down in that painful way that cats have. I'm always surprised they don't turn themselves inside out.

"I'm pretty sure," Sharon answered. "Although I read the book several years ago, so it's hard to remember."

"And Dustin is living downtown with Troy?"

There was another big *GLURP* and then a gag as I slipped out of the room.

"Probably. I mean, this was a few months ago I was hearing about it. But they were roommates, with one or two other young men. College-age kids. Troy's taking some community-college courses, he told me. That made me really happy to hear."

"And Dustin?"

Sharon Silverstein paused. "I don't know about that. Dustin actually struggled with reading. I think maybe Zach Wagner didn't stress that too much in the book. I'd be surprised if he went to college. It would be nice if he were, but . . ."

"Okay," I said. "So you didn't have that Anthony kid as your student, too?"

"Remind me who that is?"

"The kid in the book who was friends with Dustin," I said. "He was in for his part in the beating death of another boy."

"No, I don't think I had him," Sharon said. "But I didn't always know the kids' . . . offenses. If I didn't need to. It often wasn't necessary. And often I didn't *want* to know."

"Of course," I said. "Well, thanks so much for your time."

After I'd hung up, I stepped back into the living room. Geraldine was now sitting sphinxlike on the arm of the sofa, staring down at her own hair ball as if some other slob had deposited it.

"Glad to see you're feeling better," I told her.

As I headed to the kitchen for some paper towels, my phone vibrated again. Trenton Halliday had returned my text, saying, I DON'T KNOW HIS #. WE DON'T TALK.

Interesting. It seemed odd to me he'd have so little information about his brother. At the time of Zach's book, there had been tension between the brothers, but Trenton had at least visited Dustin in juvenile detention. I wondered why their relationship had deteriorated. Had Dustin maybe fallen deeper into criminal life?

I sat and considered my next move. I could head up to Marist Park to Shaw's and hope to hit Troy Richardson's working hours. But Jeff was getting out tomorrow, if all went well, and then I'd go back to work on Monday. Colleen Shipley—Donald

Wallace's old assistant—was likely more important than Troy Richardson, and today was the last day I could surprise her during business hours—unless I took another day off.

I refreshed the cats' kibble and left each dog with a scoop of wet food. When I got into my car, I set my GPS for Colleen Shipley's real-estate office.

Raymond Realty was one of those sad little offices with worn beige carpeting and a gumball machine full of ancient Chiclets at the entrance. As I stepped inside, I noticed an overwhelming buttered-popcorn smell—delicious on first whiff, then disgusting thereafter.

At the front desk, there was a bald man holding an open microwave-popcorn bag. As I walked in, he leaned closer to the bag and made a sputtering sound into it. For a second I thought he was using it as a barf bag.

"You caught me." He grinned. "I was sucking on the old maids."

I never know what to do with people who are this forthcoming.

"It's no problem," I said. "I've seen a lot worse."

"I'm sorry to hear that. Do you have an appointment with someone? Richard or Colleen?"

"Colleen, in fact. Well, I don't have an appointment with her, but—"

"Here for me, Greg?" someone called from the cubicle behind him.

"Yeah," Greg said.

A pair of pale knuckles appeared from behind the cubicle, followed by a woman of early middle age. Her light greenish eyes and whitish blond hair gave her a gossamer sort of presence.

"Have we met?" she asked, peering at me. "Oh! Are you the one who called about the Volker property?"

"Um . . . no. I'm wondering if we could speak privately?"

"I'm sorry. . . . What is this about?"

"I was hoping to talk to you about Kim Graber."

"Oh. And are you . . . ? Who are you? You're not Missy, are you?"

"No." I hesitated, startled. "I'm a friend of Kim's. Not Missy."

"I didn't think so. I just . . . your hair has a little red in it, and I remember . . ."

"Oh. Right. No, just a friend."

Damn it. Maybe I could've posed as Missy. I'd never have thought of that, and now it was too late.

"Why don't we talk outside?" Colleen suggested, grabbing a beige trench coat off the wall of her cubicle.

I agreed, and we left Greg to his old maids.

"Do you know what happened to her?" I asked, once the door was closed.

"What happened to Kim? In 1992?"

"No . . . uh . . . I mean, she was killed. A couple of weeks ago."

"What?" Colleen's eyes widened.

"Oh." I wasn't anticipating this—having to share this piece of news. Why had I assumed that the whole world knew about Kim? "I wasn't sure if you would have heard."

Colleen put her hand against the storefront window to steady herself.

"Oh my God," she gasped. "What happened?"

"They're not sure yet," I said. Reluctantly I added, "They've arrested someone."

"Oh my God," Colleen said again. She raised her hand to her forehead and closed her eyes. "Someone? What happened?"

"As I said, they're still not sure. But they've arrested her boyfriend."

Colleen tapped her palm against her forehead. I hesitated, unsure if I should say anything while she was processing this tragic information. Was it possible that she was closer to Kim than Missy had known or let on?

"That poor girl. Are you a close friend? When did this happen?"

"They found her about a week ago."

"Found her where?"

"Outside Rowington. Near a rural road."

"What's this about her boyfriend? Did he beat her? What?"

"I'm not sure. I just know he was arrested."

Colleen put her hand down. "I'm sorry, dear. Did you know him, too?"

"Not really," I said.

Colleen reached her hands into her deep pockets and produced a napkin with the Subway logo on it. "What's your name, now?"

"Margery."

"Margery. Okay." Colleen blew her nose with the napkin, crumpled it, and returned it to her pocket. "Kim must've mentioned me, then?"

"Yes. And . . . um . . . She showed me the footage you gave her."

"The footage?"

"Of herself as a kid. Her interview."

"I see." Colleen pulled her coat tight around her chest. "Now, why did she show *you*?"

"We were good friends."

Colleen gazed at me. "I imagine you're grieving. I imagine this is very difficult. But why are you here now, hon?"

"I know Kim wanted some questions answered. I know this thing she had about Donald Wallace was important to her."

"Yes. It seemed to be." Colleen's face tightened. "But what can I do for . . . you?"

I paused. "Can you tell me why you gave it to her?"

Colleen studied me for a moment more, then gave a resigned shrug. "Kim struck me as very confused. I thought that it might help her to sort things out."

"Why did you have that stuff, though?" I struggled to keep my tone curious, matter-of-fact. "Shouldn't that have been filed at the D.A.'s office or the police department or something?"

"It wasn't." Colleen folded her arms. "It was in my garage."

"And now it's . . . where?"

"I gave it to Kim. I don't know what she did with it."

"You don't have a copy?"

"No. It was just something I had in a box in my garage. I'd have no reason to make another copy."

"What did you expect Kim to do with it?"

Colleen shook her head and gave me a pitying look. "I don't know if I'm the right one for you to be asking these questions. Are you sure you don't need a few more days to process what's happened before—"

"I've had quite a few days. Please. *Please*."

The desperation in my voice was real, even if the ostensible reason for it was not.

Colleen unfolded her arms and rubbed her forearms. "Hon, I expected her to watch it. That's all."

"You know she was looking to make a sort of video about Donald Wallace, right?"

"Yeah." Colleen wrinkled her nose. "That seemed like a funny idea to me, frankly. I thought the old footage might help her find a little peace. She was only ten years old back then. She was a pawn in that case. She didn't do anything wrong. I think seeing herself back then, and the way she was asked those questions, would help her forgive herself for her role in that case. Because it seemed to me—and maybe I'm being presumptuous here, since you probably knew her better than I did—it seemed to me that was the real issue. That she didn't really care if Donald Wallace won or lost."

I hesitated.

"Am I far off on that?" she asked.

"No . . . uh . . . I don't think so."

We were both silent. We both watched as a car marked STUDENT DRIVER moseyed into the parking lot and backed into a space, out of it, and into it again.

Once the car was gone, Colleen turned to me. "The business with Jenny's brother . . . that had always disturbed me."

I took a breath. "The part about Kyle Spicer, you mean?"

"Was that his name?" Colleen sounded more relaxed now. "I don't remember."

"Probably you mean Kyle," I said.

Colleen shrugged. "Don didn't share my feelings about it. And he doesn't change his mind about things, generally."

"What were *your* feelings about it?" I pulled out my knit glove and started picking one of the knots at the wrist.

"Well . . . that the things she said about Andrew and Jenny weren't trustworthy, given what she said about the brother. I mean, you always have to be really careful with child witnesses."

Susan Halliday's lawyer had said the same thing in Kim's interview. It seemed as if this was a theme Kim had been trying to build.

"Did you watch the footage before you gave it to her?" I asked.

Colleen seemed to notice my glove but didn't say anything about it. "No, I didn't."

"Did Donald Wallace know you had this stuff?"

"No. It was temporarily stored at my place, and then it was forgotten."

"Temporarily stored?" I shoved my glove back into my coat pocket and stomped my feet for warmth. "In a person's private garage?"

Colleen's gaze met mine. "It's not as shocking as you probably want to think."

It felt to me as though Colleen was confessing something with that statement. I wasn't sure, however, what that something was.

"Would Donald Wallace be angry if he knew you gave this to Kim?" I asked.

"Most likely," Colleen said, still watching me carefully. My hand fingered my glove in my pocket.

"Especially now," I said softly.

"Especially now?" she looked puzzled. "Oh, I don't know.

These politicians are always in damage-control mode. I think Don could handle the likes of Kim."

"But what if she released it?" I asked.

"Excuse me. *Released* it? From where? To whom?"

"Oh . . . like on YouTube."

Colleen rolled her eyes. I could see she was more of my mother's generation than my own with regard to YouTube. It wasn't real life. It was all celebrity meltdowns and kittycats on treadmills.

"Kim thought parts of it would be controversial," I added.

"Maybe she was right. But nothing Don couldn't handle, I don't think."

"Are you sure?"

Colleen gave me a sad little smile. "I see you share Kim's belief that people have the time to care."

"So when you handed this stuff over to Kim, you weren't afraid you'd get in trouble?"

"No. Given what happened to Andrew Abbott, I've often wondered how *none* of us ever 'got in trouble.' Maybe that's one reason I sat on those tapes. It felt as if someone, someday, ought to come along and ask me about my role in the whole thing, small as it was. And when Kim came out of nowhere, it felt like a sort of reckoning. Something I was almost expecting. I thought it might help her forgive herself and get on with her life. It seemed like the least I could do." She paused. "And screw the consequences."

Despite her age, I had a feeling Colleen normally would've said "fuck the consequences" with anyone she'd known longer than our fifteen minutes. Or maybe I seemed prudish to her. It was a flattering notion, really.

"Has Donald Wallace contacted you since you gave that tape to Kim?" I asked.

"Tapes, not tape. It was a lot of footage."

"So they were unedited?"

"That's right." Colleen gave me another smile, the meaning of which I couldn't quite discern. "Unedited."

"Was there ever an edited version? It seems like we're talking about footage that never made it into the courtroom when Andrew Abbott was on trial."

"It sure seems that way, doesn't it?" Colleen patted me on the shoulder. I couldn't tell if this was supposed to be reassuring or condescending. "Listen," she said, glancing away from me, "I had little kids then. What happened to Jenny Spicer terrified me."

I nodded, unsure how to respond to this admission.

"So . . . *has* Wallace contacted you?" I asked.

"Why would he?"

"Because . . ." I wasn't sure if I should tell her about Kim confronting Donald Wallace. "Because maybe he heard about her having the tapes?" I said. "Wouldn't he be angry?"

"Yeah," Colleen said. "I suppose he would. But given what happened to Andrew Abbott—given that we helped it happen to him—I figured Don could withstand a little discomfort, if it came to that."

I couldn't discern whether there was any vengeance in this statement—behind the rather matter-of-fact delivery.

"I see," I said.

Colleen threw up her hands, signaling an end to our discussion. "I'm really sorry about your friend," she said. "I hope they string up the boyfriend."

"Thanks," I muttered.

"I should get back to my desk. I'm expecting a call."

She began to open the glass door to the realty office but then turned around and looked at me.

"Who has the tapes now, hon?" she asked.

"I don't know," I admitted.

"Her parents, maybe?" she suggested.

"I really don't know."

"That's interesting," Colleen said.

"It is," I said.

She nodded and went back inside.

String up the boyfriend. String up the boyfriend. It was all I could think of as I drove away from Raymond Realty. My hands were shaking so badly that I had to stay in the slow lane. I wanted some calming music, but my iPod was disconnected and I was too distressed to mess with it. I hit FM radio—always tuned, by default, to the classic rock station.

Janis Joplin was singing "Piece of My Heart." I relaxed into the song for a moment, but then it made me remember something: Jeff and me doing homework in front of the TV, as was our habit in high school. There was some special on about John F. Kennedy's presidency. When they got to the assassination, Jeff said, "I've seen this so many times, sometimes I could swear I remember it."

And I knew exactly what he meant. Not about John F. Kennedy per se. For me it's Woodstock. It's Jimi Hendrix playing "The Star-Spangled Banner." Sometimes, for a moment or two, I feel like I was there when it happened.

Maybe it was something about our parents. Maybe it was the kind of TV we watched. We both felt like we were spending our youth reconstituting Boomer memories. I remembered now the odd feeling that Jeff could articulate a thought I hadn't quite realized I'd had till he said it.

Hitting the OFF button on the radio, I took the next exit and parked at a Mobil station. Once I'd stopped the engine, I tried to take a deep breath but felt like I was choking on it. I glanced into the backseat and wished I had Wayne there to talk to. Surely Wayne would understand on some level. Surely any of my animals would. They'd all been torn away from their siblings at some point, I had to assume.

I took out my phone and discovered a message from Zach: DEPT. MEETING CANCELED. WORKING @ STARBUCKS TILL 4:30. CAN U MEET?

Cute text shorthand from a professional English smarty-pants.

I'LL BE THERE IN 15, I texted back.

When I arrived at Starbucks, Zach was waiting for me at the best window table. His laptop was open, and a giant brown cookie sat on a plate beside it.

"I thought we could share it," Zach said. "Do you like ginger molasses?"

"Of course," I answered. I wasn't hungry at all.

"This one even has baking soda in it, I'm pretty sure."

"Bonus," I said. "Are you working on your next book or what?"

"Yeah." Zach sighed and closed his laptop.

"Can I ask what it's about? Does it have a memoir element, like the last one?"

Zach sipped from his enormous cup of coffee. "It's about . . . well, I guess the simple answer is that it's about gambling, and gambling addiction to some extent. There are smaller sections about Atlantic City and the Connecticut casinos, but the majority of it is about Las Vegas. I mean, in a sense."

"Have you been traveling to research it?" I asked.

"Yeah, some." Zach broke a sliver from the cookie and pushed the rest toward me. "Last summer, and the January before that."

"I take it that's the personal part? Your travels?"

He shrugged. "Uh, sort of. The real personal part is about the year I spent in Vegas when I was twenty. Counting cards at the blackjack tables."

"Really?"

"Yup," he said. "I earned most of my first year's college tuition that way. They want me to make a lot of that in the book. A corrupt Vegas coming-of-age. A twisted realization of the American dream or something. They kind of want it to be a big book. But I read parts of it that I've written lately and it doesn't feel big enough somehow."

I nodded, although I totally couldn't relate.

"You know," Zach continued, "I'm surprised you and I haven't talked more about Margery Kempe. I've wondered if I should include her in one of my classes."

"It *is* the first autobiography written in English."

"Do you think it's a very accurate autobiography?"

"Have you read the whole thing?" I asked.

"No," he admitted.

"Because aside from the accounts of the pilgrimage to Jerusalem and some of the encounters with church authorities, a lot of it is quite humdrum. Petty disagreements with people in her town, getting kicked out of a church where the priest couldn't stand her wailing, explaining why she was or wasn't abstaining from meat or fasting on Fridays. I think most of it was accurate. If she was worried about its being a good yarn, she would've edited herself differently. You probably read the best parts, in an English-literature anthology, right?"

Zach nodded.

"Yeah," I said. "I may be biased, but looking at it as a whole, I don't think she took a great deal of license. The funny thing is, she was clearly trying to model herself after St. Bridget of Sweden and Mary of Oignies, two famous holy women of that era who had what Marge would've considered to be similar experiences—they were both married women who had visions of Christ, and Mary of Oignies also convinced her husband to allow her to swear a vow of chastity. But Marge doesn't exaggerate her own life story enough for readers to take her as seriously as they might those women. She comes across very much like a wannabe."

Zach nodded and motioned toward the front counter with his coffee mug. "Can I get you a coffee?"

"No thanks," I said. "My nerves are pretty much shot this week."

He put down his mug. "So you wanted to talk about that kid Anthony?"

"Well . . . yeah. But I have a pretty good lead to find Dustin, through one of his other friends. So it might not be as important as I thought yesterday."

"I think you're right that there are better ways to find Dustin. I doubt that Kim would've been able to find Anthony without his real name either."

"Unless she asked *Dustin* about him."

Zach looked perplexed. "Why would she ask Dustin about him once she'd *found* Dustin?"

"Well. Dustin says Anthony's the only person he's ever told everything about the night his father died. Maybe . . . well, I guess not."

"What? Say."

"You said Dustin seemed unstable. Maybe she wanted to see if what he told *her* matched up with what he told Anthony?" It sounded pretty lame now that I said it out loud. I'd simply wanted to look at Kim's probable steps from every angle.

"Possible," Zach said charitably.

"But not likely, probably. Can you tell me what you know about him?"

"Not much more than what's in the book, quite honestly."

"You know his name," I hinted.

"Yeah." Zach opened his laptop again. "I had to look it up in my notes."

"You mentioned there were confidentiality issues."

"Yeah. Most of the kids agreed to be interviewed only if their names were changed."

I suppressed a sigh. "So . . . you can't give me his name or anything?"

"I've been thinking about that. I'll give it to you, under the circumstances. I think this business with Wallace's old assistant is actually much more unsettling than her chasing after these kids, but just in case it's of some use to you . . ." Zach lowered his voice. "His name was Michael Johnson. I've done some sniffing around online, but I can't find him. I mean, with a name like that, it's difficult. I'm almost certain he'd be in college now.

His parents seemed pretty intense. They wouldn't have it any other way. They were considering relocating the whole family once he finished his sentence. I wouldn't be surprised if he even changed his name."

"With parents like that, I'm surprised they agreed to let you put him in the book."

"I changed some identifying stuff. Their jobs. The kid looked different from how I described him." Zach reached his hand into his back jeans pocket and pulled out a folded piece of paper. "Stuff like that."

"What did he actually look like?"

"Oh, he had black hair, and I said it was brown." Zach unfolded the paper. "I said he was short when he was actually tall. Really basic stuff."

I shrugged and made a mental note of this information: Black hair. Tall.

"You mentioned you had something else for me?" I said, sensing Zach was eager to show me what he'd found. "Something Kim wrote?"

"Yeah. Now, I don't know if you read her piece on her friend Jenny or not—maybe you've been too busy."

"No. I read it. Pretty well written, I thought. But sad."

"Yeah. But I'd forgotten that one piece she wrote, she didn't share on the site. You know, it comes up with a couple of students every semester. There's something they want to write about but they don't want everybody in the class reading it. Sometimes I give them a pass, sometimes I don't. Sometimes I tell them you shouldn't write anything down you wouldn't want the whole world to read. And have them pick a new topic. Depends on how nasty I'm feeling that day."

"But with Kim?"

"I gave Kim a pass. Her stuff was so hit-or-miss. Seemed I should set her up for a hit. Anyway. She handed this in. I only thought of it because you mentioned Jenny Spicer's brother. It's probably nothing, but I thought you might want to see it."

I took the paper from Zach and read Kim's essay.

Funny that one of your prompt suggestions is "First Kiss."

I hate it when people talk about The First Kiss. And I want to puke when I see one of those sweet, innocent lemonade-commercial first kisses on TV. Do that many people really have such an inspired first kiss that it needs to be a Thing? What about all of us who had terrible, icky, wrong-place, wrong-time first kisses? I suspect there are more of us who've had those than not.

My first kiss was with an Older Boy. It was one of those days, in a smelly-carpet suburban basement. Coulda been a kiss. Coulda been Nintendo. Coulda been a tired old board game like Sorry! Coulda gone any of these ways. Even the day of the kiss, there was much more than a kiss. Not everything. But more. I didn't feel an ounce of guilt or shame that day, or on the ones following it. Soon after, there were things of so much more consequence to be ashamed of.

Only when I looked back years later did I notice the absence of shame—like I'd been missing something that other girls had as inherently as their big blue eyes, their thin wisps of hair around their temples, their delicate white hands.

Is it possible some of us are born with more innocence—or capacity for it—than others? I'm not bitter, because I don't think innocence was taken from me. I'm pretty sure I was never innocent. I threw myself into it because I knew it would make me special. It would make me bold.

I knew early I wanted boys to look at me. Does innocence need to be cultivated? It's simply something my parents wouldn't think to value.

Every time some sap or other says "When was your first kiss?" I say something like, "Oh, maybe about six months ago." Everybody laughs. Not because it's funny. It's just a successful deflection of the question. No one has ever countered with, "But really, though . . ."

The boy I shared it with was special to me and still is. He didn't ever seem to have much innocence either.

I never told him, but the kids at school called him Snake Eyes. That is, before something Terrible happened to his family and he was forgotten for everything else. He told me later: When something like that happens, people try to forget all the things they hated you for.

We've been broken up awhile, but whenever I roll Snake Eyes, I still think of him. Him and me. Two of a kind. Undesirable but symmetrical. Rolled together on the basement floor.

"She was experimenting with capital letters," Zach offered.

"I can see that," I replied. I was glad to have something to respond to besides the content.

"What do you think?" Zach asked.

"This is . . . intriguing," I admitted.

Zach shrugged. "Something else I probably shouldn't be sharing."

"But thank you for doing it anyway," I said.

"Probably not useful to you, but . . ."

"It actually is," I said.

"I remember writing on it that she should put in more 'sense-of-place details' and that I'd appreciate a few more specifics about Snake Eyes so I could picture him better. Now I feel kind of like a creeper for that."

I was distracted, wondering if I should tell him about Colleen Shipley. Surely there was some drama and confusion surrounding Kyle and Kim kissing in the basement. And surely it had factored significantly in Kim's mind. But what it had to do with Jenny or Andrew—or Donald Wallace, for that matter—I couldn't quite make out yet.

"I'm sure she didn't think you were a creeper," I said. "I'll bet she was flattered you were interested enough to ask for more."

"The piece is clearly spare for a reason. It was a painful memory. She'd said enough, actually. I don't think a smart reader would need much elaboration."

"Maybe, maybe not," I murmured.

I was only half listening to Zach. Whatever this meant, I could think of someone who might be more frightened of it than Donald Wallace. If I had the timing right, Kim had been too young to be doing *anything* in a basement with an older boy around the time of Jenny's death. And this older boy was the brother of her dead friend. How had that affected her testimony about Andrew Abbott?

Zach seemed to sense my distraction.

"You mentioned that shortly before she died, Kim had talked to Janice Obermeier, who works at the *Chronicle*," he said. "Would you like me to give her a call? Do you think that would help?"

"Jeff talked to her already," I said. "She thought Kim was a crazy person, going on about some special footage she had."

"She might be more forthcoming about the details if she's talking to . . ." Zach paused. "To a colleague."

"She might. I don't know how it works with you journalist types."

I watched a young mother park her little boy in one of the black Starbucks chairs. She handed him a cookie studded with M&M's, then settled across from him with her laptop.

"While you're putting your journalistic brain on it, do you all know how to get a hold of politicians' home addresses?" I asked.

"*What?*" Zach said. "Theresa, if you really want to check out Donald Wallace, he's doing a lot of campaigning. You could probably catch him at—"

"Never mind." I didn't need for Zach to know I was headed for crazy town. "Sure, try Janice Obermeier. If you want. I mean, I don't want you to be sucked into this if it's going to get you in trouble."

I watched the boy take a big bite out of his cookie.

"Theresa."

"Yeah?" I turned my attention back to Zach.

"I don't feel 'sucked in.' I've been thinking a lot about all this since you told me about those tapes. These situations scare me." He took a long sip of his coffee. "Situations where people can take advantage of their power and think they can get away with it. Corruption from the people who are supposed to be the good ones. Or at least the ones who are supposed to be *lawful*. I saw a great deal of that when I was younger, actually. More than I even put in my book."

I sensed him hesitating, waiting for a response. "What do you mean?"

"Well, I *didn't* mean to make this about me. I'm just telling you why I'm taking this seriously. Some people don't believe that this shit can happen. I've seen that it can."

"But what are you referring to?" I asked.

"Well, when I was in detention . . ." he began.

Then I felt him hesitating again. Most likely he didn't want to say what he'd seen go down in a juvenile-detention center. I had a brother in a county facility—and who might even go to a real maximum-security prison—both of which were surely much worse. It seemed to me he was trying to think of a way to distract me from my own question—but wasn't thinking fast enough.

"*Say,*" I demanded.

"There were these incidents with prison guards. There were scheduled fights, and guards were betting on them. One kid nearly died. Fell into a coma. Brain damage. I doubt he completely recovered."

"The guards?"

"Yeah. That's what I'm saying. People with power doing shit you wouldn't believe. Some people might hear you speculating about Donald Wallace—or someone connected to him—having something to do with Kim and think, 'No way.' But not me. I'm not a skeptic when it comes to abuse of power."

"Did you put that thing about the guards in your book, Zach?"

"No."

"Why the hell not?" I couldn't help but ask.

"Sarah—that's my ex-girlfriend—she asked me the same thing."

Did he say "ex-"? Yes, he did. I wondered if Sarah was the young lady I'd seen who'd reminded me of Kate Middleton.

"And?" I said.

"Well, it didn't happen to *me*. It was just something I heard about, and I never got quite the full story, because stuff was covered up so much. And I was worried how it would look to the facilities and staff I used in the present-day part of the book. Like Sharon Silverstein. Those people were really good to me, really welcoming. If I shared a story like that about my own experience, in the context of a book mostly about kids in *their* comparatively well-run facilities . . . I worried about the implication. Especially when I doubted I could verify it to begin with. And I had a feeling it might be a whole other book, delving into that story."

"It might still be," I said. "Were you with Sarah when you wrote the book? Did she help you decide what to put in and leave out?"

"No. We got together after the book was out. I met her at a reading."

I nodded.

"We broke up this summer," Zach added.

So Sarah *was* Kate Middleton. And it didn't sound like there was anyone else. "I'm sorry."

"Thanks." Zach looked at his cookie, which I hadn't touched. "I suppose you're not hungry, looks like?"

"I'm sorry. Not really."

"Because I was going to ask if you would let me treat you at that falafel place a couple doors down."

"Maybe after my brother gets out," I said. "He gets out tomorrow. Maybe I can be lucid company after that."

"Oh my God. I didn't even ask you about bail. I meant to. I'm sorry."

"It's high, but we're managing it. We'll have him out first thing tomorrow morning. Maybe you and I can have falafel sometime after that."

"Probably you want to be with your family," Zach said. "I shouldn't intrude."

Zach reached up and gripped my shoulder, giving it a quick but reassuring squeeze. I allowed myself to meet his gaze. His eyes were warm and engaging. But the mention of Snake Eyes in Kim's garbled essay reminded me that I needed to get back to Nathan's lair. I had to get my hands on that footage.

"Can I keep this?" I said, waving Kim's essay.

"Sure."

As I started to walk out of the shop, I thought about Nathan for a moment. I thought about his George Michael earring and his fresh-frozen mice. Then I looked back at Zach as I opened the Starbucks door. It made me a little sad to leave him there, gazing down at his big ginger-molasses comfort cookie.

But I had to get back to Nathan for Jeff's sake. Besides, there had always been a clear difference between the sort of guy I wanted and the sort I deserved.

Before Nathan, though, I wanted to drop in on Kyle Spicer. If I left right away, I could get to Carpet World before it closed. I fed Boober and the cats, hooked a leash on Wayne, and drove to Ricksville.

It was already getting dark when I got to the Carpet World–Beverage Superstore strip mall. At first I kept my distance from the building, standing by my car with Wayne, watching people entering and exiting the liquor store in the twilight. But I was afraid I might miss Kyle when he left. I crossed onto the storefront sidewalk and cupped my hand to peek into the front window. The lights were on, but I didn't see any movement. For a few minutes, I watched Wayne sniff around a lilac-brown wad of chewing gum flattened into the sidewalk.

"Let's see how you do this time, Wayne," I whispered to him. "Get me some more leads and you'll get another hamburger. No, don't *lick* that thing, man."

"Well, if it isn't Margery Lipinski," someone said from behind me.

It was Kyle Spicer, approaching from the parking lot with a large paper coffee cup in his hand. "And is that Wayne?"

"Yes," I said. Wayne looked up from his gum and gave a sharp yap in Kyle's direction. "And you can call me Margie."

Kyle looked different from last time. Not laid-back, exactly. Just less oily. There was less shine in his hair and less snap in his eyes. I prayed he wouldn't yell at me again. This time I might have to yell back, and I wasn't sure where that kind of sass was going to come from.

"I don't work for Donald Wallace," I offered.

"Yeah," he said, unlocking the shop door. "I figured that out after you left. How did you end up with old Wayne here?"

"So you know Wayne?"

"Of course I know Wayne. He lived with me for a little while. When Kim and I were together."

"Did you and Kim get him together?"

"No. She got him when we were broken up for a short time. I'm not an animal person. He and I weren't buddies, really."

"That explains why he doesn't seem to . . . uh . . . recognize you."

Kyle sipped his coffee and wiped his lips with his thumb. "Are you planning on standing here all evening?"

"No." I looked down at Wayne, who hung out a noncommittal tip of his tongue. "But I'm sure dogs aren't allowed in Carpet World."

"True that, Margie," Kyle said. "Especially not this clown. I still have his bite marks in my Ekornes recliner."

"I don't know what that is."

"It's a fancy chair. I watch TV in it. Now, you never said how you got Wayne."

"Kim gave him to me to take care of for a weekend. And then she never came back."

"Oh. Why didn't you tell me that the first time you came?"

"I tried. You kicked me out first."

"You didn't try very hard."

"Maybe not. But I'm here now."

"And *why* are you here now?" Kyle rubbed the bridge of his nose and squeezed his eyes shut for a moment. "Are you offering Wayne to me?"

"No. I wanted to ask you about a few things you said that day. In light of what's happened, I thought you might be willing now."

Kyle extended his coffee cup. "You mind holding this? I'd

kind of like to smoke. If it's not gonna bother you too much."

"Nope," I said, taking the cup from him. It wasn't warm at all. Kyle produced a lighter and a cigarette from his back pockets.

"Have the cops talked to you yet?" he asked.

"Um . . . no. Did they talk to you?"

"Yeah. Of course. Kim's my ex-girlfriend."

"Did you talk to them about Donald Wallace at all?"

Kyle grimaced as he took his first pull on the cigarette. "No. Her boyfriend killed her. That's mostly what they asked about."

"But last time I came here, you seemed to think Donald Wallace was after you."

"I didn't say that." Kyle exhaled smoke through his nostrils. "Nothing that dramatic."

"Do you think he was after Kim?"

"'After' her? What does that mean?"

"Well, he was aware that she was trying to get him some bad press, right?"

Kyle studied me for a moment, then harrumphed. "Yeah. Typical Kim. She goes up to him on the street and gets right in his face."

"Now, when was that?"

"Just a few weeks ago."

"Did she mention the tapes to him?" I asked. This was why I had come here—to bring up the tapes and watch Kyle's reaction. But I hadn't planned for it to come out at exactly this moment.

He paused to breathe out a bit of smoke. "What tapes?"

"The tapes she got from Colleen Shipley. She didn't tell you about those?"

Another draw on the cigarette. Kyle kept his gaze focused on

Wayne and then, when he'd breathed out again, returned it to me. "I don't know a Colleen Shipley. Should I?"

"Oh. Well, no. Um . . . what was Donald Wallace's reaction when Kim confronted him? Do you know?"

"I wasn't there. But she bragged about it later. She said he looked like a deer in headlights when she even brought up Andrew Abbott. You know who that is, I take it?"

"Of course."

Kyle smoked silently for a moment. "I think what really surprised Wallace was to know he was talking to one of the kids involved in that old case—his most badly fucked-up case—all grown up. To be faced with such a person on the street, without any talking points. I don't think there was anything in particular she said or did that really scared him. It was just a hell of an unexpected surprise."

"But then what gave you the idea, later, that one of Wallace's people had approached her?"

"Because one of his campaign people *did* approach her at her apartment. She called me up to brag about it."

"Brag about it, really? Or did she seem threatened by it?"

"It seemed more like bragging to me. If she was scared, she didn't tell me."

"What did they say to her, exactly?"

"She said they acted like they wanted to negotiate with her."

I thought of Kim's question to Jeff right before she left—the "hypothetical question" she posed about being paid for silence. "Did they offer her money?"

"I don't think so. She would've told me. She would've been *real* proud of that. No, they said they wanted to 'understand where she was coming from.' She probably was planning on jerking them around a little, enjoying getting to control the situation. Controlling powerful people. She kinda loved the idea of that, I think. Do you know what she was doing in Rowington before she died?"

"No." I was startled by the question. "Do you?"

"I think so. There was supposed to be this town-meeting kind of thing, with Donald Wallace, in Fisherton, which is only about ten miles from Rowington. It was early that Saturday morning. She intended to go to that event and waylay him again. She told me."

"Have you told the police this?"

"Yeah. Of course."

Kyle was holding his cigarette so lightly, so casually, that I was afraid it would slip and drop onto Wayne's fur.

"What do you think she wanted to get out of all this?" I asked, pulling Wayne to my side and wrapping part of his leash around my wrist.

"That's a good question. I really don't have an answer. You know, that's a big part of the reason we had to break up. I got tired of trying to figure her out."

Kyle sucked on his cigarette again and, when he released the smoke, added, "I do miss her, though."

"You were together a long time. She told me that you were really young when you got together."

"Yeah. We were."

"All this must be hard for you."

Kyle dropped his cigarette on the ground and smushed it with his shiny black shoe. To me, patent leather ought to be off-limits to any grown man who's not either getting married or doing magic tricks.

"Is that what you came here to ask, Margie?"

"No. I just wanted to ask you about this Donald Wallace stuff. It's starting to concern me, what I'm hearing about Kim's interest in him recently."

"Did you know her boyfriend?" Kyle asked.

I watched Wayne sniff at the cigarette butt. "Only a little."

"Whatever she was up to . . . what they've got on him seems more significant to me."

"Yeah. Well, in any case, I'd still like to get to the bottom of it. This Wallace thing."

"Get to the bottom of it?" Kyle stared at me. Though his eyes had looked tired for most of our conversation, they now seemed to be brightening some and sharpening their focus. "What do you think you're going to find at the bottom?"

The question was meant to make me appear foolish. I gripped Wayne's leash hard and took a breath. "I feel like there was, in all the flailing she was doing, something she legitimately wanted to say about Donald Wallace, or at least about what happened in 1992. I'd like to help clarify that for her."

"That's kind of you." Kyle gave me a sardonic little smile. "But if *she* couldn't figure out what she wanted to say, how can *you*?"

I shrugged and avoided his gaze. "Maybe not clarify, then. Maybe see that she's heard. However garbled the message is."

Kyle extended his palm out to me. It took me a moment to realize he was beckoning back his coffee. His cold fingers brushed mine as I handed it to him.

"You know," he said quietly, "she never mentioned you to me."

"We'd only just become friends," I said. "When she died."

"And now you want to get to the bottom of things," Kyle said, his voice lowering still.

He opened the door to the store.

"I'm freezing," he said. "You want to come in here and warm up for a minute? Before you go?"

"No thanks," I answered. "I have somewhere I have to be."

"Okay. Then see ya, Margie. See ya, Wayne."

Wayne stared after Kyle, as if trying to remember where he'd seen him before. I nudged him out of his sitting position and hustled him to the car.

"I have a feeling I'll have more to say to Kyle," I said to Wayne as I handed him a Burger King patty. I couldn't find a Wendy's in Ricksville. "A lot more."

Wayne sucked the meat down in about thirty seconds.

"First, though, I have to get my hands on those tapes—or copies of their contents. My best bet for that is still Nathan. Right? And I need to look at whatever other footage Kim had saved. Plus see if there are any VHS tapes lying around. Probably she wouldn't have left anything that important at his house, but if she hadn't digitized it yet, you never know. . . ."

Wayne was too busy eating my cheeseburger wrapper to answer. I yanked it away from him and tossed him a couple of conciliatory french fries. While he gobbled them, I called Nathan to ask if he wanted to get together after his shift.

"Has Peaches ever gotten out of her cage?" I asked Nathan, playing with the pewter pendant hanging from his neck. It was a knotted Celtic symbol of some sort. Between his jewelry, his Asian tattoos, his Hare Krishna upbringing, and whatever else I had yet to learn about him, Nathan was like a dozen of Jeff and my I'm-thinking-of's sewn together Frankenfashion.

"Not while I've had her," Nathan said, pulling a blanket over us both. "But I know she did with her previous owner once. When she was younger and smaller."

"So you know she has those skills."

Nathan shrugged and put his hand on his upper chest. I tried to ignore the scratchy sound of his fingernails against his abundant chest hair.

"She didn't have as good a cage then," he explained.

Our "date" had started at The Lab, the insufferably hipster bar downtown. They were serving bacon and strawberries with dipping sauces—chocolate, maple, and caramel. I'd had three pieces of bacon. Nathan had stuck with the strawberries, since he was a vegetarian. When I'd kissed him, I wondered if I had hickory-smoked breath.

I'd like to see your place, he'd whispered between kisses.

It's a mess, I'd whispered back. We'd come in separate cars. *Next time. Meet you at your house?*

"Is this kind of fast for you?" Nathan asked now, changing the subject from Peaches.

"What?"

"What's going on here with us."

"Why, is it too fast for you?" I tried to sound casual and wondered if I sounded slutty instead. "Does it bother you?"

"No. It doesn't. I just wonder what this is. Are you ever going to want hang out during daylight hours?"

"Have we not?"

"No."

Nathan fell back into his pillow. Crooking his elbow and resting his hand behind his head, he displayed his super-long, glistening underarm hair.

"You promised me you'd tell me more about where you grew up," I said, snuggling closer to him and averting my eyes from his armpit.

I needed for Nathan to fall asleep at some point. And in my experience men fall asleep pretty fast after you request intimate conversation of this particular kind.

"We've already talked about me too much." Nathan stroked down the flyaway hairs around my forehead. "I want to ask something about you."

"Okay."

"Why aren't you finished with your dissertation yet?"

"How long have you lived in Thompsonville, Nathan?"

"Three years."

"I see. Well, you should know by now—living that long in a university town—that unfinished dissertations are a dime a dozen. It's nothing unusual."

Jasper—the old greyhound I'd met briefly as I'd rushed out of Nathan's house earlier in the week—crept into the room and made eyes at Nathan. Nathan patted the mattress and Jasper climbed onto the bed, settling on the other side of Nathan with a contented sigh.

"Sure, it's nothing unusual. But there's a story behind each one, right? Maybe a more interesting story than for the finished ones."

"No. The story is almost always motivational deficiency."

Nathan rubbed Jasper's brown-spotted back. "There must be more to it than that."

"Yes, well. I wrote about two-thirds of it. It was called 'Margery Kempe and the Carnality of Piety.' I took a really long break from writing when I got a divorce—like six months or something—and when I came back to it, it felt like I needed to start over. I'm about halfway through writing the new version. Sometimes I think maybe I just don't want it to end. I was inexplicably sad the first time I finished Marge's book cover to cover. It ends rather abruptly. You don't get to know how she died, because of course she can't narrate her own death. I didn't want it to end, so I turned back to the beginning and started it again. As repetitive as some parts are, she's so real and flawed that I found her book comforting. I think part of me expected her to go on and on, weeping and exasperating people into eternity."

"Maybe she did," Nathan said. "Maybe she doesn't need you."

"Of course not," I sniffed, unsure whether to consider this reply dismissive or endearing. "But maybe *I* need her. You know, this is a depressing topic. I'm happy to talk to you about Marge's life, but I don't really want to talk about the thesis itself."

"Okay. Then tell me another story about Marge's life."

I considered my catalog of Marge stories. "I think I've told you all my favorites. Or— Well, have I told you about the time she was interrogated by the archbishop of York?"

"No."

"Oh. Great." I could stretch that one out pretty well. "So it wasn't unusual for Marge to raise suspicion in her travels. She didn't ever curb her wailing and her lecturing for the sake of being a gracious visitor. Wherever she went, she raised the eyebrows and the ire of the locals, and she was arrested more than once for possible heresy. Probably the most dramatic of these incidents was the one in York."

"Uh-huh." Nathan's eyelids were already drooping.

"She was dragged into the archbishop's chapel on suspicion

of heresy—but more generally for her usual perplexingly assertive and unconventional behaviors and simply overstaying her welcome. She'd promised a priest she'd stay two weeks but stayed on beyond that."

Nathan's eyes were closed now.

"On the day of her hearing, a crowd of locals screamed and swore at her and wished her a prompt burning at the stake. She turned to them and told them they'd go to hell if they kept up their swearing. Then, as she waited for the archbishop to appear at the chapel, she said a silent prayer to God, who assured her that all would be well. When the archbishop arrived, he asked her why she wore white, called her a 'false heretic,' and had her handcuffed. While she waited for him to return with his clerics, she shook with unaccustomed terror. Things had rarely gotten this serious. After their arrival, as they were arranging themselves in their seats, Marge gave one of her great and startling cries, astounding everyone in the chapel, by her account. When her fit was over, the archbishop demanded an explanation. And guess what Marge's response was?"

Nathan murmured, "Hmmm?"

"She said, 'Sir, you shall wish someday that you had wept as sorely as I.'"

Nathan's eyes opened. "What does that mean? What did she mean?"

"Well, aside from being a very sassy answer from someone who was practically peeing her pants a few minutes before, she was kind of saying she was more righteous than he was. And she continued to imply that throughout the interrogation. Anyway, the archbishop and his clerics examined her on the Articles of Faith, and she answered everything right. That's the thing about Marge—her *behavior* was weird, but whenever people asked her doctrinal beliefs, she was always by the book."

Nathan closed his eyes again.

"One cleric came forward and said he'd heard Marge preaching, which was of course not permitted, since she was a woman. And Marge defended herself, saying, 'I do not preach, sir. I do not go into any pulpit. I use only conversation and good words, and that I will do while I live.'"

"Mm-hm," Nathan said, clearly struggling to sound more awake than he was.

"And the cleric added that he'd heard Margery telling a terrible tale about priests. So the archbishop demanded that Marge repeat it."

Nathan was nestling his head deeper into his pillow, so I launched into the tale. It was about a priest who went for a walk and then spent the night sleeping beneath a pear tree full of beautiful blossoms. In the morning a bear came along, ate all the blossoms, turned his butt to the priest, and shat them all out. Then a pilgrim came along and explained to the priest the meaning of what he'd seen: that the priest was like the pear tree. He gave beautiful sermons, but he lived sinfully. So his "beautiful blossoms" came to nothing.

By the time I was finished with the story, Nathan's arm felt very heavy on mine.

"Anyway. The archbishop liked the story. Besides, there wasn't much to convict Marge on. He let her go on the condition she skip town quickly. Which she didn't exactly do, and which got her in a little more trouble later, but that's another story."

I finally stopped talking. I couldn't hear anything resembling a snore, so I picked up Nathan's hand gently and dropped it. It flopped heavily onto his royal purple pillowcase. I waited a few more minutes before I crept out of the bed and down the hall to the office. One floorboard gave a whimper as I started to cross the room to Nathan's swivel chair.

I prayed as I moved the mouse—prayed Nathan's computer was on, that he hadn't gotten wise and password-protected his desktop. He hadn't. I returned to the Wallace folder and clicked on "Wallace stuff 2."

This was the footage with Missy that I hadn't finished the last time I was here.

"Yeah, they questioned me for a few hours altogether. My mother was there in the room. Wasn't your mom there when they talked to you?"

"On and off," Kim said. "She took breaks. She went out and got me McDonald's. At least that's how I remember it."

"Do you think you felt pressure to say something that wasn't true?" Missy asked.

"Aren't *I* supposed to be interviewing *you*?" Kim said.

Missy rolled her eyes. "What's the difference? We were both there. Why don't we just talk instead?"

The young women proceeded to have a lengthy discussion about what would be a "more compelling format." I paused that interview, eager to see what else Kim had stored. After all, I'd already heard what Missy had to say. I'd go back and finish that interview later.

I clicked on "Wallace stuff 3."

Dustin Halliday appeared on the screen. His long hair was pulled back, with a couple of oily-looking pieces falling over his eyes. His chin was tilted downward, but his eyes were rolled upward, gazing into the camera with a bored expression.

"Okay, *now* we're all set," Kim said from behind the camera. "So we're here because you had something to add to our last interview."

"Yeah. That's right." Dustin's expression didn't change. "*All* set."

"Why don't you say everything you want to say?" Kim's enthusiasm seemed out of place with the sole visual of Dustin's sulk. "And then I'll ask follow-up questions."

"All right." Dustin finally blinked, and he even gave a slight smile. "So there were some things I didn't say in my last interview."

"Why are you changing your mind now?"

"Because we know each other now."

"Okay."

"And people don't ask me about this stuff much anymore. Since you actually care, it seems important to be honest."

"You weren't honest in the last interview?" Kim asked.

"I'd rather you just threw that interview away and started over with this one."

"Okay." Kim sounded a bit impatient. "So what did you want to say now?"

"Well. I can't just start with that night. I should explain a few things about my parents. About my mother, mainly."

"Go ahead."

"I loved my father." Dustin pushed a piece of hair out of his eyes. "He wasn't a very emotional guy, but he loved us and he worked hard for us. I was closer to my mother than to him when I was little, so maybe I didn't see that so well. My mother shouldn't ever have been married to him. That probably sounds like something lots of people say. But I mean she shouldn't have been married to *anyone*. She wasn't normal."

"Wasn't normal. I'm sure you'll want to be more specific."

"She would get these ideas in her head," Dustin explained, "that she needed to arrange things to happen a certain way, no matter how it affected the people around her."

"Okay," Kim prompted.

"She had a way of making you do things," Dustin said, glancing away from the camera.

Kim sucked in a breath. "Things like what?"

"Well, just . . . making something seem right, that when you thought about it later wasn't right at all. Like the time she got me to tell my aunt she needed a nose job."

"Your aunt?"

Kim zoomed out. I recognized the bluish green–and–white sofa Dustin was sitting in. They were filming the interview in Kim's apartment.

"Her sister-in-law. My mom hated her. So I guess she wanted to make her feel like shit once in a while."

"I see." Kim hesitated. "So you're saying your mom maybe isn't the nicest person in the world?"

"Um. I wasn't going to put it that way."

"Oh," Kim said. "How *were* you going to put it?"

While I'd been surprised at what a decent interviewer Kim had been thus far, I wasn't impressed with her behavior here. It seemed like she was annoying Dustin—just when he was poised, I suspected, to say something important.

"I feel like I already said it." Dustin folded his arms. "She had a way of making you do things."

"By 'you' you mean yourself?"

"Yeah. Me. And my brother. She was a master manipulator."

"And how does that apply to the night your father died, Dustin?"

Dustin covered his face with his hands. He sat like that for a minute or two. Somewhere in the background, I could hear Wayne barking.

"Nobody got it right," Dustin said finally.

"Including Donald Wallace?"

Dustin finally uncovered his face. "I'm not talking about him. I'm talking about my mother. My family."

"Okay. Sorry. Go on."

He swallowed and said, "She told me his gun wasn't loaded."

Wayne's barking came closer.

"Shut UP!" Kim said.

Dustin smiled weakly, then bent down out of the camera's sight—presumably petting Wayne. "Can you stop the camera for a minute?"

"No," Kim said. "Let's just—"

"Really," Dustin said, straightening up again. "Stop the camera."

The footage ended there.

"Damn it, Wayne!" I whispered.

What did it mean? That Dustin had shot his father by accident? Where was the next part of this video?

There were no more materials left in Kim's folder. Of course, it was possible Kim had stored other footage elsewhere on

Nathan's computer but under a less obvious file name. I was convinced she had, because there was stuff on her draft "commercial" that wasn't contained in her other files. I switched to the desktop but found that Nathan kept it very clean. I'd have to dig a little deeper. Would she have stored videos on iPhoto? I was clueless about this sort of thing. I didn't ever film anything and didn't deal with those sorts of files in my stodgy academic life.

Before deciding how to proceed next, I started to look through Nathan's overhead cabinets in hopes of finding VHS tapes. The left cabinet contained a mug full of Sharpies and an empty tub of something called Dr. Harvey's Incredible Canary Food. The right cabinet had DVDs piled on the lower shelf and two stacks of VHS tapes on the upper one. I picked up the top one: "Orlando-Bowman." A wedding, of course.

"Couldn't sleep?"

I gasped and fell back into the swivel chair.

Nathan was leaning against the office doorway in his boxers. When he turned to face me, I saw he was holding Peaches gently on his arm. She was slithering toward his palm. I shrieked in surprise.

"It's okay," Nathan said, stepping closer to me and taking the tape with his free hand. "She doesn't bite."

"Uh-huh." I rolled my chair backward a couple of inches, knocking into Nathan's desk.

"What were you watching?" he asked softly.

I wasn't sure what he'd seen.

"*Tootsie*. Sometimes it's loaded up on YouTube. Or at least clips of it. I was watching clips of it on your computer." I could hear myself babbling, but I couldn't seem to stop. "When I was in high school, it was one of the few movies we had on tape. My dad taped it off the TV. So whenever I was desperate to watch something to cheer me up, like in the middle of the night when nothing much was on, I'd pop that in. We didn't have cable or anything."

Peaches dipped her head under Nathan's wrist, then changed directions, slowly moving back up his forearm.

"I guess you didn't have cable growing up either. Or a VCR for that matter?"

"No." Nathan frowned. "Well, not exactly. The commune did have a VCR and a TV, actually. We would watch Hindi devotional dramas sometimes."

"Oh," I said, getting up.

"So you'd watch *Tootsie*," he prompted. "When you were a kid."

"Yeah. When I couldn't sleep. Do you know who Dustin Hoffman is?"

Dustin. It must've been this name that had made me think to use this old habit as my brilliant cover story.

"Yes," said Nathan.

"Well, in *Tootsie* he plays an actor who's desperate for work. He dresses like a woman. It's really funny."

"I've seen the movie," Nathan whispered.

"Oh."

"That's really what you were doing in here?"

He waved his arm in the direction of his computer. I was terrified he'd fling Peaches at me.

"Yeah," I said. "Or I was about to."

Nathan sank into his chair. I inched out of Peaches' striking distance. Nathan moved the chair gently back and forth with his feet, avoiding my eyes for a few moments.

"My therapist says I'm destructively trusting," he said.

"My therapist says I'm desperately charming," I replied.

"Really?" Nathan looked up at me.

"No," I admitted. "I don't have a therapist."

He sighed and shook his head.

"I mean, I wish I had one. I'd probably have one if they were free."

"So you do this—you watch *Tootsie*—when you need comforting?"

"Yes," I said. This part was actually true.

"You need comforting for something?" Peaches' tongue flickered out, and I jumped.

"Just . . . I mean . . . not sleeping."

Nathan nodded and then looked at Peaches for a few moments. She began to curl up on his palm.

"That's why they call them ball pythons," Nathan said. "Because they tighten up into a ball."

"Don't all snakes?"

He didn't answer.

"Some people have trouble trying to sleep in a bed that's not their own," he said after a moment.

"Th-that might be it," I stammered. "Although I didn't have trouble last time."

"No," Nathan said. He bit his lip and took a deep breath. "But now you do."

I didn't reply.

"Now you have trouble," he said.

"Uh-huh."

"Maybe that's the solution. Maybe you need to get back to your own bed. If you're gonna lie to me."

Peaches flickered her tongue in agreement. To escape her

blood orange stare, I went to the bedroom and gathered my shoulder bag and phone. I didn't say another word. Nathan walked me through the living room and opened the front door for me.

"Bye," I said.

"Good-bye, Theresa," he whispered, and closed the door.

Boober was awake when I got home. I was too distraught to give him any real attention, so I opened a can of Iams.

"Why did I walk out of that house?" I asked him. He yipped for his food. I scooped the contents of the entire can into a dish and slammed it down on the floor. "What was I afraid of?"

Boober ignored me and began chowing down. Wayne waddled in, so I opened another can. As I set down another dish, Rolf came in to give me a look of noncommittal disgust, then leaped onto the top of the refrigerator.

"Maybe that was all the footage she had on his computer anyway," I said, trying to reassure myself. "Probably she stored the bulk of it only on her own laptop, which is probably with either her family or the police, so . . ."

Not a reassuring thought after all. I stared at the dog-food spoon, tempted to stab my eyes out with it. I hated myself for walking away from Nathan without being sure I'd seen everything I could. Or at least figured out how to e-mail the Dustin footage to myself. How hard could that have been?

But then what did that footage mean, exactly? Was it very significant?

It felt to me as if Dustin was going to say he'd had some part in his father's death. Certainly such an admission would be of great consequence to Dustin and perhaps other members of his family. But what of Donald Wallace? Would Donald Wallace really care about any of this? Even if this was a big bombshell with regard to the Halliday case, it wasn't necessarily Wallace's fault that the authorities had never gotten the truth out of that family.

Was *this* the special footage Kim had bragged to Janice Obermeier about having? Or some other, additional footage of Dustin explaining himself further? Or was it the elusive footage from Colleen Shipley?

I wanted to talk it through with someone. Zach was of course out of the question at this hour—nor did I wish to elucidate to him how I'd worked my way into Nathan's home and life. Tish was a possibility, but I'd have to explain too much. Plus, Penelope was a terrible sleeper, Tish was always telling me. If I woke her with the phone, Tish would likely be up with her for hours.

Jeff, I decided. I'd discuss it with Jeff. He was going to be out first thing in the morning. Tomorrow, after my parents were assured he was okay, we'd have the luxury of a private conversation. And I'd have things to tell him. I wished I had more, but at least I had more leads now than the day they hauled him off.

"He'll be home tomorrow," I told Rolf, who didn't acknowledge the good news.

I said it again to Boober, who looked up from his food and licked his lips.

"Good boy," I said. "I'll bring you with me. He'll need cheering up."

The picture of Boober licking Jeff's face as he emerged from the county jail filled me with warmth. I took a deep breath. I made a cup of tea and burned an Evening Hearth candle while I drank it. I went to bed.

Friday, October 25

My father is the one who went in and actually bailed Jeff out. Though my mother and Ned provided more of the cash, likely she considered it a dad thing—like buying a fishing pole or a first razor. Mom and I waited in the county jail parking lot—fenced in outside the brick administrative building.

As I let Boober sniff around the cyclone fence, my mother followed us, clutching her yellow leather handbag to her chest for warmth. Once again she was wearing a breezy little cotton dress beneath her fleece jacket.

"I wish you hadn't brought Boober," she said. "I'd hoped we could all take your brother out for a bite somewhere."

"I want to cheer Jeff up," I explained. "He loves Boober. You three can go if Jeff is feeling up to it, and I'll catch up with you guys later."

"When's the last time you were at work, Theresa?"

"Whitlock gave me some unpaid time off this week," I said. "But I'll be going back in on Monday."

"Good," Mom said. "It's important to maintain some sense of normalcy."

"Important for who?" I asked.

"I don't *know*. That's what they say, isn't it? Have you been working on your thesis?"

I was surprised she brought it up, but I obliged with an answer. "Not since Jeff was arrested, no."

Boober barked. My mother sighed and fiddled with the hair around her ears. "What's taking so long? I hope to God there's not some holdup."

"Legally, I don't think anything else can get in the way."

Boober began sniffing Mom's beige pumps. We both watched him till my brother and father came around the corner of the building. Jeff was sporting a gleaming white Festival Cruises T-shirt my dad had apparently just given him, along with a patchy starter beard and a painfully strained smile.

"There you are!" Mom cried, rushing to Jeff and embracing him.

When she let go, I picked up Boober so I could thrust him into Jeff's arms.

"Lick his face," I muttered into Boober's ear. "Be a good wiener. Keep it light."

As I approached Jeff, Boober let out an unaccustomed snarl. Maybe he didn't recognize Jeff with so much facial hair. Or maybe he could smell the nasty jail aura on him. I gave Boober a quick bite on the very edge of his ear.

"Theresa, *what* are you *doing*?" my mother cried.

"She's bringing Boober back to himself," Jeff mumbled.

As he said it, I heard a *bzzzz . . . click*.

All four of us looked toward the noise. I realized Boober had already been looking in that direction.

Another *bzzzz . . . click*.

A young woman was stepping toward us, holding a digital camera. She had beautiful big eyes, long brown hair, an elegant neck, and large, eager front teeth.

"Jeff?" she said. "Jeff, I'm with the *Courier*. Can you talk for a minute?"

"Did you just take our picture?" Dad asked.

"Yes, sir. Would you like to make a statement?"

"No thank you, dear," Dad said, unlocking his car door.

"I think she's talking to me," Jeff said. "No, I wouldn't. Theresa, let's go. I'll ride in your car."

"But where are we going?" my mother asked. "We wanted to take you somewhere nice. Shall we all meet up at that new Indian place?"

"Can you open your door, Theresa?" Jeff asked, and then he took Boober from my arms.

I did what he asked.

"We'll talk about it at Theresa's," Jeff said, getting into the car with Boober. I was relieved to see that Boober had calmed down. Clearly it wasn't Jeff that had set him off. It was the girl with the camera—who was now staring at me.

"Are you Jeff's sister?" she asked.

I got into the car without answering.

"Get me out of here," my brother said.

Boober clawed at Jeff's sweater, then licked his hairy chin. I started the car.

We convinced my mother that takeout was a better idea. She was happy with a mild-spiced chicken tikka masala and garlic naan. Jeff got only a dal, claiming he needed to "detox" off strange meats. My father ordered a goat dish and bragged about eating alligator on one of his cruises. Sensing my brother's exhaustion, my parents were gone within an hour.

Once they'd taken off, I filled Jeff in on everything I'd discovered over the past few days.

"But how did you get Nathan to show you all that stuff?" Jeff wanted to know, as I'd glossed over that part.

"Oh, I kinda cozied up to him." I tried to look busy petting Sylvestress.

Jeff nodded in reply but didn't comment.

"So what's your current theory, then?" he asked.

"Well, I was thinking that someone might have wanted to silence Kim about whatever was in those old tapes—the ones from Colleen Shipley. But then I saw this thing with Dustin. Now I'm not so sure. Either way I think maybe Kim really *did* have something on Donald Wallace. Or got herself into trouble trying to find something. I want to check in with her roommate and see if she knows anything about the VHS tapes. I'm gonna start there. Then I was thinking I'd go looking for Dustin. Starting with the Shaw's in Marist Park."

Jeff shrugged. "Marist Park's an hour's drive. You want company?"

Before I could answer, I felt my cell phone buzz. It was a text from Zach: DO U CARE THAT WALLACE IS @ SALLY'S RIGHT NOW?! STUDENT JUST TOLD ME. IMPROMPTU CAMPAIGN STOP, I GUESS.

"Sounds good," I said to Jeff. "I'll probably go tomorrow. Listen, I've got to run a little errand right now. Can you come back for dinner tonight?"

Jeff looked disappointed but not surprised. I told him I wouldn't be more than an hour.

Sally's is College Street's answer to the Donut Dip. They sell coffee and overpriced desserts, but students go mostly for the free Wi-Fi, occupying tables for hours on end. I hadn't been there in years, though, as the place started to make me feel old after I hit thirty.

As I drove there, I decided it wasn't important, for now, that I didn't have Colleen Shipley's footage. What I wanted to find out was what Donald Wallace's reaction would be if he *thought* someone had it.

Sally's was packed, but I wasn't sure if Donald Wallace was the draw. A sign in the window said HALF-PRICE CHEESECAKE BITES! It was crowded enough, in any case, that one didn't need to buy anything to justify one's presence. A fair number of people were just standing around listening to Donald Wallace hold court about his support of an increase in federal college aid.

I moved closer to him as he spoke.

His voice surprised me. It was low and confident but also had an eager, breathless quality that didn't match his fairly stodgy physical presence. His lipless mouth twisted and jerked dramatically as he spoke, but his eyes remained still and expressionless.

"My opponent has said he'd support the Branson plan, which would cut that aid significantly," he was saying.

He said it in a singsongy, scolding sort of way. I wondered if the kids here felt a bit condescended to. There was a touch of suburban-high-school principal to Wallace. I could more easily see him pulling apart two wrestling punks in a cafeteria than addressing the U.S. Senate, but maybe I lacked imagination.

"Now, I find that quite troubling." Wallace shook his head and sucked in his nonexistent lips. "You don't kick the door closed once you walk through it yourself. That's not how the American dream works."

I heard a low snort from someone behind me—and saw a girl with black lipstick rolling her eyes over her coffee cup. Still, the line earned him a hoot from the back of the shop, followed by a smattering of applause.

As Wallace continued to speak, I watched him more than I listened. His sleeves were rolled up tight around his elbows. I suppose this was meant to look casual, but he looked really uncomfortable, as if it were cutting off the circulation in his arms. Also, someone really ought to have told him to unbutton his collar and loosen his tie.

"I'm happy to take questions," Wallace said in conclusion. "I plan to stay here a bit longer and have a piece of Sally's delicious pumpkin bread. Who knows—maybe I'll have two!"

A couple of kids—probably from the College Dems and clearly feeling obligated—laughed out loud at this painful attempt to appear relatable. Apparently Wallace thought all the Thompson kids had a folksy familiarity with the Sally's pumpkin bread. Anyone who knew anything knew that Sally's was known for their custard pie. But maybe it was weird for a politician to mention custard. Maybe it sounded too European or something.

After the girl behind the counter handed Wallace his slice of pumpkin bread, he began to move through the crowd, alternately chatting with students and taking enthusiastic hearty-man bites of his bread. As he moved in my direction, I dug in my bag till I found a receipt and a pen. I scribbled my phone number on the receipt, finishing just before he reached my corner of the room.

I folded the receipt and mashed it into my palm. As Wallace began to pass me, I extended my hand to him.

"Nice to meet you, sir," I said, shaking his hand.

"What's your name?" His smile began to shrink as he felt the paper in his hand. "Did you have a question for me?"

"I'm a friend of Kim Graber's." I could hear the tremor in my voice, but I kept going. "She gave me a copy of those tapes before she died. Call me if you want to talk about it."

The black-lipped girl gaped at me, but thankfully no one else seemed to have heard.

"Excuse me?" Wallace wrinkled his nose, squinting at me. "Kim . . . Graber?"

"Yes. From the Andrew Abbott case, remember? She gave me a copy of those tapes before she died," I repeated.

I could see this time that the information actually sank in. I thought I saw Wallace's eyes pop a little before he arranged his face into a solemn expression.

"She died?" he said.

"Yes." I held his gaze, looking for some hint of real emotion. "She was strangled."

Wallace stared back at me, his mouth still frozen into a thin, unconvincing frown. Black Lips watched us both, taking a blasé sip of coffee.

"Mr. Wallace?" A woman in a tailored navy suit tapped him on the shoulder. "This young man here has an interesting question about your stance on military spending."

"The tapes that Colleen Shipley gave her," I said softly, in case Wallace was still unmoved.

I thought I saw another eye twitch at Colleen Shipley's name.

"Mr. Wallace?" his aide said.

"I'm sorry for your loss, young lady," Wallace muttered.

I watched him turn away, keeping my eyes on the hand that had received my phone number. He slipped it into his pocket as his aide steered him off.

Donald Wallace shook hands with a bespectacled student sporting a leather messenger bag. He listened to the kid, but before he opened his mouth to answer him, he glanced back at me. Five minutes later he thanked the whole crowd for their support—and then he was gone.

On my way home, I considered whether this man I'd seen in the flesh could've killed Kim for something she was going to expose. He was on the elderly side—although he had a strong build. Or maybe he'd *had* her killed? I hadn't thought of that before, but wasn't that how these powerful men operated? On the other hand, I didn't get a distinct feeling of power from Wallace. A *wish* for power, yes. And that had just as much potential for malice, I supposed. Maybe more.

I wondered if he would call me—thinking I had whatever damning footage Kim had possibly died for. Or if he would show up at my door. It would be scary if he did. But I could think of scarier things.

Saturday, October 26

Jeff and I started out for Marist Park in the late morning, after giving my mother the satisfaction of watching Jeff scarf down a substantial diner breakfast. I decided to make a pit stop at Kim's old apartment, as I didn't want to avoid the most obvious possible place to look for those old VHS tapes: where Kim used to live. Of course, we agreed that Jeff should stay in the car and parked out of view of the apartment. I debated taking Wayne with me but ultimately left him with Jeff.

Brittany didn't seem surprised to find me at her door. She had a towel on her head and a bottle of Windex in her hand.

"Oh, hey," she said softly. "I've actually been thinking of you."

"And I of you," I answered. "You must've been shocked, too."

"It's really scary. So sad. Her poor family."

"Yeah," I agreed.

"Did you hear they arrested that Jeff guy?"

"I did, yeah."

"Do you want to come in?" Brittany asked.

I stepped inside and followed her to the couch. The room looked even cleaner than it had the other day. The hairy bean-bag chair was gone.

"I just wish I knew that things had gotten so bad." Brittany shook her head.

"What do you mean?"

"Well, you know how much he *drank*?"

I managed a shrug.

"See that there?" Brittany pointed to a dent in the wall behind the television. "Jeff did that. He came here one night stumbling drunk and threw this big glass candle at the wall."

"A large jar candle?"

At Jeff's request I'd used my half-price employee discount on a Candle Supreme—our biggest jar candle, outrageously priced at thirty-six dollars, retail. Baked Apple, Jeff had advised me, was Kim's favorite.

"Yeah. Did Kim tell you about that?"

"What scent was it?"

"I don't know." Brittany looked puzzled. "It was red."

"What did he say when he did it?"

"Well, first he said, 'I got that candle you wanted.'"

"Okay."

Brittany lowered her voice. "And then he's like, 'Maybe you can cover up the skank smell in here.'"

"Oh."

"He was pissed about her calling Kyle and stuff, I guess. But Jesus. I didn't think he had it in him."

"What happened after he threw the candle?" I asked.

"He and Kim fought for a little while. Then he threw up and passed out on our couch. I mean, it would be one thing if he was our age. But Jeff's like *middle-aged*. And acting like *that*? I should've known then that there was something seriously wrong with him. I should've said something. But it wasn't my business, you know? I just chalked it up to Kim's bad taste."

I glanced away from Brittany and took a breath. "Did that kind of thing happen often with him?"

"No. But I know he and Kim drank a lot together."

"But that was the only time you saw him be . . . like, physical."

"Yeah. Yeah, I guess. Mostly he seemed like a loser to me. Not like a *killer*. But isn't that the sort of thing people usually say when this stuff happens?"

"Uh . . . abso*lute*ly." My voice cracked. I hurried to add, "Listen, I wanted to ask you about something specific."

"Yeah?"

"Did Kim have any VHS tapes that you know of? Did you see anything like that around?"

"Huh. You know, she asked me if I had a VCR or I knew anyone with one. But I didn't see any actual tapes."

"You think there might be some in her room?"

"Maybe. The police were here right after she died, of course."

"So it's possible they took them, if she had any."

"Possible. It didn't look to me like they took much. They took her computer, but they left her clothes and some other stuff. Her family didn't take everything yet. But maybe they forgot. I don't know. Probably it's hard."

"Do you mind if I take a peek into her room?"

"I guess." Brittany shrugged. "What's the deal about these VHS tapes anyway?"

"Kim was working on a little video project. She and some other friends of mine want to complete it for her. A sort of tribute."

"Video project? Like of Wayne?"

"Yeah. It was like a compilation of all of her pets. That's why the old VHS."

"Oh. That's . . . uh, sweet of you."

She thought I was lame. But that was good. Lame is harmless. Lame is trustworthy. Lame is clean. It's easy to trust lame. And damned if she didn't just lead me right into Kim's room after that.

It was pretty spare—all that was left of Kim was a queen-size bed and a large bureau painted chartreuse.

"See, her family didn't have a truck for the big things," Brittany explained. "They just put everything in plastic bags. It feels weird, though, to still have a little bit of her furniture here."

I opened one of the green drawers. It was empty. "Can I look in the closet?"

"Sure."

I did. Also empty.

"Sorry. I didn't realize they took *everything*. I never actually looked. Didn't feel right."

I started out of the bedroom. "It's okay."

"You know, I really *was* thinking of you just yesterday," Brittany said quietly.

"Of me?"

"Yeah. 'Cuz I remember you asking about Kim mentioning Donald Wallace, and I remember thinking how weird that was."

"Uh-huh."

"Hold on a sec," Brittany said, then disappeared into her bedroom for a moment. When she returned, she handed me a folded-up piece of paper.

I unfolded it—another printout about the Hallidays. The headline read SUSAN AND TODD HALLIDAY: "A CASE OF OPPOSITES ATTRACT."

"I found this in our magazine basket in the bathroom a few days ago. I guess Kim had shoved it in there. I don't know when. But I thought of you because it has Donald Wallace in it. Near the end."

"Thanks," I said. "I . . . uh . . . know she was interested in this case."

"Seems interesting." Brittany shrugged. "I read it through when I found it. It's kind of a crappy article. And I don't know why Kim cared."

I agreed, thanked her, and returned to my car.

"Wayne, she didn't even ask about you," I said as I opened the door.

"Shhh," Jeff said, and pointed to Wayne sleeping in the back-seat.

I didn't look at Jeff. Instead I read the article.

May 3, 2005
Cranford Reminder
Susan and Todd Halliday: "A Case of Opposites Attract"

By Ruthie Benoit, Our Towns columnist

CRANFORD, MASS.—As the prosecution continues to lay out its case on Court TV, locals are asking themselves how this could ever have happened to the Hallidays, such a well-known and well-liked Cranford family. Still others of their neighbors and friends are admitting that they saw some subtle signs of tension in the family for the past couple of years.

Susan and Todd Halliday have lived in Cranford all their adult lives. Sweethearts in their early twenties, they married when Susan became pregnant with their elder son, Trenton. Dustin followed two years later.

"They were a case of opposites attract," says Todd's childhood friend and longtime Cranford resident Sam Mc-Bride. "At least in the beginning. Susan liked fashion, parties, and romantic comedies. Todd liked fishing, working hard, bowling league, and going to church."

Susan was the spender, according to many friends, and Todd was the saver.

"There was definitely some disagreement about how those boys should be raised," says McBride. "Todd didn't grow up with much. He didn't think the kids needed hundreds of dollars' worth of toys on Christmas and birthdays, and all sorts of phones and computers in between. He truly felt that that sort of thing screwed up kids' values, made them into unhappy adults."

Marybeth Blunt, a friend of Susan's, explains the Hallidays' conflict differently: "Susan didn't spoil the kids. She just wanted to make sure they had the same advantages as the kids around them. She thought Todd was too severe. She wanted to find the right balance."

For seven years they lived in a modest house on Wagon Ridge. Most people on the street knew them as a hardworking dad and good-looking mom with two smiling, rambunctious boys.

On Tuesday of this week, at a Wagon Ridge/Yardley Street Neighborhood Watch meeting, several of the Hallidays' neighbors chimed in on the subject.

"I don't usually believe in curses," remarked Ron Bishop of Yardley Street. "But it did start to feel, around the time of the thunderstorm last fall, like the Hallidays were cursed."

"They had a terrible string of bad luck," agrees neighbor Krista Hammerbacher. "Starting when Todd's office closed. He found a part-time job to keep the household afloat, but it was an hour away, and I think he was exhausted from all the driving. Then there was the damage their house had from that thunderstorm in September. Then the fire in November. And their dog died in that fire, poor thing. Not to mention the kids were traumatized because Todd barely made it out. They ended up having to stay at Todd's sister's place for a few months while their place was being fixed up. I don't think it's been a positive time for them, being displaced from their home like that. Having to stay crammed in at someone else's place. When they already weren't getting along anyhow."

Other friends cite the time at Todd's sister's as a source of strife.

"Dustin was having serious difficulties in school," explains Donna Hewitt, a coworker of Susan's. "Susan believed that it was because he felt unsettled in her sister-in-law's home. They argued a great deal about money—about renting a place while their house was being fixed. Todd refused."

A month before Todd's death, the family moved back into their Wagon Ridge home. But while their house was fixed, Blunt says, the damage to their relationship was now quite serious.

As District Attorney Donald Wallace has made much of in court this week, Susan Halliday began a romantic relationship with her coworker at the DMV.

"I don't believe that Susan was by nature a cheating sort," Blunt claims. "I think the home situation with her in-laws made her feel the need for some kind of escape. It's a shame what that prosecutor is saying about her. She needed an escape. She needed someone who would love her and not criticize her all the time. That doesn't mean she was a murderer."

"Susan is one of the kindest women I know," agrees friend and neighbor Peggy Straight. "Very devoted to her sons. She'd do anything for them. She made a mistake. But it's a mistake that, under those conditions, I can see a lot of people making. I hope the jury will be smart enough not to judge her based on that mistake.

"And their home was unoccupied for so long I believe that it was a likely target for a home invasion. I don't think Susan's story is so far-fetched, given those circumstances.

"These are people who've had some terrible luck in the past year. That's how these things happen, isn't it? Tragedies lead to more tragedies."

At the bottom of the last page, Kim had scribbled:

I know what it's like to be swallowed whole by a story. I know how hard it is to uncurl yourself from its warm, wet stomach, climb up and out of its vile throat, and feel the cold truth. You think I don't know?

"What's that?" Jeff asked.

"Just another article about Dustin's parents," I said, handing the paper to him. "From a local paper."

Jeff read it as I pulled out of Barton Village. I expected him to comment on Kim's note at the bottom, but he simply re-folded the article and placed it on the console between us.

"Did you give Kim that candle I got for you?" I asked once I was on the highway. "The big Baked Apple one?"

Jeff fiddled with my iPod. "Yeah."

"Did she ever burn it?"

"Yeah, I think so." Jeff looked up, frowning. "Why?"

"Oh, it just smelled pretty nutmeggy in there. I guess her roommate likes it."

"I guess." Jeff settled on some old Flaming Lips.

"So, Jeff," I said.

"So, Theresa."

"Things were getting tense between you and Kim a couple of weeks before she died?"

"Yeah." Jeff gazed out the window. "They were."

"Have you told Gary Norris everything about it that he should know?"

"Haven't we already been over this?"

I stared ahead at the highway "I don't know. Have we, for real?"

"For real?" Jeff repeated.

I passed a sluggish blue Ford.

"I mean, how bad did it get?" I asked. "What was the worst thing?"

"The worst thing was me following her up to Rowington and sleeping in my car. I've told you that."

"What about when you guys were drinking together?"

"I did go overboard occasionally. So did she. I blacked out a couple of times. I'm told we fought pretty bad once or twice when I was blackout drunk. Why, was Kim's roommate talking about me?"

"Fought pretty bad? Like what?"

"Like Kim told me I kept calling her roommate Dolly Pumpkin. Like 'Get out of my way, Dolly Pumpkin.' 'Got any soda or chips, Dolly Pumpkin?' I feel kind of bad about that."

Oddly, the name did seem to fit Brittany. What didn't fit was *Jeff* saying it to her face. That was a nastier Jeff from the one I knew. What he was trying to tell me, it seemed, was that he was a mean drunk. I'd never seen it—but we hadn't ever done much hard stuff together. Only beer and wine with takeout.

"And you don't remember it?" I asked.

"No. Haven't you gotten blackout drunk before?"

"Is that what they call it? Is that a thing? 'Blackout drunk'?"

"It's when you don't remember—"

"Of course I know *that*. I just never heard it said like that before."

"Well, they say it's hereditary. Some people are more apt to black out when they drink too fast than others. I mean, I learned that online. When I looked it up after the first time it happened. I had a lot of time on my hands, you know?"

I shrugged. "I had some benders in college. But I always remembered everything, pretty much. I never liked doing shots, and it's hard to drink beer fast enough to black out, I think. And I don't remember you ever drinking that much either. When we were that age. Even when everyone else was."

"That was a long time ago," Jeff said.

I was behind a semi truck now, and I felt too depressed to pass it. I stared at its HOW'S MY DRIVING? sign as Jeff continued.

"You don't know what it's like to spend all day by yourself," he said. "Going back and forth between watching the news and trying to find little Band-Aids for your latest past-due bill or your broken laptop. Find something you can sell on Amazon or eBay. If you can borrow someone's computer to do it on. Or trying to find out if one of your credit cards has a little bit of credit left on it. You don't know what it's like, I don't think, to be drowning in that stuff so much that you can't focus long enough on the big picture to get out of it."

"Not financially, no," I admitted. "But I've had other situations where I felt like I was drowning."

Jeff turned away from me. "Drowning in your own self-made academic situation isn't the same thing."

My fingers tightened over the steering wheel. "Okay."

"But sure. You and I are used to disappointment. Anyway, when Kim came along, there was suddenly, weirdly, a part of my life that *wasn't* about drowning. Every night wasn't some long abyss. Suddenly. And for a few months. But when I realized she was getting tired of me—when I realized that all it had ever been was to pass the time when she wasn't with Kyle, to maybe even get Kyle's attention—I couldn't stand it. I could've dealt with the hole that was in my life if she hadn't come and fixed it. Before she came and fixed it, it was just a ragged hole, wearing itself bigger at the edges. But slowly. Then she came and filled it. And when it looked like I was losing her, it wasn't slow and natural anymore. It was a giant black hole. Torn wide open. Not only at night anymore. All the time. *All* the time. Because I'd made a mistake. I'd let myself think things were getting better for me. I was stupid."

I held my breath and slowed the car down, realizing I'd been tailing the semi too close. I wasn't sure where Jeff was going with this.

"It wasn't Kim's fault. Kim was involved in her own crazy shit, whatever that was. But for a little while, I let myself think she'd *made* the black hole. And that it would close up if I could keep her."

HOW'S MY DRIVING? HOW'S MY DRIVING? HOW'S MY DRIVING? I had to focus on keeping that sign at a safe distance, because Jeff's words had begun to weigh on my body, drawing down my shoulders and straining my foot on the gas.

"So what are you telling me?" I gripped the wheel so hard my knuckles hurt.

"I'm answering your question. I'm telling you why I started drinking so much. Which is what I thought you were asking. Right?"

Was it? My mind felt scrambled. I took a moment to find the words with which to form a reply.

"Right. How much did you drink the night you followed Kim to Rowington?"

"I can't really remember. I drank Jack and ginger ale in the car when I got to the hotel. I felt like I needed a little something to build up the courage to confront her and whoever she was meeting there. I was sure it would be Kyle. But no one came."

"And you kept drinking."

"Till I fell asleep," Jeff admitted.

"How long were you asleep?"

"I don't know. It was daylight when I first woke up."

"You told me it was like five."

"I'm not sure, Theresa." Jeff took off his seat belt and reached into the backseat to pet the sleeping Wayne.

"You probably should try not to drink too much while you're out on bail," I offered.

Jeff turned back to me. "You're funny, Theresa."

"Funny?" I repeated. How did he go from "try not to drink too much" to "funny"?

"You're funny if you think drinking is the main temptation now. My main problem now."

I finally passed the truck. In front of it, there was a clear expanse of highway without any other cars. Everyone who was in a hurry had passed us by.

I started thinking about Jeff "preparing" my dad for the possibility that the DNA under Kim's fingernails would be his. It occurred to me that he was perhaps preparing me, too. Maybe something had happened between him and Kim that night— something he was now trying to distance himself from by reminding me that alcohol was in the mix. Maybe he thought this would make it easier on me somehow. Or easier on himself.

"There's nothing more depressing than a New England highway this time of year," I said, to stop this train of thought.

"Nothing?" Jeff replied dully. He clearly didn't want a response.

Because, I thought, you could still remember the vibrant color that was there just a few weeks before. And you asked yourself, *Where the hell was I for that? How come I didn't swallow it, make it a part of myself, somehow save that color for now? And now how will I survive till spring?*

It wasn't merely about surviving till spring this year, though. This spring might be terrifying. Spring could bring Jeff's trial, even Jeff's conviction. Spring might bring beautiful mornings full of blue skies and crocuses that Jeff would never get to see. And spring might become for Jeff something pat and plastic—like a candle description, supplied to him by his sister during Saturday visiting hours.

Once we were parked at Shaw's, I asked Jeff if he wanted any groceries.

"I'll look and feel a lot less conspicuous if I actually have something to buy," I explained.

"Twix," Jeff said. "I was craving one the other day in the clink. And get Detective Dog here some Milk Bones or something. Now, remind me who this Troy kid is?"

"A friend of Dustin Halliday's," I said.

Jeff responded with a lethargic nod. I tried not to let his boredom bother me.

Inside, I asked for Troy Richardson at Customer Service. The cool, slick-haired girl behind the counter seemed unsurprised by the question and led me to a tall young man with dreadlocks.

"Here he is," she said. "Mr. Troy. Best damn bagger in the business."

Troy rolled his eyes at the girl.

"Can I help you, ma'am?" he asked, after she had walked away.

"My name's Margery Lipinski. I'm a friend of your old teacher, Sharon Silverstein."

"Oh. Ms. S? How's she doing?"

"Pretty good. Um. We both became concerned about Dustin Halliday recently, and I was wondering if you could help."

"Uh-huh. Well, he used to live with me. I'm concerned about him, too."

"So he doesn't live with you anymore?"

"No. Not for a couple of weeks." He turned to the customer whose groceries he'd been packing and said, "There are your eggs, sir."

"Do you know where he went?" I asked.

Troy started packing his next customer's endless tins of cat food. "He's staying with his brother."

His brother. The brother who'd told me just a few days ago he hadn't heard from Dustin in months?

"Trenton?" I said.

Troy looked up, apparently surprised I was so well informed as to know Dustin's brother's name. "Yeah," he said. "How did you say you know Dustin?"

Either Troy or Trenton was lying.

"It's complicated," I said, then added my own lie to the mix: "I was his teacher at one point, too."

Troy pushed a piece of hair out of his eyes. "I don't remember you."

"His teacher from a long time ago. Before he got in trouble. We go back a while."

Troy frowned. "Oh. Um, why don't we talk outside for a second?"

I agreed and followed him out of the store's sliding glass doors. Once we were outside, Troy leaned against a wall of shopping carts.

"Dustin's not in great shape, Ms. . . . ?"

"Lipinski."

"Ms. Lipinski. He's been kinda . . . uh, crashing and burning for a few weeks now. He got beat up and mugged a couple of weeks ago, outside that Farley's bar. Know the place?"

I nodded, just to make things easier.

"Then, a few days ago, he took a bunch of some kind of Oxy pills or something. Me and the guys finally called his brother and asked him to help us. He was real upset when this new friend of his died, this girl . . ."

"Kim?" I offered.

"Yeah. Kim." Troy rubbed his arms for warmth. He had only a thin sweater beneath his bagger smock. "So you know about her?"

"Yes. He told me a little about her. Did you ever meet her?"

"She came to the house a couple times. I don't know if they were, like, together or anything, though. She wanted to meet him 'cuz she read about him in that juvie book. His first groupie. You know about that book?"

"Yeah, I do. So what do you know about Kim?"

Troy looked at the pavement. "I didn't really like her, I've got to admit. I know I shouldn't say that now, but . . . I didn't like how Dustin was being with her."

"How's that?"

"I don't know how well you know Dustin, how well you know his whole story. He really needs to forget all that shit that happened with his parents and move on. But any excuse he had to dwell on that story, that night, he'd take it. And that Kim, she was quite an excuse. He said she was videotaping him talking about it or some shit like that? Like she was gonna get him all over the Internet talking about how wrong they all had it? Like the first fifteen minutes he got weren't painful enough? Or the second, with that stupid book? He wanted fifteen *more*?"

A young man who'd been corralling shopping carts came up and slammed a bunch of them into the collection already behind me. He and Troy exchanged private little waves. Kids that age always make me self-conscious, harking back to my Comp-teaching days. I always felt like they were secretly laughing at me—for what I don't know.

"So you didn't like Kim because she was encouraging him to dwell on the past?" I asked once the cart kid had drifted back into the parking lot.

Troy shrugged. "Listen. Normally it would be none of my business, how much someone wants to feel sorry for themselves over some trauma like that. But that girl doesn't understand that with Dustin, asking him about his parents is like creating a monster. A monster no one else around him can stand."

"Can you explain that a little bit? Give an example?"

"An example." Troy rubbed his hands together, then shoved them into the front pouch of his smock. "Well . . . that shit about the intruders the night his mother shot his father? They're black and white one day, two black dudes another, two white ones another. Once it was a Hispanic guy and an Asian. I wouldn't be surprised if someday it was a man in a chef's hat and an Indian chief. Seriously."

"So you're a good friend of his—and you don't believe his story about those intruders?"

"It's *because* I'm a good friend of his that I don't believe it. Anyone who knows him well doesn't believe it."

I tried not to look too perplexed by this statement. "Then do you ever ask him what happened? So he can talk about it for real?"

"He doesn't want to talk about it for real." Troy rubbed his nose and sniffled, regarding me skeptically. "I don't know how well you know him if you don't know that."

I did my best to maintain an even, teacherly composure and redirect. "Well . . . what about in the book—did you read the book he was in?"

"Parts of it." Troy shrugged again. "Dustin had it. Although I don't know if he read it himself. He just liked that his name was in it. He kind of likes . . . drama, don't you think?"

"Sometimes, yes. I've noticed that. So in the book, when he said that there's only one person he told everything about that night?"

"I don't remember that part too well," Troy said. "Was that part of that whole thing about his little white friend?"

"Yes."

Troy shook his head. "Yeah, that was bullshit. Dustin made out like that kid was his only friend 'cuz there weren't many white kids. Just drama, like I said. I was pretty close to Dustin, and I don't even remember that kid."

"Were you and Dustin in detention at exactly the same time?"

"No." He lowered his voice. I realized he probably didn't want me talking too loudly about that time of his life. "He was there much longer than me, that's true."

"Were you interviewed for the book at all?"

"No. That writer asked me, but I said no. It didn't interest me. But that sure as hell interested Dustin. A chance to get back in the spotlight."

"It seems like you're pretty frustrated with him."

"Look. I'm not trying to talk bad about him. He's the nicest guy when he can, you know, focus on the right things. That's why I took a chance and suggested he try living with me. I wouldn't have done that if I didn't think he could pull himself together."

"Okay," I said.

Troy noticed my tentative response. Probably a blank look had crossed my face as I struggled to come up with another question.

"I really ought to get back to work," he said.

"Of course," I said. "But before you go . . . do you have any idea where Trenton Halliday lives?"

Troy didn't have the house number, but he'd said it was the only light blue house, he was pretty sure, on Hammond Avenue. Hammond was crowded full of big houses with tiny yards, but Troy had been right about there being only one painted pale blue. My view of the front porch was almost entirely obscured by an overgrown hedge.

"Unfortunately, that'll keep you from being able to see me," I said to Jeff. "In case there's any trouble."

"Are you expecting any trouble?" asked Jeff, leaning into a kiss from Wayne, who was sitting on his lap in the passenger seat.

"Should I bring Wayne with me, you think?"

"If it's for personal protection, I'd say no. Wayne's not great in a crisis. If it's to make you look eccentric and nonthreatening, go for it. As long as you accept that that can backfire."

I looked at Wayne, who had his front paws mushed into Jeff's lap. He pawed Jeff's chest, digging for more biscuits. Jeff had already given him three in the fifteen-minute trip from Shaw's.

"He has a weight problem, remember," I said.

"This is a special occasion," Jeff said. "But okay. I'll make him work for the next one."

"I'll go by myself," I mumbled, and got out of the car.

There were three different doorbells on the porch, but they were marked with weather-faded cardboard labels. None of them was fully legible, but I could see that the second-floor card ended with DAY. I pressed it resolutely, impressed with my own sleuthing.

I deflated a bit, however, when a young woman answered the door. She was unhealthily bronzed but still ridiculously pretty and wearing a black-and-white polka-dotted head wrap.

"Hi there," I said. "Is Dustin here?"

The girl squinted at me. "You want . . . *Dustin?*"

"Who's that?" a man's voice demanded from behind the door.

"Oh," I said cheerily. "Is that him?"

"Um. No. It's—"

The door swung open, and a burly guy with thick glasses appeared. He nudged the young woman aside with his elbow, stepped onto the porch, and closed the door behind him.

"How can I help you?" he asked.

"I was told Dustin was staying here. Are you Trenton?"

"Who told you that?"

"His friend Troy."

"Well, he's not here, I'm afraid. Who are you?"

"My name's Margery. I believe we exchanged e-mails and a text."

"Oh. Yes." Trenton touched his hand to his chin. He had one of those circle beards, where the mustache meets the beard and forms a trim frame around the mouth.

"So he's not here?" I said, trying to tame the skepticism in my voice.

"No. I haven't seen him in several months. Like I said in my text."

I nodded slowly, uncertain where to go from here. I didn't think Troy would have much reason to lie to me, but I wasn't sure how to call Trenton's bluff.

"I'm sorry I can't help you," Trenton added. He turned and put his hand on the doorknob. "We were just getting ready to go out for some dinner. I'm sorry."

"I'll let you go, then," I said reluctantly.

"Bye now," he said, and entered the house.

Back in my car, I stared up at the house. "Out for dinner, my ass," I said. "I bet if we sat here for an hour, nobody would come out."

"But since we're not gonna sit here for an hour," Jeff mumbled, "I guess we'll never know."

"I think he's lying to me, though."

"Why would he lie to you?" Jeff asked.

"Because he doesn't want me to talk to his brother." I glanced up at the windows, wondering if anyone was looking back at me from behind the blinds.

"Why not, do you think?"

"I don't know. But I'll bet Dustin's in there."

"Doing *what*, Theresa?" Jeff sounded impatient.

"Hiding, probably."

Jeff pulled a biscuit out of the Milk Bone box and snapped a piece off with his teeth. "The pink tastes the same as the brown," he said.

I sighed. "I know."

Maybe he didn't remember, but we'd test-tasted all the flavors back in the Jedi days.

"I want to go home, Theresa."

Said the man who'd spent four nights in jail. I had to honor the request.

I wanted to ask him why he had so little faith in my investigation. But it was easier to simply hit the ignition button and drive him on home.

Once we got on the highway, Jeff opened the second Twix package and offered me one. I shook my head. I'd bought him four packs altogether, in hopes it would help him bulk up.

"I think you would be a good mom," he said after he'd gobbled down the candy. "If you ever wanted to be one."

"Why are you saying this?"

"Because of this candy. I mean, because you know how to take care of people, when you're interested enough."

"Question is, would I be interested enough in a kid? I'd hate to get one and then discover that I wasn't."

"And because I know what happened with you and Brendan," Jeff added.

I stayed quiet. Brendan—and all the things that had come with him—felt like the distant past now. Almost everything that came before this day, this trip with Jeff—Jeff's eerie talk about "blackout drunk"—felt insignificant. How gentle—how folksy, even—my difficulties had been up till the last few hours.

"I saw Tish at Marshall's, back then. I think I was buying expired peanut brittle or something. She was all excited, though.

Because she was buying this pair of pajamas with duckies on them. Two pairs. Same pajamas."

"Oh," I said after a moment. I wished Jeff had said something back then, when it would've mattered, or not at all.

"I said, 'Oh my God, Tish—twins?' And she looked at me like I was crazy. Like it should be obvious why she was buying two."

I shook my head. "It didn't occur to her that not everybody makes an announcement the day they pee on a stick."

"Why didn't you tell her not to tell, then?" Jeff asked.

"I *did*. But she's so close with her family, I think she must not have realized that I wouldn't have— I mean, I'm not saying that we're not . . . uh . . . close . . . but . . ."

"I'm not asking for an explanation. I just wanted to say that I thought you'd be a good—"

"You don't need to say anything else."

"I mean, just look how good you are with Boober and the cats."

"I mean, you *really* don't need to say anything else, Jeff." I hated when children and pets were discussed in relation to one another. Little depressed me more.

"Sorry. I just— With all the time I had there in the prison by myself, I started thinking about what things I needed to say to people. Like, if something happened to me. Things I wouldn't want to say through a glass partition."

"Nothing is going to happen to you," I said, wishing I sounded more confident.

Jeff put his wrappers in the grocery-store bag and tucked it into the slot on the car door.

294 • Emily Arsenault

"If I go to maximum security, something might."

Wayne chose that moment to begin whimpering for more Milk Bones. The sound was so pathetic that I felt the need to talk over it.

"I think people do okay if they decide to keep their heads down," I said. "Not to get into any trouble or get involved in any gangs or whatever."

Jeff snapped a Milk Bone and raised a skeptical eyebrow at me.

"Where are you getting your information from, sis? *Shaw-shank Redemption?*"

I began to tell Jeff what Zach had said, about wardens betting on prisoner fights.

"That sounds a lot like something that happened at Sing Sing," Jeff said. "Just a couple of years ago. I saw it on CNN."

"So it's maybe more common than people realize," I said.

"Yeah," Jeff said, shoving half the broken biscuit into Wayne's mouth. "Maximum-security prisons are bad motherfucking places. Now that we've established that, will you accept that I'm telling you I think you'd be a good mother? And that you should be one if you want to?"

"What? Why are we talking about this now?"

"It's not too late for you, if you really want that. You don't need to be married either. You have a house and you have a decent job. You have friends, like Tish, who'd be happy for you and who'd help you out."

Jeff handed the second half of the treat to Wayne, more gently now. More pink crumbs collected on the front seat's upholstery.

"Do you know something I don't know?" I asked.

"No. I can just see you using me as an excuse not to get on with your life if I end up in jail. I'll be your new Marge."

"Marge doesn't keep me from getting on with my life. Marge is *part* of my life."

Jeff rolled his eyes. "You're not really listening to me. I'm trying to tell you that if it doesn't work out for me, you shouldn't go to heroic efforts to try to get me out. You don't need to be like that Hilary Swank movie. You don't need to go to law school for me."

"I don't know that movie."

"Because knowing you and graduate programs . . ."

"Jeff." I passed a car on the right, then got caught behind a pickup truck. "None of this is going to happen."

"I hope not. But I'm just telling you, if it does . . ."

I got into the fast lane. "It *won't*."

"Slow down, Theresa," Jeff said gently. I glanced at the speedometer. I was going well over eighty.

"I think I might have some holes from that night," he said. "In my brain, I mean. Not enough to have done what they say, but enough not to know one hundred percent of what happened. I didn't keep track of every minute. Even every hour. And I don't know where that screwdriver came from. So how can I convince them I didn't do anything wrong?"

"You *need* to." I breathed deeply, resisting the urge to press harder on the gas pedal. "The fact that you can't account for every minute doesn't mean you deserve to go to prison for the rest of your life. *Does* it, Jeff?"

He closed his eyes. We were almost at our exit when he spoke again.

"What gets people in trouble," he said, "is when they start

convincing themselves of what they *deserve*. What do any of us really deserve anyhow?"

I didn't know what this meant and wasn't entirely sure I wished to.

"You don't deserve to go to *prison*, Jeff," I repeated, practically screaming now.

He was silent again.

"SAY SOMETHING," I demanded, revving the engine as I turned off the ramp to Thompsonville.

Jeff was back to looking out the window, ignoring Wayne, who was nudging his elbow with his moist nose.

"You want me to say something, Theresa? After I told you that I don't remember everything that happened that night, you want me to say something to reassure you?"

"I didn't say anything about reassuring."

"You didn't need to," Jeff murmured. "That's how it's always been. I'm the one with all the shit luck, but still *you* need *me* to cheer you up."

"Shit luck, Jeff? *Shit luck?*" I sounded like our mother, repeating phrases back to him like a deranged parrot.

"Take me home, Theresa."

I was out of questions and out of energy. I did as he asked and wept all the way home.

When I stepped into my kitchen, I found Sylvestress on the counter in the bread-loaf position, staring into nothingness.

"Sylvestress," I whispered, sitting next to her and scratching her lower back. "Why don't you like my brother?"

She turned to me and blinked her beautiful yellow-green

eyes but didn't offer so much as a purr. When I scratched more aggressively, she got up and left.

"That wasn't actually a question," I called after her, watching her feather-duster tail float away from me and disappear down the hall. "It was a cry for help."

I poured myself a large glass of Shiraz, but after one sip I knew I didn't really want it. All my brother's talk of "blackout drunk" had ruined me for the stuff—maybe forever.

On the television there was nothing absorbing or stupid enough to meet my distraction needs. There was little to clean, and the notion of working on Marge was a joke. Desperation began to settle in. I tried to call Nathan but got no answer. I had no idea how I'd manage to justify myself to him anyway. There was probably no getting back into his home and office anytime soon.

I stared at my phone and prayed for it to ring—with a scared and willing Donald Wallace on the other end. Each second that it didn't, my throat tightened a bit. After about ten minutes of this, I felt like I couldn't breathe.

I called Tish.

"I'm glad you called," she said. "I've been wondering how you're holding up. And how's Jeff?"

"Tish, why do you think I've been working on my Margery Kempe thing for so long?" I asked.

Tish was silent for a moment. "You really want to talk about that right now?"

"I'm your oldest friend, and this is a tough time. Why don't you just indulge me?"

"Um. Okay. Why do *you* think you have?"

"Fuck that, Tish. Did you learn that trick in marriage counseling?"

"Fine. I think you can't finish the damn thing because you're flummoxed by anyone who has faith in anything."

I'd never heard Tish say "flummoxed" before. I didn't know how to feel about her saving it to describe me.

"That's not true," I protested.

"I think you think she's silly. Amusing. For believing that God talks to her. For believing that she, a regular lady, is possibly saint material. For thinking her crying is connected to God. For believing in *anything*."

"Have you actually *read* her book?"

"Yes. Once you got me a copy of the modern-English version. Like five years ago. Because I said I was curious. You didn't think I would care enough to read it, probably. Or that I'd have the attention span. You never asked what I thought."

"And you read it?"

"About half of it. I couldn't get all the way through. That Margery is a piece of work. I liked the part where the other pilgrims on her boat, like, short-sheeted her bed or something? Am I right? Did that happen? Because they found her so annoying?"

"Let me ask you a question. Do you believe Jeff is innocent?"

Tish took an audible breath. "I believe you need to be strong for your brother," she said after a moment. "And that might require *you* to have faith in something."

"You didn't answer my question."

"Do you want me to come over, Theresa? I could bring Ben & Jerry's. My neighbor Helen is always happy to come over as long as Penelope is sleeping. She likes to watch my HBO."

"I haven't had ice cream since my divorce," I said.

It wasn't true. But it *could* be true, as far as Tish was concerned.

"Or something else you'd like to eat."

"I'm really not hungry at all these days."

This was true. In fact, I couldn't remember if I'd eaten anything after the coffee and apple I'd had this morning. Maybe I'd nibbled on some mixed nuts I had in my car.

"You still haven't answered my question," I whined.

"I'm saying I can come over, and we can talk."

"But you're trying to let me know gently that you can't say the things I need you to say. You're going to make me wait an hour and eat a pint of ice cream before you can work up the courage to say so."

Tish was silent for so long I thought we had a bad connection.

"Tish?"

"Theresa, you know what I thought was interesting about Margery Kempe?"

"Tell me five years ago."

"I thought it was interesting that she didn't have any of what she *thought* she had. She thought she was going to be a saint. She thought she was so holy and so divinely gifted. You could tell reading it that that wasn't exactly it. She was as annoying as hell, going on and on about how sinful and confused everyone else was, and how good she was because she had fantasies about being cut up into pieces and made into a stew for God's love, if memory serves . . . do I have that right?"

"Yeah," I mumbled. "She said that a few times."

"And no one was ever going to reward that with sainthood.

But she had a kind of religious hardiness to her. Nothing was going to kill her spirit. She was like a holy fucking cockroach."

"That's brilliant, Tish. I'm going to have to start my thesis all over again."

"Absolutely. Select all. Delete."

"Let me go get my laptop."

"Seriously, Theresa. I'd like to come over. It's not good for you to be by yourself right now."

"I'll be all right."

"Theresa?"

"Yes?"

"I love Jeff. You know that."

"Yeah."

"We both do."

"Yeah." I fell into a chair and closed my eyes.

"I'm here for you."

"Good-bye, Tish," I said, then threw the wineglass at my kitchen wall.

Monday, October 28

As I got out of the shower in the morning, I heard Wayne barking like a lunatic. Then I heard the *thunk* of my front door closing.

"Jeff?" I shouted through the bathroom door.

"It's your mother!" my mom called back.

"I'll be out in a second," I said, feeling strangely relieved.

My mother rarely brought emotional surprises. I knew how this conversation would feel and vaguely how it would end. When I came into the kitchen, spiffy in my work clothes, Mom had already laid out an assortment of Dip doughnuts on a plate.

"You don't get the *Courier*, do you?" she asked, so quietly I knew something grim was coming next. The *Courier* was the townie rag that came out only on weekdays.

"No. I don't read newspapers."

My mother nodded and pulled a folded *Courier* out of her purse. "I thought you ought to see this before you went to work," she said, handing it to me.

Below the fold was the headline GRABER MURDER SUS-

PECT OUT ON $200,000 BAIL. Beneath that was a photo of Jeff, my parents, and me in the county jail parking lot.

My mother was wearing her polar fleece with a dress covered in dusty purple roses.

My father was tilted sideways, scratching his knee. Jeff's expression was neutral but tired. He was looking at me as I bit Boober's ear. My lips were pulled up in a canine expression as Boober's ear was falling out of my mouth. A blond tendril curled down the left side of my face, hiding my left eye. My right eye looked slightly crazed.

I was wrong about my mother bearing no emotional surprises. Handing the paper back to her, I tried to breathe normally—the way they tell you to do on airplane videos that teach you how to use those snout masks right before you're about to die.

Clearly this was the universe answering my recent doubt. I just didn't know what it was telling me. It was like all the penis visions God sent Marge when she doubted him; the message was garbled at best.

"At least Jeff looks okay," my mother offered.

"Yeah. He doesn't look particularly criminal, if that's what you're getting at."

"And your hair looks nice," Mom added.

"Right. I look fabulous."

I could feel my mother waiting for a more dramatic response. I took a sip of coffee.

"Why did you bring this here?" I asked.

"I thought you'd want to see it before you headed back to work."

I dumped some more sugar in my coffee and took a gulp. "This really makes it difficult for me to carry through with my plan. My plan to go in confident and dignified and business-like even though everyone will surely know that my brother's been arrested for murder one. This makes it ten effing times harder."

My mother slid the newspaper out of my view. "Would you rather someone at work showed you?"

"Who would be insensitive enough to do that? Give me those doughnuts, please."

My mother pushed the plate closer to me. "Save a couple for your brother. I'm going to his place next."

"What, you think I'm going to scarf them all down?"

"I don't know. *I* might, if there was a picture in the paper of *me* eating a dog's ear."

I grabbed the ickiest, gooeyest pink-frosted doughnut from the plate—an act of self-hatred. "Jesus, Mom. Did you come here because you wanted to make me feel better?"

"Mostly I came because I was worried about you. You didn't answer when I called last night."

"You called? I was here."

I knew she'd called. I hadn't answered. Probably she was here now to sniff around and see if I'd been with a man the night before.

"Theresa?"

"Yes?"

"Do you . . . have someone in your life right now?"

Exactly.

"Mom, does that *really* matter to you at the moment?"

"Of course it matters. It matters to me how you're doing. It's a rough time. It actually would make me feel better to know you have someone who's supporting you. Like I have Ned."

I looked down at my napkin to find one bite of doughnut left. I couldn't remember eating the first bites or what they'd tasted like.

"I've got everything I need," I said. "Let's just focus on what Jeff needs. I'm sorry to cut this short, but I have to fix my hair."

My mother regarded me with a frown. "I'd like to meet him," she said.

"I'm sure you would." I smiled.

I knew that my mother would take this as a personal challenge, but I didn't care. My brother was accused of homicide, and there was a picture in the paper of me looking like a circus geek. My mother's interest was now officially one of the more positive elements of my life. Maybe I could learn to embrace it.

At Whitlock's I kept my head down and worked on copy for our new Cocktail Candles. The marketing plan was to push them hard in retail stores in college towns like ours—so I was to make the copy young and snappy.

I started with the Margarita Buzz candle. The note on the sample said this was to be the "kickiest" of the Cocktail collection. It was pale yellow-green with a grainy, "salty" appearance. I sniffed it and scribbled:

A refreshing citrus blend with a dash of salt. Kick back. You deserve it!

No, no, *no*. I erased *"You deserve it."* College-age kids didn't need to be told they deserved anything. They just went ahead and took it. Also, "dash" felt vaguely middle-aged, too. Like Mrs. Dash salt substitute. I scribbled:

Want to get fucked up? For the price of this candle, you can probably buy a decent-size bottle of Cuervo.

That made me feel younger, but not much better.

I set aside Margarita Buzz and looked at the other candles on my list: Midori Sour, Jell-O Shot!, Beer Pong, Pomegranate Martini, and White Russian.

Beer Pong was of course the worst. The others were clearly for sorority girls. Beer Pong was so they'd have something to buy their boyfriends, I guessed.

I put my pen to my notepad:

Certainly you already know that you are growing up in a culture that wants to market everything to you ten times over. You're supposed to buy stuff that reminds you of something else you bought. Like if you enjoy red velvet cake, you have to try the red velvet ice cream and the red velvet deodorant and of course the red velvet candle. But let's get real here. Don't let us market your own degeneracy back to you, my friends. Nothing can really smell like Beer Pong but Beer Pong, and thank the sweet Lord for that. Someday you might really, desperately need $20 for something and not have it. In these uncertain times, I can't promise that won't happen to you, sadly. But if it does, you might at least feel infinitesimally better about it had you not, at this carefree point in your life, spent $20 on a candle that smelled like molasses and beer burps.

I put aside Beer Pong and leaned back in my chair, raised the Midori Sour to my nose, and inhaled it until I felt light-headed. I'd probably been sniffing at that thing for twenty minutes when my cell phone rang.

"I was wondering how you're holding up," Zach wanted to know.

"I take it you saw my picture in the paper."

I heard him take a deep breath.

"You are talking to a famous woman," I said, to save him the trouble of having to come up with something reassuring to say.

"Are you sure you're all right?"

"Did I say I was all right?"

"I guess you didn't."

Zach was silent for a moment, and so was I.

"Did you go check out Wallace's appearance the other day?" he asked.

"No," I lied, since the slipping of the phone number would surely sound pathetic. "I tried, but by the time I got there, he'd moved along."

"Oh. Well, I spoke to Janice Obermeier. And she told me something really interesting."

"What's that?"

"Kim claimed to have footage of Andrew's original confession. And a few hours of his questioning beforehand. It showed coercion on the part of the police."

"Really?"

"Yeah."

"That would damage Donald Wallace quite a bit. If he'd seen it and it never made its way into the original trial."

"I checked," Zach said. "There was never any mention of a

videotape of his confession in the original trial. It wasn't standard practice back then."

"Now . . . why didn't Janice Obermeier take that seriously?" This didn't sound right to me. "Why didn't she demand to see the tapes?"

"I think she thought Kim was nuts. Still does. Seemed surprised I was asking about her."

"And why would Colleen Shipley give Kim such a thing?" I asked.

"I don't know," Zach said.

"Maybe it was in a box with the other footage," I suggested. "Maybe she gave her the wrong thing or gave it to her by mistake. I think Colleen Shipley was operating on a vigilante sort of level to begin with."

"What makes you say that?"

It was time to come clean. "Zach—I've met Colleen Shipley. The day I saw you for coffee."

"Oh." He paused. "Why didn't you tell me?"

"Hold on," I said, getting up and making my way out of the office, down the stairs to the Whitlock's employee parking lot.

Once I was a few steps from the building, I started to tell Zach about my trip to Raymond Realty.

He interrupted me. "I think we *really* need to find whatever footage Kim had."

"Easier said than done. I've had a few leads. And none of them has yielded anything."

"What leads?"

"I don't have time to tell you everything. I'm supposed to be working, and everybody's keeping a pretty sharp eye on me today, considering."

"When do you get off work?" Zach asked.

"Four-thirty."

"Maybe it's time you let me buy you dinner. I'll get takeout at the falafel place. Is that good? You want to do your house or mine?"

"Mine," I said. I didn't want to neglect my animals any more than I already had. I gave him my address.

"Great. How about . . . six?"

When I returned to my desk, I sat and stared out the window at the giant Whitlock's candle for a good ten minutes. *Light,* my mind ordered it. *LIGHT.* Then I heard myself say the word out loud.

I wasn't embarrassed, though, because I had no embarrassment left. A little despair, maybe. Maybe a lot. But no embarrassment. I buried my head in my hands and wondered what had ever made me expect the world to service me with little miracles.

I didn't go crazy cleaning up for Zach. I figured that a guy who was still interested after seeing that picture in the paper was likely into quirks. Nothing says eccentricity like cat-haired couches and empty yogurt containers full of pennies. I did, however, light a Peony Patch candle to cover up any pet smells I might've grown immune to in recent weeks.

Zach arrived in a cloud of spicy-bean smell, his hair tousled and his hand outstretched with a big brown take-out bag. There is something so sexy about a man bearing prepared food. In that moment I wished I'd done a bit more primping. Applied some mascara at least.

Over the baba ghanoush, I told Zach about going to Kim's

old apartment and finding nothing. Explaining about Nathan was a little harder. For that I waited till the main course. First I detailed the easy parts—about how Jeff knew that Kim had been using Nathan's video-editing software and equipment. And that he did some VHS-DVD conversion for people's old wedding videos.

"I've gotten to know Nathan pretty well over the last week or so," I said slowly.

"You didn't know him before?" Zach asked.

"No." I decided to get it over with as quickly as possible. "But I kinda wormed my way into his place. We hung out a little. I managed to take a look at some of what he had. After he went to sleep."

A falafel ball fell out of Zach's sandwich and onto his paper plate.

"I think I get what you're saying," he said, then covered the ball with a napkin, as if it embarrassed him.

I quickly avoided a lengthier discussion of the matter by describing the footage I'd seen of Dustin.

"Dustin's a pretty confused kid," Zach said.

"What about his brother?" I said. "You said you got to know him a little better."

Zach shrugged. "Not much better. But my sense was he was much more able to take care of himself than Dustin was."

"He seems a bit devious to me."

Zach made a face at me. "Based on *what*?"

And then I had to tell him about that adventure, too—my brief encounters with Troy Richardson and Trenton Halliday.

"It may just be that Troy's mistaken. Maybe Dustin told him he was going to be with his brother but took off on his own. Alternatively, he's with Trenton and Trenton's being protective—understandably so, if Dustin really is in a bad way right now. If Trenton doesn't know what you're up to, he may not be willing to put you two in touch."

"I bet he'd trust *you*, though. He knows you well enough that if you asked, he'd tell you where Dustin is and what he's up to."

"I wouldn't go that far. But I can try. I'll have to think of a reason I'm asking, one that he'd buy. I'll work on that. I'm still thinking, though, that the footage from that Shipley woman is what's gonna get us somewhere on Wallace. *That's* what I'd like to get my hands on, if I were you. *That's* what I think Kim was probably going to confront Wallace about when she went to that town meeting."

Rolf strutted in and did a flying leap onto the fridge.

"Wow," said Zach.

"I do wish I had that footage of Dustin," I said. "For what it's worth. Maybe I could leverage it somehow."

"Leverage?" Zach looked skeptical, his expression matching Rolf's.

"Nathan's onto me now, though. I don't think I'm getting back in there."

Zach ate in silence for a few minutes, thinking about this. His pita bread was coming apart, getting yogurt sauce all over his fingers.

"Maybe if you just explained to him how much is at stake, he'd let you have one more look?" he asked.

"I'm afraid if I explain that, he'll hand everything over to the police and we'll never see any of it again."

"Are you really that distrusting of the police?"

"Given everything I've been hearing, and the possibility that someone as powerful as Donald Wallace could be involved, I want to be careful. And make sure Jeff has everything *they* have."

"Okay. I get it."

Zach broke a piece of pita off his mangled sandwich and nibbled on it, staring up at Rolf, who'd begun to doze. "I've got a couple of ideas," he said.

"Okay?"

"Wallace did some advocacy work early in his career that connects pretty well with some of the stuff I usually write about. At-risk youth. I could ask him to do a story on that, set up a time to meet. Maybe I could surprise him and tell him I have the tapes. Or know about the tapes. See what happens."

"Maybe . . ."

"If I connected with his office, I'd bet they'd jump on it. A feel-good story about his advocacy work would do him some good right now."

"But then you'd have to *write* that story," I pointed out.

"Nah," said Zach. "I could take my time with it. And then if it doesn't run before the election, no one will follow up or care."

"But Donald Wallace probably isn't going to go for a bluff," I said, thinking of his unthreatened expression at Sally's. "None of this is going to work if we don't have it. I . . . just have that feeling."

Zach nodded. "You're probably right. And I think Nathan is our best bet for that."

"I told you he won't—"

"Maybe you shouldn't ask him for it," Zach said. "Maybe you should just take it."

"How do I do that? Storm his house with an automatic weapon?"

Zach stared at his hands as he wiped them with a napkin. "Do you know his work hours pretty well?"

"Sort of. He works till eleven most weekdays, I know that. Much later on Saturdays."

"You're forgetting my roots, Theresa. I'm pretty good with locks and that sort of thing."

"Like . . . picking them with a credit card?"

"Uh . . . that general idea. Don't you think I learned anything up there in juvie?"

"That's a crazy idea."

"Is it? If it helps Jeff?"

I watched Zach as he collected our paper plates. He wouldn't look at me. Did he think I was a wimp? That I didn't care about my brother enough to do something crazy? I had already hopped into bed with someone I barely knew, just for a glimpse at a stash of amateur video footage. The issue was not how low I was willing to go but whether I wanted to drag someone else down with me.

"That's a, um . . . a sweet offer. I'm gonna have to think about it."

"Yeah," he said, finding my trash under the kitchen sink and tossing the plates. "Think about it."

"I think you should think about it, too. I'm gonna give you a little time to come to your senses."

"I'm not going to."

There was something defiant in his posture that I hadn't seen in his office or at the student center. It was easy to forget that years and years ago, in a remote and peculiar past, Zach had been some kind of a badass kid.

"Why are you trying to do this for me?" I asked, rising to rinse our glasses in the sink.

He studied me for a moment, then turned back to the table to clear the silverware. "Two reasons. One is that this isn't what people like Donald Wallace are supposed to do with the power they've been granted. Like I said. If this is really happening, it's too evil *not* to do anything. I mean, I can't believe this was someone I was about to *vote* for."

"What's the other reason?" I asked. There needed to be more. Maybe it was just the way I was raised, but political outrage rarely felt real to me.

Zach glanced at my kitchen floor. "Actually, there are three reasons. The second is that it annoys me that there was a story here all along and I didn't see it when Kim came to me."

He took both glasses from me and set them on the counter resolutely.

"And the third?" I asked.

He leaned forward and kissed me. A quick, soft kiss at first. And then—presumably because I didn't pull way—a longer, stronger one. It was just short of aggressive, which I liked.

"Zach?" I said.

He didn't reply at first. He seemed to be holding his breath.

"You don't need to help me break into someone's house to get me to kiss you."

Zach shook his head and exhaled.

"You look like you've shocked yourself more than me," I said.

He smiled. "I guess I never thought I'd kiss a medievalist."

I laughed and led him into the living room, where he sprawled on the couch. Boober apparently picked up on his sheepish expression and jumped into his lap to comfort him. Zach gingerly put his hand on Boober's little head.

314 • Emily Arsenault

"Do you have any pets?" I asked.

This seemed an important question—if we were going to be kissing and all.

He shook his head again. "No. I've been thinking of getting a dog. But I go away too much. For my book research and everything. It might not be a good idea."

"Did you have any pets growing up?"

"Yeah. We had a Samoyed."

"Those are such beautiful dogs. Aren't they really expensive, though?"

Zach was quiet for a moment. Boober leaned his head back and made eyes at him as Zach scratched behind his ears. "Oh. Sometimes, I guess. My mom got him from her boss, who decided he didn't want him. Barked too much. He was a sweetheart, though. We called him Licky Mick."

"Licky Mick?" I said.

He nodded. I watched him pet Boober down his back and wondered if we could really work as a couple. I'd grown tired of Brendan's drive and Brendan's accomplishments as my own had diminished. And Zach was so goddamned optimistic, too.

I wanted to be that way. I never would be. But I supposed it couldn't hurt to kiss someone who was. I sat next to Zach and kissed him again.

It was different from kissing Nathan. Nothing left my head. Marge didn't start singing or weeping. Nor did Jeff Buckley. When it was over, we were both still here.

It didn't go any further than that kiss and a few more. I sort of wanted it to, and I think Zach did, too—but the little bit of

Catholic still left in me drew the line at two different men in less than a week.

I rested my head on Zach's shoulder, and he said softly, "Tell me about the house."

"What house?"

"Nathan's. Do you remember anything about the doors or the windows? Oh—is there a garage?"

"Yeah."

"Okay. That might be the ticket, then. Unless he's super security-conscious, garage is the way to go. Most people don't know how easy it is to break into some garages. Does the garage have windows?"

"I think so."

"I can't promise it'll work. I wouldn't want to fiddle around for long, but we could try it. If it's the right kind of garage, it won't take more than a minute. If it's not, it won't take long to make that determination and leave."

"You learned this in juvenile detention?"

"No. Not this. I saw this on a news report about how easy it is for burglars to get into your garage. But juvie's where I first started being interested in this kind of thing. The weaknesses of various security systems and different ways people can get into your shit. It can make you sort of paranoid, once you know a little bit about it. You can be sure *my* garage door has a security clip on the safety latch."

"Do you miss . . . ?" I started to ask a question, but I was unsure quite how to formulate it.

Sometimes I wished I'd had something more specific to overcome in my youth than general inertia. I'd been driven to get into and stay forever in one of the country's top universities, just because it was there in my hometown, waving itself in my face. It wasn't actual ambition. There had never been much need to be fierce or lawless or brave.

"Do you ever miss being in survival mode? In do-whatever-it-takes mode?"

Zach looked surprised by the question. "All the time," he whispered.

That was when I knew we were really going to do this.

The plan was relatively simple. We'd park my car on Nathan's street, but not in front of his house. It had been parked on that street a few times this week and wasn't likely to be noticed among all the student cars anyhow. Zach would go check out the garage door. If it was a no-go, he'd come back to the car and we'd be off on our way. If the safety latch was easily seen, he was ready with a wire hanger that we'd fashioned into a hook and a ready-to-send text message that said I'M IN if it all happened correctly and the door to the house was unlocked. We were dressed to look like students at a glance—Zach with a baseball cap on, me in a ponytail bun, with a backpack. We both happened to be wearing jeans anyway. Zach had readied a memory stick from his briefcase. He'd work on the computer, saving any video files that looked useful, while I'd go through all the VHS tapes and pack up any unmarked or promising-looking ones.

The moment he left the car, I began to regret what I'd set in motion.

"'There is no gift so holy as is the gift of love,'" I whispered to myself. It was from the Book of Marge. I repeated it again and again, reminding myself that this was a demonstration of faith. I had faith in Jeff. Even if I shouldn't. Even if it did not make logical sense. That's how faith worked.

"'There is no gift so holy as is the gift of love. *Thereisnogiftso-holyasisthegiftoflove.*'"

I must've said it thirty times before my cell phone jumped: I'M IN.

My heart pounded as I opened the car door. I closed it quietly but casually. I didn't rush till I was at the end of Nathan's driveway and saw his garage open about one third of the way. Zach was waiting for me on the inside. He put his finger to his lips as I ducked in, then closed the garage door.

The bulb at the back of Peaches' cage allowed us to tiptoe through the living room without turning on any lights.

"See, there's his snake," I said softly.

Zach nodded and whispered, "Office?"

I led the way.

Just as I flipped the light switch of the office, an awful shriek came from the room.

"Jesus!" I screamed.

"Shhh!" said Zach.

"That wasn't me!" I whispered loudly. "The first scream, I mean."

We both peered into the room. In front of the computer desk was a black, arch-topped cage that was almost as tall as me.

"You didn't tell me about that," Zach said.

There was another, louder scream. Inside the cage was a cauliflower-colored bird nearly as big as a toddler, with a yellow curl on the top of its head. Its freaky eyes looked like tiny black marbles poking out of a poached egg white.

"This wasn't here when I was here," I whispered.

"Well, it's here now," Zach said, sitting at the computer. "Let's just do this as quick as we can."

I leaned over him, rummaging quickly through the overhead cabinet where I'd found the VHS tapes. The first said "Stark-DeFransciso." A wedding, clearly. I put it aside. An unmarked one. I put that in my backpack. "Our Beautiful Wedding." Put that one aside. The next one had just a number on the side, typed. The next was the same. Both of those went into my backpack. There weren't many that were unmarked, but some had cryptic titles. None had obvious labels like "Andrew Abbott." Anything that could potentially be Kim's, I stuck in the backpack—and ended up with seven tapes.

"There's a file named 'KG Backups,'" Zach said. "Have you looked at that stuff yet?"

"No!" I answered. "That sounds promising."

"Okay. I'm saving that along with the stuff in the Kim file."

"Awww," whispered the bird.

I watched its black mollusk tongue move up and down in its sharp black beak.

"He loves animals," I whispered, opening the door to the room's small closet. "Nathan, I mean."

"You'd have to," Zach said, tapping Nathan's mouse. "That thing is heinous."

Surely Zach was wondering about my judgment. It was one thing to hang out with guys who owned snakes. Guys with birds—maybe. But guys with both? Not so much.

The closet had mostly clothes in it—a couple of suits and an obnoxious-looking black cowboy shirt with red roses across the chest. On the floor were a few packages of printer paper from Staples.

"I'm done," I said. "Are you?"

"Almost," Zach murmured.

Then I heard a squeak. And not from the bird.

"Did you hear that?" I whispered.

"No. What?"

I heard it again. It was the storm door of the house opening. Then there was a noise that sounded very much like a key.

"Oh, God," I said.

Zach pulled the memory stick out of the computer and stuck it in his back jeans pocket.

"Out the window," I said, trying to yank my backpack's zipper closed.

"What?" Zach whispered.

"AWWWW!" screamed the bird.

"You go out the window," I whispered, yanking the shades all the way up. "I'll greet him at the door. I'll tell him I wanted to surprise him or—"

I pulled up the window, and Zach pulled up the screen with the finger tabs.

"Surprise him?"

"Go!" I said.

"You can make it, too," Zach whispered as he climbed out. "Come on!"

I could hear the shuffling make its way down the hall.

"I don't think so."

In that split second, I decided it was better for me to make my presence look like a casual drop-in. I could tell Nathan I'd come to talk to him and found the door open. If I made it to the bedroom before Nathan saw me, it would be more believable.

And Zach was already no longer visible from the office. If he could get out of the yard, we'd probably be okay.

I slammed the window shut and jumped into the hallway. There I nearly ran smack into a man who wasn't Nathan. He had a giant belly, only half covered by an orange Thin Lizzy T-shirt.

"Who are you?" he demanded. He smelled peculiarly like baby powder.

"Hi. I'm Nathan's friend. Who are you?"

"I'm his *best* friend," Thin Lizzy said, so possessively that I expected him to put a haughty hand on his hip.

"Oh," I said softly.

"What are you doing in here?" he asked.

"Nathan wanted me to meet him here."

Thin Lizzy scratched the back of his neck, below his stubby blond ponytail. "Nathan's not getting back till one. That's why he called me to check on the new bird."

"That's funny. Nathan asked *me* to check on the bird, too. She's cute, isn't she?"

It was the smell of talcum powder that had me taking chances like this. Between that and his belly sticking out, Thin Lizzy seemed nonthreatening, like a giant bouncing baby boy.

"It's a he. Not a she. Are you Theresa?"

"Yeah," I admitted.

"I don't think Nathan would've asked you to come here." Thin Lizzy gave me a hard stare. "He told me about you."

One of the VHS tapes chose that moment to tumble from

my overstuffed backpack. When I reached down for it, two more fell out.

"Oh, *damn*," I said. It came out so fake that I knew I was doomed.

Thin Lizzy took a cell phone from his pocket, pressed a button, and put it to his ear.

"Who are you calling?"

"Nathan," he said. "But he's not answering." He hit a few more buttons on his phone. "Hello, yes. I want to report a break-in."

Tuesday, October 29

October 29, 2013
Thompsonville Courier

THOMPSONVILLE, MASS.–Police are investigating a possible break-in reported on Higgins Court last night. Officers were called to 428 Higgins Court at 10:02 pm. According to initial reports, a friend of the owner of the home came to feed his pet cockatoo. When he entered the home, he found Theresa Battle, of Willow Street, in the process of removing video equipment from the home. She had entered through the garage.

Battle's brother, Jeffrey Battle, is currently awaiting trial for the murder of his girlfriend, Kimberly Graber, a Thompsonville resident whose body was found on Highway 114 on October 18.

Police are investigating reports that a man in his thirties resembling Jeffrey Battle was seen fleeing the scene through the Higgins Court backyard.

The Thompsonville police had trouble determining if I'd really come into Nathan's house uninvited. He told them he thought I might have had a "misunderstanding" about his desire to see me again and refused to press charges. I insisted that my brother had not been with me—that I'd come for a romantic interlude.

Still, the story was in the paper for all to see the following morning—a tiny story, but front page, below the fold, due to the connection with my brother's soiled name. Zach had been calling all morning, leaving messages, saying he was starting to watch the files on the memory stick and babbling about how he should turn himself in so the police would be certain it wasn't Jeff helping me. I ignored the calls, hoping to clear my head and determine my next move before talking to him—or anyone. First of all, I decided I couldn't endure work that day. Reluctantly I picked up my cell to call Tish.

"What were you thinking?" she demanded, answering after one ring.

"If you call your dad for me and tell him what bad shape I'm in, I'll treat you to our next ten dinners out."

"You don't need to do that, okay? You just need to be *careful*. You know you could've gotten Jeff into even more trouble? Good thing he had a solid alibi."

"Who's that?" I said. "What're you talking about?"

"He was with *me*, Theresa."

"Why . . . ?"

"Yes, I'll call my dad. He won't care." Tish cleared her throat. "He says you're creating a big distraction anyway."

"A *distraction*? Is it my fault that my personal life is more interesting than finding fifty ways to say 'Smells like cinnamon'? Does your dad know how easily distracted these people are?"

Tish hung up on me.

Jeff with Tish? Apparently he'd decided to go ahead and tell her all the things he didn't want to say to her through a piece of glass. And apparently she'd wanted to hear them.

Next I called Zach to tell him to quit worrying and go teach his morning class.

"You just leave the memory stick for me in your box in the English office," I said. "I want to watch it all myself."

"Okay," he said. "There's nothing much useful, though. As far as I can tell. I watched most of it. I didn't see much that you didn't already describe to me before. Nothing from the nineties, with Donald Wallace."

"Even in that new file you found?"

"A lot of people saying what a shame it was about Andrew Abbott going to jail. No one saying anything new."

"I'd like to pick it up anyway," I said, clinging to his "most of it" for hope. Most was not all. He may have missed something. We might still find Jeff's saving grace.

I spent the morning watching all the footage on Zach's memory stick.

There was, as Zach said, no footage from the early nineties.

All Kim had saved on the "KG Backup" were longer versions of the interviews she'd excerpted in her "commercial"— Andrew Abbott's cousin, the young guy who worked at the nonprofit New England Project for Justice. Nothing that would set Wallace's campaign on fire.

I was glad for the chance to watch the Dustin interviews again, though—particularly the second one.

The most interesting exchange came near the end, before Wayne interrupted the interview:

"She had a way of making you do things," Dustin had said.

"By 'you' you mean yourself."

"Yeah. Me. And my brother. She was a master manipulator."

"And how does that apply to the night your father died, Dustin?"

I'd certainly noticed the mention of Dustin's brother the first time I'd seen this. But so much else had been going on at the time—inside this footage and outside it—that I hadn't given it a great deal of attention. I'd wondered since then if Dustin had been set to reveal something about his own involvement in the shooting. Now I wondered if he'd been poised to reveal something about his brother. Had his brother ever gotten wind of it?

I had given up easily on the Hallidays because I'd been with Jeff at the time. Now I was on my own, and I had an afternoon to kill.

I sipped a cold latte while I sat in my car outside Trenton Halliday's house, turning on the heat occasionally and listening to NPR: first an interview with someone who'd written a book on Internet technology's impact on the U.S. Postal Service, then a story about the history of chocolate chips. It reminded me of the old days—of when Brendan had to have NPR constantly piped into his car, our kitchen, our marriage bed, even—on a few Saturday mornings when neither of us was enterprising enough to reach over and press SNOOZE.

After about an hour and forty-five minutes, a young man and woman emerged from the front door and approached a light green compact car parked on the street. The woman was the one I'd encountered two days earlier. The man, however, was not Trenton Halliday. This man was younger and skinnier, with floppy skater hair. It was Dustin. He got into the passenger side of the car as the woman unlocked it. I started my car and then pulled behind them as they zipped onto the main road.

I followed them for about five minutes, and then another car came between us. After about two miles, the green Easter egg pulled in to an office park. I followed but lingered near the entrance while Dustin's car drove right up to one of the buildings. Dustin got out, and the car sped away.

By the time I parked, Dustin had disappeared into the building. I followed him and studied the office map in the front hall. On the first floor, there were two dental groups and a chiropractor. On the second was an ear, nose, and throat doctor and two "licensed therapists." The third had drug and alcohol counseling and another dentist. Dustin had likely headed to floor two or three, but I decided to stay put at the entrance and wait for him to come out.

As people left the building, I amused myself by guessing which specialist they'd seen. Finally Dustin emerged from one of the elevators.

"Dustin?" I said, my heart thudding.

He walked right through the glass doors, avoiding my gaze. Maybe he hadn't heard me, I told myself. I followed him outside and into the parking lot.

I repeated his name—louder this time.

His steps slowed, then quickened. He made his way to the landscaped divider that separated this parking lot from the next property.

"Dustin," I said again.

He finally whirled around. "Yeah? Do I know you?"

"No. But I believe you knew my friend Kim Graber."

"Kim? Yeah. I did. She was your friend? What's your name?"

"Margery," I said. "Would you mind talking to me for a minute? I know you two were in contact shortly before she died."

"Someone's about to pick me up." Dustin took a step away from me.

"Just a couple minutes. Till your ride gets here."

He hesitated, then looked alarmed. "How'd you know I'd be here?"

"It's a long story," I said. "I really need to talk about Kim, man."

The "man" actually seemed to defuse his anxiety.

"I'm sorry about Kim," he said, flashing me an exaggerated frown that I supposed was meant to be sympathetic.

"I appreciate that."

"It's been kind of hard for me, too," he said. "Even though I didn't know her long. We got pretty close."

"She mentioned that," I said, stepping closer to him.

"Really?"

"Yes."

Dustin slid a pair of puffy gloves out of his coat pocket and began to put them on. "What did she say about me?"

I hesitated. "Um, well. Were you angry with Kim the day she disappeared?"

He wrapped his arms around his chest, then nodded. "I was."

"Why, though?" I asked softly, trying to keep my tone kindly and commiserating.

"Because she stood me up. We were supposed to hang out the night before, and she didn't show."

"Was she going to interview you again?" I asked.

Dustin's eyes widened. "She told you about that stuff?"

"She told me pretty much everything," I said, giving an apologetic shrug.

"That Friday night we were just supposed to hang out." He sighed. "As friends. I guess she wasn't interested in that, once she realized I wasn't going to be as useful as she thought."

"What does that mean?"

Dustin just shook his head.

"The weekend she disappeared, you texted her," I said. "You referred to a video. Were you angry with her about something related to that?"

"No. That was something else."

"Something else?"

"Just something stupid I e-mailed her from my phone."

"Do you still have it? Can you show it to me?"

He stepped away from me again. "It wouldn't interest you. It was just something I had on my phone. Someone I know being a jackass. Anyway, my phone was stolen about three weeks ago. Someone clocked me in the back of the head while I was drunk coming out of Farley's and took my wallet and my phone. So I don't have it."

"That's why you weren't answering your phone for a while?" I said.

"Yeah. It took me some time to get my number reestablished."

I nodded. "I saw the interview where you were saying your mom told you the gun wasn't loaded. You were saying she made you do things."

"Uh . . . yeah?"

"Like what, Dustin?"

He glanced at the office building before meeting my gaze. "I just met you," he said.

"Sometimes I find it easier to talk to strangers," I said. "Isn't that why you come here to this office anyway?"

"But why do *you* care?" Dustin asked, unfazed by my bumbling response.

There was something so sad and so boyish in his question. I wondered if he wasn't even more damaged than everyone had described.

"Because I want to finish what Kim started," I said quickly, before my conscience could have a chance to mess up this opportunity. "She told me your story. Everything."

Dustin folded his arms. "Okay. My mother made me tell that story about the intruders. And saying that was easier than saying what I really saw."

"Which was what?" I demanded.

"I saw my mother shoot my father. I saw him die."

The words stunned me. They weren't exactly surprising. Just horrifying. Not words you ever expect to hear out of anyone's mouth, under any circumstances.

"There were no intruders," he said softly.

He said these words as if they were somehow more significant than the first. Of course there were no intruders. Wasn't that obvious to everyone?

"Kim was disappointed to hear it," Dustin said. "Are you?"

"I–I . . . um . . ." I stammered, feeling wretched. "I don't know. . . . That wouldn't be the word I'd—"

"Kim was the first person I ever told. And I could tell she was disappointed."

The police and the prosecutors *had* gotten it wrong, in a sense. The right person was in jail. But Dustin hadn't woken up when he'd heard a gunshot. He'd actually seen the shooting take place. And after years of repeating his mother's story, it was significant to *him* to finally admit that it was untrue. Kim, of course, had been after something else. If Donald Wallace had a *pattern* of wrongful convictions, Andrew Abbott wouldn't so much feel like her fault.

"What about your friend from juvenile detention?" I said. "Michael Johnson?"

"Who's Michael Johnson?" Dustin asked.

"Your friend in juvenile detention. Wasn't that his real name? In the book you said he was the only one you felt you could tell the whole truth about what really happened that night with your dad."

"The book?" he repeated.

I was starting to wonder if Dustin was a little bit baked.

"Zachary Wagner's book. *Juvie.*"

"Oh, right. The book. I guess I may have said that. May not have. Fifty-fifty."

"So that wasn't accurate?"

"Do you believe everything you read, lady?"

I chafed at being called "lady." "Are you saying that something in the book wasn't fair?"

"Oh, I didn't say it wasn't fair. That's different."

"Okay, then . . ."

"You know what my brother says about that book? 'Fair is when everyone is portrayed how they want to be and everyone's okay with it. Accurate would be if everyone was portrayed exactly as they are.' Something like that."

This conversation was getting too philosophical for me.

"Dustin, what did your brother think of what you were doing with Kim?"

He shrugged. "He didn't know about it until after she died. We hadn't seen each other for a while, till a few weeks ago."

"But what did he think of the things you were telling her? Did it bother him?"

Dustin shook his head. "My brother knows what my mother was capable of. He learned earlier than me. He learned it when she had him start a fire in the kitchen. That didn't turn out how it was supposed to—the house didn't burn down. Our dad got out. But it made her more confident. Because no one suspected a thing. She thought she could get away with *anything.*"

More sad revelations, but none that Kim would've found useful.

"What did Kim say when you told her all this?" I asked.

"She was very sympathetic. For a little while. But I didn't have anything she could use to slap Donald Wallace with. And that was when she lost interest. She wanted everything to be about Wallace. I'm not one to talk, but that girl had some issues. Sure, she was part of a big, tragic mess when she was a kid. But Donald Wallace didn't create the mess. He just sewed together a story about it that made sense, at the time, from the pieces he got to see. I kept wondering when she was gonna maybe figure out he wasn't the right one—or at least the only one—to be mad at. That she should be mad at whoever gave him those pieces."

"And who was that? In Kim's case?"

Dustin sighed heavily, as if he didn't know where to begin.

"Did she ever tell you anything about her boyfriend?" I asked.

"The one they arrested? Or the old one?"

"Um . . . either one."

The little green hatchback buzzed into the parking lot and

stopped in front of the building from which we'd just come. Inside the car I could discern a figure craning her neck to see if Dustin was behind the glass doors. Dustin seemed to spot her but kept talking.

"All Kim ever told me about the guy she was with was that he was clueless about her history. She said he wouldn't understand, because he'd never seen or done anything bad in his whole life. She said he was sweet, like a little boy."

Dustin saw me cringe.

"I know," he said. "Look how *that* turned out."

"Halliday!" someone yelled. It was Dustin's driver—she'd caught sight of us talking and was now leaning out her car window.

"Ignore her," Dustin said. "She'll wait, trust me."

I thought it was odd, but I was eager to finish this conversation regardless.

"She's not very smart," he added.

"And about Kyle?" I hurried to ask. "Jenny's brother? The old boyfriend?"

"She said she didn't think she could've ever done this project if she was still with him."

"Because?" I prompted, growing anxious about Dustin's little friend.

"Because when she was with him, she was always afraid. That's what she said."

"HALLIDAY!" the young woman yelled again.

"Afraid of what?" I asked, trying to ignore her.

"I don't know, exactly." Dustin glanced toward the waiting car.

"Was she afraid he would do something to her? Physically?"

He shook his head. "She never said anything like that. She

didn't strike me as someone who would stay with a guy who pulled that kind of stuff. She didn't take any shit."

I didn't think it was so easy to identify who would take what kind of shit. That was something I knew about relationships that the young Dustin perhaps did not.

The woman circled and parked in the lot, pulling up close to us.

"Trenton!" she called to Dustin.

"Why's she calling you Trenton?" I asked.

"Insurance," Dustin replied. "She's so dumb she thinks the doctor in there might hear if she calls me by my real name."

"Insurance?" I said.

"I'm using my brother's insurance."

I paused, thinking about this. Of course Dustin didn't have any medical insurance. He wasn't in school, didn't have a job, and didn't have any parents to fall back on. But Trenton probably had a decent plan, if he still worked at the cable company.

"That's how my brother operates. Like I was saying about the book. Little lies are okay. As long as everybody's either happy or clueless and no one gets hurt."

"TRENTON!" the young woman screamed.

"She is so damn dumb. All she needs is a sparkly purse with a teacup Yorkie. I can't believe my brother likes her."

"Sometimes it's best not to overanalyze a sibling's taste," I offered.

Dustin smirked. "I'll say."

"Who do you think killed Kim, Dustin?" I asked.

"It's pretty obvious, don't you think? The guy they've arrested."

The young woman had reached us now. She grabbed Dustin's arm.

"Why didn't you answer me, *Trenton?*" she said.

"Because that's not my name, *Riley*."

Trenton's girlfriend looked stunned.

"In *most* of these cases," Dustin said to me, "it's the obvious person."

"What are we talking about here?" Riley demanded.

Dustin turned and headed toward the Easter egg. "Let's go, Riley," he said.

Riley followed, hissing scolds at him. Watching them walk away, I felt an unfamiliar anguish settling in my core. I'd hung so many of my hopes on finding Dustin and demanding an explanation for his texts and his anger. But it was clear now that his revelations were not going to magically transform into a smoking gun. He was another wounded soul who had thought, for a little while, that Kim cared about him.

For a moment I racked my brain to come up with an idea to pursue for the rest of the afternoon. None came to me. And in the absence of ideas, there was a raw pain that nearly knocked me to my knees. I had no choice now but to let it wash over me. I sat on the cold dirt and grass of the divider and closed my eyes. I breathed the pain in and out. Not till I was used to it—as I knew I never would be. But till I was ready to stand up and go home.

As I drove back into Thompsonville, I stared up at the Whit-lock's candle and thought about Marge. There was a particular passage in the latter part of her book that I had always found surprisingly touching. When she was old, after she'd all but abandoned her husband for a life of celibacy and pilgrimages, he (by then living alone, as per an agreement with Marge) took a bad fall and thereafter required constant care. Margery was reluctant to go back to living with him, fretting that his needs would interfere with her prayers and her church attendance (and making much of the fact that he was now incontinent). But God told her to return to her husband and "look after him for my love." And she did.

By doing so she showed an understanding of faith as something that is at least *sometimes* quiet, humble, unglamorous, and relatively egoless. It feels as if Marge may finally have begun to mature in her old age and to see faith differently. Maybe she even saw her husband differently—saw that his patience and love for her had quietly helped her to lead the unconventional life she'd wanted.

I wondered now what my later-in-life service was going to be. Would it be visiting my brother in jail for years to come, trying to throw together enough funny Boober and Rolf stories to fill a few decades of Saturday visiting hours? Being the holdout supporting his innocence? Stalking Donald Wallace into the U.S. Senate and perhaps the White House, till the FBI put me in a rubber room? Or, more humbly, simply attempting somehow to ease my parents' suffering over whatever fate had in store for us?

I could take on any burden but acceptance of Jeff's guilt. I prayed to the Whitlock's candle for a sign of what was expected of me. It remained as tacky and as dim as ever. I would have to find comfort in that somehow.

I hadn't even had time to feed the cats when there was a knock on my front door. Wayne howled once. Boober began yipping and wouldn't stop.

Nudging both dogs aside with my foot, I opened the door a crack and saw Kyle Spicer on my front steps.

"Well, if it isn't Margery Lipinski," he said.

"Uh . . . hello," I said, startling at the sneer on his lips.

"I hear your dog." Kyle stuck his foot in the door. "Is that the one from the picture in the paper?"

"Hey!" I yelled.

"I'm coming in." Kyle put his hand on the door and narrowed his Snake Eyes at me. "Because I need to talk to you."

"I'm going to call the cops if you come in here." My heart was racing.

"Really? Because I have something that I think you want. I saw that weird picture of you in the paper the other day, *Theresa*." He emphasized my real name. "Then today I saw that thing about you breaking into Kim's friend's house. And it's all been pretty illuminating. Because he doesn't have it—what you're looking for. *I* do."

I touched my phone in my pocket. I could reach it if I got into trouble. Kyle could very well intend me harm, but I was willing to take the risk. *There is no gift so holy as is the gift of love.* I let go of the door, took a step backward, and let him in.

Kyle made a big show of making himself comfortable on my couch—loosening his slithery satin salesman tie and plumping the cushions. I took that opportunity to review possible self-defense tools in my home. There was the cutlery in the kitchen, of course. But was there anything closer? Maybe I could clock him with a lamp or strangle him with Boober's leash.

"So when I saw the picture of you with your brother and your dog the other day," he said, "boy, did I feel like the world's biggest dumb-ass. I really thought you were Margery Lipinski, mystery dogsitter. 'A friend of Kim's'? I knew her well enough to know she didn't make very close friends. Girlfriends especially."

Wayne approached Kyle—panting, his tongue looking obscenely long. Kyle pushed his snout away gently.

"Not now, slobber boy. It finally makes sense, though. You don't really care about Kim. You care about your brother."

"It's not—"

"It's fine." He interrupted. "Really. It makes more sense than trying to get to the bottom of Kim. Trust me, there is no bottom. I'm glad I don't have to bother to explain that to you. Because you don't care."

"I actually—"

"*No*," Kyle said, and he reached into the wide right pocket of his brown leather blazer. He pulled out two DVDs in clear plastic cases, and I shut up. He put them on the couch beside him.

"So I'll only explain the parts that I need to. How about that?"

I nodded. Wayne, seeming to sense the tension in the air, turned and left the room like a champ. Boober's gaze followed him for a moment, and then he did the same. *Way to look out for your mistress, boys.*

"I was twelve and she was ten," Kyle began. "I was almost

thirteen, I guess. Is that sick? Is that weird? Probably. If I'd had a normal life after that, maybe I would've felt really bad about it. Maybe someone would've called me out on it. But they didn't. Because you know what happened?"

"What?" I whispered.

Kyle closed his eyes. I scanned the room for more potential weapons. There was a Banksy coffee-table book. Not deadly, but it could buy me time, probably, if I angled it just right and jabbed him in the eyes. Then I could run for the leash in the hall. Or just run.

"Kim came over a lot, to see my sister. But after a while we started kicking Jenny out. We'd lock her out. Well—*I'd* lock her out. To be with just Kim. I'd only done it a couple of times when Jenny decided one day to go walking by herself. Probably to the store to buy Bazooka gum. They'd sell these big boxes of Bazooka for a dollar. Jenny thought it was the best deal. And she didn't like to wait once she had a taste for Bazooka. She banged on the door a couple of times, asking Kim to come with her. But we didn't answer. And then Jenny never came back."

Kyle tapped his knuckles on one of the DVD cases.

"I can't watch this. I tried one for a few minutes. Kim is so young in it. Too young. She was a little *kid*."

I could feel myself breathe now. I had the distinct feeling I would not need to strangle this man with a dachshund's leash.

"If it was Andrew who killed Jenny, then it wasn't our fault. If Andrew was a sick kid who had set his sights on Jenny, it was only a matter of time. If it was Andrew, then it wasn't about that one day. It wasn't just about the wrong place at the wrong time. It wasn't about what we did or didn't do that day.

"I believed Kim when she told everybody Andrew was messing with Jenny. I was so angry. What a sick fuck. I didn't think those words when I was twelve, thirteen, but that's how I put it for years after that.

"It was only when I tried to watch this that I asked myself where she might've gotten that material. Did Jenny really tell her all that? I couldn't remember Jenny acting that different, in those last days, from how she had before. I couldn't remember her being troubled. I couldn't even remember her being all that close to Kim. She was better friends with Missy. Kim was the outlier. Kim was the maverick. Can you say that about a kid? That's what I liked about her.

"I don't know if these things matter." Kyle tapped the DVDs again. "I don't know if Donald Wallace has much to answer for here. I don't know if he'd care enough. But it seems to me awfully convenient for him that Kim died right before she could do anything with it."

Kyle's gaze met mine, and I tried to hold it. Then he glanced down at the DVD cases.

"You're trying to save your brother. I don't know if you can. But I don't want to get in the way. Just because I couldn't save my sister doesn't mean you shouldn't have a chance to save your brother.

"That's like what we did to Andrew Abbott. We put it on the easiest person. I don't know what your story is. I don't know what your brother's is. But I'm not going to be a part of doing that to anyone else.

"The day before she drove to Rowington, Kim dropped these at my place. For safekeeping, she said. But I don't want to be responsible for them." Kyle gently tossed one of the DVDs to me. "I don't want to be responsible for any of this. When Kim and I broke up, it was supposed to be over. I want it to be *over*."

Then he tossed the other. It missed the couch and fell at my feet.

"Thank you," I said, bending to pick it up.

"You'll leave me alone now, Margery Lipinski." Kyle stood up.

"Okay," I whispered, unsure if I should get up, too.

"See you, Wayne," Kyle called down the hall. Wayne came running, giving a confused *woof* in Kyle's direction, but Kyle was gone by the time Wayne reached the door.

I ran to the window and watched Kyle get into his car.

Once he was gone, I opened up my laptop and put in one of the DVDs. I held my breath as the player began to load.

The shot was grainy, but the two figures sitting at the table together were clearly a young girl and a young woman. The girl had pretty dark hair, pushed back with a rhinestone headband. Her hands were folded primly before her, and her face was arranged in a sweet smile. The woman was a younger Colleen Shipley with a fluffy perm.

"You did a great job talking to Officer McCarthy, Kim," she said. "Now we want to go over a few things you said, okay?"

"Okay." Miniature Kim nodded.

"We're going to start with the week *before* Jenny disappeared and some of the things you said about that."

"Sure," said Kim.

I was struck by how self-possessed the young Kim was.

"So you said that Andrew would try to kiss Jenny. When would he do that? Did you *see* that happen?"

"Um. Mostly she just told me about it. Because it was in private?" I noticed the question in Kim's voice.

"It was in private. Okay. But did you ever actually *see* it?"

"Once. In the basement."

"Whose basement?" Colleen asked.

"Jenny's basement." Kim's voice lowered slightly.

"Andrew came over to Jenny's house? Who else was there?"

"Oh. I meant, Andrew's basement."

"Andrew's basement. Are you sure, Kim?"

"Yeah. We were in his yard drawing the horses and the unicorns, and it started to rain. And we went into Andrew's basement."

"Andrew invited you in?"

Kim touched her headband, then pushed a stray strand of hair behind her ear. "Yeah."

"All three of you? You, Missy, and Jenny?"

Kim bit her lip, thinking. "Mmm. I don't think Missy was there."

"So you and Jenny and Andrew were in the basement working on your drawings?"

"Yeah."

"And then what happened?"

"Andrew . . . Andrew, uh . . ."

In an instant, Kim's composure collapsed. Her face crumpled. She heaved and then sniffled. It was so sudden and so sad. And she looked awfully small.

"It's okay, Kim. Take your time."

"It's okay, honey," said another female voice from outside the shot. Kim's mother, I presumed.

I stared at Kim: minus the crooked lipstick, minus the cell phone, minus the cocktail glass.

"I was in Jenny's basement?" she said, and Colleen Shipley nodded.

"I was in Jenny's basement with Kyle," Kim said, pulling her shoulders up high, then releasing them. "Kyle was teaching me how to kiss."

"When's this? The same day?"

"No. I don't know. It was the third time, I think. We locked Jenny out. She banged on the door, but we didn't answer."

"And that's when Jenny went to Andrew's?"

"Probably, yeah."

"Wait. So we're not talking anymore about the day you saw them kissing, are we?"

"*No.*" Kim was clearly frustrated. "I'm talking about the day she DISAPPEARED."

"Okay. We were going to get to that."

At that moment a man entered the shot, pulling up a chair.

"Kim," he said. "I know this is hard. Let's just take it one step at a time, okay?"

Clearly this was Donald Wallace. I recognized the length of his face and the swoop of bangs across his forehead—more brown then than gray.

"Okay," Kim said, wiping her nose with the cuff of her sleeve.

"Now, I know you feel bad about what happened to Jenny. We all do. We all feel terrible. But it's not your fault. And it's not Kyle's fault. Nothing you could have done would have changed what happened. We want to start with Andrew bothering Jenny. Because he shouldn't have been kissing her and touching her if she didn't want him to, right?"

Kim shrugged. "I don't know."

"Jenny can't tell us what Andrew did." Donald Wallace handed Kim a tissue. "So if *you* saw anything, you *need* to tell us. Okay?"

"Okay," Kim said, wiping her nose again.

"Good. Now let's start over. Did you ever see Jenny and Andrew kissing?"

"Yes."

"Where was this?" Wallace asked.

Kim thought for a moment. "In Andrew's backyard."

"When was this?"

Kim looked away from Wallace. "In the summer."

"Did he try this with you, too?"

"No." Kim shook her head. "I . . . saw from Missy's yard. We were looking over the fence, and we saw."

"Missy saw, too?"

"I think she did." Kim paused. "Yeah."

"So Andrew didn't know you two were watching."

Kim hesitated again, then nodded.

"I see. *Now* I see."

Kim sniffled and looked relieved.

Kim had apparently cut that footage from the rest—the screen went blank there. I paused the footage. Colleen Shipley was right. That *was* a little disturbing. Election game-changer disturbing? Probably not. But disturbing nonetheless. I took out my cell phone. I wanted Zach to see this.

"I'm glad you called," he said when he picked up. "I've been worried—"

"Come over," I interrupted. "I have the footage."

"Okay," he said. "I'm leaving in just a minute."

I minimized the window with the DVD footage and went online to look at Zach's class blog. I wanted to read Kim's piece on Jenny again.

The prompt for that week had been:

Write a conversation between your present-day self and a younger version of yourself.

OR

Write about an experience of a song that represents for you a particular moment or era in your youth.

I flipped past Jeff's piece about "Stranger on the Shore" to get to Kim's response.

Kim had chosen the second prompt and written about Jenny and the Cranberries. I paused when I got to these words again:

> There is, in the end, only Jenny. Pretty like a girl on TV. Pretty like a girl who won't last. Old as I was at ten, how is it I didn't know that? How is it that of all the things I told her, I couldn't tell her this? How is it that I didn't open that door?

That last line, which I hadn't much noticed on the first read, made painful sense now. It was interesting that Kim had not chosen the first prompt that week. If she'd been willing to take a step back and see her ten-year-old self from an adult perspective, she might have been able to forgive herself.

I felt rather sad for the smaller Kim. It was very clear to me—and should've been clear to any adult, I felt—that she was trying to say something different from what actually came out. Was it so clear to the older Kim, when she watched it?

Could she possibly have forgiven herself, once she saw all that? Maybe she had. But probably not. It had obviously fueled her anger toward Donald Wallace. Maybe he had always been her boogeyman. He reminded her of a mistake she'd made when she was very young, and he became ever more powerful as she grew up. It may well have driven her a little bit crazy.

As I began to click out of this section of the blog, I noted the due date of the assignment: April 12.

I stared at the date. Kim had written it somewhere, hadn't she? On one of the articles about the Hallidays?

It took me a few minutes to locate the articles—in a pile on my ironing board, under a few bills and a checkbook. I skimmed all the articles but didn't find it.

Then I found my copy of *Juvie* and flipped through.

Kim had written *April 12* on the section about the kid named "Anthony." I reread the passage she'd marked:

> "I think that a big part of it was that Liam picked me out to harass. If he'd been harassing someone else, I think I could've been cooler about it, you know? If it happened to someone else, I'd have told that person, 'Hey, just tell him you're not interested. Or tell him to go to hell, if you want. And then walk away.'
>
> "But since it was me, I somehow wasn't able to do that. In the moment it felt very personal. Like, I was so sick of that shit. Just because you're a little quieter, a little smarter, a little nicer, people think you're gay."
>
> "So your friends wondered about your sexuality?" I try to clarify. "And you went along with them to put a stop to that?"
>
> "I don't know what other people wonder," Anthony replies, a hint of impatience in his voice. "I just know

346 • Emily Arsenault

I was angry. Not only at Liam. At the boxes people wanted to put me in. That night I didn't want to be a nice guy. I wanted to tear the fuck out of that box, in a big way."

"Do you wish now that you had told the guys no when they challenged you to trick Liam?" I ask.

"Well, yes. Of course."

"Would you say you're afraid of gays? Or they make you angry?"

"Neither. I'm not like that at all."

"But do you think there was real anger in what you did? Anger at people different from you? Or was it just about the moment, about the other guys?"

"There was anger, yes. But it wasn't at people different from me. It came from somewhere deep inside me, I think, and had nothing to do with Liam. I feel like I came to my senses, though, when I saw Patrick whaling away at Liam. Like, what have we done? How did I get here? But by then it was too late."

"Do you think you are in control of your anger now?"

Anthony sighs before answering. "I hope so."

I considered April 12. I considered the question about having a conversation with your younger self. I thought about all the terrible situations Kim, Missy, Dustin, and Trenton had been in when they were young and how painful that question could potentially be. Zach certainly knew that as well as the rest of them.

Zach—who, as a kid, had started a house fire to help his mother.

I put down the book. But *Trenton* had started a house fire—under vaguely similar circumstances.

A twisting seized my stomach. How was it possible that Zach's and Trenton's stories were so similar?

I hit EJECT on the first of Kyle's DVDs. If Colleen Shipley's footage was on this DVD, what was on the other? Kyle had assumed that it was more of the same, but given the brevity of the contents of the first, I suspected not. I prayed it was footage of Andrew Abbott's original police interrogation, as Janice Obermeier had indicated to Zach. Maybe that would have something much more damning to Donald Wallace. And maybe that would ease the suspicion that was creeping up my throat and making it difficult to breathe.

I put Kyle's second DVD into my computer.

I started to close the class blog to watch the DVD, but then I remembered something my brother had written in his essay "Stranger on the Shore," and I went back to check.

I didn't know till after my grandfather died what the song was. He left me his black Buick Regal Grand National with all his cassette tapes still in it.

Why hadn't this bothered me the first time I'd read it? Maybe I'd been distracted by the weight of Kim's "Jenny" piece that day. Anyone who read Jeff's essay would be able to locate my brother's car quite efficiently in a parking lot or on his street.

Heart still hammering, I hit PLAY on my laptop.

The screen framed a poorly lit room—the walls had a sickly yellow glow.

There were two figures slumped down low on a formless brown couch. A soundless TV flashed behind them.

The figure closer to the camera was Trenton Halliday. His hair was longer, but it was clearly him. He appeared to be dozing while holding a beer.

Next to him was another young man of similar build. He was too big to be Dustin, but I couldn't see his face very well.

"It's like the kids you went to high school with are sort of dead to you anyway, right?" he was saying. "When you move up and on in your life? So when I think that he's gone, it doesn't feel real. Len would be *gone* to me anyhow now, right? That part of it is still surreal. That he's really dead."

The voice sounded familiar, but I wasn't entirely sure.

The guy sat up and stared down at Trenton, then glanced at the TV, clasping his hands in front of him. From his profile I could see it was indeed Zach.

"I kicked him while he was still standing up," he murmured. "While it was still kind of an even fight. Once he was down, I walked away. I don't kick a man when he's down—whoever he is.

"I mean, I learned my lesson. I did the time. More time than I think I deserved, but I did it."

Zach mushed his hand into his cheek and swiped it clumsily across his mouth.

"Doug, he's still doing real time. But he kicked Len when he was down on the ground, so . . . you know, get what you deserve. I mean, yeah. I'm lucky I had a good lawyer. Everyone should have a good lawyer. I'm not gonna feel bad about that. My parents work hard for their money, they could afford a decent lawyer, so I didn't get screwed. It's a shame some people don't have that. It shouldn't be a *luxury*, and that's a shame. But that doesn't mean I should feel bad that I had that right."

"Totally," Trenton piped up, without opening his eyes.

"And even Connor and Doug didn't mean for him to die. They just wanted to teach him something. It's okay to be gay, whatever. You just don't fling yourself on people. And that's what he was doing.

"I'm not saying he should've died for that. It just went further than it should've. Nobody meant it to go *that* far, you know?"

"Totally," Trenton said again, softer this time. Then there was a *clunk*, and Zach jumped up from the couch.

A scoff came from behind the camera—I assumed it was Dustin. From what I could gather, Trenton had dropped his beer as he'd nodded off. The picture went dark right after that.

All the swear words I'd ever known jammed in my throat at once, so not a single one could make its way out.

When I could breathe again, I hit PAUSE on the DVD and tried to do a Google search on "Zachary Wagner" and key words that might fit the crime of his youth: "hate crime" and the like. But I couldn't find anything. I wasn't surprised. Based on our ages, the incident would've been from before newspapers—or much of anything—was online. Back then "bullying" and "hate crime" weren't such buzzwords anyway. Such a crime likely wouldn't have gotten quite as much press at the time as it would now. And then I thought of something else—Zach saying of Anthony's family, *They were considering relocating the whole family once he finished his sentence. I wouldn't be surprised if he even changed his name.*

And the name "Michael Johnson" had probably been made up on the fly. I hadn't actually bothered to Google it. But Zach must have known that such a common name would yield nothing definitive or satisfactory.

I hit PLAY again, in case Kim had saved anything else on the

DVD. There appeared to be a few more minutes of footage left on it. Probably dead air, but I wanted to be sure.

After about thirty seconds of blackness, I picked up my cell phone and called Janice Obermeier. When she answered, I introduced myself as a friend of Zach Wagner's.

"Oh. Zach," she said. "It's been a while since we've connected. How's he doing these days?"

"Not bad," I said uneasily. "Um, he told me what you said—about Kim Graber offering to show you footage of Andrew Abbott's original police interrogation."

"Excuse me?" Janice said. "Kim Graber never said anything about that to me. She said *footage*, but she didn't specify . . . and I haven't talked to Zach in weeks. Did you say he gave you my number?"

As she asked the question, a new picture appeared on my computer. It was a fuzzy light blue-gray—as if the camera lens were pressed against fabric.

"Sorry, misunderstanding, I guess," I said, hung up, and turned my computer volume as high as it would go.

"That's definitely you," an assured female voice was saying.

"No, it's not," a male voice snapped back.

"Even if you try to say it's not, it'll do some serious damage." The voice was Kim's.

"I think maybe you should leave," said the guy, who sounded very much like Zach.

Kim snorted. "I don't think you want me to leave just yet, do you? Don't you want to think about it? Listen, Professor Wagner. I didn't go after this. It just plopped into my lap. Dustin sent me the footage. He's all like, 'Don't ask *that* guy to help you. He used to hang out with my brother, and he's an ass.

Get a *real* writer.' I defended you, though. I told him I couldn't think of anyone better to help me. But it's now or never. Time is running out. The election's not really that far off."

The blue-gray on the screen shifted, and then Kim spoke again.

"You said yourself that Janice Obermeier is a good one for these sorts of sensationalistic stories. I've got her number right here. Hold on a second."

"Kim, come on now."

"Shhh. It's ringing," Kim said in a singsong voice. "Oh. Voice mail. Hello, Ms. Obermeier. My name's Kim Graber. We spoke last week. I just wanted you to know I've got some special new footage you might be interested in. Slightly different story. Call me back if you get a chance? You have my number."

After a moment Zach said, "I doubt that'll be enough to hook Janice, Kim."

Kim sighed or breathed heavily—I couldn't tell which. "I've told her I've got special footage. It'll either be about Donald Wallace or about someone else—you know what I mean?"

There was a long silence. While I waited for more, I heard the gentle thump of Rolf jumping off the countertop.

"Juvenile criminal records are sealed," Zach said.

"Records? Sure. But that footage Dustin sent me, that's something else altogether. When was that taken? Two years ago? You don't sound very sorry. You sound pretty gross, actu-ally. Imagine if this video went viral. It'll make an interesting story. An up-and-comer at this very liberal university. But such a mark on his past. A horrible, hateful act. And a fair amount of sloppy dishonesty in his writing to boot."

"What do you *want*, Kim?" Zach demanded.

"I want you to help me with this video I'm doing. I want you to put a story about it in *Waltham's*. I want your name on it."

Zach sighed. "Do you really think that's going to help you? Do you really think you're going to affect the outcome of the election at all? Listen, Kim. I have some money I've been saving for a trip."

"Okay," Kim said skeptically. "So?"

"Maybe that would help you do some things you'd like. Take some time away. Get your mind off all this Donald Wallace craziness."

"I've told you what I want," Kim said sharply. "I don't want money. And it's not craziness."

"Or do something nice for Andrew Abbott. How about *that*? Write an anonymous check. He'd probably like that better than this bizarre project you're engaged in."

"I don't want money. I only want you to help me. Because people listen to you. For some reason."

A few moments of silence followed Kim's words.

"I'm going to have to think about it," Zach said quietly.

"I'm going to a town meeting that Wallace is having near Rowington. I want someone there from an important publication. To cover it when someone ambushes him about his past."

Both Kim and Zach were quiet for a moment.

"I'm ready to act, Professor Wagner. One way or another."

Zach remained quiet.

"This is the easier way. You agree to cover the town meeting at least. You meet me in Rowington in the morning."

Zach exhaled. "Okay."

"Okay, good. I'm glad."

I'd heard enough. I had to get out of here—and quickly, with that DVD safely in hand. I slammed the EJECT button on my computer.

"Whatcha been watching?" a voice said behind me.

"Omigod!" I yelped, jumping up.

It was Zach. It hadn't been one of my cats in the kitchen. Zach had come in quietly, and I could tell by his dull tone that he already knew very well what I'd been watching.

"Theresa," Zach said softly. "It's not what it—"

"You're not going to say, 'It's not what it looks like,' are you?" I muttered, snatching the emerging DVD from under his approaching hand.

"Of course not," he said.

I stood up from the couch and ran out of the living room.

Zach likely would've caught up with me, but Boober was between us, yapping at the excitement in our quick movement, tripping up Zach's mad dash.

I slammed the bathroom door in Zach's and Boober's faces and locked it.

"Damn it, Theresa!" Zach pounded on the door.

Geraldine, who was using the litter box near the toilet, looked stunned.

"Shhh," I told her.

Geraldine swiped her paw at the litter and glared at me.

"Theresa, come out," Zach was saying. "I'd like us to talk about this."

"You helped beat a kid to death? Because he was gay?" I asked.

"It wasn't ever supposed to end like that," Zach said quietly. "I was very young. I've had a lot of time to think about what happened."

"Really? Because you didn't seem all that remorseful in that footage Kim had. She was right about that. You look like an entitled asshole, on top of everything else. You never cared about finding Kim's old footage, did you? *This* is what you were looking for."

"What? *No.* Theresa, why don't you come out so we can talk face-to-face?"

Zach knocked gently now, instead of pounding. He'd decided to reconsider his strategy and his tone.

"I'm fine here," I said through the door. "We can talk like this."

"What do you want to know, Theresa? I'll explain anything to you if you just give me that thing."

"I want to know about the fire you set when you were a kid. Did that really happen?"

He hesitated. "No."

"You got that story from Trenton and used it like it was yours?"

"Only a little of it. I made it into a better story. I gave it more heart, less dysfunction."

Something about this statement made my pulse race even harder. It sounded so calculating and so cynical.

"The idea was to pique people's interest," he continued. "I gave all those kids a voice. But I needed a story that would draw people in."

"Why didn't you use your own story? The real one?"

"Because no one wants to read a story by someone who did something so terrible."

I wasn't sure that was true. But whether a university would want to keep such a person on staff—especially the way he appeared in that relatively recent footage—was a different question.

"Really, I'd intended all along to tell the truth about myself." There was pleading in Zach's voice. "But when it came down to doing it, it was just too painful. To tell it straight. So I made up Anthony and gave the story to him. It was stupid, I know."

I could hear Zach's heavy sigh through the doorway. Was I supposed to feel sympathetic? I couldn't tell what effect he was going for, which scared me.

"Didn't Trenton care at all?" I asked. I patted my pockets, hoping I still had my cell phone on me. I did not. It was on my kitchen table.

"No. Dustin told me about the fire in my original interview. When I asked Trenton about it, he asked me not to put it in the book. So I didn't. At least not in a way that involved him. Which was all he really cared about."

"And you didn't think he'd notice that you changed it a little bit and put it in another part of your book?"

Zach paused. Then I saw the bathroom doorknob twitch.

"You didn't, did you? You think that little of your subjects?"

I closed the toilet and sat on it.

"He contacted me when the book came out," Zach said. "But it didn't really bother him, no. Not as long as I kept him and his brother looking okay. And I gave him some cash now and then, from the book. Everyone was happy with that arrangement."

An *arrangement*. I was beginning to understand.

There was a paperback of a modern-English translation of *The Book of Margery Kempe* on the toilet tank. I picked it up and thumbed its browned pages while I waited for Zach to continue. He didn't.

"You got pretty comfortable with Trenton, I guess," I prompted.

"Trenton and I are fine with each other. Everyone got what they wanted out of that relationship."

I opened my Marge book. "It is a great grace and miracle that you still have your wits," Jesus tells Margery, in one of their many heart-to-hearts. I'd marked that with a smiley face back when I was an undergrad. If I could have a conversation with my past self, I'd tell her what a dweeb she was. Beyond that I had little wisdom for her. After all—look where I'd ended up.

"I get it," I said after a while. "You paid him off to cover a mistake you made. Just like your parents did for you when you were a kid."

I saw the doorknob move again—more subtly this time. Maybe he was trying to figure out a way to pick the lock. I slid off the toilet and quietly began to unlock the bathroom window.

"You just didn't think dopey old Dustin was paying much attention," I said as loudly as I could, hoping to cover up the sound of the window. "And you didn't expect some random person like Kim to go sniffing into it later."

Outside the bathroom door, there was a long silence followed by a horrible squeaking yelp that surely came out of Boober.

"So I'm holding your little dog here," Zach said. "What did you say his name was?"

"Ripley," I said softly. Like "Margery Lipinski" the first time, it just slipped out. I didn't want to give Zach any more power than he already had.

"What else did you want to know?" Zach asked.

I heard Boober whimper.

"You're okay, Ripley," Zach said softly. "Because Theresa is going to come out of there soon, and she's going to give me that DVD."

"Right, Theresa?"

I didn't reply. I needed to figure out a way to save Boober *and* the DVD. I considered tossing the DVD out the window but worried Zach would hear me push the screen out—and I didn't want it to leave my hands.

"Theresa?"

"Hold on a sec," I said, opening my medicine cabinet and scanning its contents. Dental floss. Did I have the brute strength to strangle him with that? Band-Aids. Advil. My eyes focused on a nail file. I slid it out of the cabinet as quietly as I could and gripped it tightly in my fist.

I closed the cabinet and gazed at myself in the mirror, nail file drawn. Did *I* still have my wits? Likely not, as I'd allowed myself to be played by this creep. So I had nothing to lose, then.

I stuffed the DVD into my jeans.

"Theresa?"

I threw open the door and flew at Zach. My intention was to go for his eye, but I lost my nerve at the last second and slammed the file into his upper arm. Boober escaped from his grip, but Zach grabbed me by the wrist and pulled me close, locking me around the neck with the crook of his arm.

"Where's the DVD?" he said, dragging me into the bathroom to look for himself.

He pushed me against the wall. Boober barked.

Zach pressed his hand against my throat and his chest against mine. The DVD case knocked against the snap of my jeans.

Zach smiled, reached in, and slipped the DVD out. I stabbed his hand with the nail file, tearing downward as hard as I could.

"Ow!" he yelled, dropping the DVD case. I kicked it out of the bathroom. Zach let go of me and tried to scramble after it. I beat him to it, and he grabbed me again. This time he dragged me into the living room, holding my nail-file hand to my back.

He pushed me onto the couch. Wayne had emerged from my bedroom and was barking hysterically now, the same *ROW-ROWROW* that he usually reserved exclusively for the mailman.

Zach put his hands around my neck.

"You framed my brother," I gasped. "You knew exactly what kind of car he drives. And you know how to break into an old car. You killed her because she threatened to show this around, and then you pinned it on my brother."

"I never meant it to go this far," Zach said.

I tried to breathe. Zach's hands got tighter.

"But it seemed a smart idea to throw off the police," he whispered. "And Jeff was so *easy*. Alcoholic tendencies and all. When I pulled in to that hotel parking lot, there he was, passed out there in his car, for God's sake. I don't know what the hell he was doing there. Do you? And then you waltz into my office a few days later and let me hear that he's getting drunk out of his mind at Stewie's. All I did was put the screwdriver in his car, and the cleaning stuff. He did the rest. I just needed a distraction for the police. They came to me early because of calls to me on her cell-phone records. I needed to do *something*. I didn't think they'd run with it like this."

Wayne jumped up Zach's leg. Zach kicked him away. Wayne leaped right back, and Zach kicked him harder. Wayne let out a yowl. I loosened one arm from Zach's grip and grabbed his hair, yanking his head sideways. I felt around for my nail file but couldn't find it.

"And Donald Wallace?" I croaked, thinking that if I kept talking—or kept Zach talking—I could somehow survive.

"That was a good distraction for *you*, since you were poking around a little too close. Kind of a fanciful adventure, wasn't it? Going after the powerful politician, trying to uncover his deep, dark, murderous ways?"

My vision started to feel speckled.

ROWROWROWROW, Wayne was saying, as things turned from speckled to black.

"I liked you, Theresa," I heard Zach whisper. "I'm telling you this because I don't want you to go out doubting your brother. I saw doubt in your eyes that day after they arrested him. And I thought that was a shame."

There was a moment of blackness. I wasn't sure if it was anger or death—or both.

Then I heard a door. A door to the next life?

"Hello-hello-hello?" I heard someone say. A woman.

I felt like I was choking on my own breath and thought I might be hallucinating the voice through the sound of Wayne's barking.

Marge? I thought. Was she greeting me at the entrance to purgatory? Surely not hell. Because I'd at least tried, in this life. Sometimes. Zach had been right about my doubt, but was it that easy to get sent to hell?

"Theresa, hon?"

At those words Zach's grip loosened and my vision returned. I sat up.

"Do you realize that your indoor cat is sitting outside on the lawn, Theresa?" My mother's voice came closer to us. Zach, stunned, let go of my neck and eased his hands down to my shoulders. "Just staring bug-eyed at your car like it's the mother ship. Shut up, puggle-face. *Shut up!*"

Wayne was still going ballistic when my mother reached us.

"Oh. My. God," she said. "I'm *so* sorry. I'm interrupting."

I managed to wriggle away and stand up.

"You're not interrupting, Mom. Give me your phone."

"Oh, dear. I should go. Hon, I was just checking in. And I'd stopped at the Dip for dessert. Did you know they're having an éclair special?"

My mother smiled at Zach. "Did you even know there's such a *thing* as a pistachio éclair? Leave it to the Dip, though—I think it's pistachio Jell-O pudding on the inside."

I picked up the DVD case off the floor. "Give me your phone, Mom. Jesus!"

My mother shot me the evil eye but handed me the phone anyway. "I don't believe we've been introduced. I'm Theresa's mom, obviously. Do you like éclairs? I'd have bought more if I realized she'd have a guest."

"Um . . ." Zach struggled to catch his breath. "I . . . don't . . . Well, yeah. Yeah, I do."

I went into the kitchen as I dialed 911, then ran back into the living room with my biggest kitchen knife.

"I have an intruder in my home," I said to the 911 operator. "And he tried to strangle me."

Zach stared at me as I gave our address.

"Theresa!" my mother screamed, dropping the white bag. "Are you out of your mind?"

"You can run." I shoved my mother's phone in my back pocket so I could hold on to the knife with both hands. "Or you can stay here and have one of my mother's pastries while we wait for the cops, since she's already offered. As long as you don't touch either one of us."

At that, Zach turned and ran from the house. When I heard his tires squeak, I hoped Geraldine had managed to stay out of his way.

My next thought was realizing that my mother of course had seen Zach's car in the driveway before she came waltzing into my house.

My mother stepped closer to me and put her fingertips to my neck.

"This is for real?" she asked as the conspiratorial smile finally left her face.

I dropped my knife and put my arms around her.

Thursday, April 24

It wasn't really warm enough to eat supper outside, but we were all willing to pretend it was. I'd just given Boober and Wayne baths, and the whole house smelled like wet dog and flea shampoo. None of us wanted to stay inside—particularly Nathan, who'd spent an hour making us a ginger-chickpea recipe he'd insisted would be *transcendent*. We were eating early, before he had to go to work.

It was a special occasion. We were celebrating Jeff's new job driving a bread truck. Tish had used one of her many family connections to help him get it. It wasn't a dream job—I had no idea what Jeff would consider a dream job— but it would buy him security, days away from his dreary apartment, and some time to think about his next steps.

He was free now.

It hadn't happened overnight.

After my final encounter with Zach, I made copies of Kim's DVD—one for myself, one for Jeff's lawyer, and one for the police. It forced the police to give Zach another look, but they still didn't take him seriously as a suspect.

Zach denied everything, and they didn't have enough to take him in. They still had their sights set on Jeff anyhow.

Then the DNA tests came back from Kim's fingernails. And the profile didn't match Jeff's. That's when they took it seriously. That's when they tested Zach.

Over the past few months, he'd changed his original plea from not guilty to guilty. His lawyers were hoping to get him a reduced sentence, since the murder wasn't, they claimed, a premeditated act. Zach had driven down to Rowington with the intention of going along with Kim's plan. They'd met at the Denny's and were planning to drive over to the meeting together in Zach's car. According to his account, she began talking about Dustin's footage again and making further demands of him. Zach lost his temper and stabbed her in the thigh with a screwdriver he had in his car. She started screaming. He panicked, jumped on her, covered her mouth, and strangled her in the heat of the moment. The prosecution was claiming he couldn't have done this in the parking lot of the auditorium where the town meeting was to take place—that someone would've seen the struggle in the car. Zach, they said, probably took Kim to a secluded place, which indicated premeditation.

In any case the police dropped the charges against Jeff just before Christmas. Zach was arrested on Christmas Eve.

By then, of course, Donald Wallace had won the election.

"Seconds?" Nathan asked now.

"I'm not sure I need more," I said. "I can handle only so much transcendence this early in the evening."

This thing with Nathan didn't happen overnight either. I went to Wiley's on a frigid evening in early February, feeling uninspired by Marge that night—and half hoping Nathan would be there. He was. He'd read about my brother by then. It had occurred to him to call me, he said, but he'd been busy. With the two jobs and now a night class, he had a lot on his plate. Plus, he was still looking for a home for the cockatoo and now a painted turtle he'd been saddled with as well. But he missed my stories about Marge.

"I've been thinking of getting a couple of tattoos," Jeff said.

"Really?" Nathan asked. "Don't go anywhere but Tasty Pain, I'm telling you. They do beautiful work."

"A cup of cappuccino on one bicep," Jeff added, deadpan. "And a croissant on the other."

"Oh, really?" I said. "Well, did I tell you I'm considering growing a soft, downy mustache?"

"I'm considering growing an exoskeleton."

"I'm thinking of growing my own kombucha mushrooms."

"I'm thinking I'll Twitter that."

"Oh, *please*," Nathan said, standing up from the picnic table. "I can't stand this game."

"Tell me about it." Tish folded her arms.

"You just don't have the hang of it yet," I said.

"I don't ever want the hang of it." Nathan picked up the chickpea platter, his plate, and mine. "I'm gonna bring in a few things."

"I'll come," Tish offered. "I've got to whip the cream."

Tish had insisted upon making a chocolate pie, to counteract any woo-woo health benefits of Nathan's entrée. Now, the thing with Jeff and Tish *did* seem to happen overnight. Not that I was sure, even now, what this thing was. But they both seemed pretty happy with it, so I didn't ask a lot of questions.

"I've been thinking of using the expression 'Oh, my stars,'" I said. "Not every day. But on good days."

"On that note, Theresa, I've been thinking of saying 'Huzzah' now and again."

I sighed and Jeff stretched. We were both spent, and nobody had won. Maybe we were, at long last, getting too old for this.

"Half these things we talk about we're thinking of doing," I confessed, "I actually kind of want to do."

"I know," Jeff said.

He didn't add, "Me, too," I noticed. Maybe he didn't feel the same.

"I'm thinking of dropping Marge. I'm thinking of withdrawing, finally. Maybe I'd rather spend the fee on a trip this year. A 'Good-bye, Marge' trip. A pilgrimage to England, even. I could stop by her hometown and say an official good-bye. It might be more fun than torturing myself for another year."

I had managed to meet my deadline of presenting pages to my department and done fairly well, but I had felt no victory in it. Some persistent insecurity had impelled me to keep a toe in academics long after my heart had lost interest. I was fairly certain I was ready to take it out now.

"You're serious?" Jeff said.

"Yes."

"Well . . ." He ate a single chickpea, looking a bit sad for me. "Think a little more."

"I am." I stood up to collect the rest of our dishes. "I will."

As I reached for my glass, a golf ball flew past me, missed my head by an inch or two, and bounced off the seat of my picnic table.

I stooped and plucked it out of the grass.

"Oh, my stars," I whispered. "First wayward golf ball of the season."

"What is that, like, good luck or something?"

"If we want it to be," I said, and tossed it to my brother.

Acknowledgments

Many thanks to: Ross Grant, Laura Langlie, Carrie Feron, Nicole Fischer, Joanne Minutillo, Lisa Walker, Nicole Moore, Danny Arsenault, Jennifer Purrenhage, Jennifer Breuer, Jessica Grant Bundschuh, and Cari Strand.

For modern-English excerpts of *The Book of Margery Kempe*, I used the Barry Windeatt translation.

For additional information about Margery Kempe, I relied on the following works: *Memoirs of a Medieval Woman: The Life and Times of Margery Kempe,* by Louise Collis; *Mystic and Pilgrim: The Book and the World of Margery Kempe,* by Clarissa W. Atkinson; and the Norton Critical Editions *The Book of Margery Kempe,* translated and edited by Lynn Staley.

About the author

Read on

Insights,
Interviews
& More...

Meet Emily Arsenault

EMILY ARSENAULT is also the author of *The Broken Teaglass, In Search of the Rose Notes*, and *Miss Me When I'm Gone*. She lives in Shelburne Falls, Massachusetts, with her husband and daughter. ∾

Q&A with
Emily Arsenault

Your last two books were mysteries that involved female friendships. What made you decide to write about a brother-sister relationship this time?

I have two brothers, so it's an important relationship in my life. In my experience these relationships can be very close but still have awkward, uncomfortable holes. Theresa and Jeff clearly care a great deal about each other and can be about 80-percent honest with each other concerning their lives. It's the other 20 percent where things get interesting. There are things they will never say to each other. There are things they both know about each other but will probably never address. I can't speak for all siblings, but this is how it is for me, and I wanted to capture that with Theresa and Jeff.

Who were your inspirations for Jeff and Theresa? Are you very much like Theresa? Does Jeff resemble someone in your family?

Though they are nothing like Jeff and Theresa, my initial spark of inspiration came from my mother and her brother— my uncle. They live in the same town they grew up in, within walking distance of each other. My mother goes out to eat a great deal, and her very frugal brother often comes over and steals the doggie bags from her fridge. I started with that— an adult sibling relationship in which the brother and sister are very much in each ▶

other's daily lives. They are sort of like gadflies to each other. (I should say, however, that my mother and uncle might not characterize their relationship exactly that way.)

I have some of Theresa's qualities (spotty commitment to academic interests, high emotional investment in pets, general slovenliness), though I wouldn't say she is me. She is bolder and more spontaneous than I am.

When I was in college, I very much thought I wanted to enter a philosophy Ph.D. program and be an academic. For a variety of reasons, I decided during my senior year to "take a year off" from academics. I got a job at Merriam-Webster, got married a few years later, then taught for a while, had some other adventures, and never thought much about philosophy again. I think of Theresa as a sort of alter ego for me—how I might've ended up had things gone differently and had I pursued academics more seriously. I can imagine losing my drive somewhere along the line but clinging to the "idea" of getting a Ph.D. as a sort of intellectual security blanket.

Aside from an interest in origami, which he shares with my older brother, Jeff doesn't resemble either of my brothers. (Where credit is due: The idea to write a book called *How to Win Chicks with Origami* comes from my brother's brain, not mine.) The *relationship* between Jeff and Theresa, however, borrows some elements from my relationship with my older brother. For example, we tend to indulge each other's pessimism, as Jeff and Theresa do.

Why did you choose Margery Kempe as the subject of Theresa's dissertation? Did you know much about her before you wrote the book? How did you research this topic?

I wanted Theresa to have an eccentric subject, since she's somewhat eccentric herself. I first encountered Margery Kempe in a survey class on early English literature years ago. I had, since then, wanted to learn more about her, and this book seemed like a good excuse to do so.

My main research was reading *The Book of Margery Kempe* a few times. Margery gets self-righteously repetitive at times, but it's still a fascinating glimpse into the life of a medieval woman who conducted herself in such unconventional ways.

Two other sources I used for research were *Memoirs of a Medieval Woman: The Life and Times of Margery Kempe*, by Louise Collis, and *Mystic and Pilgrim: The Book and the World of Margery Kempe*, by Clarissa W. Atkinson.

Can you explain the book's title?

The title comes from a quote from Jane Austen's *Mansfield Park*: "What strange creatures brothers are!"

This is how I felt about my brothers growing up, and I imagine this is a common sentiment between siblings of both genders and all ages.

"What strange creatures" can probably be applied to nearly all the characters in the book, actually. Love and tragedy make them do strange things. Of course, it ▶

makes us *all* do strange things. A lot
of characters in this book really don't
understand their own behavior—past or
present—try as they might. I also liked the
phrase because it connected to Margery
Kempe's—and occasionally Theresa's—
habit of referring to herself as a "creature."

***This is your first book with some political
and legal elements. Any particular
reason?***

Years ago, while researching for another
book (a book that never really came to
fruition), I started to become interested
in some of the Satanic Panic criminal
cases in the 1980s and early 1990s. The
case of the West Memphis Three is the
most famous of these, perhaps, but there
are many more. I became particularly
interested when I saw that one disturbing
case (in which the convicted party was set
free over a decade later) actually involved
a politician whom I had voted for. I'd been
oblivious to her past, because it wasn't
discussed much in the press. It always
seems strange to me that we don't talk
more about that odd era in American
justice. I made this part of the backdrop
of the story, rather than a central question,
because I'm not a legal expert and I didn't
want to get preachy about it. But it's a
question that perplexes me a great deal,
since so many of those cases were such
big news when I was growing up. And
now, for the most part, it's as if they
never happened. ⤳

Have You Read?
More by
Emily Arsenault

For more books by Emily Arsenault check out

MISS ME WHEN I'M GONE

Author Gretchen Waters made a name for herself with her bestseller *Tammyland*—a memoir about her divorce and her admiration for country-music icons Tammy Wynette, Loretta Lynn, and Dolly Parton that was praised as a "honky-tonk *Eat, Pray, Love.*" But her writing career is cut abruptly short when she dies from a fall down a set of stone library steps. It is a tragic accident, and no one suspects foul play, certainly not Gretchen's best friend from college, Jamie, who's been named the late author's literary executor.

But there's an unfinished manuscript Gretchen left behind that is much darker than *Tammyland*: a book ostensibly about male country musicians yet centered on a murder in Gretchen's family that haunted her childhood. In its pages, Gretchen seems to be speaking to Jamie from beyond the grave—suggesting her death was no accident . . . and that Jamie must piece together the story someone would kill to keep untold.

IN SEARCH OF THE ROSE NOTES

Eleven-year-olds Nora and Charlotte were best friends. When their teenage babysitter, Rose, disappeared under mysterious circumstances, the girls decided to "investigate." But their search—aided by paranormal theories and techniques gleaned from old Time-Life books—went nowhere.

Years later, Nora, now in her late twenties, is drawn back to her old neighborhood—and to her estranged friend—when Rose's remains are finally discovered. Upset over their earlier failure to solve the possible murder, Charlotte is adamant that they join forces to try again. But Nora was the last known person to see Rose alive, and she's not ready to revisit her troubled adolescence and the events surrounding the disappearance—or face the disturbing secrets that are already beginning to emerge.